TABLE OF CONTENTS

        Special note: Historic events associated with
Surprised by Love – 1913 Great Miami River Flood in Troy,
Ohio. Other notable cities flooded are Dayton, Hamilton,
and Middletown. Known as Greatest Natural Disaster in
Ohio history.

FRED'S GIFT

By Bettie Boswell

Dedication:
To my husband David, my children,
their family, and the memory of my dad

"Jingle bells, jingle bells..."

Students laughed as they watched the class clown do a reindeer dance. The video projected on the music classroom's white board focused on the rascal. Several children whispered about his antics during their recent holiday program. A knocking sound drew Dawn Kyle's attention away from the merry scene. As she opened the door a shiver shook the confident teacher. Her good friend and cousin, Marsha Edmunds, motioned her out into the hallway. Marsha's welcoming school counselor smile was not evident as she wrapped her arms around Dawn.

"It's your father, Fred. I'm afraid the news isn't good."

"Is he..." Dawn paused, afraid to know the answer.

Marsha released Dawn from her tight embrace. Her face registered concern as she reached out to join their hands.

"The assisted living administrator at Bright Manor said to come immediately. Fred's been placed in hospice care. There isn't much time."

Dawn's heart took a dive as she stood outside her classroom. She'd waited too long. Should have taken time to visit Pop, but life had been busy. Especially since her husband Joe passed away a year ago. Being a widowed mom filled her days with basketball and music lessons. Preparation for the early December holiday program last week hadn't helped.

Noise from inside the classroom interrupted her reverie.

Marsha's professional smile returned. "I'll take care of your students until the office gets a substitute."

The two friends entered the classroom and immediate quiet returned as students once again focused on the video.

Marsha's eyes searched Dawn's face. "Do you need someone to drive you?"

Dawn swiped tears from her eyes. "I can do this."

"Are you sure?"

"I'm on my way. Just need to grab my purse and see if Sally can watch David and Molly for a few days."

Marsha gave her one more hug. "I've got you covered. They can stay with us. My kids would enjoy having their cousins over for a while." She gently pushed Dawn toward the door. "Take care of yourself and don't forget, I'll be praying for you."

"Thanks." Dawn forced confidence into her voice and pulled her bag from a nearby cabinet. She would need to talk to her children before she left them with Marsha. If only she had taken them to see Fred more often. So many regrets, so little time...

ʕ ʕ ʕ

Dawn had no regrets as she sat by Fred's bedside at Bright Manor. A few days turned into a week as she held her father's hand and quietly conversed with him. Her presence and the care of the visiting hospice nurse seemed to bring him some peace.

Marsha made the hour drive, from Toledo to the heartlands of Ohio, so Molly and David could say farewell to their Pop. They gave hugs and kisses to their grandfather. He blessed them all with a sweet smile. Talk was not an option as raspy breaths signaled the sounds of fading life. She prayed with him and hoped he listened. A few hours after the children left, he was gone.

ʕ ʕ ʕ

Two days after the funeral, Dawn stepped into the room where Pop had lived for the last two years. The Bright Manor staff had been there for him when she wasn't. At least there were a few days at the end to say her good-byes. Hopefully that made up for some of her lost time. She picked up Fred's ancient flannel shirt and held it close. She breathed in the woodsy scent of her father's aftershave that lingered on the old garment. What she wouldn't give for another day with him. A tremor shook her body as she wrapped the warm shirt around her shoulders.

Then her eyes focused on Mom's tattered Bible that lay open under a tabletop Christmas tree. Could Pop have taken up reading the Bible? She could only hope. The well-worn book had been closed and covered with dust the last time she had visited.

Beneath the little tree, Christmas cards were scattered across the antique bedside table that Pop had given Mom as a wedding gift. A stack of letters cluttered up a corner of the table's square top. It was going to take a while to clean things up.

Her older sister and brother had cleared town as soon as the funeral was over. They had work obligations. Being a teacher gave her an advantage. She had the rest of Christmas break to sort things out before school resumed. What a way to celebrate the holidays.

A knock at the door drew her attention from the remnants of her father's life. A dark-haired, blue-eyed man with an expression of concern entered the room. It was Austin Bradley, a recent addition to the Bright

Manor staff, who served as their administrator. The Superman look-alike carried a small cardboard box in one hand and dangled a large manila envelope from the other as he rested against the doorframe.

She'd tried not to notice that his hands bore no wedding ring when he came by to visit during Fred's last days. Why she checked was beyond her. This was a time to mourn. Her husband Joe had only been gone for a year, and now Pop. She needed to concentrate on this room and then make time to celebrate Christmas with her kids.

"Thank you for being part of the memorial service. Dad would have gotten a kick out of the kind words you extended on behalf of Bright Manor."

"We enjoyed having Fred as a resident. I wish I could have gotten to know him better." He set the box in Pop's lift chair and placed a warm hand on hers. "Though I only knew him for a short time, I really enjoyed his stories."

Dawn stared at their joined hands and then pulled away as she fought the warmth spreading into her heart. "Pop was good at telling stories. Hopefully you didn't have to hear the same ones over and over again." She attempted a weak smile. Her gaze traveled down the tall man's broad chest. Then she looked away to blink back tears of sorrow.

"No problem. I like to remember the good tales. They're worth keeping. Someday I may write a book featuring sage words from these wise elders. Your dad's stories would hold a special place in the publication." The expression on Austin's face shone with the compassion he had for those he served at Bright Manor.

She shifted her eyes to the box and envelope that now took up residence in Pop's favorite space. The chair had served him well as it became harder for him to reach a standing position on his own. He had it placed beside his computer and television. His phone was within easy reach. He called it his communication center.

She'd need to cut off services to all three devices. The computer would go home with her. David and Molly would appreciate having the up-to-date model. Pop's hard drive was newer than the computer at home. Their television was showing its age, too. Her siblings had given her their blessing to claim whatever she wanted and dispose of the rest.

Austin cleared his throat, breaking into her thoughts. He picked up the envelope. "I'm not sure what's in this, but Fred said it was very important that you get it after everyone else left. He said it was your Christmas gift this year. He asked me to give it to you if something happened to him."

Dawn took the precious envelope and pushed it deep into her tote. The envelope was thin, probably one of Pop's writings. Those could be good or bad, but it was his last message. "Something special for

Christmas" was written on the outside of the envelope in shaky penmanship. "Thanks, I'll put it under my tree. What about the box?"

"These are things that Fred had on our community Christmas tree. The staff thought you might enjoy having them."

Tears began to flow in earnest as he handed her the overflowing box. She couldn't stop them. Austin's left hand touched her back as he retrieved the box and set it back on the chair. Words were not needed as she let grief course from her body and into the stream flowing down her cheeks. Austin handed her a tissue. His silent support was as warm as the hand on her back.

A few minutes later, Dawn sniffed and wiped a final tear. "I needed that." A deep breath filled her chest. She had found some peace. She just hoped Pop had found his before he'd gone on.

"Don't worry. Fred is in a good place."

"I hope so." She tried to sound positive as she moved the box of ornaments to the patchwork quilt covering the bed. "Tell the staff I appreciate them for taking care of Pop. I know he wasn't always the most patient man but I loved him anyway."

"I'll let them know. If there's anything we can do to help, just give us a call." The handsome administrator turned to leave and then hesitated, making eye contact. "I've only been here a few months but I found your father to be quite pleasant and patient."

"He must have liked you. Thanks for sharing." Dawn waved good-bye and turned to the task at hand. What to keep, what to give away? The closet might be a good place to start.

The few shoes found in the bottom of the closet went to the trash. Pop never liked to shop. The scuffed up loafers and slippers provided evidence of his thrifty ways. Mom would have been embarrassed to find the holey underwear that Dawn tossed in the garbage.

His pants and shirts would make a nice gift for a needy person. She had personally restocked those when Pop had entered Bright Manor two years ago. There was money then and a husband who helped provide it. She'd had time to show Dad that she cared. She should have checked on his underclothing sooner.

She set aside a few flannel shirts. Those she would save. Her best memories as a little girl featured a flannel-clad father walking down a country lane with his adoring daughter. Back then he was her superhero. He was the one who brought home treats, the one who danced around with her feet riding on top of his shoes.

Pop was the one who managed to find the perfect cedar tree each year for Christmas. Only he could reach high enough to put the star on that tree. He was the one who read the Nativity story from Luke's second chapter on Christmas morning.

Christmas used to be his favorite time of the year. Then Mom got sick. The world got worse. Pop got cynical and gave up on church and Christmas.

Tinsel from the little tabletop tree shimmered in a sunbeam as if to mock her thoughts. Since when did Pop start having a tree in his room? One of the aides must have sweet-talked him into the little plastic evergreen. Dawn had tried some decorations the first year he was at Bright Manor and received a firm 'not interested.' Maybe someone put it there after he got too sick to object. That had to be the answer.

A soft knock at the door heralded the entrance of Mary, one of the aides who helped with Pop's care. "Hey Miss Dawn, I came to help you fold up any clothes or linens." The plump woman spread her arms wide and Dawn fell into the aide's warm embrace.

"Oh Mary, I'm going to miss the old bear so much."

"I know, sweetie. He loved you, too. Every time I came in here he was bragging on what a great teacher you've become."

"A teacher who got too busy to come see her dad in the last few months. I knew he was getting worse, but I let other things get in the way."

"Now sweetheart, don't you start that guilty talk. Fred understood. He was a teacher a long time ago himself, wasn't he?"

"Dad was one of the reasons I went into teaching. He loved his time in education and encouraged me to follow his calling. Students respected him. They nominated him for teacher of the year several times." Dawn took the cardboard box off the bed and set the pillows to the side.

"Fred was real proud you followed in his footsteps. He loved you and your children. Every time I saw him, he was talking about how the kids were playing ball or giving recitals. I saw their videos on his Internet. Boy, was he good on that computer. He was better than some of the younger ones around here." Mary chuckled.

Dawn pulled the patchwork quilt from the bed and handed one end to Mary. "We did keep in contact that way. I guess he must have appreciated getting our messages."

"You know he did. I think it made his day when he got something from you or one of your darlings. Now quit being so down and tell me about this quilt."

"Mom gave him this quilt one year for Christmas. See that blue square over there? The material was from one of my favorite dresses. That flannel patch on your end was from the shirt Pop was wearing when my brother was born. He was so proud to have a boy that he took it off and wrapped the new baby in the shirt."

Mary shook her end of the quilt and they folded it in half. "He sure did love his flannel and your mama. Is there something from her on here?"

"This pink floral square was from the dress that Mom was married in." Dawn pointed to a section that lay on top of their last fold. "They couldn't afford a fancy wedding so they got married in the preacher's parlor. This coverlet represents so many happy memories."

"Good. That's what you need to start thinking about. Fred would want you to remember the happy times." Mary stowed the blanket in Fred's laundry basket with the flannel shirts and turned to help fold the sheets.

"You've been a great friend, Mary. Let's keep in contact."

"Sure thing, Hon, you know where to find me. If you need to stay over to work on Fred's things, you're welcome to hit my couch."

"We'll see. I'm not sure if that would work out with the kids."

"All right, I'll leave you to sort through the stuff on the table." Mary pulled Dawn into another bear hug. "Take care and God's blessings."

"Blessings to you too, Mary...wait a minute. Do you know where the tree came from? Pop hasn't celebrated Christmas in a long time." Dawn couldn't keep the hopeful tone from her voice.

"I could be wrong, but I think Fred may have purchased it with his Bingo money. That tree's been sitting there since the first of December for sure." Mary smiled and left the room.

Dawn scratched her head and eased into the lift chair. Maybe Pop had found his Christmas spirit. Only God knew for sure. She kicked off her walking shoes and leaned against the lift chair. A push on the down button glided her into a reclining position. It was time to sort the mail.

🎄🎄🎄

Austin tapped lightly on Fred's door. No answer. He pushed the door open and peered in to see if Dawn was okay. From the doorway he spotted red and green Santa socks peeking out from the elevated footrest of the old guy's recliner. The afghan-covered lump attached to those holiday clad feet could only be Dawn.

He hated to disturb the poor woman, but her cousin Marsha had called. Dawn wasn't answering her phone, and there was an issue with the children. It sounded important.

"Dawn. Wake up." Austin reached out and touched her soft cheek. A jolt of awareness shook his senses as she rolled over and moaned in her sleep.

Fred had pointed out that this daughter was his little angel. She looked heavenly right now with her gently mussed hair and peaceful countenance. Too bad he needed to wake her up to the realities that she faced.

Fred had taken every opportunity to tell Austin about his sweet daughter. The loveable old matchmaker often mentioned that she was widowed. Subtlety had not been in the old man's character.

6

Austin reached for the sleeping woman's hand and silently prayed for her. *Lord, give her strength through this time of grief. Watch over her children and the difficulties they are facing right now. Help her to find peace and enjoy this Christmas, in spite of losing her father. In Jesus' name, Amen.*

At least she had a father who cared for her during his lifetime. His own dad died before he knew him. Mother did her best. He could not fault her for his upbringing. She was the one who set the example by working hard to keep them above the poverty level. It was a pattern he had embraced since he obtained his first work permit.

By working two jobs or more at a time, he had slowly worked his way through college. One of those positions led to his love of elder care. His social life became wrapped around sweet senior citizens and left no time for dating.

Maybe Fred was right. Perhaps he did need to expand his social life a bit. He raised the hand that he held and brushed his lips across Dawn's knuckles. It was time to wake this sleeping beauty.

♻ ♻ ♻

Something tickled her hand as Dawn fought to emerge from her exhausted slumber. Dreams of Christmas trees and superheroes merged as she blinked her eyes and tried to focus on a blurred image that looked a lot like Superman. Not Superman, it was Austin Bradley. He spoke her name as he patted her hand. Did he say something about Marsha and the children?

She sat up as well as she could in the recliner. "What was that about the kids?" She pulled her hand from his and fumbled for the controller. Where was the up button for this contraption? She fought waves of panic. Did something happen to one of her babies? Not that they were babies any more. They hadn't been babies since they'd changed Dad's name to Pop.

Austin took the chair's controller from her and pushed the up button. "I'm not sure what's going on. Marsha just said she couldn't reach you on your cell phone. She needed to ask you an important question concerning the children." He offered his hand when she reached a near-standing position. "Do you need to borrow my phone?"

Dawn lost herself in his eyes before she jerked her hand away. "I'm good. I just need to find my phone. It's got to be around here somewhere."

A muffled ring sounded from the depths of the upright lift chair. "Now, that's what I call perfect timing." Austin reached deep into the cushions and fished out the buzzing device.

She grabbed the phone and answered, "Hey Marsha, is everything all right?"

"Nothing to worry about, the neighborhood kids organized a couple of sleep-overs. I'm watching the boys and the girls are going to be at the Joneses'. I just wanted to see if David and Molly could participate."

7

"Sure, that's not a problem. I may do a sleep-over of my own. Mary offered me a place to stay for the night. I think I'll stay here and get this done." Dawn sighed in relief. No drive home. No worries about her children. The extra time would be a blessing.

She signed a thumbs-up to Austin as he waved good-bye from the door. Marsha chattered on for a few more moments about some of the neighborhood news before they hung up. Dawn reached for the Christmas cards and letters. She had to make it through them this time.

She opened a bright red envelope and pulled out a hand-made card.

Merry Christmas Fred, I appreciate your prayers so much. It's been good to see you taking your turn offering the blessing. You've given me something to look forward to at dinner time.

Pop prayed? Dawn checked the signature and recognized the name of one of Bright Manor's residents. Interesting... She reached for another card.

It was from the men's group at the local church. A folded letter fell out as she opened the envelope.

Dear Fred, We're so glad you joined our Thursday Bible Group at Bright Manor. Your insights have added depth to our studies. We all get a kick out of your sense of humor. You're the best!

It was signed by five men who each added positive comments about Pop.

Peace flooded through Dawn's heart as she filtered through the missives. Messages that spoke about her dad's renewed faith were added to the 'keep' pile. Her smile grew as the stack of letters piled up.

"You're looking happy." Austin stood in the hallway with a large basket of multi-colored flowers. "The florist got this order too late for the funeral so they sent them here. Would you like them?"

"I think Dad would want to share them with his friends. Could you put them in the dining room? That way everyone can enjoy their beauty."

"So, it's Dad now, not Pop?"

"Yeah, these letters have reminded me of the Dad I knew before he lost his Christmas spirit. I just wish I'd made time for him in the last few months. I'm sorry I missed seeing him happy again."

"He was a pretty happy guy. He seemed to know what he wanted and where he was going. His faith was very important."

"That's good to know. He was lost for a long time. Mom's death hit him hard."

"Fred talked about going home to meet her. I think he knew he'd better shape up his faith so he could see her in heaven."

"They were a sweet couple." Dawn reached for Mom's Bible and gave it a hug before she added it to the stack of Christmas cards.

"He told me about their courtship. He couldn't help hinting that I should try some courting of my own."

She didn't miss the wink he sent her way.

"I'll keep that in mind." She returned his wink with a smile. Dawn could not believe she was flirting. It was great to know that Dad had turned his life around. She would blame her mood on that good news. Maybe it was time to move on. Dad sure had. Austin seemed like a great guy.

ひ ひ ひ

On Christmas morning, Dawn sat in a sea of wrapping paper as Molly and David compared their gifts. One of Dad's flannel shirts covered her pajamas as she hugged his unopened envelope to her chest. She pictured him pounding out his message on the computer keyboard or scribbling it in his scrawling handwriting. It was time to view his final letter, be it good or bad. Her hands trembled as she slowly pried open the manila envelope.

Dearest Dawn,

Don't worry about missing my last few months. The truth is I didn't want you to see your old man fading away. I asked the doc to keep things quiet. I wanted you to remember me the way I was. Make that the way I used to be before I let the things of this old world get to me.

After I got the bad news from the medical experts, I started thinking about what your mother would have expected of her honey. I'm sorry I wasn't so sweet lately but I've been making up for it. I even convinced grumpy Gerald to join me at Bible study recently. I'm starting to notice some changes in his life. God has given me a second chance during these last few months.

I know things have been kind of rough for you this year without your Joe. Don't make the same mistake I did. Grab on to life. Live your faith. Keep that young man and lady of yours on the straight and narrow. Don't let anyone tell you that you shouldn't love again.

Hopefully you have met our handsome new administrator by now. He's single and I've thrown a few hints in his direction. I even sent him an email with your picture attached. I may have given him your contact information. I hope you'll check him out. He's a keeper.

Speaking of keepers, I want you to know that I am giving you the old home place. It's yours, your own little piece of the Ohio heartland. Your siblings had no interest in it. It's not much but it meant the world to your mom. She was so proud when she told everyone how I built that thing with my own hands. It's nothing fancy but the old home has stood the test of

9

time. I know you thought I sold it to pay for Bright Manor but I couldn't part with the house. Your cousin Jim has been taking care of it for the last two years. My lawyer has a copy of the deed for you.

It will mean a little longer commute for you but what's a half hour these days? By the way, I heard a rumor that your old music teacher is retiring next year. I put in a good word with the current superintendent. He's one of my former students. A country school might be a good place for my grandchildren.

Did I mention that it's only a half hour from Bright Manor and a certain available administrator?

Have a Merry Christmas, dear daughter. I guess my return to Jesus is the best gift you get this year. I could tell you were worried about my soul. I'm happy to be back in His grace. See you on the other side.

Dad
P.S. Austin lost his mother a while back. He'll be celebrating Christmas alone this year. You should give him a call.

A happy tear traced down Dawn's cheek as Molly pulled a cardboard box from under the tree.

"What's this, Mom? Did we forget to put some ornaments on the tree?"

"They were my Dad's ornaments. He made them during the last month he was living at Bright Manor."

"Maybe we can we put them on our tree each year to remember him." David pulled a glittery star from the box and held it up to the tree.

Dawn gave him a warm hug. "Oh sweetheart, it reminds me of the one Dad used to put on our tree when I was your age."

Molly pulled out a small picture frame. "Look at this one. It's a picture of Pop in a Santa suit! I wonder if he gave out any presents."

"Pop gave us the best present. He renewed his trust in the Lord. He's also given us the old home place. How would you like to take a trip this afternoon and check it out?"

"Cool! I've missed going there." Molly started to dance around the room.

Dawn gathered her courage and looked at both children. "Would you mind if I invited someone to go with us? Pop wants you to meet his friend, Mr. Austin."

"Is he the guy that looks like Superman? I like him. He was nice to us when we said good-bye to Pop." David joined Molly's dance.

"I'll take that as a yes." Before Dawn could reach for her phone, it began ringing.

"Hey it's Austin. I just opened my gift from Fred. It was your phone number. I hope you don't mind…"

Dawn started to dance with her children as she answered. "We were just talking about you. Come and celebrate Fred's Christmas gift with us."

Bettie Boswell is an author, illustrator, and composer for both Christian and children's markets. She holds a B.S. in Church Music from Cincinnati Bible College and a Master's in Elementary Education from East Tennessee State University. She lives in Bowling Green, Ohio.

Her numerous musicals have been performed at schools, churches, and two community theater events. When she isn't writing, drawing or composing, she keeps busy with her day job teaching elementary music in Sylvania, Ohio.

Inspiration: *Fred's Gift* was inspired by my father, who did leave me a portion of his farm. My dad was a proud veteran of WW2 and an avid genealogist. His historical records and tales are providing inspiration for future stories. My husband and I met before my father retired. We are enjoying a long marriage and are currently enjoying our grandchildren, so this story is not biographical.

Learn more about her online:
https://sites.google.com/view/bettieboswellauthorillustrator/home
Twitter: @BboswellB
Facebook: Bettie.Boswell.9

EVIE'S LETTER

By Cindy Thomson

Diana Johnson carried her husband's piece of chocolate cake into the dining room while holding the letter in her free hand. She wanted him to read it but convincing him would be difficult. As postmaster of Cardington, he was forbidden to open mail that should be forwarded to the Dead Letter Office in Washington, D.C. And he took his responsibilities seriously.

"What's this? A confection at the mid-day meal and it's not even my birthday?" Wade's face brightened when she placed the dessert on the table in front of him.

"Since I've been baking so much for Christmas, I thought we might as well enjoy some treats now." She sat next to him, sliding the letter under his fork.

His brow wrinkled. "I thought you understood not to bring these letters written to Santa to my attention." He nudged away the envelope as though an ant had crawled across the linen tablecloth.

"Oh, Wade, this is different."

He shook his head.

She put her hand on his wrist. He never could resist her touch. "Will you not believe me when I tell you it is a critical matter I simply must share with you?"

He sighed and sipped from his china cup. "I do believe you, my dear. However, you must remember how tenuous my position is."

"Surely not so much now that Grant is president." Wade had been postmaster for two decades when he and over a thousand other postmasters across the union were removed for being Republicans by President Johnson's chosen Postmaster General. Now that he had the prestigious assignment back, he didn't want to risk the wrath of the Washington office by not following the rules.

He sighed and cast her a somber look. "If a letter given to the postmaster is addressed to a fictitious person the postmaster must send it to the—"

"Yes, I know, dear. And that is why I retrieve them from the counter. I am not held to such rules."

"And the ladies of the town, they are your companions. You should be showing this to them."

"You must see it as well. With your own eyes." An idea came to her. She nudged his half-eaten cake to the side. "You know, the rules say you must not open the letter. You haven't. I have. You don't have possession of it, and you don't even have to hold it. If I were reading the letter and you, being such an attentive, caring husband, were to look over my shoulder…"

He stared back at her, his blue eyes rounded. She knew he would comply, though he would not agree explicitly. They'd been married so long words were no longer required. She pivoted in her chair, opened the letter, and stretched out her arms. Wade's vision wasn't as good as it used to be. He needed some distance. As she sat there feeling his warm breath on her neck, she re-read the note silently.

> *Please, Santa, do not bring me any presents. Gifts make my Ma peevish. She says we require no charity. Just last week the ladies from the Methodist church brought us a ham and stayed for coffee. She pretended she was mighty grateful, except she was really afraid. She has been unhappy since Pa died in the war and we had to come to Cardington to live with Uncle Burt. Except Uncle Burt was not here, he died, and Ma did not have enough money to go back to Kentucky. She is afraid folks will learn that Pa fought for the Confederacy. Folks here would say Pa was a rebel and we'd be ragamuffins, if'n they knew. So, Santa, instead of bringing me presents this year, could you bring Ma something? She does not like fancy dresses, she has enough stockings, and she cares none for candy. I know what she would really like. Dear Santa, could you bring Ma a friend?*
>
> *Your admirer,*
> *Evie Ratliff*
> *P.S. You can find us at Uncle Burt's house. We live there now.*

A grunt, and Wade returned to his chair, picked up his fork, and resumed eating. He hadn't fought in the war, being nearly fifty years of age when it broke out and also legally exempt because he was postmaster. Lincoln had deemed postmaster a crucial position that must remain filled by those who had been appointed. Still, Wade talked to folks, read widely, and knew a lot about the war years. Certainly his conversations with U.S. Congressman James Beatty, a local war hero who attained the rank of Brigadier General during his wartime service, should shed light on Evie's mother's misgivings and what might be done about it.

"But, what do you think?" She heard the choke in her voice. The letter tugged at her heart even though it wasn't the first time she had read it.

"I think you should be her friend. Emma is the girl's mother's name, I believe. What's the quandary?"

"Well, certainly I shall, but the other ladies —"

"Need never know." He took a swig of his coffee and then wiped his mouth with a perfectly starched and pressed napkin.

She hoped he did not take any of the others she had folded to use later. She drank from her water glass before continuing. "It's too late."

"You told them about this? I thought you were asking me first. Wasn't that the point of this conversation, Diana?"

She added honey to her tone. "Wade, darling, the point of the conversation was to inform you that one of the women plucked Evie's letter from the stack at our meeting and read it aloud." She had always known her husband to be fair and compassionate, but he occasionally lacked sufficient sensibilities. During those times, she dutifully brought it to his attention, delicately, as a good wife should.

He grunted, swallowing a mouthful of cake.

Wade's main occupation was proprietor of a wagon-making business, but his status in Cardington came from his position as postmaster. He was also an ordained minister in the Methodist Episcopal Church, though he did not pastor a congregation, only preached funerals and helped out when needed. He came from a long line of devout Christians. He should have some wisdom to share on this matter beyond his suggestion that Diana befriend Evie's mother.

He tapped his fingers on the table top. "I see. I suppose Mabel Walker was at that meeting?"

"She was."

"And Doris Shelby? Alice Rice and her daughter?"

"They were all in attendance. And not any of them kind."

"I expect not. They suffered much at the hands of the Confederacy."

"But, even so, Evie and her mother Emma, they should not be blamed."

Wade reached over and took her hand. "Indeed, they should not. I'm sorry to have been so cantankerous, my love. You were right to bring it to my attention."

Chocolate cake always softened him up. "Excellent. They will be here shortly."

He pulled his shoulders back as though she was speaking in Greek.

"Our meeting. It's my turn to host. I am serving chocolate —"

"Diana, you aren't suggesting I attend this gathering."

"But you know much more about the war than I do. You'd be the perfect mediator."

He eyed the rest of the cake sitting on the sideboard atop a cut glass stand. "This will not be an easy task."

"Think of poor Evie. Christmas is almost upon us. I have plenty of cake and coffee."

He stood. "All right. Let me instruct the clerk at the post office and stop in to see how the Pennington brothers are coming on the undercarriage they've been building in the shop. I shall return in one hour."

She kissed him and helped him into his overcoat. "Don't be late. We only have two new letters to consider."

He huffed and stepped out into the cold December afternoon.

Not long after her husband left, Diana was entertaining the ladies who had undertaken the role of Santa in the town.

"Little Lizzie wants a doll with blond hair tied back with a gossamer ribbon." Doris gazed over her spectacles at the letter she held. "I can take this one."

"Are you certain?" Mabel asked. "Times are hard. We understand."

Most of the toys they'd be delivering had been handmade by generous townsfolk. What had to be purchased was done through sacrifice.

"I am certain," she answered.

Diana knew that probably meant going without something. She would ask Doris to join them for supper soon.

"Did Morris finish the Nine-Pins?" Mabel asked, glancing around at the packages littering the parlor.

"Indeed he did," Diana answered. She held up the box. "I'm sure Alexander and his brothers will spend many hours playing that game now."

Mabel nodded, sending her white curls bouncing. "Excellent. Rolling hoop? Dominos?"

Sarah, Alice's daughter and the youngest of their group, tip-toed through the toys. "All accounted for!"

As they finished discussing their assignments, Diana stared at the closed parlor door, willing her husband to walk through it.

Doris clapped her hands. "Attention, ladies. It is agreed that we shall meet at Mabel's house next week to wrap the gifts and dispense them to the children's parents?"

"And divide up some to be delivered," Alice added.

A murmured approval swung through the room and then Doris prepared to close with a blessing before the cake was served. "Heavenly Father," she began in her nasally voice. "We thank thee for these dear children. We thank thee for guiding us as we become thy hands and feet during this blessed season. Bless the refreshment we are about to enjoy and the hostess who has so lovingly prepared it."

There was a resounding amen and then excited chatter.

Diana went about serving despite the sinking feeling in her stomach. Little Evie would not get her Christmas wish if these women's hearts were not changed, and quickly. She needed help. Where was Wade?

Like an actor responding to a director's cue, Wade emerged onto the stage through the parlor door.

"Greetings, Mr. Postmaster," Alice said, handing Wade a cup of coffee.

"Thank you, Mrs. Rice." He bowed toward the center of the room. "Ladies. I do hope you'll permit me the pleasure of your company." He winked at Diana.

Oh, how she loved that man! He sat next to her on one of the kitchen chairs she'd brought in for the meeting.

After several minutes of chatter and pleasantries, Wade stood.

"You aren't leaving so soon, are you?" Mabel asked.

"Indeed not. Ladies, it has come to my attention that there is a serious matter you have not yet addressed. Isn't this so, Diana?"

"It is."

Doris glowered. Diana ignored her, turning her attention to Wade.

"Mr. Postmaster," Doris said, setting down her coffee. "I understand that you ignore our answering these letters to Santa."

"I do not," Wade said. "I simply permit you to collect the letters before they are officially delivered to me. My wife was very concerned over one of them, and I was distressed to see her so melancholy, so I read the letter over her shoulder."

"Evie's letter," Sarah said. "She wants her mother to have a friend."

Wade turned to her. The girl was only fifteen, but old enough to have heard stories about the war, including the events that had personally affected her. "That is correct, my dear. And let me say to you all, I understand how dismayed you are to have memories of the War Between the States stirred up again."

The women fell silent. They respected Wade. No other person could approach the subject with these women and be heard. Diana knew this from the maelstrom that had occurred when the letter first came to light.

Wade sat back down. "If you will allow, I'd like us all to hear how each of you has been affected. You may not even know the whole truth of each story."

Doris seemed the most reluctant as she kept her gaze on the carpet.

Wade used his preacher's voice. "I promise I shall be as delicate as possible. And Diana and I will require nothing of anyone here."

Nods compelled him to continue. "Mabel?"

She looked up, her hands fidgeting in her lap. "My son Matthew died at Andersonville."

"A battle?" Sarah asked.

Mabel shook her head. "A prison in Georgia at Camp Sumter. I would spare you the details."

Diana went to her and put a hand on the woman's shoulder. "I would like to understand your heartache as best I can, Mabel. We know he died in the war, but if you would not mind it too much, please tell us what happened to dear Matthew."

Mabel drew in a deep breath. "My husband Charles sometime later told me what some of the men who had been at Andersonville with Matthew told him."

Diana prayed silently that God would strengthen this woman. "Go ahead if you can."

The older woman dabbed at the corners of her eyes with a handkerchief. She glanced at Wade. "What do you know of this place?"

"I understand there was much overcrowding. The prison was not built to hold so many men. And, by that time in the war, the Confederacy was low on supplies, food, just about everything. The Confederates held tens of thousands of Union men there. Had they released them, they would strengthen their enemy. Holding them resulted in mass starvation, disease, men going without proper clothing — misery as none of us have ever seen. They hung the prison commander when the conflict ended, for violating the laws of war."

Wade was right. This was a depressing, sorrowful story to hear. Diana rubbed the top of Mabel's shoulder. "And Matthew?"

"He was shot for crossing the deadline. At least his death was quick."

Sarah put a hand to her heart. "He tried to escape?"

"No, dear," Mabel answered. "There were posts set up inside the prison and our boys were instructed to stay inside the penned in area. It seems Matthew thought he could reach a cleaner part of the stream from the other side of the deadline, that's what they called the boundaries. He was reaching underneath it when one of the guards fired at him." She gasped and put her hand over her mouth.

"I am so sorry," Diana said. She choked back her own tears. Of course she'd heard stories, but folks rarely talked so intimately about what had happened. It was difficult to awaken sorrows folks preferred to bury. Somehow her husband, or perhaps God's hand through him, was now opening hearts that could hopefully heal.

Wade spoke to the others. "To die for your country is, to most folks' minds, a noble death. Defending a line in battle or rescuing a comrade, these are considered to be heroic acts. But shot inside a prison for trying to get water? That was an act of murder, I would say." He pivoted on his chair to better face the weeping woman. "Let me tell you, Mabel, your son died a hero. He volunteered to fight for the Union. He endured hardships to answer Lincoln's call. Our president was also murdered. You can be proud that Matthew was willing to defend the Union. We mourn beside you and pray for God's comfort."

The woman pinched her lips together a moment and then sat straighter. "I am glad to talk about it. Thank you all for your support."

Doris Shelby had been quite verbal about shunning Evie and her mother. Diana watched to see how the story had moved her, but she could not tell by Doris's somber expression. Doris taught a women's Sunday school class. Her father had been an itinerant preacher when Doris was a girl. She quoted Bible verses as though they were written on the inside of her eyelids. Diana knew Doris's husband had gone off with John Beatty and was killed in the war, leaving her a young widow. She hadn't seemed bitter in all the years Diana knew her, and yet her reaction to Evie's letter had been the most severe.

"Not many Southerners come to Cardington," Wade said, moving cake crumbs around his plate with a fork. "Certainly there have been those opposing war, and particularly conscription, but not many Confederate sympathizers remain around here."

The women murmured agreement. Diana could not imagine where he was going with this.

Wade continued. "Doris, I believe the others would find your forgiveness touching, though the story is tragic. Congressman Beatty has shared some of it with me. Would you like to tell it here among friends?"

"Well, I don't know. Seems improper to speak of such sadness."

"We would like to honor your husband, Doris," Diana said to encourage her. "Would you allow us?"

Her face brightened. "I suppose that is proper."

Diana returned to her chair and leaned back, bracing herself.

Doris patted the Bible in her lap. "As you all know, Samuel was with Beatty's men in the mountains of Virginia. John Beatty says the folks in those mountains were poor as church mice. They knew nothing of wealthy plantations and slaves. They were fairly isolated, except they'd been told some untruths, isn't that right, Mr. Johnson?" She looked to Wade who acknowledged her with a nod.

"They thought our men had come to confiscate their farms and to slay their children."

A gasp encircled the room.

"We know better," Doris said. "But they didn't. They thought to defend their homes. Samuel was part of a picket, that is to say, the guards sent ahead of the main army. It was a dangerous position, to my understanding." She turned to Wade who encouraged her to continue. "A farmer got off an accurate shot as his young ones cowered behind him." She shrugged. "Protecting his family, at least to his mind. I can forgive."

Diana was stunned. "That's mighty gracious, Doris." She wanted to ask why she'd been so vehement about not accepting Emma, whose husband had also been killed, but she wasn't sure how to ask.

Suddenly, as though a storm cloud had moved in, Doris's demeanor changed. "It's the Rebels I blame for Samuel's death. The men in the southern army."

"But it was a southerner who shot him," Diana said.

Wade held up his hand. "Please, Doris, go on."

"The farmer was not the one who spread the rumors," Doris said. "It was the one wearing the butternut coat. I suppose one like Emma's husband. I can't forgive that." She folded her arms tightly across her stomach like a stubborn child.

Diana opened her mouth to protest. After all, Emma's husband was dead, but Wade jiggled his head and she refrained.

"We are sorry for your loss, Doris," Wade said.

"Indeed we are," Diana agreed.

"Doris, your husband did his duty. Of that, you can be proud," Wade said.

"Thank you," Doris mumbled, holding her handkerchief to her mouth.

Then Wade turned to Alice. She was hugging her daughter to her side. "You do not have to talk about your Robert," he said to her. "But we are eager listeners if you'd like to."

Alice took a deep breath. "I do not mind talking about Robert. To not mention his name makes it seem as though he never lived a normal life. And he did." She smiled at her daughter.

Diana knew that Robert Rice resided at a home for disabled veterans, not those who'd lost limbs or eyes, but those whose minds would never recover from the trauma of the battlefield.

"We just visited him this morning, as a matter of fact," Alice said.

"Oh, how is Robert?" Mabel asked. "I've been meaning to bring him some of my gingerbread."

Alice smiled. "He would like that. Thank you."

Sarah scooted to the edge of the settee. "Daddy speaks a little now. Doctors say that is some improvement."

A good sign, Diana thought, but after all these years Robert would never be the husband and father he was before the war. "We shall have to bring him some baked treats soon," she added.

Alice sighed. "I know it isn't right, Mr. Johnson, to dislike Emma and Evie Ratliff just because the rest of us despise what was done to our men, but it's hard. I don't mean them no harm, just would rather not socialize with them, you understand."

They let Alice's words settle uncomfortably in the room for several minutes. Finally, Diana found her voice.

"Ladies, no one can make up for the hurt you feel. Your feelings are to be expected." She looked at Wade. "I suppose those in the south, the widows and mothers who lost children, experienced some of the same?"

"They certainly did," he said. "Some lost their farms and all their worldly possessions, and many did not even know why they were fighting, other than to defend their homes." He held out a hand toward Doris. "We may never know who spread those rumors about our men in those Virginia mountains, but certainly it could not have been the entire southern army. I am convinced the good Lord wept over what happened on both sides."

Doris pursed her lips.

Diana patted her arm. "Doris, your Bible? Would you mind looking something up? Something that has just come to my mind."

The woman opened her well-worn Bible.

Diana pointed to the pages. "From the Book of Leviticus, the nineteenth chapter. There is something there about not bearing a grudge."

Mabel got to her feet. "Surely you do not accuse us of merely bearing a grudge, Diana. Our husbands and sons are lost to us forever."

Wade spoke up. "No one means to offend. Please, may we just listen? We accuse no one of anything."

She plopped back down on the parlor chair.

Diana was not convinced Mabel or any of them would truly listen. *It's in your hands, God.*

Doris began to read. "Thou shalt not avenge, nor bear any grudge against the children of thy people, but thou shalt love thy neighbor as thyself; I am the LORD."

Wade stood. "Ladies, you are not the only people in this great country who puzzle over how to follow this command. Look at the quarreling still going on between the North and South. Our previous president was impeached over disagreements in policy and how laws should be carried out and by whom. Shall we not start here, in our own small town, to heal this divide? With Evie, whose only wish this Christmas is to see her mama happy again? Is that not within our power in some degree?"

Diana stood next to her husband and put her arm in his. "God was speaking to his people in that ancient passage, and I believe he still speaks to us today. 'Thy children' are our children. Was this not what our soldiers fought for? For a union?" She stretched out her hands, encouraging her friends to come to her.

The women rose and joined hands, although no one spoke again except to thank her for her hospitality and say goodnight as they left.

🍂 🍂 🍂

When the time came to distribute the gifts to the men and women who would be Santa's helpers, Diana still was not sure if the women would respond to Evie's wish favorably. She hoped the girl's letter would be the beginning of healing for the Cardington women, but she wasn't sure. She would visit Emma that very evening, however, and make sure Evie knew her mother had at least one friend.

Lizzie's mother accepted the fair-haired doll with the pink ribbon in her hair. "She's only had a rag doll to play with. I cannot thank the women's society enough."

Mabel seemed delighted to have granted that wish. "Please, take her a peppermint stick as well."

Not all the wishes would be given so openly. Part of their task had been to discern who would welcome the charity and who would need to accept wrapped gifts left on their porches. The undertaking certainly made them all feel goodwill and cheer. But Diana couldn't help but wonder if that was truly what charity was supposed to affect.

Wade paid a visit to help. Or perhaps to snag some of Mabel's gingerbread. After he greeted the others, Diana whispered to him. "Shouldn't the spirit of giving at Christmas involve offering more of ourselves? More than our time and funds?"

She had not realized Sarah was standing close enough to hear, but when she turned around she saw the girl tug on her mother's sleeve. Alice approached them.

"Diana, Wade, we would like to thank you for the other evening. Talking about our men was…well, comforting. We are pleased they are remembered."

This was good, but not all Diana had hoped for. She put on her best smile and led Wade to a table where they worked on making bows.

The door opened to let in another parent. Diana turned to welcome the visitor so she could search for the appropriate gift. She was stunned to see Emma standing on the threshold.

"Come in," Doris said. Her voice was tight. "You have heard about our mission to grant wishes the children in our town make for Christmas?"

Emma did not take off her hat. "I was not aware my daughter had written a letter to Santa, so I was surprised by your invitation. However, I will make sure my daughter gets presents this year. You may give whatever you planned for her to another deserving child."

Diana and Wade exchanged surprised looks. What were they going to give this woman?

"I am afraid we cannot do that," Alice said, reaching for Emma's muff. "Please, come in. This wish can only be granted for her."

Emma reluctantly gave up her wraps. "Very well. I cannot stay long. She's waiting at home for me."

"Please, sit beside me," Doris said as she patted the velvet upholstery on Mabel's sofa. "We haven't gotten to know you since you've come to town. I do hope you'll forgive us."

Emma sat as though she was afraid the furniture might collapse.

Diana and Wade sat in chairs facing them. Diana wanted to welcome Emma as well, but the other women filled all the silences.

"My little brother knows Evie from school," Sarah said. She handed Emma a gingerbread cookie. "He says she's nice. And smart too."

Emma's defenses seemed to soften. She bit into the cookie. "This is quite good."

Mabel beamed. "Thank you, my dear. I shall box some up for you to take to your Evie."

"About that wish," Doris said. She too seemed more relaxed. "We were quite humbled by it."

"And ashamed, truth be told," Mabel put in. "But we mean to remedy that right away."

Wade squeezed Diana's hand.

Emma shrugged. "I'm afraid I do not understand."

Alice stepped forward. "We have not been good neighbors. We vow beginning now to change that. We will no longer look at any family and ask ourselves which side they were on during the war. The war is over. We shall not fight it all over again. You are one of us, Mrs. Ratliff."

Tears welled in Emma's eyes. Sarah handed her a napkin. "Please, call me Emma."

"We shall call you..." Doris hesitated, then reached for Emma's hand. "We shall call you friend, if that's all right with you."

Emma nodded while blinking back tears. "This was Evie's wish, the thing she asked for in her letter?"

"It was," Diana answered. "Merry Christmas!"

Cindy Thomson is the author of eight books, including her newest novel, *Enya's Son*, third in the Daughters of Ireland series based on ancient legends. Being a genealogy enthusiast, she has also written articles for *Internet Genealogy* and *Your Genealogy Today* magazines, and children's short stories for *Clubhouse Magazine*. She has also co-authored a baseball biography. Most everything she writes reflects her belief that history has stories to teach. Cindy and her husband live in central Ohio near their three grown sons and their families, and can be found online at: *www.cindyswriting.com*, on Facebook: *www.facebook.com/cindyswriting* and on Twitter: *@cindyswriting*.

COURTESY TURN

By Rebecca Waters

"Your friends are right, you know," Leah told her mother-in-law as she helped clear the Thanksgiving table at Lori's house. "You do need to get out. Maybe the Carol Fest at church. You always liked the rehearsals and baking cookies as much as the caroling."

"Maybe," Lori murmured, her thoughts traveling back five years when the carolers made their way to her own home. John had been too weak to meet them at the door, but insisted she sing along by his bedside. It had been hard. They had both known that would be his last Christmas. "I get out. I shop and go to church."

"I don't want you driving at night by yourself." Ethan scooped another dollop of whipped topping on his pumpkin pie. "If you want to go to Carol Fest, get a ride with someone from church. Understood?"

Lori's mouth fell open, but before she could respond to her son's demand, he was headed back to the family room.

"Have you thought about going back to work?" Leah asked.

Lori shrugged. "Not really. Don't know what I'd do."

"Are you kidding? Mom, you were such a great editor."

Lori smiled. Her daughter-in-law had always been supportive as if Lori were her own mother. "Thanks, but my technology skills are limited and everything has changed in the last few years anyway."

"I can't believe *Priority Care* let you go in the first place." Leah clenched her jaw. "You were the best editor they ever had."

"I'd rather not rehash all of that," Lori said as her two grandsons ran into the kitchen.

"Well, if you were anyone else I'd suggest you try dating, but of course I know you're not interested in that."

"Mom, can we go outside and throw the football?" Aiden asked.

"It's okay with me and maybe Grandma will go with you." She turned to her mother-in-law. "I'll get these last few dishes, Mom."

Lori joined the bundled boys as they tromped through the back yard chasing the football. *Maybe this is where I belong*, she thought, *with six- and seven-year-olds.* Somewhere along the way, roles had switched.

I'm treated like a child. Humph! Ethan practically ordered me not to go out at night. He may as well have said, "You are too old to be out late." Lori retrieved the football from the deadened lilac bush for Aiden and Jack for the umpteenth time. *Fifty-seven isn't old.*

Fifty-seven wasn't old. Not by anyone's standards except her son's. *And what did Leah mean when she said if I was anyone else I might be interested in dating? Does she think I'm too old to care about such things?* Lori loved her family dearly but wondered why she was experiencing this growing frustration with them and with Ethan in particular.

Maybe I should consider going back to work. But what would I do? Those last years as an editor had been difficult. Her work for the nursing journal, *Priority Care,* had been quietly dismissed as the corporation owning the publication decided they needed an editor to "take them into the digital world." It would save the corporation time and money. No more print versions going out. Nurses would download the entire journal online, take the accompanying quiz and earn the continuing education credits they needed to renew their credentials.

Lori drew in a deep breath. It was the right decision. Learning the publication end of a digital digest had been too much to take on with John's cancer looming large over them. She had allowed the company to replace her duties piece by piece, telling herself she would reinvest herself in the work once John was cured. *I've done that with everything in my life. Allowed others to take over. I've allowed my own children to practically bully me!*

"Grandma! Run out deep for a pass!"

Lori shook herself from her dismal thoughts. "No tackling!" she called back. She jogged toward the end of the yard, turned and nearly caught the ball, much to the delight of her grandsons.

I brought this on myself. The three ambled back toward the house. *I've acted so lost. So afraid of, well, everything since John died. Maybe it's time for me to reclaim my life.* "I'll do it!"

"Do what, Grandma?" Jack asked.

Lori put her hand on her grandson's shoulder as they walked. "Thinking to myself, sweetie." *I'll need help with this, Lord. Didn't you say something about not being timid and fearful?*

Armed with new resolve, Lori ventured back into her house, thanked her daughter-in-law for cleaning the kitchen and passed Ethan as he sat glued in front of the television, watching a football game.

"Maybe if you're a good girl, Santa will bring you big screen TV for Christmas," Ethan called after her. Lori grunted. His joke only punctuated her decision to change.

Upstairs in her bedroom, Lori pulled her Bible from the nightstand. It took her a few minutes to locate the verse she wanted, but when she found it she read it several times over. Sasquatch jumped up on the bed beside her. "Listen to this, cat.

"For God did not give us a spirit of timidity, but a spirit of
power, of love, and of self-discipline. 2 Timothy 1: 7."

Lori wrote the verse on the back of an old offering envelope. This
would be her new mantra. She would no longer live in the shadows of fear
and doubt. She was a strong, capable woman. She would live like a strong,
capable woman.

"I am woman! Hear me roar!" she said out loud. Startled at her own
voice, Lori put her Bible away.

Sasquatch turned his head sideways, gave a wide yawn and a look
that said he did not know what the fuss was about, nor did he care.

"And you know something else, cat? It would be nice to have dinner
with someone of the opposite sex from time to time." Sasquatch tilted his
head upward. "You don't count. I want to talk to someone who talks
back." The cat stretched, licked his rough tongue against Lori's hand, and
jumped down. That was the problem. The good guys were taken. The only
ones left were the kiss-and-run kind like Sasquatch.

When John was alive, they had enjoyed an active life and the
company of many friends. Closest church friends still invited her to
functions like picnics and concerts. She knew too, though, that they often
got together as couples to go out to the dinner theater in Springboro or to
attend one of the Cincinnati Reds' baseball games. She wasn't included on
those "couples" outings.

Their square dance friends were different. John and Lori had taken
up the activity when their son left for college. Never one to dance, John
surprised her by suggesting they try it. "It's the United States' official folk
dance, Lori. Just one lesson," John had said. "Consider it a date night.
We'll try it and if we don't like it, we'll bail out."

One lesson and they had been hooked. They finished the lessons,
joined a local square dance club and set about making lasting friendships.
During his illness, the square dancers made sure the grass was cut, fixed
the washing machine when it broke, and came by with meals to share.
Other friends brought meals, but left them for John and Lori to eat alone.
Their square dance friends had stopped by with food enough for all of
them. They had entertained John and kept Lori from losing her mind in
isolation.

If I were to "get out," maybe it would be to go to a square dance. "I haven't
danced in so long, cat, I'll probably have to go back to lessons." She looked
at the calendar by her bed. Classes would begin again in January, a little
over a month away.

Lori opened the bedroom door and returned to her family. Sasquatch
raced ahead and jumped in Ethan's lap.

"There you are, Mom." Leah smiled "We were just talking about

27

Christmas. What do you want?"

"I already told her she needs a bigger TV," Ethan said, and laughed.

"Ha. Ha. We weren't asking what you want." She turned expectantly toward Lori.

"I want a garage door opener," Lori responded matter-of-factly.

2

The Hayloft Barn was a flurry of activity the first Tuesday in January. The smell of hot buttered popcorn and freshly baked chocolate chip cookies greeted the new students and square dance helpers as they climbed the stairs to the upper floor of the two-story barn.

"Well look who's here," Marta Mason, the main organizer of the lessons cried out as Lori walked across the wooden floor. "I haven't seen you in a month of Sundays. Good to have you back!"

Lori returned the gracious hug. She had anticipated such a greeting and had prepared herself for several more from old friends.

"I haven't danced in over five years, so I decided I needed a little refresher course." Lori glanced around the room but didn't see anyone else she knew. "Where's the old gang?"

"Oh, you know, every year we have a few who stop coming, but we always pick up a few new angel helpers for students."

"I guess I'm a student." Lori stuffed her purse under one of the chairs lining the walls.

Marta handed her a registration form. "A retread. People who are just brushing up on the moves, we call retreads."

Lori took the paper, the obligatory stick-on nametag, and helped herself to a cup of coffee.

"So why do they call the people helping *angels*?" a voice asked from the registration table.

Lori turned to see a woman with short black hair, reaching for a cookie. Her nametag identified her as Iris.

"Tradition, I guess," another woman responded. "Or maybe it's just because some man like my husband came to take lessons and they said, 'Heaven help us all!'"

"I know! I couldn't believe Hank agreed to come to these lessons."

Okay, Iris and Hank. Lori took a deep breath. *This may be harder than I thought. There seem to be a lot of couples here.* Experience told her there would be singles as well. Probably more women than men, but the people in charge would split up angel couples to make sure all of the students had an angel partner to guide them through the dance moves.

"Welcome!" a man's voice boomed over the microphone. Everyone looked up to the front of the large room where a man stood on a makeshift stage. "My name is Greg. It's good to see all of you here for our first night of square dance lessons. I would like to ask all of you to join hands and form a large circle around the room."

The bevy of students, retreads, and angels quickly joined hands and stood expectantly looking toward Greg.

"Good. Let's get started," Greg challenged as he turned on the music. "Move your circle to the left, keeping time with the music. Now circle to the right. Excellent. Now drop hands and face me." Everyone stopped and looked toward their leader.

"Good. I am your square dancing caller. You just demonstrated to me you already have the three things you need to know to be good dancers. You listened to the caller, you moved together in a circle with the music, and *most* of you know your left from your right."

At this the entire group chuckled.

"Now I want you to move around until you are standing in a boy, girl, boy, girl configuration," Greg instructed. He then walked them through some basic moves.

Lori was partnered with a short, balding man by the name of George. She guessed him to be at least in his mid-nineties. He had difficulty hearing the calls and even more trouble completing the moves. At one point he grabbed Lori and turned her around so fast, he caused her to stumble into the couple behind them.

"So sorry," she told the man who caught her by the arm. Looking up, Lori could see he was tall. Tall and good looking with a mass of wavy dark brown hair graying at the temples. He was obviously a helper. He was dressed in a denim western shirt, making his blue eyes stand out even more. A club badge was pinned to his shirt, but she had little time to note the name.

"No problem," came the answer in a strong but friendly voice.

Lori felt her heart do a little flip-flop. Embarrassed, she shook herself, thanked the man for the rescue and turned back to George, who seemed oblivious to the break in action they had caused. The music started once more. Lori took another glance at her rescuer.

That man looks like an honest to goodness cowboy.

Marta came over after a few minutes and partnered George with someone from a local club. She asked Lori to dance instead with a more experienced dancer, so the dancing went much more smoothly for the second half of the evening.

Greg sorted the groups out into squares with four couples in each square. He was explaining how two of the couples were the heads of the square and two were called the sides. "Now that guy or gal standing right beside you is your partner. Your nearest neighbor is your corner. Gals, your corner is to your right. Fellows, that gal standing to your left is your corner. Say hello to your corner." He began a series of calls where the head couples would do-sa-do and then he would ask the sides to do the same. "Now do-sa-do your corner." The first lesson continued this way until Greg had taught the group enough moves to put them all together for a simple dance.

Lori's group progressed nicely through the first lesson. She couldn't help but notice Old George was now in the same square as The Cowboy. The older man was moving on every call instead of waiting his turn, causing great confusion to the other dancers in the square. The Cowboy was patiently helping George without ridicule. The Cowboy's eyes met hers for a moment from across the room. He smiled. Lori felt her heart do that same little flip-flop, causing her to draw her hand to her face. Was she really blushing? At her age?

Ridiculous.

As the evening ended, Lori watched as the man she called The Cowboy donned an honest to goodness cowboy hat and left a minute or two before she did, going into the parking lot. She sat for a few minutes in her darkened car. The image of The Cowboy came unbidden to her mind.

There is no way I am interested in a man, she thought. *This is crazy.* Overcome with the unexpected feeling, Lori quickly started the car and made her way slowly toward the main road. *Well, that's the end of that. I tried. I don't need to be square dancing anyway.*

The Hayloft Barn was located in a county park within the city limits of Cincinnati. To get to the main road, Lori had to weave her car through the park along a dark, tree-lined road. A pair of headlights moved slowly up behind her car. At first, Lori felt a sense of comfort, knowing she wasn't alone on the rarely traveled road through the woods, but then noticed the car turned left onto the main road leading out of the park just as she did, and then made a right turn behind her onto the city street that would take her to her neighborhood. Lori tried to shake the notion that she was being followed, but was unsuccessful when the headlights turned onto her own street only a few car lengths behind her vehicle. She was forming a plan to drive past her own house and go somewhere else when the car made a sudden turn left and disappeared.

Lori pushed the garage door opener button in her car and praised God Ethan and Leah had not only purchased it for her for Christmas as she asked, but had it installed, and Ethan showed her how to use it.

"Sasquatch, you have a foolish old woman for a friend," Lori confessed to her cat as the big-footed creature rubbed against her leg in greeting as she stepped into the house. "That car was probably a dancer leaving the Barn just like me."

"Four to six inches of snow?" Lori asked.

"That's what they're predicting," Leah told her over the phone. "It should start coming down late tomorrow night. Do you want to come to our house?"

"No…no. I'll be fine. I don't have to be anywhere. We haven't had much snow this year. I'm kind of looking forward to it."

"I know. Too bad it didn't come for Christmas. I always liked a white Christmas."

"I liked the movie, but can't say I enjoy the white stuff when I have to drive in it."

A quick assessment of the pantry was in order. "Well, you're all set," she told Sasquatch. "Plenty of cat food and kitty litter. If I want to live on green beans for the next few days, I'm in good shape, too. Whadda' you think?"

Sasquatch gave a noncommittal twitch of his nose before sauntering off toward the living room.

"Humph. That's what I thought."

Lori glanced at the clock. She grabbed her keys and purse. "Be back in a jiffy, cat!"

Although a small grocery was located within a couple of miles of Lori's house, she preferred the large rambling market called Jungle Jim's located a few miles away. She liked the fresh produce and the wide selection of international foods available at what locals called "the jungle." If a snowstorm was brewing, it would be nice to have fresh vegetables and fruit, along with foods that would keep, should the electric go out.

Jungle Jim's was crowded with people like Lori, anxious to purchase food before a nasty winter storm made travel impossible. Lori picked up a loaf of bread and a box of cereal. She put a few bags of chips and jars of salsa in her cart. *Love salsa. Oh, cheese and crackers are always nice, too.* Lori grabbed a box of crackers and a small brick of Colby Jack cheese. The meat was packaged in large "family size" quantities. Lori found a small ham and a package of chicken thighs. *Four thighs? That's four meals for me.*

She had just rounded the corner leading to the fruits and vegetables section of the store when her heart leapt. Turning down the next aisle was The Cowboy. She only caught a glimpse of his back, but it was him. The height, the way he walked, even the hat was distinctive. He was coming down the open aisle on the other side of the squash. What was he picking up? Eggplant? Something purple looking. Between the banners and signs hanging down describing each item and the tables of vegetables themselves, Lori could see the bottom of The Cowboy's face and had a clear view of his shopping cart. Three apples, a small hand of green bananas and a couple of baking potatoes. *I bet he lives alone.*

A plan started forming. *If I turn my cart around now, we'll probably meet at the end of this aisle near the cabbage. I'll look up. He'll tip his hat and say something like, "Well hello, again. We met at the Hayloft Barn last Tuesday, remember?" I'll offer a slow smile of recognition. "Oh, of course. I remember." Then he'll give his name and I'll offer mine. Maybe we'll have a cup of coffee at the Starbuck's right here in Jungle Jim's.*

Lori looked over the zucchini. The Cowboy was gone. She looked both ways. He had vanished. *What was I thinking?* A little laugh escaped.

Grabbing potatoes, some cabbage, and bananas, Lori made her way through the store, picking up a bag of brown rice, a few canned vegetables and the makings for her famous bean soup. *Some milk and eggs and I'm out of here.*

The dairy aisle was bottlenecked with shoppers. She sampled a new Greek yogurt offered by a young woman at the end of the aisle. She bent over a bin containing two varieties of the creamy yogurt. As she stood up to compare the calories of the two, a corduroy-clad arm reached past her.

"Oh, pardon me, Ma'am. I was tryin' to get that blueberry yogurt."

The Cowboy.

"No problem." Lori smiled.

The Cowboy tipped his hat, dropped a blueberry yogurt in the basket and pushed away.

I should say something. Maybe, I could be the one. I could say, "Don't I know you from somewhere?" No. That's lame. Lori bit her lower lip. *"Were you at the Hayloft Barn Tuesday?"* No. Maybe *"Pardon me, but did we meet at the Hayloft last Tuesday?"* Much better. Then he'll probably say, "Why yes." Then he'll offer his name and I'll offer mine. *Would we have coffee? I really need to get these groceries home. Maybe exchange phone numbers.* No. That would be rushing it.

"Excuse me, ma'am, but could I reach past you? I need the fat-free yogurt."

Lori blinked her eyes back to the reality of the grocery store. A young redheaded woman with a redheaded infant in her cart was smiling sweetly at her.

"Oh, yes, I'm sorry. I guess I was blocking the way." Lori put both yogurts in her shopping cart and pushed forward.

The Cowboy was gone. She grabbed a quart of milk and a dozen eggs before making her way to the checkout line. No cowboys were anywhere to be seen. "I'm an idiot," she said to no one in particular. The dark-skinned man behind her grinned.

♡ ♡ ♡

A sense of relief washed over Lori Tuesday afternoon when Marta called to say the lessons at the Barn were cancelled due to inclement weather. She had pretty much decided she would never show her face there again, anyway.

But why? "I feel goofy, that's why." *Of course The Cowboy was clueless. He could even be married. Or a weirdo.* "He didn't say anything at the store." *Guess I didn't make much of an impression on him.* "Humph!"

Lori changed Sasquatch's litter box, the cat silently following her every word and every step.

"I can't tell anybody else all this, you know. You're the only one I can talk to, cat. Truth is, I don't need a man in my life anyway. I have a perfectly wonderful life. I have friends. I have more sensible hobbies like crocheting and cooking. Maybe I could take up aerobics or something, but what's the point? No, cat, I think everything is just right as it is. What more could I want?"

4

The snow was a memory by Sunday. Sitting with Carol for the worship service, Lori noticed her friend fumbling through the contemporary songs on the screen. She enjoyed the older hymns as well, but there was a vibrancy to these new songs that touched her heart.

I hope I never stop embracing new ways to praise God.

Pastor Mike stepped up to the pulpit to deliver his sermon. Carol leaned over. "Wonder why we even have a pulpit. You know he'll be out from behind it before the first sentence is out of his mouth." It was true. Pastor Mike was not a man to stand still. He never used notes and he had the scripture memorized. He was a dynamic speaker, which probably accounted for the surge of growth the church had experienced since hiring him three years ago.

"We've all made New Year's resolutions at one time or another. At first we do okay, right? Usually about two or three weeks in, we start to wane. How about now? It takes four to six months to make a behavior a habit. Our first Sunday of the New Year, I asked each of you to write down a goal you have for this year. Remember? We talked about a Scriptural Growth Goal. What goal did you set? Did you resolve to read through the Bible this year? Maybe your goal was to memorize a passage of scripture. I know some plan to learn the books of the Bible in order. Maybe you decided to study one book. Whatever your goal, now is the time to renew that challenge you gave yourself. Now is the time to recharge your internal battery."

"I haven't done much to keep up that Bible challenge thing," Carol admitted after the service. "I said I would read my Bible every day for fifteen minutes, but I bet I've only opened it twice and that was on

Sundays! You want to grab some lunch? Bill has to go see his mother today."

Ten minutes later as the two sat at a small table at Skyline Chili, conversation returned to New Year's resolutions.

"I quit making resolutions long ago," Carol said. "Just decided to try this Spirit Growth thing for Pastor Mike."

Lori laughed. "I think it's *Scriptural* Growth Goal. Although Spirit Growth doesn't sound half bad."

"I can never remember what it's called. I guess spirit growth sounds a bit like a cheerleader." Carol wiped the napkin across her mouth. "So how about you? Do you make resolutions every year?"

"Actually, I do. At least for years I did. I'd make a physical goal — you know, like lose weight or something. John used to tease me. He would tell people I lost 200 pounds and they would look at me in awe."

"Two hundred pounds! You were never that big,"

"Yeah, well, ten pounds a year for twenty years. It adds up."

Carol laughed. "Leave it to John."

"I always had a learning goal, too."

"I remember that! A few years ago you learned to speak Spanish."

"*Si.*" Lori scrunched her face. "I don't know how much I remember or if I could ever use it in a real conversation. I didn't make any resolutions the last year John was so sick and really none for the years since he died. Until this year."

"Care to share?"

"Well, for the physical one, I decided to get more active." Lori hesitated. Should she tell Carol about going back to square dancing? Was she going to follow through with it? *It is what it is.* "So for that one, I decided to go back to square dancing."

"That's great! I remember how much you enjoyed those dances. I used to wish Bill would give it another shot." Carol sipped her coffee. "So did you set one of those scripture goals like Pastor Mike suggested?"

Lori raised her hand as she finished chewing the bite of ham and cheese sandwich. She took a drink of the hot coffee before continuing.

"Well, I thought about trying to read through Proverbs. I mean there are thirty-one chapters and I once knew a woman who read a chapter for each day. You know, chapter one on the first of the month and chapter twenty on the twentieth and such. I always thought that could be kind of neat to do."

"Well, I'll tell you what. You encourage me and I'll encourage you."

"It's a deal." Lori looked across the table at her friend. *Should I tell her how I secretly long to share life with someone again? Is that even a goal?* The moment passed.

Carol was chattering on. "And oh, by the way, Anna Fowler emailed me the other day. You know they moved to Florida for the winter. I don't think Guy could ever convince Anna to move away full time and leave her grandkids. I guess they love it though. They're in one of those retirement communities. She said there's always something going on."

The lunch had been fun. Relaxing. But now, Lori jumped up and mumbled something about needing to get home to the cat. She raced to her car.

Anna and Guy Fowler. The image of the energetic couple loomed large. They were maybe three or four years older than her and John. Best friends until John's illness scared them away.

Not such good friends after all. How dare they live out their dreams? "It just isn't fair, God!"

Lori drew in a deep breath.

"Okay, God. I know. Life *isn't* fair. I know deep down everything will be okay, but sometimes I feel so…so crushed. So cheated."

The drive home was mindless. Lori fought back the tears.

Spent, she plopped into her reclining chair. Sasquatch jumped into her lap.

"You're the oddest one, aren't you, cat? How did you know I was feeling down?"

Lori reached for her Bible. Proverbs. *Was that a crazy goal?*

"It was the only thing I could think of at the time, cat. Hmm… It's already the seventeenth. Do I try to catch up on the reading I missed? No. I guess I'll read the seventeenth chapter, but I doubt I'll find anything there for me today."

She read the text as she stroked the warm, furry body of Sasquatch. "What?" The cat lifted his head, his ears perked. "Listen to this, cat. Verse 22. 'A cheerful heart is good medicine, but a crushed spirit dries up the bones.' How about that? Just how I was feeling. Like a crushed spirit. Old and spent. Dried up and without hope. Friendless. Sad. Without a plan for the future." Lori bolted out of the chair sending the cat flying to the carpet with a squeal. "I have an idea."

5

Lori smoothed the hem of her dress and tugged at the tight waistband as she stood by the car. *I was never crazy about these fluffy square dance dresses when I danced regularly. Why did I think this was a good idea now?* The two-day project of cleaning out her bedroom closet had unearthed more than a few square dance skirts with their matching crinolines. Lori had shoved most of the frilly dresses, slips and pantaloons into a large black trash bag she now retrieved from the trunk. Perhaps some new dancer would like the clothes. Three of John's western shirts were in the pile as well. Lori knew Marta would welcome the donation.

After handing the bag over to Marta, Lori scanned the room. No one she knew. Not yet. The Cowboy wasn't there either. *Just as well.* Lori donned her nametag and introduced herself to two new dancers standing nearby.

Greg started the music and the group formed a large circle. "Let's see if we can get in boy-girl-boy-girl formation." After a bit of shuffling, the dancers looked expectantly to the front for their next set of instructions.

"Some people say square dancing is friendship set to music," Greg announced from the small stage. "So right now, we're going to review grand right and left. Do you remember that one? Let's have the girls face left and the boys turn to the right. Now reach out like you're going to shake hands. Say hello to that person. Exchange names." A bit of shuffling and exchanging of names followed. Lori looked around. There were probably close to forty people in the circle. Half of them were the angels.

"Good," Greg said. "That is going to be your partner. Now gents, pull her by, ladies walk on forward to meet the next person with your left hand. Pull by. Good. Now we're going to turn on the music and move all around the circle. Every other hand. A right pull by then a left pull by until you meet your partner. Remember who that was?"

The music started. Lori smiled as she made her way around the circle. She might not care much for square dance attire as a whole, but the swish of the crinoline made her feel pretty. Feminine. Cheerful. She was nearly back to her partner, a man named Todd, when she spotted The Cowboy sauntering in the front door of the hall. Her heart did a little flip. Greg and Marta sorted the dancers into squares. Marta moved a few dancers around so that new students were paired with more experienced dancers.

Once the shuffling was complete, The Cowboy was standing to her right. Her neighbor. Her "corner" in the square. Members of the square introduced themselves.

"Pleased to meet you, Lori." The Cowboy tipped his hat as he read her nametag. "Name's Axel. Axel Calhoun." His name even sounded like a cowboy.

Lori smiled warmly. "Where are you from, Mr. Calhoun?"

"Originally, Jackson Hole, Wyoming, ma'am, but I've been living in these parts for a few years now."

Lori wanted to know more, like what made him move from Wyoming to Cincinnati, but the music was starting again, signaling everyone the lesson was about to begin.

What does a cowboy do for work around here?

Greg gave a short lesson about the history of square dancing. He explained the influence of French court dances on what eventually became the American folk dance. Lori had a hard time focusing. She pictured Axel on a horse, rounding up the dairy cows she saw on Ohio's farmland.

"Now ladies, put your right hand at the small of your back with the palm out. Gents, you're going to reach out, take that gal's left hand, and put your right hand there where she has her right hand and gently guide her around like this." As Marta moved toward him, Greg reached out and guided her in a small circle until she was standing beside him. "That's called a courtesy turn. Let's let our angel couples in each square demonstrate the courtesy turn."

Axel's partner moved in the middle of the square and faced Axel. As she moved toward him, he took a step back, reached for her hand, placed his other hand on her hand at her back and guided her in a small circle until she stood beside him. The remaining six dancers in the square took turns learning the move before Greg turned on the music and incorporated it into a simple dance. The group learned two more moves before Marta announced it was break time.

Students met around the snack table. The Cowboy took one of the brownies Lori had baked. He gave an appreciative "M-m-m, good."

Lori considered striking up a conversation with him when a man named Hank came at him from the other side. *Hank. Ah, yes, Iris's husband.* Lori looked around, took her bottle of water over to the other side of the room, and sat down next to Iris.

"So how are you liking the lessons?" she asked.

"We love them. Even Hank was disappointed they were called off last week. I was amazed."

"I know what you mean. The first time my husband and I came, well, I was surprised he came to begin with. Then on our way home he started naming all the people we knew who might like to learn. I knew he was hooked then."

"Sounds like Hank. Is that your husband over there, talking with Hank?"

"Uh, no. Uh… my husband died a few years ago. I haven't been dancing in a while, so I came to brush up." *Please Lord, I hope I didn't sound flustered. Or pathetic.*

"Oh, I'm so sorry to hear that. I mean, about your husband. But it's good you came back."

"Thanks. Square dancing is fun and you meet so many good people. Some of my dearest friends, I met through square dancing."

Marta tapped on the microphone. "It's time for announcements, so I need everyone to take a seat." She stood quietly and expectantly while the crowd shuffled back to the main area and settled into the folding chairs lining the perimeter of the dance floor.

"Good. Now a few announcements. I hope we don't have any more bad storms like we did last week, but if we do we'll call. One of the gals suggested we set up a calling tree. We have one in the back for you to sign. The way it works, everyone will call two people and we'll get the word out sooner than we did last week." A few heads nodded in agreement.

"And I want to tell you that in a few weeks we're having a party. It's a Super Bowl party right here at The Barn on Super Bowl Sunday. We're asking everyone to bring food. We'll supply soft drinks and water and coffee. No alcoholic beverages. Alcohol and dancing don't mix.

"We'll have some games and do some dancing. The callers will call moves you can do. And we'll have some of what we call Mainstream. Right now, you're learning Basic. The next step up is Mainstream. We'll have a few dancers who can dance Mainstream so you can see what's in store. So mark your calendars. Wear your favorite team colors. We'll have a lot of fun."

"What time is the party?" someone called out.

"Oh, yes. The party starts at four and we'll be here until six-thirty. That'll give everyone plenty of time to get home for the game."

The second half of the Tuesday night lesson progressed smoothly. Once the last goodnight was said, Lori picked up her empty brownie pan and headed toward the door.

"You make those?"

Lori turned to see The Cowboy standing near the registration table, a paper in his hand.

"Guilty."

"They were great." He put the phone tree sign-up sheet back on the table.

"Thanks. Axel, right?"

"That's right. And you're Lori."

"Right. Loretta, really, but nobody calls me that."

The tall man fell in stride with Lori as they left the building.

"So I see you're part of a club in Wyoming."

Axel absently touched the plastic club badge pinned to his shirt. "Yeah, haven't officially joined one here, yet."

They stopped when they reached Lori's car.

"Well, I guess I'll see you next week. Thanks for walking me to my car."

Axel smiled and tipped his hat. Lori got in, locked her door, and started the engine. She watched in her rearview mirror as Axel headed toward a big dark green car parked on the other side. *Probably has cow horns on the front.*

Darkness shrouded the parking lot. As the cars exited, most turned right toward the city. Lori cautiously pulled across the intersection, crossing through the dark wooded park to get to the main road leading to her suburban community to the north. As the road straightened, headlights appeared behind her, seemingly from nowhere.

Again? I should have gone the long way around. Lori reached in her purse to make sure she had her cell phone close at hand and nearly swerved off the road's narrow shoulder. The curvy road was a lonely place to travel. *Well, lonely is a relative term. I do seem to have company.* Lori shivered. John always said if she was out and fearful someone was following her, she should never let the other car pass her. She guided her car to the center of the road. Finally, the main road appeared. The traffic light marking the intersection turned green as Lori approached. Only as she turned and let out a long sigh of relief did she realize she had been holding her breath.

She looked in the rearview mirror. The mysterious car's headlights were still behind her. She slowed down. So did the dark car. She increased her speed as she went through a yellow light. The trailing car went through the light as well. When she turned right, the car behind her turned right. When she turned left, so did the other vehicle. She now remembered another piece of advice John had given her. "Never go home in such a situation. Go to a well-lit, highly populated place or the police station," he had said.

Lori approached the turnoff to her street. The car followed close behind. Lori pushed the gas pedal down and drove toward the police station. The car didn't follow. Lori pulled into the police station.

Now what? Should she tell the police someone was following her? *Was someone following me?* Beneath the glaring lights of the police station, the event was less menacing. Still, she had read of widows falling prey to strangers in such circumstances.

Picking up her cell phone, Lori dialed her son's number as she pulled out of the lights surrounding the police station and back onto the shadowy winter streets. Ethan picked up on the second ring.

"Hey, Mom. What's up?"

No need to sound like a frightened child. "Hi, sweetie. Just thought I'd check in and see how you're doing." Now all she had to do was keep him on the phone for the next five minutes until she was safe in her garage.

"We're fine. Say, where are you?"

"What do you mean?" *So far so good.*

"You called on your cell. You hardly ever do that."

"Oh, I went to square dance lessons tonight. Just on my way home and thought of you."

"Isn't it kind of late for you to be out driving?"

Ignore that. "Listen, I wondered if you and Leah and the kids are doing anything on Sunday. I thought we might have lunch."

"I'll have Leah call you. She may be going to her sister's. I don't know."

Lori hit the button to open the garage door. *Whew.*

"Mom? Are you there?"

"Right here. I'm home now. I was just getting my stuff out of the car."

"Oh, good. You're okay, though, right? You're always telling me to stay off the phone when I'm driving."

"Oops. Yeah, well, I'm fine. I was just thinking about getting together, so I thought I'd call before it got too late."

"Actually, I was going to call you tomorrow. I'll need your tax stuff. Some of it should be arriving in the mail soon."

"Look, Ethan, I probably should go. I'm home now. I need to check on Sasquatch. And Honey, thank you again for the garage door opener." *Taxes? Really? Still, I'm safe and that's what counts right now. And Ethan was there when I needed him. That's the second time a car has practically followed me home through that dark section of the park.*

Sasquatch didn't need her. She couldn't even find the cat at first. Lori hit the button on her answering machine.

"Hi, Lori! It's Carol. Checking in to see how you're doing with your scripture goal. I'm reading, so I guess we're both doing fairly well so far. Talk to you later. Bye." Click. No more messages.

Well, she may be doing great. "Here I go again, cat. Forgot all about reading a chapter in Proverbs. Probably nothing in there for me today, anyway."

Lori changed into her sweatpants and sweatshirt. She headed toward her chair, the Bible on the table beside it. Sasquatch mewed and rubbed against her leg.

"Okay. I guess I'll read it."

Lori sat down in her chair and reached for her glasses. Sasquatch jumped in her lap and laid down, his eyes half closed. Soon, Lori's eyes were closed, too.

A loud banging sound caused her to jump up from her chair, sending Sasquatch and her Bible flying in different directions.

6

Light poured in the front window. At first, Lori feared her house was on fire and the rescue squad was outside. There was a definite banging on the front door.

Okay, not so much a banging, maybe more of a knock.

Lori raced to the front door of her house. The fog in her head cleared with the chill of the morning air. There were no emergency vehicles with their floodlights aimed at her. Only the bright morning sun reflecting off a new layer of snow.

40

The young woman standing on her front step shivered. She looked familiar.

"Hi, it's Angie." The woman pulled down the scarf wrapped haphazardly around her face. "From across the street?"

"Oh, of course, Angie. Come in. Where's your coat?"

Angie let out a nervous laugh. "In my house with my keys. Could I use your phone? I accidently locked myself out."

"Yes, yes. This way." Lori led her frozen neighbor into the kitchen. "I was about to make a pot of coffee. Would you like some? Or I could make you some tea."

"Coffee would be great, thank you." Angie lifted the phone and dialed.

Lori cleaned the coffee pot. The clock on the microwave read 8:42. *I must have fallen asleep in that chair.* She looked in the windowed door of the microwave, hoping to assess her appearance in the darkened reflection. Angie was talking to someone about bringing her a key. *Probably her husband.* Lori remembered him as a scruffy sort of fellow. The coffee on, Lori slipped out of the kitchen as Angie made a second call to her office.

A bit frumpy maybe, after sleeping all night in the chair with her cat, but a quick brush of the teeth and hair and a trip to the toilet and she was as good as new. *Presentable anyway.*

Angie was looking at the pictures of her grandsons plastered all over the refrigerator when Lori made her way back.

"My grandchildren." She pulled two large mugs from the cabinet above the coffeemaker.

"How many do you have?"

"Two."

"They're gorgeous kids."

"I think so. Cream? Sugar?"

"Just cream, please."

Lori carried the cups to the kitchen table where the two women sat down. "I've locked myself out a couple of times. And I was always losing my keys. My husband used to make fun of me." She smiled at the memory. "Not in a bad way, mind you. All in fun."

"Danny says I'm scatter-brained. But I don't think he's teasing. He's pretty upset he has to come home from work to rescue me. Said he has a big meeting today he should be getting ready for, so he won't be here for at least a half hour or more." She bit her lower lip.

"Not to worry. You can stay right here until he comes home. Or if it would help, I could drive you to your work..." *Why did I say that? It's snowy out there.*

"Oh, no, I wouldn't have you drive me all the way to work. I work downtown. Danny will be here soon."

41

The two women sipped their coffees silently for a moment.

"Did you eat breakfast? I think I have some cinnamon rolls in the fridge." Lori pushed her chair out.

"None for me thanks. I don't usually eat in the morning."

"Oh." Lori lowered herself back into her chair.

"You can have some."

"No, that's okay. I'm trying to cut down."

More silence.

"I have an idea," Lori said. "Why don't you have an extra key made and leave it here? That way, if you ever get locked out again, you won't have to call your husband."

Angie bit her lip and looked down at her coffee mug. *Mistrust?* Lori was about to change the subject when Angie looked up. "You wouldn't mind?"

"Not at all. And if you like, it can be our little secret." Lori's stomach growled. "I think I'll make those rolls after all."

"I might have one, too."

Lori turned on the oven, retrieved a small round cake pan from a lower kitchen cabinet, banged the side of the cylinder holding the cinnamon rolls on the edge of the counter, and in a few minutes the rolls were in the oven.

"When I was your age, I made these things from scratch."

"I don't think I've ever made anything from scratch."

"I used to love to cook and bake, but now that it's just me...well, there's not much point to it anymore."

"To tell the truth, Mrs. ..."

"Lori. Just call me Lori."

"Okay. To tell the truth, Lori, I never learned how to cook. My mother didn't want anyone in the kitchen when she cooked, so I never really learned."

"Well, if you decide you want to learn how to cook, let me know. I can teach you what I know. It'd be fun."

"I may take you up on that."

"I take it you haven't been married very long."

Angie squirmed. "We're getting married in June. Danny said we should get the house first."

"Oh, I see." *Don't judge. Don't judge.* "Saw 'Morgan' on the mailbox. Are you planning a big wedding?"

"Not too big. We put most of our money in the house. Morgan is Danny's name."

Change the subject. Change the subject. "It's a great neighborhood. A great place to raise a family." *Should I have said that?* Lori found her eyes drawn to the young woman's stomach. *Maybe she's pregnant.*

"Yeah, we like it here so far. We haven't gotten to know many neighbors yet, though. We met the people on either side of us and the family behind us. They have a huge dog that keeps digging under the fence."

"The Bakers. I know the dog."

The smell of hot cinnamon began to fill the room. Sasquatch, who had disappeared at the sign of company, now appeared at the door. He lifted his head as if to ask if the cinnamon rolls were for him.

"I didn't know you had a cat!"

"His name is Sasquatch. Do you like cats?"

"I love 'em. Dogs, too. Danny says I can't have any pets, though, because we both work so much."

"They do need to have people around. Even cats. Actually, Sasquatch was my son's cat. He found it as a kitten in a cardboard box on the side of the road. When Ethan left for college, the cat sort of became attached to us. Every once in a while, Ethan says he wishes the boys had a pet like Sasquatch. I've said he should take him back now that he has a family, but then I don't know what I'd do without the silly creature."

"Did your son name him?"

"Yes. He has six toes on one paw. Like Bigfoot – Sasquatch."

"I get it. How old is he?"

Lori pulled her elbow up on the table and rested her chin in her hand. She tapped her lip with her finger. "Let's see. I think he found him when he was sixteen or so. He's thirty now. Oh my, that cat has to be at least thirteen or fourteen years old. I still tend to think of him as a kitten."

The oven timer sounded a single ding. Lori removed the cinnamon rolls, leaving the oven door open. "Might as well not waste the heat." She found two dessert plates and served her morning guest the hot roll. She placed the little tub of icing that came with the can of rolls on the table with a butter knife. "If you want icing. I don't care for it myself."

The two women finished their impromptu breakfast just as Danny Morgan pulled into the driveway across the street. Angie hurriedly finished her coffee.

"Thank you so much for your hospitality, Lori. I better get over there."

"It was a pleasure to meet you, and don't forget about the spare key." Lori watched from the door as Angie trekked through the snow on the sidewalk and crossed over to her own house. Danny had unlocked the door and met her on the driveway as he returned to his car. Lori couldn't hear, but could tell from the way he gestured with his hands, and the way Angie looked down at the ground, the verbal exchange was not pleasant.

She closed the door.

7

Snow fell continuously throughout the day. The weatherman on the late night news promised the worst was behind them, so Lori prepared herself mentally to bundle up the next morning and shovel her driveway

The snow glistened like diamonds in the morning sun, but much to her surprise, her driveway was totally cleared of the white stuff. The bright sunshine had already dried the concrete surface. Danny was about to finish clearing his own drive. He looked up and waved. Lori waved back, offering a hearty, "Thank you!" sending her words out against the chilling wind. She waved again as Angie opened the garage door, then popped back into the warmth of her house.

"Well, cat, my first impression of that little couple wasn't all that great. Especially that Danny. But maybe they'll turn out okay after all. What do you think? It was nice of them to clear my driveway."

Ethan called near lunchtime. "Don't have much time to talk, Mom, but thought I should see if you need anything. I could stop on my way home and clear your drive, I guess."

"My drive is fine, honey. The neighbor did it. But if you want to stop by, I could use some more eggs and bread."

"Oh, uh, well, if I have time. As long as you're okay."

Lori drew in a deep breath. *At least he called.*

Later in the day, she decided to bake. She cut half of the pan of brownies into uniform squares and carefully stacked a half dozen on a paper plate, covering it with plastic wrap. She carried a single brownie to eat and the plate with her to the front window. No lights were on across the street. Angie and Danny rarely got home before seven-thirty or eight. Lori set the plate of brownies on the end table and watched.

Lori knew this would be a good time to read her Bible. Carol would likely call later. It would be nice to report she had done her reading for the day.

"It's a good thing I'll read this one book of the Bible all year, cat. Maybe by next December, I'll actually have read every chapter." *Why was it so hard to get into this habit?*

She opened the text to chapter twenty-one. "Listen to this, cat. 'All a man's ways seem right to him, but the Lord weighs the heart.'" Lori pulled her mouth tight. *Oh, Ethan. Sometimes I wonder about your heart. You're such a sweet man and I know you mean well, but sometimes you ignore those closest to you. Not just me, either.* "Please, Lord, help Ethan remember what is most important in his life. You. His family. Life isn't all just work and watching sports on television."

Lori pressed on with her reading. "The whole book is like this, cat. A bunch of little sayings. A lot about money and quarrelsome wives. Why did I ever commit to this?"

Headlights flashed across the front window and Lori saw the garage door open across the street. Danny's car.

"I think we'll wait for Angie to get home." What did she really know about her new neighbors? Nothing, really. Only their names and that they worked long hours. They drove nice cars. "I don't even know if they like brownies." Angie's car moved slowly down the street and pulled in the drive. "But I'll soon find out."

Lori bundled herself in her winter coat, tying a scarf around her face. She tugged at the winter boots by the door. The struggle caused her to heat up like a furnace. Finally, carrying the plate of brownies, she welcomed the cold blast of winter air as she crossed the street and rang on the doorbell of red brick house.

The porch light flipped on and Danny stood shirtless behind the glass storm door. It took him a moment to recognize his neighbor. *Probably the goofy scarf wrapped around my face.* "Hope I didn't scare you."

Danny pushed the door open a crack, a frown on his face. "I didn't know who it was."

"Just me! I'm Lori... from across the street?" Lori pointed to her house. She was beginning to shiver.

"Oh, sure...sure. Come on in."

She stepped across the threshold as Danny shouted toward the back of the house, "Angie, the lady across the street's here to see you."

"Uh....actually, I came to see both of you." Lori held out the plate of brownies. "I wanted to thank you for shoveling my driveway this morning."

Danny accepted the plate. "Thanks, but I didn't do it."

Angie appeared around the corner, dressed in a pair of navy fleece pants and a gray sweatshirt. "Sorry. I had to get out of those work clothes. Come on in, Lori. Have a seat." The two sat down on the soft brown sofa. "Oh...uh, Lori, this is Danny. Danny, this is Lori."

"We met. I'll leave you two alone, I'm gonna go pick up the pizza." Danny pulled a sweatshirt over his head, grabbed his car keys from the table and took his coat from the back of the chair.

"Would you like to have pizza with us, Lori?" Angie smiled sweetly as Danny headed out the door leading to the garage.

"Oh, no, sweetie. I just brought over some brownies. They can be your dessert."

"I love brownies! I may have to take you up on that cooking lesson."

"Anytime. I just wanted to thank you for clearing my driveway this morning. Danny said you did it."

Angie's shoulders sagged. "I don't know why he said that. I didn't do it."

"Oh, I mean...I think... what he said was he didn't do it. I figured that meant you must've done it."

"Sorry. It wasn't me. I saw some man out there when we got up this morning. Do you want your brownies back?"

Lorie laughed. "No. I still want you to enjoy them. But it's a mystery." Her brow furrowed. She stood to leave.

Angie opened the front door. "Looks like you have company."

Lori looked through the glass. A long, dark car was backing out of her drive. Before she could make it to the sidewalk, the vehicle was moving down the block.

Angie stood on her porch and called to her. "Everything okay?"

"Don't know who that was. Probably just somebody turning around." She turned and headed toward her own home. *I should have left the porch light on.* As Lori reached for her door, she shivered in the realization she hadn't locked the door behind her when she left. A quick look over her shoulder assured her Angie was watching. *I wonder what she'd do if I screamed. Call 9-1-1? What's wrong with me? I've never been afraid to enter my own home before.* Lori shook her fear away, grabbed the doorknob, and stepped inside, turning only to wave goodbye to her new friend. Angie stepped back into her own home quickly, causing Lori to do the same. She hastily slammed the door shut and in a single move, turned the deadbolt lock in place. A noise in the kitchen made her jump.

8

"I jumped out of my skin." Lori stirred the creamer in her coffee. "I don't know what got into me. I've had that cat forever."

Carol tore open a sugar packet. "I understand completely. You weren't expecting it, that's all."

"I kind of geared myself up for it." Lori didn't intend to tell anyone about the dark car following her home from square dancing or the fact a dark car like it was in her driveway when she left Angie's house. She had already discussed the issue with Sasquatch and thought it resolved. Now, over a second cup of coffee at the Hilltop Coffee Shop, the following morning, the words spilled out like a tidal wave.

"I didn't tell you this, Carol, but for a bit there, I thought someone was stalking me." Lori looked up to see if her friend was laughing at her. *No, thank goodness.*

Carol leaned in. "What happened? When?"

Lori spent the next few minutes outlining details of the mysterious car tailing her through the darkened woods. *Funny. It sounded better when I told the cat.* "Then the very same car came to my house late at night, pulled in my driveway with the lights off, and then pulled away suddenly. Just lucky I was across the street with Angie." It was an embellished version, but sounded more menacing that way. She threw in an exaggerated shiver for effect.

"Did you get the number on the license plate? Or the make and model of the car?" Carol was very thorough. She watched all of the latest crime shows on television.

"No." Lori shook her head slowly. She twisted her napkin and looked down at the table. "Actually… I'm not one hundred percent sure it was the same car."

"You should call the police anyway." Carol sat back in the hard plastic chair. "Women are targets. Especially if someone figures out we live alone."

Carol still has her husband. Easy for her to be brave. "What's this 'we' business? You don't live alone."

"I'm speaking on behalf of all women everywhere. I'm telling you, you need to call the police."

"I'm not calling the police."

"Then tell Ethan and Leah. They should know you're in imminent danger."

"Maybe, but I don't feel as though I'm in imminent danger. Not the way you make it sound."

"Didn't you just tell me you were so frightened when Sasquatch tipped his dish in the kitchen, you jumped into the living room lamp and broke it? I call that feeling in imminent danger."

"I'll think about it."

"You know what it is, Lori? It's the Evil One. Old Satan knows your fears and that you want to overcome them, and he's messing with you."

"Hmmm…I bet that's it! And that stuff about a stalker is probably him making my imagination go wild."

"Probably. Of course, I still think it would be wise to keep your eyes open and maybe buy yourself one of those pepper spray things."

Once she was back home, Lori located a pencil and jotted "pepper spray" on the running list of groceries she kept hanging on her refrigerator.

I wonder where you buy pepper spray. She couldn't ask Ethan or Leah. They would worry. It was a puzzle. Angie? She was young and probably knew about all that sort of stuff. *Maybe Angie.* Lori made a mental note to ask her new neighbor the next time they talked.

But of course, days went by without even seeing Angie. By the time the weekend rolled around and Lori thought the girl might be home for a while, she wasn't. "Out shopping," Danny told her.

Lori trudged back across the street to the warmth of her own home. No way was she going to ask Danny anything. What was it she read this very morning that made her think of him? She settled into her chair and picked up her Bible. Proverbs 23:9. Yep, there it was. "Do not speak to a fool, for he will scorn the wisdom of your words." *He would have laughed at me for even thinking someone might be stalking me.* "Humph! Sometimes I wonder which one of us is the fool. In some ways, I hope it's me."

There was, of course, only one thing to do. Go to the store and ask. She needed a few grocery items anyway. She'd stop at the grocery and then head to the anti-stalker store, wherever that might be. Surely someone at the grocery could tell her.

Grateful for the sunny weather and clear roads, Lori drove to the nearest store to pick up the items on her ever-growing list. She knew she needed coffee and bread. Add to that bananas, orange juice, oatmeal, and oh yes, that meant more brown sugar. She also needed cheese and definitely an assortment of dried beans for her fifteen-bean soup. By the time she made it to the meat department, Lori had nearly forgotten her mission to find out where to buy pepper spray. *Someone in this store should be able to tell me.*

"Could you split this package of chicken breasts for me?" she asked the butcher. "I need them in individual packages."

The man pursed his lips as if to question her, but simply said, "Sure, no problem." He returned a couple of minutes later, handing her the package. "I wrapped each individually then wrapped them together on the tray. Hope that works for you. Anything else, Ma'am?

Lori took the package from his hand and thought a minute. "Uh...no, that's all. Thank you." *Asking for pepper spray and getting individually wrapped chicken breasts. Could anything scream "woman living alone" louder?*

Her next target was a young man stocking the end cap with cereal. "Pardon me, but I wondered if you might know where I could buy some...uh...pepper spray."

"Oh sure, aisle five."

"Aisle five. Thank you."

"No problem." The confident stocker went back to lining up the boxes of cereal on the shelf.

Who knew? Lori pushed the cart back to the other end of the store and headed down aisle five. "Great. He obviously doesn't have a clue."

The employee arranging the spices turned to Lori. "Are you looking for something special?" the young woman asked.

"Well, I was looking for pepper spray, not pepper. It's a..." but before

48

Lori could finish the sentence, the young girl reached in her pocket and pulled out her key ring. On it dangled a small cylinder.

"Like this?" she asked. "The kind we girls need to carry for protection?"

We girls. Lori smiled. "Exactly. Where did you get that?"

"My dad. He said if I was going to get a job and be out after dark, I had to carry this."

"Do you know where he got it?"

The girl fished her cell phone out of her pocket. "No, but I'll ask."

"I hate to make you go to so much trouble."

"No problem." The girl punched in her text message. "It'll be a minute or two. He always texts me back, but it takes him a bit to figure out the right keys."

"I'm impressed he can do it at all."

"He's learning, but takes no shortcuts. He spells every word and proofreads every text. He's a writer. He's home, so I know he'll answer."

Lori's admiration for this man she didn't know was growing. "What does he write? Anything I might know?"

"I doubt it. He writes technical stuff. You know, users manuals for your lawn mower and stuff like that." Her phone beeped. "Ah... he says he bought mine at the sporting goods store at the mall."

"Thank you so much and tell your father I said thanks, too."

"No problem."

No problem must be the store's mantra. Now that she had perishable groceries in the car, a trip to the sporting goods store would have to wait. But not for long. The same dark car she had seen earlier was driving slowly past her house as she turned down her street. Who was that? Was it the same car that followed her from The Barn? And, more importantly, what did he want?

9

"I met a girl at the store whose father writes technical support manuals. It got me to thinking about maybe doing a bit of freelance editing." Lori searched Ethan's face for a reaction.

"Like in the medical field? The stuff you used to do?" Ethan lifted the meatloaf out of its pan and placed it on the serving platter.

"Freelance. I could edit all sorts of writing. Mostly nonfiction, I think. I could do line editing for fiction writers, but there's all sorts of content editing I wouldn't trust myself to touch." She put a dollop of butter on the bowl of hot mashed potatoes.

"You lost me, but if you really think you want to go back to work...I mean this is a 'want to do' thing, right? You're not hurting financially or

49

anything?"

"No, I'm doing okay. I mean, your dad set everything in order and I have some savings."

"You haven't taken out a second mortgage or anything? You know, Mom, I could help you with all of that."

Lori opened her mouth to protest, but thought better. Ethan was only showing care and concern, but did he trust her to be able to make wise choices? *I gave my kids reason to question me. I've lived ensconced in fear and gave over all my decision making to them.* She drew in a deep breath and handed her son the bowl of vegetables to put on the table.

"Ethan, I am solid financially. I think when your dad died I was tired and lost. I felt totally spent. I still have a lot to offer. I just think it's time I live a productive life again."

Leah put her hand on her mother-in-law's arm. "Good for you!"

"Of course, Mom," Ethan stammered. "I guess I just thought you were kind of happy not having to work. I mean, isn't it everyone's secret dream to retire early? I know I'd like to not have to go in every day."

"Well, I'm thinking about working from home. I probably need to upgrade my computer though. That desktop is archaic. Fine for emails and Facebook, but I'll need something with an updated operating system. And I think I might like a laptop."

Ethan stood by the dining room table, his mouth open. Leah took the bowl of mixed vegetables from him and set it on the table. She headed back to the kitchen for the rolls. "Mom, you amaze me," he finally said. "You say your tech skills aren't great, but you talk the talk."

Lori laughed. "I can handle word processing and document revision on a computer, son. I just can't make the technology work all the magic I think it's supposed to be able to do." She pulled out a chair and sat down. "Let's eat. Ethan, will you say our blessing?"

Ethan mumbled a short prayer and started spooning food onto his plate. Leah filled the boys' plates and stared at her husband eating hungrily. "You'd think I never feed the man."

"Mom, you make the best gravy in the world." Ethan spooned an extra portion of the brown gravy over his mashed potatoes.

"It's true. My gravy is always lumpy." Leah never appeared threatened in any way when Ethan raved over his mother's cooking.

"My gravy was lumpy, too, Leah, until one day when my own mother-in-law shared a little secret. It's all about the temperature. Most people put the flour in the hot milk and water and broth and it cooks it up like miniature dumplings. You need to mix it first and the bring the temperature up."

"Dumplings! I haven't had your chicken and dumplings

since…well…I can't remember, Mom." Ethan looked at Lori expectantly.

"Well, I'll tell you what. You two come next Sunday and I'll make you chicken and dumplings for lunch." *It's so good to have people to cook for.*

"Thanks, Mom, but we can't. Next Sunday's the Super Bowl and we're going to a party and all at Leah's brother's house."

"Yeah, and I have to take dip or something. I don't know what to make." Leah frowned. "I wish I was as good a cook as you."

"I forgot about the Super bowl." Lori prayed her disappointment didn't show. *The Super Bowl's in the evening. They could come for the lunch. Let it go.* "Well, sometime soon, then."

Leah finished cutting up Jack's meat, instructing him he needed to clean his plate before he could leave the table.

Like a script. I remember saying that very thing to Ethan.

The boys toyed with their food. Leah turned to her husband. "Ethan, I could use a little support here."

Lori watched as her son challenged the boys to each take a bite of potatoes.

"You know what, Mom? You could come with us to the Super Bowl party. I know my brother wouldn't mind."

Lori hesitated. What was that look her son shot his wife? "Actually, I have a Super Bowl party that day myself. I nearly forgot."

"You're going to a Super Bowl party?" Ethan's amused tone pierced Lori's fragile heart. She bit the inside of her cheek.

"Why not? I'm not exactly over the hill no matter what you think, son."

Leah smiled. "Where's the party?"

"It's at the Hayloft Barn. A square dance."

"I think it's great you're back to dancing. I know you loved it." Leah spooned another dab of mashed potatoes onto her plate. "Maybe someday when the boys are bigger, we'll try something like that, right, Ethan?"

"Maybe," he said.

"And I think the idea of taking on some editing jobs is perfect. You were always so good at that. I'll go with you to look at computers if you like. Too bad you didn't ask for one for Christmas."

Lori smiled at her daughter-in-law. "Well, just so you know, I love my garage door opener. It was exactly what I needed. And thanks for the offer to help me shop, but as it turns out, my new neighbor across the street is in the computer business. His…uh…Angie said he'd be happy to fix me up with a laptop at a great price and give me free tech support when I need it."

Ethan's head shot up. "The guy at the Bronskis' old house? Isn't he kinda sleazy?"

"Whatever makes you say that?" *I can think it, but what makes you say it?*

"I don't know. I've just seen him outside a couple of times and he drives that expensive car. He doesn't exactly look the part of a businessman. I don't know. Where's his business located? I mean, is it a store or what?"

"He's a distributor. He says most of the computers are made by only two or three companies and sold under different names. They all come from China, you know. At least that's what I've heard."

"Just promise me you'll check everything out before you buy it. Take me or Leah with you, okay?"

"I'm not a child, Ethan."

"No, but I don't want to see anyone take advantage of you, either. I know a little more about computers than you do."

Leah wiped gravy from the edge of the table where her youngest was sitting with her napkin. "Maybe you and I could go to a couple stores and check them out. Ask questions and find out exactly what you need. Then we'll know for sure if the guy across the street is giving you a good price or not."

Lori considered Leah's offer. "Fair enough. Would that satisfy you, Ethan?"

"Sure. Do what you want. I don't know why you want to go back to work anyway." He pushed away from the table and headed toward the family room and the television.

"Was John ever like that?" Leah asked.

"Addicted to sports? No. Well, football, I guess."

"Honestly, Ethan prefers watching any sport on television to spending time with his family. He says that watching sports is a guy thing and the best way to spend time with the boys." Leah stood to clear the dishes from the table.

Lori looked toward the family room. It was good to have her son here, but if this was all there was to him, she could see how it would wear thin on his wife. *Please, Lord, help my boy see the treasure in front of him that is not on TV.*

10

"Listen to this, Sasquatch. 'By wisdom a house is built and through understanding it is established.' Ethan wants me to make a wise decision about buying a computer and Leah says if we shop a bit for the laptop, I'll know what I need. I'll have understanding. Get it?"

The cat rested motionless on the arm of Lori's recliner.

Lori pushed on to read through the rest of the twenty-fourth chapter of Proverbs but stopped at the thirteenth verse. "'Eat honey, my son, for it is good; honey from the comb is sweet to your taste. Know also that wisdom is sweet to your soul; if you find it, there is a future hope for you, and your hope will not be cut off.' Hmm...wonder if there's any banana pudding left?"

Sasquatch jumped from the chair as Lori stood suddenly and headed toward the kitchen. She spooned the remaining banana pudding into a bowl, sat down at the kitchen table and looked outside as the afternoon folded into the gray of a winter's evening. *There is a future for you, it said.* Lori pulled a pen from the drawer under the telephone and grabbed a notepad. As she ate the rest of the pudding, she made a list of contacts for possible editing jobs. She had written nine leads she considered solid possibilities when the phone rang. She looked at the caller ID. Carol.

"Hello, Carol. Sorry I missed you at church this morning. I had to rush out. Ethan and his little family came over for dinner."

"I wasn't there. I have a cold and couldn't sleep at all last night." Carol coughed.

"I'm so sorry. I didn't know. I was so caught up in thinking about having my meatloaf ready, I didn't stop to look around."

"So how was it?"

"Oh fine. Ethan loved it."

"How wonderful! And Leah?"

"Yes, Leah loved it, too. Even the boys liked it once we put ketchup all over it." Silence. "Carol? Are you there? You okay?"

"I'm here," Carol answered. "Are we talking about the church service or the meatloaf?"

Lori replayed the conversation in her mind and laughed out loud. "Well, I was talking about the meatloaf! The service was good, too, but Ethan and Leah didn't come. I keep asking them."

"Trust God. They'll get back into church. You'll see. So what was the sermon about?"

"Hold on. I'll get my notes." Lori dug through her purse to find the folded church bulletin among an array of expired store coupons and receipts. "Here we go." She looked over the bullet points. Most of the notes were messages to herself about what she needed to do when she got home. *Guess I was only halfway listening.* She frowned. "Okay, well, Pastor Mike talked about having faith. He said, 'Let faith finish your sentences.'"

"What does that mean?"

Lori searched the scribbles on her bulletin. "Oh, here's the example he gave: 'This is a tough situation I'm in, but God will see me through it.'"

"Got it. That makes sense. If we include a simple statement of faith in every situation, we're asserting our trust that God is in control, right?"

"Uh, yeah, sure. Actually, I remember thinking after John died that he had so much faith. More than me. But I remember saying, 'I trust you, God. You'll get me through this. I know you will.'"

Carol's sigh traveled over the phone. "I guess that's what that means to let faith finish your sentences."

"Did I tell you I've been thinking about taking on some freelance editing?"

"No, that's great. You're good at the job."

"I liked my work. Now I'm thinking I should say that I'm going to take on some work if that's what God wants me to do. That's putting faith in the equation, right?"

"Right!"

"Let's see, he also talked about how we will face obstacles, so we need to be ready by praying and something else I can't read that I scribbled down. He said we should surround ourselves with fellow believers. For encouragement and support, I guess. Oh, and here is a quote I liked. He said, 'Yesterday ended last night.' Isn't that a great quote? Carol?"

Lori tucked her telephone under her chin and carried the empty bowls and spoon to the sink. She could hear Carol coughing on the other end.

"I better go, Lori. This cough is about to tear me up."

"I'll pray for you to get better," Lori offered.

A few minutes later, with the dishes washed, Lori carried her notes into the family room. She picked up her Bible and wrote THERE IS A FUTURE HOPE FOR YOU onto the top of her notebook page. She looked at the verse again. *Wisdom and honey. Who knew God would give me advice on buying a computer and eating banana pudding all in one fell swoop?* "All I can say is that God is very good to me," she said out loud to no one. Even Sasquatch was nowhere to be found. Lori settled into her recliner and reached for the TV remote control.

11

Lori spent most of Monday researching trends in the editing business. Tuesday's sunshine ushered in a newfound hope in her. "I may not make much money but at least I'll be useful," she told Marta as they spread a tablecloth for treats at the Barn Tuesday evening.

"I think it's a great idea." Marta set a bowl of freshly popped popcorn in the middle of the table. "Look at you, dancing again and getting back to work!"

"I know. It's like I've started a new chapter. Turned a page of some sort." Lori slumped into a chair. "Still, I miss John so much. I don't think I'll ever get over him."

Marta sat down beside her and put an arm around Lori's shoulder. "No, you won't. John will always be a part of you. I think he would like it that you are pushing forward, though."

People started filing in for the lesson. "Thanks for coming early. You were a great help," Marta told Lori as she moved toward the door to greet the students.

Lori found herself watching the door for The Cowboy. *Axel, that's his name. Axel. I wonder how he came by that name?* She helped Marta arrange the nametags on the table.

"Hi, Lori!"

Lori looked up. "Carol! You came!"

"Bill's parking the car. I told him this was the last day to join the lessons and to my total shock, he said, 'Let's give it a try.'"

"That's great. They'll review everything tonight and then next week they'll start learning new moves." Lori handed her friend a form to complete while she made nametags for Carol and Bill.

By the time Greg climbed onto the stage, The Cowboy hadn't shown up. *Just as well. The last thing I need is Carol and Bill...what? It isn't as if I would say something. And all he knows about me or cares to know is that I bake a mean brownie.* "Humph!"

"What?" Carol asked.

"Oh nothing, just thinking. Did I tell you I'm going to take on a few freelance jobs?"

"About ten times." Carol laughed and put her arm through Lori's. "But don't worry. I like that you're excited about it."

"I never want to bore my friends."

"You, Lori Blevins, are the least boring person I know!"

Marta whisked Carol away from Lori as the music started. *Me?* It was hard to focus on dancing. *I'm the dullest, most boring person in the world.*

Greg again went through the basic moves, linking them together for the students to dance. At a refreshment break, Lori was surprised to see Axel. *When did he get here?* She introduced Carol and Bill to Axel and the man she had been partnered with for the first half. The men were soon engaged in Super Bowl talk.

"He's a nice man and about your age," Carol whispered.

Lori rolled her eyes. "Don't even start that, Carol. We're just partnered for the lessons tonight. I'm not interested."

"I wasn't talking about that guy. I was talking about the one who looks like a cowboy. And, you wouldn't be betraying John if you were interested, you know."

Lori dropped into one of the chairs. "Technically, I know that's true. Technically. Still, I think I'd feel a little weird. And let's face it, I haven't dated a man in over thirty years."

"That doesn't mean there might not be a man out there for you. I'm just saying you should keep your options open."

Lori glanced at the men still engaged in a deep analysis of the two football teams scheduled to face off the following Sunday. Would Axel be an option? *What if God did have a plan that included a man for me? Why can't you just tell me what to do, God?*

Carol touched her arm lightly. "Don't forget, Lori. Options." She stood to greet the men as they walked toward her. Greg was back on the platform. The music started as Greg instructed everyone to find a new partner.

Axel bowed with a wide sweep of his arm. "May I have this dance, lovely lady?"

Lori stood up and rolled her eyes at Carol as she followed Axel to one of the squares. "If I were young enough to blush, I think I would be doing so right this minute," she whispered as she passed her friend.

"Options," Carol mouthed.

"Are you coming to the Super Bowl party next week?" Axel asked as the foursome gathered their coats at the end of the dance.

Bill held the door open as they filed out of The Barn. "Oh, we're not ready for any real dance. This was our first lesson."

"You're more than ready. Like Greg said, it is more like a party dance. Everything will be fun and easy for you to do," Marta added as she walked with them.

"It's a good way to get to know other dancers," Lori added.

"You folks going to Frisch's Big Boy tonight?" The four looked up to see Greg approaching them. "A bunch of us always go there after the lessons. It's fun."

Carol's eyes grew wide as her husband agreed to meet some of the other couples there. "You coming, Lori?"

"Yes, Lori. Come on. It'll be fun," Marta begged. "Are you coming with us, Axel?"

"I think I might." Axel cast a glance Lori's way. "Lori?"

Options. "Sure. It sounds like fun and it's a clear night. Why not?"

The words were out of her mouth and she was strapping her seatbelt on by the time the gravity of her decision hit her. "What was I thinking, John? I'm not an irresponsible teenager. It'll be eleven o'clock before I get home!" Images of John seated by her at Frisch's flashed through her mind. Tears threatened to cloud her vision. She bit the inside of her cheek. How many times had she and John enjoyed a meal with their square dance friends after a club dance? How many times did the two of them share a plate of French fries after lessons?

The five cars caravanned along the dark road through the county park. *At least there is a sense of safety in numbers.* All five cars pulled onto the road leading north. Every traffic light seemed to turn green on cue. *Am I really doing this?* "I should just keep driving." She spoke the words, but in a few minutes, her car seemed to will itself into the restaurant's parking lot.

12

"I had to call. Bill is actually excited about learning to square dance. Thank you so much for asking us again," Carol said.

Lori squeezed her telephone between her ear and shoulder. "I'm happy, too. It was fun having you two there last night."

"And going out afterwards? We haven't laughed that much in years."

Lori thought about the late night run to Frisch's. Three couples and two singles. What could have been awkward had actually turned into a fun time. "I have to be honest, Carol. I haven't laughed like that since John got sick. We always have a good time with that crowd."

"And that Axel guy is nice."

"Carol...."

"I'm not trying to suggest anything."

"You're not?"

"Only that he's nice. He's fun and sweet and if ever you were interested in dating again, he would be a good place to start. That's all."

"Carol, you're terrible!"

"I'm just saying that it's encouraging to know there are still some good guys out there."

"Well, I know nothing about him."

"His wife died a few years ago and he moved here from Wyoming. He and his wife used to square dance in Wyoming, so he decided to come back to it when he moved here."

"How do you know all this?"

"Bill. He was sitting on the other side of Bill, remember? Anyway, after his wife died he retired and moved here."

"Well, there you go. Who retires to Ohio?"

"His kids and grandkids are in the area. And now he's an adjunct professor at the University of Cincinnati. You should have taken the seat across from him. You would have learned a lot."

"I'm fine. I have you to tell me everything."

"Are you going to that Super Bowl party dance?"

"I thought about it."

"I think we might go. You could ride with us."

Lori stirred her coffee. It would be nice to not arrive alone. And if she agreed, she would likely follow through and not chicken out at the last minute. "Sure, I'll go if you go."

"Good. Bill told Axel we'd be sure to bring you!"

"Carol!"

"Hey, he asked. Bill said it was more than just a passing comment."

"This is embarrassing!" *But kind of nice.*

Though she intended to research laptop computers, Lori spent the bulk of her morning searching her closets for a Cincinnati Bengals shirt she recalled wearing years ago to a game with John and the kids. "Did I give that to Leah, cat?"

Sasquatch offered a noncommittal yawn and jumped up on the bed. John had had a couple of Bengal sweatshirts and a jacket. Not only would those be too big for her, they would likely be too warm for a dance.

13

Lori's inbox was full. She scanned the new messages quickly, deleting a few she knew were camouflaged advertisements for banks and jokes some of her friends felt important enough to mark as "must read." Two emails immediately caught her eye. The first was from Jim Sanger, one of the executives at *Priority Care*.

"So good to hear from you," he wrote. "Glad to hear you're getting back in the game. As you know, we have our own in-house editors, but I'll put the word out with some of our contributors and friends in the industry for you. It would sure make our job easier if our contributors hired you for a first look. (Especially some of our newer ones.) And if the freelance thing doesn't work out for you, let me know. I may have a place for you in the spring."

Interesting.

The second response to her freelance query was from a small house responsible for publishing technical manuals for medical equipment. She had worked with one of the editors there when she was still employed by *Priority Care*. Yes, he remembered her. Yes, he would keep her information on file and send some jobs her way. Lori shouted, "Yay!" causing Sasquatch to run for cover from beneath her kitchen chair situated at a small desk in the kitchen.

She danced over to the coffee pot. "Life is good! Nine leads sent out and my first two responses are good!" Sasquatch watched her from the rug by the kitchen door. "Actually, cat, I don't exactly have any jobs yet, but they'll come. I know they will."

Lori sat down and carefully crafted her responses to each editor. She created an electronic file for each business.

"I've got to get a new computer. A laptop." She made a list of needs for her new business. "And you know what, cat? I think once I get a new laptop, I'll learn how to make a little website or something for my business. Hmmm...I'll need a name. Oh, well, first things first."

Lori scanned the remaining emails. One from the church marked *Reminder: You Signed Up.* "Oh, Sasquatch, I completely forgot about Souper Bowl Sunday. I signed up to serve at the homeless shelter's soup kitchen."

Souper Bowl Sunday was at one o'clock. She did the calculations in her head. *By the time we clean up, I'll have about twenty minutes to get to the dance.* "Whaddaya think, cat? I go from no life to a full life in a matter of a few weeks

She called Leah to talk about shopping for a laptop. They agreed to go on Saturday when Ethan could watch the boys. "And I'll treat you to lunch," Lori added.

Her next call was to Carol. "I'm still coming to the dance, but I'll have to drive myself. I forgot I had signed up for the Souper Bowl Sunday at the homeless shelter."

"We could still drive you," Carol offered.

"No, I'll be coming from Hamilton. It'll be faster if I drive myself rather than you picking me up at my house or meeting you somewhere."

Sunday morning broke with warm sunshine pouring through the windows. "It feels almost like spring, cat!" Lori found herself humming as she readied herself for the day. The black and orange Bengals jersey she purchased for herself at the sporting goods store made her look fit and trim.

"Well, mostly," she confessed to her cat as she looked in the mirror. "At least strong and empowered," she said. "Of course, buying my own laptop and picking up that pepper spray may have had something to do with it." Another glance in the mirror confirmed she was ready to take on the world. Or at least the Souper Bowl crowd at the homeless shelter. "Church, the shelter, and a square dance, cat. What a day!"

Lori squirmed during Pastor Mike's sermon. Her mind wandered to the dance. The image of Axel came to mind. *He'll smile when he sees me. I'll smile back. He'll walk over and ask me to dance.* The image of him asking her for every dance played over and over in her mind. *I could even dance mainstream. It hasn't been that long.*

Serving soup at the homeless shelter interfered with Lori's daydreams. *Just as well. I'm starting to act silly.* Expecting a long line of scruffy men like those she had seen in the movies, Lori wasn't prepared for the droves of young families. Children, the ages of her own grandsons, ran through the soup line grabbing bread and crackers. Young mothers coddling babies gratefully accepted the bowls of soup Lori delivered. The shelter offered grilled cheese sandwiches, apples, chips and beverages to accompany the four different types of soup. One of the supporting churches had decorated the hall for the annual football event. A youth group organized games and activities for the children.

"You staying for the party?"

Lori turned to see a nicely dressed man about her age, drying a freshly washed serving tray. "No, I have another commitment. You?"

The man snickered. "I'll be here for the whole shebang. Thanks for comin' though. Maybe you'll come back. I'm here every Tuesday to Friday."

Lori smiled. "How good of you. What a ministry."

Pastor Mike walked up and patted the man on the shoulder. "You don't need to be drying those trays, Ernst. We're here to serve you today." He took the towel and tray from the man's hand.

Lori's mouth fell open. "I thought he was one of the volunteers!"

"Yeah, ol' Ernst has had a tough life, but he's a good man."

"He said he's here every Tuesday through Friday."

"Yep. He goes to the Missionary Alliance dinner on Mondays and then gets a meal at St. Bartholomew's on Saturdays. He's a regular here, though."

Lori lifted a tray from the stack. "Well, I think this is my last tray to take out. I need to leave by three-thirty at the latest. Is that okay?"

"Of course, Lori. We appreciate all you've done today. Leave when you need to."

"I'll just take these three bowls of soup out. We had a couple of latecomers. Then I'll head on. I think the cleanup is well underway." Lori loaded the tray with soup, bread, and apples. Someone else would be handing out the chips and beverages.

She started to lift the Styrofoam bowl of chili from the tray to hand to an elderly gentleman when SWOOSH! one child chasing another cut right in front of her, causing her to lose her balance as well as her grip on both the bowl and tray. Chili splattered everywhere, with the bulk of it landing on Lori.

"Are you okay?" One of the men bent to help pick up the now empty bowls of soup scattered on the floor.

"I'm fine. I hope it didn't get on you!" Lori looked around for help.

"No, ma'am, we're fine."

Pastor Mike was running toward her with a handful of paper towels.

"At least no one was burned," Lori managed to tell him. She tried to smile and assure the guests all was well. Another worker appeared with a mop while still another brought fresh bowls of soup to the table.

Lori locked herself in the women's bathroom, looked in the mirror and burst into tears. "My beautiful shirt!" She pulled the Bengals jersey off. Even the white turtleneck shirt under it was splattered with chili. She would be late to the dance. There was no way around it. She had to go home to change clothes. "And take a shower!" she cried as she looked into the bathroom mirror.

She washed her face and opened the bathroom door. A little boy stood in her way.

"I'm sorry, ma'am."

"Tell her what for," his mother prompted.

"I'm sorry I ran into you." He held his cookie out to her.

Lori felt her heart soften. "Well, I'm okay. Thank you for such a nice apology. And I'll tell you what. I'm not super hungry right now. Could you keep that cookie for me and maybe eat it for me during the game?"

The child offered a toothless grin and turned to his mother. "Can I, Mom?"

Lori texted Carol to tell her she was running late but would be at the dance as soon as possible. By the time she got home, the smell of chili permeated the car.

14

No cute Bengals jersey. No bright white turtleneck. No Bengals colors. Lori ran a brush through her hair. "I'm not letting this stop me, cat. I've been looking forward to this all week." She rummaged through her closet and drawers. The closest to team colors she could come was a black long-sleeve pullover. She slipped out of her chili-stained black slacks and pulled on a pair of jeans. "What do you think, cat? It's a casual dance anyway, right?"

Lori wrapped foil around her pan of brownies. "My secret weapon, cat. He likes my brownies!" She glanced at the clock on the stove. "By the time I get there, the dance will be in full bloom." *Who would Axel dance with in her place?* "What am I thinking? There are plenty of women."

Alone in her car, Lori found herself second guessing the decision to show up at the dance at all. "It's not like he asked me specifically to come with him." She tried to remember the conversation. *Maybe it was more the way he said it. He looked straight at me, though. I know he did. And then he did talk to Bill about me coming, right?*

Lori turned the key to start the ignition, then quickly turned it off again. "What am I doing?" *I'm acting like a schoolgirl.* The inner argument was leaning toward walking back in the house. "No. I want to dance, and even if he doesn't speak to me, I'm going." She turned the car on and put it in reverse.

By the time Lori arrived, the dance was already in full swing. She climbed the stairs, dropping the pan of brownies off on the refreshment table as she peeked around the corner into the nearly full hall of dancers. Everyone, dressed in their team colors, danced to the basic moves called by Greg. Several women she recognized from local clubs were wearing square dance skirts she suspected they made just for the occasion. Lori scanned the room. Axel was in a square near the front. She didn't recognize his partner. The woman was younger. *Younger than me, anyway. Younger and thinner.* The long prairie skirt fell gracefully to mid-calf on Axel's partner, where her stylish soft leather boots accentuated her tiny feet.

"Ugh." Startled at the sound of her own voice, Lori pulled herself back into the hallway. She slipped into the bathroom and stared at herself in the mirror. *Dowdy. That's the best word to describe me. Old and dowdy. And thick.* Lori turned to view herself from the side. *Definitely thick. Why would he want me when he can dance with Miss Super Model?* Lori sighed. *Okay, she may not be exactly a super model, but she is stunning.* "What were you thinking? You're crazy, you know it?" Lori cracked the door open and peered toward the hall.

The music was still going strong. She could slip out now and make her escape. No one need know she was ever there. *Aerobics. I can take up aerobics at the YMCA. An all women's class. That would be so much better.* The music stopped and dancers started milling around. Some headed for the refreshment table. Axel guided his partner toward the table and poured her a glass of water. She, in turn, fixed a plate of goodies and handed it to him. *Humph! So he brought a date! Jerk!* Two women headed toward the bathroom. Lori jumped into one of the two stalls and locked the door. She made a lot of noise with the toilet paper roll and waited. The ladies took turns using the other stall and left, chattering all the while about some man named Cliff. Lori waited until she heard the music start up again. She had just eased past the refreshment table and was heading down the stairs when she heard her name called out. *Marta.* Lori turned.

"Sorry I can't stay, Marta. I'm not feeling well, but I promised to bring brownies, so I dropped them off. See you later." Lori didn't give her friend a chance to speak. She raced down the stairs and flew out the door to her car. Once settled behind the wheel, she texted Carol to tell her she didn't feel all that great.

Dropped off the brownies. Didn't see you. If you would, could you bring my brownie pan home with you?

Lori didn't wait for a reply. She knew Carol wouldn't see the message until after the dance anyway. What would Carol say?

The minute she was safely home, Lori plopped into the nearest chair. Sasquatch jumped in her lap. "You always know, don't you, cat? The truth is, I really don't feel great. I feel old and ugly and silly. I'm turning into the very sort of person I've always avoided. I'm turning into a sad and desperate woman!" The cat purred as Lori massaged his furry neck. "I could kick myself for acting like a silly teenager. Never again, cat. Never again."

Lori grabbed the remote. Pre-game shows on two stations. The second held her interest for a moment. It was a preview of some of the expected Super Bowl commercials. *Super Bowl! Everything revolves around the Super Bowl!* Lori flipped through channels searching for a movie or a house makeover. Nothing seemed to hold her interest. "John was right, cat. Sixty channels and nothing to watch!" Lori pressed the search button one more time before giving up.

A Dateline Mystery, now half over, offered a recap. "Fifty-year-old Marge Krane thought she had found love again after losing her husband of thirty years. But was the cowboy who rode into her life the man who was now trying to kill her? Dateline continues in The Case of the Man on the Horse." Lori sat up. *A murderer!* "Oh, cat, that woman could be me!" Lori watched the story unfold with horrifying fascination. *Yes, he pretended to be a cowboy. No, he was nothing like Axel.* "Still, cat, a woman has to be careful."

A loud horn on a car outside her window drew Lori momentarily away from the mystery unfolding on the television. "What in the world?" A number of cars parked on either side of the street signaled a party at the Morgan house. The offensive horn belonged to a sleek gray sports car. A man leaned out the window, yelling obscenities at a van stopped in front of him. Danny Morgan was out in his shirtsleeves trying to direct traffic. Angie was walking up Lori's sidewalk.

"Come in!" Lori called as she opened the storm door.

"Sorry for all this. Danny invited everybody and his brother to watch the Super Bowl at our house. It's crazy over there!"

"I can see. Want to hide out here until they're all gone?"

"Actually, I was going to see if some of our guests could park in your drive."

Lori looked out at the mass of cars lining the street. "Of course they can. I'm not going anywhere."

"But I thought you had plans."

"Plans change. Your friends can park in my drive if it helps."

"Thanks, Lori. And if they get too rowdy, I may take you up on ducking in here!" Angie popped out the door and gave a thumbs up to Danny as she stepped off the porch.

Lori watched as several young men carrying coolers and six packs made their way into the Morgan house. *I hope you do come back, Angie. For the sake of both of us.*

The Dateline Mystery was over. At least for those who watched the entire episode. "Well, cat, I'll have to come up with my own ending. And just because he brought a date to the dance doesn't make him a murderer. Doesn't even make him one of the bad guys."

Three messages blinked on Lori's machine by the time she returned from having the oil changed in her car Monday morning. She pushed the button and listened while she fixed herself a cup of coffee and a peanut butter and jelly sandwich.

"Hey, Mom! Just checking in. We didn't get home from Leah's brother's house until after eleven. Great game though, huh? Let me know if you need any help with your laptop. Should be easy enough, though."

Lori smiled at the thought of her new computer, then frowned. *Eleven o'clock? I should've kept the boys. I hope they had a sitter and didn't keep them out that late.* Lori deleted the message and the next one began to play.

"Hi, Lori! Hope you're feeling better." *Carol.* "I have your brownie pan. Not one brownie left! Anyway, we had fun at the dance but went to Bill's brother's house afterward to watch the game. Let me know if you need anything." Lori sighed as she hit the delete button.

The third call was a number she didn't recognize. There was a muffled sound. A fumbling of the phone, silence, then the click of someone hanging up. *Probably a wrong number.*

Monday's sunshine mirrored the previous day, causing Lori to turn off her furnace and open the windows. "I'm telling you, cat, it feels like spring." She busied herself creating an office space in her spare bedroom. She emptied a small two-drawer file cabinet she once used to organize her crochet patterns. Turning the file folders inside out, Lori renamed the first three Edit, Proofread, and Invoice. She knew from past experience, using verbs would help her stay on top of tasks as work came in. *I wonder if I'll need these at all? I may get so tech savvy I never use paper at all.* She grinned, "Nah! Not me."

Three hours later, Lori stood at the doorway and admired her new office space. "A productive morning, if I do say so myself, cat." Three new positive emails from former clients and writers she had worked with through *Priority Care* confirmed Lori's decision to launch her business. She spent the next two hours researching writing conferences coming up in the spring. *Conferences are always good places for writers, editors, and publishers to network.*

Lori's stomach growled. Sasquatch followed her into the kitchen. The light was blinking on her machine.

"That's funny. I didn't hear the phone ring." She pushed the button. The same unrecognizable number popped up. The same fumbling. The same silence. The same clicking as someone hung up. "Cat, you have a crazy woman for a friend! I forgot to delete that silly message!" Still, Lori found the call unsettling. "I'm sure it's a wrong number, cat. At least I hope it is."

By the time Tuesday rolled around, the thought of the unknown caller was gone for good. So was the thought of ever going back to square dancing. "I still don't feel all that great," she said when Carol called. "And I'm pretty busy with getting my office set up. Did I tell you I got a job this morning? I'm trying to get it out quickly. I'll build a good reputation that way."

"Just make sure you're seeking God in all you do," Carol answered.

Lori bristled. *What does she mean by that?*

The article on new medicines to treat Alzheimer's was fascinating. Lori read it through twice before taking her virtual red pen to it. The author, a physician's assistant, was explaining the side effects of the new drugs. Lori spent three hours on the text, combing through every inch of grammar, spelling, organization, and content. She researched one of the drugs online when the author's claims seemed to contradict themselves. The problem was easy to spot and Lori suggested a new way to arrange the information to make it clear to the reader.

"Actually, working has been so much fun," she told her daughter-in-law that afternoon. "And I love my new computer."

Seven-thirty rolled around. Then eight. Only once did Lori allow herself to think of the dancers at the barn. "Just as well, cat. I have more important things to do." She settled herself in her chair and opened her Bible. Her bookmark was at chapter 27. "Wow, I've missed so many days! How did that happen? Here we are in February and I didn't finish out January!" Lori was about to flip the pages back to the sixth chapter when a verse in chapter 27 caught her eye. "As iron sharpens iron, so one person sharpens another." *Carol.* Lori leaned her head back and closed her eyes.

"You know, God, I've been so caught up in reinventing myself, I haven't really asked you what I should be doing. And this whole thing with thinking there could be some new romance waiting for me? Carol was right. I need to seek *you* first." A tear rolled down Lori's cheek.

Lori read the remaining chapters in Proverbs. She had just finished the text when the phone rang. She glanced at the caller ID. That same strange number. "Hello?" she answered tentatively.

"Oh, hi there. It's Axel. Axel Calhoun from square dancing? I, uh, I hope this isn't a misuse of the calling tree, but I heard you were sick on Sunday and then when you didn't show up tonight, I, uh, well, I hope you're okay."

"Uh, yes, actually, I'm better. I've been pretty busy and uh…"

"Oh. I hoped you'd be at the dance on Sunday. My sister was visiting from Wyoming. I wanted you to meet her. Or, well, I wanted her to meet you, I guess."

"Your sister?" Lori dropped into the kitchen chair.

"Yeah, she came through here on her way to see her daughter in Pennsylvania. Anyway, maybe you could meet her another time. I'm glad you're not sick anymore. Are you planning to come next week?"

"Absolutely!" *Oh, that sounded strange.* "I mean, I should be there next week for sure."

"Good. Maybe some of us could go out again like we did that one week."

"Sounds great." Lori smiled. *His sister.*

16

"I'm going to back the car in so you don't have to walk around it," Bill said.

"Thanks. I'm sure I'll be okay once I get inside and get some ice on this ankle. I just feel bad you and Carol had to leave the square dance lesson early because of me," Lori said.

"Don't be silly. You're sure you don't want me to drive to the emergency room? Carol thinks you should have it x-rayed."

"I think it's just a bad sprain. Is it sprain? Sounds right. A sprained ankle. So why do people say, 'I sprang my ankle'? Humph!"

Bill chuckled as he maneuvered Lori's car into the garage. "Don't ask me. You're the wiz kid editor!"

Lori gazed out the front window of her car. Carol was edging her own car into the driveway. "Bill, who is that in the dark car behind Carol?"

Bill pressed gently on the brakes and turned to look. "Only Axel. I think he lives a block or two over. He probably just wants to make sure you're okay. That was quite a spill you took."

Axel. That's why I keep seeing that car. "Yeah, well, it wasn't my fault you know."

"Nobody said it was. Old George has no business dancing. He can't hear the calls."

"He moves on every call, even when it isn't his turn. I hope he's okay, though. He seems pretty fragile."

"Fortunately for him, you were there to break his fall." Bill grinned as he backed in as close to the door as he could. "Now wait there. I'll come around."

Lori cringed as Bill, Axel, and Carol all fumbled trying to help her exit the car with her injured ankle. Each had a different idea about what should be done.

She put her hand up to call a halt to the discussion. "I'll tell you what. You men step aside and I'll get out. Carol, if you could help me swing my leg out without hitting the car…that's it. And Bill, you get on one side and

66

Carol on the other. Axel, you open the door to the house and I'll make it just fine."

The crew helped Lori hobble into the narrow hall leading to the family room. She fell into the nearest chair. "I think I may put an ice pack on it after all. There's one in the freezer."

Carol raced into the kitchen. She returned with baggie full of ice cubes wrapped in a dishtowel. "Here, honey, I didn't see an ice pack."

Axel sat down on the couch opposite Lori. "I was worried when Old George started dancing. I knew one day he'd wind up hurting somebody."

The cold ice sent a shiver up Lori. "I hate putting ice on anything."

"I'll make you some tea," Carol offered.

"I'll be fine. Really. You folks don't need to fuss."

A few minutes later, the four sat in the cozy family room sipping tea. Axel sneezed and pulled a large handkerchief from his pocket.

"So Bill tells me you live nearby," Lori said.

"Yep. Just a couple blocks over. Near the creek."

Another sneeze, followed quickly by another.

"Bless you," the other three chimed.

"Sorry, folks, I don't know what's come over me."

"It sounds like you may be catching a bad cold," Carol offered.

"Perhaps you're allergic to something," Lori suggested.

"Only thing I ever been allergic to is cats."

"Really?" Lori looked at Carol and Bill.

Axel's sneezes were coming in pairs now. His eyes watered and he started coughing.

"Axel, I hate to tell you this, but you better leave," Lori said calmly. "You see, I do have a cat and I'm afraid he's making you ill."

Axel jumped to his feet and raced toward the door, sneezing all the way. "I'm so sorry, Lori." He left.

Sasquatch came out from under the chair and jumped into Lori's lap.

"Usually, cat, I like seeing you. Not today."

Carol spent the next few minutes trying to make Lori comfortable. She grabbed a couple of pillows from the guest room to elevate her ankle.

"Axel is such a nice man. Why did he have to be allergic to cats of all things?" Lori shifted in the chair.

"I know." Carol handed Lori an anti-inflammatory. "Maybe I should stay the night with you."

"No, I'll be fine. I just feel stupid."

"What would make you feel stupid?" Bill asked. "It wasn't your fault."

"I know, but you reach an age where you really don't relish the idea of falling in front of everyone."

Carol chuckled. "I reached that age when I was thirteen. Did I ever tell you about falling in study hall? There was this cute boy I liked, and sure enough I fell flat on my behind right in front of him."

Bill chuckled. "I remember that."

"You don't remember it." Then, turning to Lori she added, "Of course I married the fellow ten years later."

"I may not have married you if I had remembered you were a klutz!"

"Stop it, Bill. You're not helping matters."

Lori sighed. "I guess it doesn't matter anyway. He's allergic to cats."

Bill scowled. "Am I missing something?"

Carol cocked her head his way. "Men! They're so clueless."

A knock at the front door caused Lori to jump.

Bill opened the door. In walked Axel, smiling and carrying a paper bag.

"You know what's really good for a hurt ankle, don't you?" he asked the group. "Cookies and ice cream."

Carol took the sack and headed to the kitchen for bowls and spoons.

Sasquatch jumped into his lap. "Well, hello there, little fellow!"

"Sasquatch!" Lori called.

"He's okay," Axel assured her. "I bought something else while I was out. Antihistamine. Sasquatch, eh?" He stroked the cat's leg and rubbed his thumb over Sasquatch's paw. "Yep, you got that name honest. Bigfoot."

The foursome sat until late in the evening, eating ice cream and sharing stories. Lori decided ice cream was indeed good medicine, but so was the company of good people. And a cat. Even though she had already made up her mind it was time for Sasquatch to go back to his original owner. She could only imagine the look on Ethan's face.

Rebecca Waters works hard to create realistic characters facing contemporary issues and stories built around faith, hope, and love. Her first novel, *Breathing on Her Own,* has garnered over 160 positive reviews. Rebecca's second novel, *Libby's Cuppa Joe,* is scheduled for release in March 2019. *Courtesy Turn* is her first novella and is based on her experiences as an avid square dancer. She has also published three books for new writers, *Designing a Business Plan for Your Writing, Marketing You and Your Writing 101,* and *Writing with E's.* As a freelance writer, Rebecca has also published several stories in the popular Chicken Soup for the Soul books, articles in Standard Publishing's *Lookout Magazine, The Christian Communicator, Church Libraries,* and *Home Health Aide Digest.* Prior to entering the writing field, Rebecca was a college professor and speaker on the Ohio Writing Project circuit. As a published author, she shares her life journey in her weekly blog, *A Novel Creation*. To learn more about Rebecca or to read *A Novel Creation*, visit her website at *www.WatersWords.com* or connect with her on her author Facebook page, RebeccaWatersAuthor.

SURPRISED BY LOVE

By Sandra Merville Hart

*Dedicated to
Brian and Kathy,
Real-life heroes to me*

1

Easter Sunday, March 23, 1913, Troy, Ohio

"There's water in the cellar." Seventeen-year-old Willy Stevens delivered the unfortunate news to his oldest sister, Lottie, and turned another page of *The Adventures of Tom Sawyer*. One blue-trouser-clad leg dangled over the arm of his cushioned armchair.

Not again. Lottie had no time to clean the cellar that flooded with every hard rain—and why had Willy waited until after supper to tell her? She rolled her eyes at her younger sister, Esther, at a loss how to make their only brother care about the work of the home. Lottie sometimes wondered exactly what did matter to Willy. He rarely listened to her anymore.

"How high?"

He shrugged without looking up. "Covers the toe of my boots."

Three inches already. She stifled a sigh for the sake of the four boarders who had joined the family in the sitting room after Easter supper. Harvey Feldman, a shy bachelor in his fifties, sometimes chose to remain in his attic bedroom as he did this evening. Their talkative reporter, Augusta Humphreys, more than made up for Harvey's quietness, but the widow was spending the day in Piqua with her former in-laws. Electricity provided lighting for the room decorated in shades of blue to match floral wallpaper. A comforting fire warmed Lottie's hands as she extended them toward the blaze in the fireplace.

Esther dropped a quilting square back in her sewing basket and retied the yellow ribbon that held her long brown plait together. ""It's no wonder with all the rain."

"It poured down today." Lottie's shoulders slumped. The responsibility of the boarding home never stopped, even for a holiday. She patted her sandy hair, surprised the side swirls hairstyle held through the supper preparations and cleanup.

"After being so lovely yesterday." Nellie McMillan, a single lady in her twenties, lifted floral curtains and stared at the darkening gray sky.

"Unseasonably so." Susannah Miller nodded, her gray hair arranged in a small knot at the nape of her neck.

"Guess we'd better rescue the canned goods from the cellar shelves." Lottie rubbed her aching back, feeling at least thirty instead of twenty. What did a real day off feel like?

Lines deepened on Susannah's forehead as she stared out the window beyond Nellie. "Be a shame to lose last summer's canning."

Nellie dropped the lacy edge of the curtain. "Doubt it will let up soon. I'll help."

Esther followed both ladies toward the kitchen.

Expecting her brother to follow, Lottie turned back. "Willy, did you hear? Cellar shelves must be emptied."

He didn't raise his eyes from the book. "I'll be along."

Susannah pushed her bulky frame from a cushioned armchair. "Frank and I will stand at the top of the stairs to take the food from you." She patted the arm of the gray-haired man next to her.

"Like an assembly line." Pressing her lips together, Lottie stared at Willy as he turned another page.

"Did someone mention a food line?" Frank Miller, Susannah's retired husband, tossed aside his newspaper. "Just show me where the goodies are."

Susannah slapped his arm playfully. "Oh, Frank. Be serious. Cans. Jars. Sacks of flour and sugar. Besides, after that big meal, I don't know how you can eat."

He rubbed his flat stomach. "No room here. That's a fact. The girls cooked a mighty fine dinner. I almost didn't have room for apple pie." His green eyes twinkled. "Almost."

Lottie laughed. "Thanks." Her sister was the talented cook, but Lottie baked the pies. "You coming, Willy?"

Henry Watson, a gray-haired widower, frowned from his wheelchair before the fire. "That boy cares more about animals and books than eating."

Willy sank deeper into the cushion.

Lottie shrugged and walked into the kitchen. These days she picked her battles with her brother or their relationship suffered.

When she opened the cellar door, a dank smell wafted into the kitchen. At the top of the stairs, the three younger ladies removed their lace-up boots and stockings. Their Easter dresses were only a few inches below the knee.

"Water's higher than Willy said." Esther was the first one down the narrow stairway. "Well above my ankles."

"Should we empty the top shelves?" Nellie looked at Lottie.

"Best be on the safe side." Susannah spoke from the top of the stairs.

The older woman's advice swayed Lottie. "We can't afford to lose food." This wasn't the first time rain had seeped into the cellar of the two-story home on the banks of the Great Miami River. It wouldn't be the last.

"Hope the river doesn't flood." Nellie passed a jar to Frank.

A jar of peaches slipped in Lottie's hand. "My father was alive the last time the river flooded enough to reach our home, and he's been gone ten years."

Nellie smiled. "Thank the Lord it doesn't happen often."

Conversation dwindled. As the younger women passed jars to the Millers, Lottie's thoughts strayed to a boy she'd known in school. Maybe Joe would return to Troy this summer and she'd pass him on the street …

No. Best not to dream. Sooner or later she must wake up and face reality.

Nellie shivered. "It's cold down here."

"Let's hurry." Lottie stared at the water line on the cement wall. A chill went down her spine. Was it her imagination or was the water higher?

♫ ♫ ♫

Rain pelted the roof. Lottie finally gave up trying to sleep. Bundled in a quilt, she sat beside her bedroom window, which faced the river. A lone boat with twin lanterns sped down the river. The pounding rain almost mesmerized her.

She relaxed against the wall. Moments of solitude seldom came.

Strange to experience loneliness in a house filled with people. Foolish hopes of meeting an eligible bachelor at church while wearing her new lilac print Easter dress hadn't come true. Nothing ever changed. No knight in shining armor would swoop in to whisk her from danger — or even rescue her from boring, everyday tasks.

She sighed. Mama's death four years ago had sealed her fate. As the oldest daughter, she quit high school and took charge of running the boarding house. Not only did her younger sister and brother depend upon her, but also her six boarders, to varying degrees.

Her teacher, Mrs. Tate, continued her school assignments in the evenings. Thanks to her kindness, Lottie had earned her diploma, though she missed the parties and dances.

She leaned her forehead against the cold windowpane. No gentleman had ever called for her. There had been no trolley rides to shows in Dayton with a young man with eyes only for her. How many times had Lottie watched Esther or Nellie stroll with a young man to the trolley for a day excursion?

Too many.

How did it feel to have a man look at her lovingly? Thoughts of Joe Bosworth nudged at her. She relived their conversations at school functions. Around the time her mother died, he'd courted Mary Kay Huffman. Lottie knew she couldn't compete with the beautiful auburn-haired girl, and pushed away her foolish dreams. Two years later Mary Kay had married a college beau and moved to Kansas.

Lottie fingered the quilt around her shoulders. Joe's college education at the University of Tennessee must be ending soon. Had he moved from Troy forever? Her only regular activity in town was church and he didn't attend her church.

It didn't matter. Some things were best forgotten.

Lottie awoke, shivering, at the window. Not only had the fire in her bedroom heat stove died, but it was also her turn to rekindle the fire in the hall stove and the fireplace. Stretching, she tied a robe around her and lit the fires. Then she dressed in a dark skirt and white blouse. Ready for a day of cleaning and laundry, she joined her sister in the kitchen.

"There's no place to prepare our meal." Hands on hips, Esther surveyed the table and counters filled with canned fruits and vegetables.

"I'll tote the food to the spare bedroom while you start breakfast." Lottie sighed inwardly as she opened the cellar door. Droplets slid down the cement walls. "Water's at least a foot higher than when I went to bed." She closed the door against the stagnant odor. "Where's Willy?"

"Barn." She indicated the direction with a toss of her head. "He left as I came downstairs."

"At least we can depend on him to care for the animals." Lottie opened the curtains to the gray light of a sunless dawn. "River's up."

Hurrying to the window, Esther gripped her arm. "It's almost out of its banks. Will it flood?"

Though wondering the same thing, she straightened her shoulders. "Doubtful. The rain has to stop soon."

Ignoring the nagging worry of the river flooding, Lottie filled a basket with jars and headed up to her parents' bedroom on the second floor. The room remained the way Mama left it and wasn't for rent.

The boarders who worked in town had eaten by the time Lottie finished. Nellie's job at the Troy Telephone Company, Augusta's at the *Troy Record*, and Harvey's at Troy Sunshade Company enabled the trio to ride the trolley into town together. Though they sometimes walked to save money, riding was the unanimous decision today.

Lottie washed clothes every Monday, which cost extra for boarders.

Everyone chose to pay it—except Henry, who had no money even for rent. Lottie never asked him for rent and had decided long ago that he could stay as long as he chose.

Even without paying, Henry complained about the way she ironed his shirts. Reminding herself that his children hadn't visited since the death of his wife two years ago, Lottie held her tongue.

"The river's still rising." Willy thrust aside a pair of trousers hanging from a line to enter the laundry room after school, as she ran a shirt through the wringer. "Canal's spilled over its banks. I'm worried about our animals."

With their home located on ten acres between the Great Miami River and the Miami and Erie Canal, this unwelcome news jolted Lottie. "Is the barn floor wet?"

"Not yet." He ran his hands through his curly brown hair. "But the barn's closer to the canal than the river."

"The canal is not deep or wide. Our house is in greater danger from the river." Lottie hung a damp shirt on one of the lines strung across the ceiling. "Rivers expand rapidly during floods."

"What about Belle and Bernice? And Bert and Ben?" He crossed and uncrossed his arms as he mentioned the cows and horses. "And the chickens. The coop's on higher ground, but isn't sturdy."

"Keep an eye on the flooding." Lottie wiped damp hands on her apron. "Augusta will know the latest news this evening."

But Augusta didn't come home for supper. Neither did Nellie or Harvey. Lottie whispered a prayer for their safety as water trickled down the windowpane.

🦙 🦙 🦙

A thoroughly soaked Harvey arrived after supper. "I walked home to monitor the rising water levels. Townsfolk are mighty skittish. Canal flooded last night. River's up." He removed his boots at the door and set them on the porch before closing it against the draft.

Quite a speech for a man who normally spoke about fifty words daily. Lottie propelled him to the cozy fire in the sitting room. She and Susannah removed his soggy coat as he shivered.

"Did you see Nellie or Augusta?" Henry wrung his hands from his wheelchair.

He shook his head. "Thought they'd be here."

A chill shot through Lottie. "Change into dry clothes while we heat your supper." She carried the coat rack closer to the fire to dry the coat.

He complied and trudged up the stairs in the back of the sitting room.

"I'll clean those boots." Frank stepped outside, closing the door behind him.

"Maybe you should call Nellie." Susannah clutched her crochet hook, her hands unmoving on a nearly completed lavender shawl.

"She may have heard from Augusta." Esther tilted her head toward the hallway where the telephone hung on the wall.

Good idea. Crossing to the hall, Lottie turned the crank and held the receiver to her ear. "Nellie? Is that you?"

"Lottie! Yes, I'm still working. It's crazy. Everyone calls for news." Nellie sounded both excited and scared. "We operators are calling townspeople to warn of rising waters. Were you contacted?"

She shifted closer to the wall as the others gathered near. Henry's wheelchair creaked as he crept closer. "No."

"Move food and valuables to upper levels as a precaution. Remember to store dry wood upstairs for heat stoves. Is there water in the house?"

"Just in the cellar."

"Good. That's what everyone is saying. With our house being so close to the river ..." Someone spoke to Nellie in the background.

"What's she saying?" Henry turned his good ear toward the phone.

"Someone's talking. I can't understand what he said." Lottie listened to several voices. None of the words made sense. The door creaked as Frank stepped inside.

"Don't expect me home this evening. I believe Augusta's staying in town—you know how she hates to miss a story. Don't worry about us. We won't come home in this deluge."

Harvey's socked feet thumped on the stairs.

"That's a relief." Lottie's fingers tightened on the receiver. "Keep us informed. Without close neighbors, we won't know what's happening."

"Will do." She sounded distracted. "Look, my switchboard's all lit up. Pray the rain stops soon."

"I already did." Lottie replaced the receiver and passed on the information.

"I'll carry the chickens to the barn loft." Willy grabbed his coat and hurried out into the rain.

A chilly draft entered the room with the opened door.

Frank held the door open. "He has to jump puddles." He closed the door. "Our valuables are in our room. What can we do?"

"Let's move the rest of the food from the kitchen first. Then firewood, pots, pans, dishes. As much as possible." Lottie met Harvey's concerned gaze. The bachelor was so dependable, like her father had been. His presence lightened her burden. "Harvey, eat your supper. If we all work together, it won't take long."

Two exhausting hours later, all chairs and small tables were stored in her mother's room, along with kitchen supplies and her grandmother's music box from the time of the War Between the States. The grandfather clock, which had belonged to her mother's parents, was too bulky to easily move, so it remained in the sitting room and chimed on the hour. The sway of the pendulum clicked a steady rhythm. She didn't want to lose the finely crafted timepiece and prayed the river receded before reaching their home.

Henry occupied the only bedroom on the first floor. Before she died, Henry's wife had arranged everything within his easy reach. The bathroom was on the first floor along with the dining room and sitting room, so he had no need to venture upstairs. Confined to a wheelchair, he never went anywhere except church.

The stubborn man didn't see any reason to change that policy for a little rain.

"I'll sleep in my own bed, thank you very much." With a mulish expression, Henry folded his arms across his scrawny chest.

"What if the river rises while we sleep?" Susannah spoke in a reasonable tone.

"I ain't goin' nowhere." He lifted his stubbly chin in the air.

"I'll carry you to a comfortable bedroom upstairs." Arms extended, Harvey took a step toward him.

"Leave me be." He brushed Harvey's hand away.

"You can sleep in my mother's bed." Lottie's shoulders tensed.

"Bah! The bedding probably ain't been changed in better than four years."

"Those sheets are clean." Lottie clenched her jaw. "But I'll change them."

He shook his head. "Don't bother. I ain't going up there."

"We tried." Susannah shrugged. "Best grab what sleep we can."

It seemed a good suggestion since Nellie hadn't called back. Lottie tried to convince herself that no news meant everything was fine.

2

"Help! Somebody help me!"

Instantly awake, Lottie shoved her arms into her robe and ran to the stairs. She picked up the lantern always kept lit on the hall table and began to descend. She paused as running footsteps hit the stairs behind her.

"What is it?"

"What's happening?"

"Is that Henry?"

Everyone spoke at once. Henry screamed in a panic-stricken yelp.

Esther gasped. "There's water in the sitting room. That cup is floating."

Lottie's gaze followed her sister's pointing finger. She clutched the banister as blackness threatened her consciousness.

The river had invaded their home.

"You all right, Miss Lottie?" A fully-dressed Harvey grasped her arm as she swayed.

"Don't worry about me." She tightened her grip on the banister. "Let's see about Henry."

Icy water swished over Lottie's ankle the third step from the bottom. She gritted her teeth and forced herself to continue until her bare foot squelched into the sitting room rug.

Willy waded past her. "I'll see to the animals."

"Stop!" Harvey's normally quiet voice boomed.

Willy halted.

"First things first. Henry's in danger." The big man spoke in a gentle yet firm tone. "We'll rescue him and then see what can be done for your pets."

Willy glanced at the door and then turned as quickly as knee-deep water allowed.

Thankful her brother obeyed, Lottie waded through foul-smelling water. Esther, Harvey, and Willy trailed her as she knocked on the bedroom door. "Henry! Can we come in?"

"I don't see how you can do anything for me from the hall." The panic in his voice lessened.

Harvey put his massive shoulder to the door and heaved it open.

Lottie lifted the lantern high. Water covered the seat of the wheelchair and the mattress. Her shoulders drooped. She reached for the light switch and then stopped short, wondering about the safety of electric wires.

"Look how high it is." Esther covered her mouth with her hands.

"Stay strong." Lottie glanced at her weeping sister. "Light another lantern."

Robe wet to mid-thigh, Esther trudged toward the kitchen.

Harvey bent over the frightened man. "Evenin', Henry. This fine young man and I will carry you safely upstairs."

Henry shrank against the wet pillow, causing little ripples. "You young whippersnappers will drop me."

"Never happen." Harvey's deep voice softened.

Willy met Harvey's gaze. His posture straightened. "We promise not to drop you."

Lottie's lips curved at her little brother's confident tone. This life-saving task was within his grasp. He knew it.

"Gotta get you away from the rising water."

Henry's tense face relaxed at Harvey's reassurance.

Lottie shared the gray-haired man's faith in Harvey. Her mother had leaned on him, too. The strong man instilled confidence. "No time to waste—the river's pouring in."

Harvey scooped the small man into his arms as easily as if he lifted a child. "Hold his legs, Willy, and lead the way. We'll return for the wheelchair."

"It's probably ruined." Henry's brow puckered.

Did the man ever look on the bright side? Then Lottie wondered just what the bright side could be as her sister's lantern lit their way. Lottie pushed the chair to the stairs.

Harvey retrieved the wheelchair within moments. "Come on up, Miss Lottie. I can't rest easy while you're down here."

She followed him to the second floor where her brother leaned out an open window, gazing toward the barn.

Henry crouched on the bed in the spare bedroom. His bewildered expression tugged at her heart.

He peppered Susannah, who towel-dried his chair, with advice on her task and then demanded dry clothing. "You folks would just as soon see me catch my death of cold in this wet nightshirt. Then you won't need to bother with me anymore. That's your plan, ain't it?"

Lottie gritted her teeth. "I'll fetch the clothes."

As she descended the stairs, she spotted Willy and Harvey climbing through an open porch window. "Be careful," she admonished. The front door remained firmly shut, preventing another foot of water from entering.

The unnatural presence of muddy water created a spooky atmosphere. Lottie didn't tarry in the sitting room. Henry's bedroom in back faced the river. She lifted the bedroom curtains to peer out in the moonless night.

Waves lapped against the house. Screams for help echoed from town. Her pulse raced as she whispered a prayer for those in peril.

The river she'd swam in as a child had become an enemy.

Lacy curtain fell from nerveless fingers. She must pull herself together. Everyone depended on her. *God, I prayed earlier for You to spare the grandfather clock. That's the least of my worries. Now I'm asking You to spare our lives. Please protect us.*

She lifted the lantern high. Her heart dropped to her cold, wet feet. Even in the time it had taken to carry Henry upstairs, the water level had risen. Murky water covered all the furniture in his room, custom-made years ago to be within comfortable reach of his wheelchair, including the top drawer of both chests containing his clothing.

Lottie tripped over something and caught herself against the brass footboard. His shoes? Gingerly she groped in the water. Finding them, she dangled the old leather shoes as far away from her body as possible. Foul-smelling river water poured out. Might they be saved? His clothing was ruined, along with his furniture.

Then she remembered the newly laundered clothes. Wading to the laundry room, she piled all the clothing from the lines in her arms and returned upstairs with the smelly shoes flapping against her robe.

Frank took the offensive footwear with a grimace. "I'll show him what they look like now so he'll feel better after they're cleaned."

"Good idea." Susannah gave a heartfelt sigh and took the clean clothing from Lottie. "I'll fold these." She carried them into her bedroom.

Henry twisted his wedding ring. "My shoes are ruined."

"We'll dry them." Frank spoke soothingly. "But first, let's get you into dry clothes."

Fanning herself, Lottie carried the dripping shoes to the heat stove in her room.

Shaking her head, Esther followed her. "I wish he'd show a bit of constraint in times like these."

"He's frightened." Hard rain bounced off the roof. They had more pressing concerns. "Mama used to say folks complain about little things to keep their mind off bigger worries."

"I guess." Esther tied back the curtain to stare into the darkness. "The river's rising so fast. Do you suppose it will reach the second floor?"

Her heart skipped a beat. She stepped behind her sister to stare into the darkness. Waves smacked their home. She squeezed Esther's shoulder. "It'll stop raining soon. If not, we'll build an ark." She waited for Esther's tentative smile. "Let's change our wet nightgowns for a warm dress in case we have to calm Henry again during the night. Then lie down and rest."

After everyone settled to sleep again, Lottie huddled on the stairs to wait for Willy and Harvey to return from the barn. Her legs shook as her eyes were drawn to the water occasionally lapping over the sitting room windowsill.

Where were they? She clasped her shaking hands together and prayed for their safety. The tick-tocking of the grandfather clock suddenly stopped. She hadn't realized she'd been listening to the rhythmic swing of the pendulum in the silent house until it ceased.

They'd lost the cherished heirloom.

She tried not to notice that water covered another step. Her nerves stretched to the breaking point. At least Harvey accompanied Willy.

She frowned at the closed bedroom doors. How could anyone sleep?

She rose and paced the spacious hallway.

The phone rang.

Her body jerked. Probably Nellie, calling to warn her about the rising river.

Lottie already knew. Unwilling to wade the first floor alone at its waist-high depth, she listened tensely until the ringing stopped. What was the news from Troy? Some homes didn't have a second floor. At least those inside this house were safe.

For the moment.

A scraping at the window.

"Willy? Is that you?"

He poked his head through the window, an adult collie in his arms. "We brought Rusty. He doesn't like it inside the house, but we were afraid to leave him in the loft with the chickens." He gave the dog to Harvey before climbing through.

Her legs wobbled. Willie and Harvey were safe. "Did the river flood the barn?"

"Not yet." Harvey negotiated his larger frame through the open window and closed it. "Moved the hen house up the slope. It's held together so far."

Willy waded over. "We tied bales of hay to the top of the stalls. They'll have plenty to eat."

"You're soaked to the skin." Lottie touched his freezing hand. "Go change. Give Rusty a good rubdown with a towel before setting him down. Susannah left a pot of coffee on the heat stove in the hall."

They went to their bedrooms. Lottie returned to her room and opened the window. People screamed for help from the south. Troy. She pressed a trembling hand to her lips.

Lord, send someone to save them before it's too late. Her heartbeat thrashed in her ears. *Save us, too, God. Send a rescue boat.*

Shivering in the chill, she kept the window open, hands over her ears to block the screams.

Minutes ticked by. As she paced from her room to the stairs, she monitored the rising water and prayed desperately.

Cries for help quickened Joe Bosworth's pace as he and his friend, Pete Morgan, ran the dark streets of Troy. He had to do something for his hometown. His gut told him that the friendly river that flowed beside Troy was about to rage at its citizens.

The fire bell had rung, alerting citizens of the emergency. Sheriff Louis Paul, the man in charge of rescue operations, would give direction on where to take Pete's boat first.

The whistle at the electric power plant blew.

Then church bells rang.

His blood pumped, the sounds urging them to a faster pace. When they found Sheriff Paul, he'd just received news of a family suspected to be in trouble a half mile from town—a boarding house owned by a family named Stevens. The family hadn't answered a call from a boarder.

"We'll take it," Joe volunteered, his heart beating a staccato rhythm. That place belonged to Lottie Stevens, a girl he'd known from school. He hadn't seen her in years, but he used to think about her a lot.

His normally fun-loving friend drew a deep breath. "You know where it is?"

Joe nodded. Though he had never worked up the courage to visit, he knew exactly where Lottie lived. "Hurry."

Searching for a distraction, Lottie brushed her hair and pinned it into side swirls. This didn't take nearly long enough. Monitoring the water rising on the steps for the last hour had almost driven her crazy.

The phone rang again. With no clock in her room, time seemed to stop altogether. She stared out into the darkness, willing a boat to come for them. The water was halfway up the steps—well over her five-foot-two-inches and probably over her tall brother's head.

Shouting from Troy continued. Lottie leaned her ear against the pane. Agonized screams sent chills through her.

As dawn lightened the horizon, she spotted a boat headed up the river from Troy.

"Over here!" She stuck her head and arms out the window into the rain. "Please, help us!"

The rowboat floated along the edge of the river, away from the swift current. In the gray mist, two men turned toward her. "Who's there?" a man called.

"Lottie Stevens." Tears blurred her vision—someone knew of her family's danger. "The first floor's flooded over our heads. There are seven of us."

"It's Joe Bosworth and Pete Morgan. We'll be over as quickly as we can."

Joe! Lottie jerked her head back inside, patting her wet hair. This wasn't the way she'd dreamed of seeing him again. "The largest window is the bedroom on the left side of the house. We'll meet you there."

Esther burst into her room. The others quickly followed.

"Don't forget me!" Henry shouted from down the hall.

"We're being rescued." Lottie gave them a tremulous smile. "Joe Bosworth and Pete Morgan are rowing to us. Oh, you're all dressed. You'll need your warmest coats."

"What's happening?" Henry yelled.

"We'll tell him." Frank clasped Susannah's hand and left with Harvey.

"The water on the first floor is over our heads?" Tears welled up in Esther's eyes.

"Esther, we must be strong." Lottie grasped her shoulders. "There's no choice. Who knows when the river will crest? It's still raining."

Esther gasped.

"Grab your coat and meet everyone in Mama's room."

Esther ran from the room, but Willy remained. He stared at her.

"Willy?" Her throat constricted. "What is it?"

"It's just ..." He stepped closer. "Are you okay, Sis?"

His concern comforted her in a way he hadn't done in a long time. "I'm fine. We'll all be fine now." She hugged him. "Let's see about Henry."

Entering her parents' room, she peeked outside the window that went from the ceiling almost to the floor. The college men struggled against the waves. "Henry, help's coming."

"I'm not leaving." Henry's jaw set.

Lottie rolled her eyes as heat flooded her face.

Wearing an old coat of Frank's, Henry sat in his wheelchair, arms folded across his scrawny chest. "I ain't gettin' in that rickety thing. We'll all drown before we're halfway to Troy."

"You'd rather drown in this house?" Harvey spoke quietly.

Henry pressed his lips together with a grimace. "It won't come to that."

"Maybe not." Lottie spoke calmly though her legs shook. "But why risk it?"

"Hello!"

She hurried to the window, a hand to her throat. "Joe, Pete, you probably don't remember me—"

"I remember you." Though Joe wore a newsboy cap, rain plastered his brown hair to his head. His green eyes twinkled as he held up the lantern. "Those days you wore two pigtails tied together with a pretty ribbon."

He remembered. Lottie touched her damp hair, grateful the pins held the side swirls in place. Shouts from the river drew her back to reality and she quickly introduced everyone.

Pete looked at Joe. "We can't take everyone in one trip. Don't want to capsize."

Blood drained from Lottie's face. "I'll stay behind."

Joe's brow wrinkled as his serious gaze met hers.

"Well, you'll not get me in that thing. No, sir." Henry crossed his arms. "No need asking me again."

Lottie's hands trembled. "Henry, please. They've braved the danger to rescue us."

Joe glanced from Lottie to Henry. "If you folks don't need rescuing, there's plenty others that do." He set the lantern down and reached for an oar.

A tear slid down Esther's cheek.

Henry edged his chair closer to the window. "Now, hold on just a confounded minute. These young whippersnappers today. Don't know when to keep their mouths shut." He fingered a button on his coat. "I'll go, but not without my wheelchair."

Pete exchanged a glance with Joe. "I'll tie it down after you get inside. You can be first." He held onto the window frame.

Harvey picked up Henry. Joe took him and positioned him in the bottom of the boat. "You'll be safe there, sir. Who's next?"

Susannah looked at Frank. "Me. Harvey, get a good hold on me." The sweet woman weighed about sixty pounds more than strictly necessary. She held Harvey's hand and reached for the window jamb before stepping down onto the rocking boat. She moved to a seat at the far end.

Frank followed and then it was Esther's turn. "I don't want to leave you, Lottie."

She held her close. "I'll be along soon. Take care of everyone until I get there."

Sniffing, Esther held Pete's hand as she climbed inside the rocking boat.

Willy put his arm around Lottie. "I'm staying with you."

Joe nodded, his expression grave. "Might be best. After we put the wheelchair in, we'll be out of room."

His prediction proved correct. The chair filled the last available space.

"Will you mind staying, Harvey?" Lottie wrung her hands.

"I prefer it, Miss Lottie."

Joe reached for her hand, his direct gaze as comforting as his cold grasp. "We'll be back."

His concern warmed her. "Please be careful."

"I'll catch pneumonia in this icy rain." Henry shivered. "Man my age shouldn't have to put up with such treatment."

Lottie reluctantly released Joe's hand. "Wait a moment." Her cheeks flushed at Henry's understandable complaints. She rushed to a linen closet and grabbed a stack of blankets. "These might keep you dry a few minutes."

"Thanks." Joe's smile faded quickly. "See you soon. I promise."

A shiver went down her back. He might arrive too late to save them. "Take care of my family." The boat floated away.

Shivering, Esther stared at her.

Joe gazed at Lottie steadily as he paddled. "Watch for us at this window."

His words seemed like a promise. "We'll be waiting."

The oars sliced through the moving river and the current took them speedily toward Troy.

Lottie lifted her eyes to the charcoal gray clouds, praying they'd return in time.

3

"I'm starving." Willy complained as the boat disappeared.

Glad for the distraction, Lottie opened a jar of green beans to heat in a pan on the hall wood stove.

"I'm hungry *now*, Sis." He clutched his stomach.

"Me, too." His brave offer to stay behind with her had touched her. "How about some peaches?"

He grinned. "Let me at 'em."

The three of them polished off a jar of fruit before the green beans began to bubble.

The water level on the stairs raised two steps while breakfast cooked. Slices of ham from Easter were eaten cold. After feeding her brother's dog, Rusty, she ventured another glance.

The river had invaded her home to the top step.

Her heartbeat pounded in her ears. Joe and Pete must return in time to save them.

Willy and Harvey ate beside the big window, awaiting the rowboat. Her brother chattered and the older man listened. Lottie didn't point out the water level to them. No need to add to their worries.

She peeked out the hall window at gloomy clouds. Heavy rains pelted the house.

Willy put down his empty plate. "Time for milking."

Lottie gasped. He didn't know?

"Can't get to the barn." Harvey's face tightened.

"I'll swim." He stood, a determined glint in his eyes.

Heart racing, she clutched Willy's arm. "Our house is flooded. You can't get to the barn. It's probably flooded, too."

"I've got to try." He shook her hand away.

Willy strode toward the stairs.

Harvey followed and grabbed his collar. "You'll drown for sure." They both looked down at their feet. A trail of water raced down the hall toward them.

Rusty barked and rested his paws on the windowsill.

"Lottie! Where are you?"

Joe's voice. Nothing had ever sounded sweeter. She ran to the window. "Is my family safe?"

"Yes." Tense shoulders relaxing, he reached for her as soon as the boat glided beside the house. "We'd best get you folks out of there."

"Hold on a second, Romeo." Pete's eyes twinkled. "Let me grab hold of the house first."

Joe flushed and waited until Pete held onto the windowsill. Then he reached for her again, his gaze fastened on hers.

His open arms invited her like a knight in shining armor. She couldn't refuse. He held her close before setting her feet onto the swaying boat. Then he clasped her hand to guide her to a seat.

"Thank you." Lottie perched on the wet seat, breathless and jittery.

Willy picked up Rusty.

Pete soon held Rusty in his arms. "Here. Hold onto him tightly."

Icy rain pelted Lottie. She welcomed the warmth of the family pet. "Willy, grab my coat and that stack of blankets on my bed."

He returned, wearing his coat, with the items requested. Harvey held the boat steady while Willy climbed aboard. Then he followed.

"Anyone else inside?" Pete asked, holding onto the window jamb.

Donning her coat, Lottie shook her head.

"We've got cows and horses in the barn." Willy's desperate gaze sought the wooden building. "Oh, no."

Lottie's jaw dropped. Their chicken coop floated on gentle waves toward Troy. Only the top half of the barn was exposed.

Joe frowned. "In some areas like this one, the canal and river met in the middle."

"Our livestock may be alive—we have to check." Willy's voice deepened.

"Doubtful." Joe and Pete exchanged a grim look. "There have been reports of people drowning. Rescue boat teams are working hard. We just can't keep up with the river."

"Please go by the barn. I may be able to save them." Willy buried his fists in his hair.

Lottie rocked Rusty back and forth, unable to believe any of their animals survived. The desperate appeal in her little brother's eyes shook her. "If there's any way to save them ..."

Her former classmates rowed silently to the barn. Lottie hardly dared to breathe until they reached the open barn doors. It was worse than she feared. She buried her face in Rusty's brown coat. The river completely covered the top of the stalls. Their animals didn't survive.

Willy peered inside the dark building and then took Rusty from

Lottie's arms. "Their stall doors were open. Maybe they ran off."

"Maybe."

Willy raised his eyebrows at Harvey's agreement.

Joe and Pete resumed rowing toward Troy.

"Where did you take my family?" In her relief to find they were safe, she'd forgotten to ask where they went.

"First Presbyterian Church." Pete gazed out at the rushing river as he rowed.

"That's also a food distribution center." Facing her, Joe glanced at her often. "Both Esther and Mrs. Miller wanted to cook for others."

She breathed easier knowing that her family awaited them on East Franklin Street in downtown Troy, though Joe's attentiveness made her wish the distance between her home and the church was greater than three-quarters of a mile. "Esther loves to cook for a crowd and Susannah simply enjoys spoiling people. I'm not surprised."

Someone shouted for help.

"They're desperately needed." Joe scanned the homes in the direction of the shouts. "Lots of hungry folks this morning."

Like her rescuers. Their mouths drooped with fatigue, their clothing was drenched. She bit her lip. "You two will come in and warm up, won't you? Rest and grab a bite to eat?"

They exchanged a resigned glance. "Can't." Joe shivered. "Folks need saving."

"Let me and Willy take the next rescue." Harvey made the offer as if they'd volunteered to take out the trash.

Lottie smothered a gasp. At seventeen, Willy never volunteered for anything at home. What if he found a drowning victim? She cringed at the possibility. She'd grown used to sheltering him since their mother died.

Pete's face brightened. "The sheriff directs the boat rescues. Pretty much any men with a boat are sent out. Joe?"

"I'm famished." Joe gazed at them.

"Let me check with my partner." Harvey turned to Willy. "Ready to save some folks?"

Willy glanced at the men, then at Lottie. He straightened his thin shoulders. "Ready."

Joe's face relaxed into a smile. "Then I won't feel guilty about taking a break. Check with the sheriff. If he's heard of someone in trouble, he'll send you there. Otherwise, row around town and help anyone who needs it."

"No problem." Smiling, he hugged his dog.

"Are you sure about this, Willy?" The overprotective sister in her couldn't hold the question back.

His chest deflated. "Don't you think I can do it?"

Harvey's gaze pierced through her. Willy didn't need her doubts. "I know you can. I'm proud of you."

He grinned. "Glad you finally realized it."

Lottie smiled at his teasing. Joe shivered again and she met his gaze. "Is there dry clothing at the church?"

He shrugged. "Hope so."

Worry for his and Pete's health grew. "I'll ask about dry clothes. I want you both to change before eating. Otherwise you'll catch pneumonia out here."

Grinning, Joe tilted his head sideways. His smile warmed her despite the rain.

"Don't mind Lottie." Willy grinned. "She's used to running things."

She felt heat rise in her cheeks. "Sorry. I do think it's a good idea though—"

Joe's laugh made her forget what she wanted to say. The others joined him. While enjoying the sound of his laughter, she noticed one more thing.

He didn't mind her suggestions.

Lottie, holding Rusty's collar, watched Willy and Harvey hurry away to talk to the sheriff as soon as they arrived at the church. A volunteer took one look at her pet and offered to keep him at her house with her three boys. Since she also had two dogs, Lottie agreed. Rusty would be happier there than in a crowded church.

Lottie sought out Henry and Frank. They sat in the crowded entry. A wool blanket covered Henry from the shoulders down.

Frank enveloped her in a fatherly hug. "I'm so thankful to find you safe."

"I don't know how well *I'm* doing," Henry grumbled. "After we changed into dry clothes, people have ignored us ever since."

She leaned to kiss his stubbly cheek. "I'm especially happy to see you, Henry. I was worried."

"You were?" Unkempt gray hair fell across his forehead. "Why?"

She leaned a hand on the arm of his wheelchair. "Because you're part of my family."

He dashed a tear away.

"Me, too?" Frank teased.

Lottie laughed. "What would I do without my adopted grandfathers?" Her gaze dropped to their feet.

"Is there any food in that kitchen? I've listened to Henry's tummy rumbling long enough." Frank's grandfatherly eyes twinkled at her.

She stood, her heart lighter to see both men well cared-for. "I'll rustle you something to eat if I have to arm wrestle Susannah for it."

As they laughed, she followed the aroma of fried bacon to the kitchen.

Thirty to forty people gathered in the large room next to the outer door. Her gaze roamed over the crowd. Joe must be changing into dry clothes.

She pushed open the kitchen door. The wooden spoon in Esther's hand clattered to the floor as she burst into tears.

"Esther, what is it?" Lottie put her arms around her. "Are you hurt?"

Esther clung to her. Biting her lip, Lottie looked at Susannah.

The kind woman patted Lottie's shoulder. "We saw one poor man riding on his roof down the middle of the Great Miami. The current lifted his house right off the foundation. He fairly flew past us ... holding on for dear life. Esther's been beside herself ever since."

"I'm glad you're all right." Esther stepped back. She swiped at her wet face with a handkerchief from her skirt pocket. "Nellie worried about us when we stopped answering the phone. She alerted Sheriff Paul to our plight."

Lottie marveled at the way their rescue came about. "Then she had a hand in our rescue. By the time Joe and Pete returned for us, water had overflowed onto the second floor."

Esther blanched. "Nellie wants you to call. She's anxious."

"At the telephone company?" A clock on the shelf showed it to be after ten. Was it still only Tuesday morning? She'd lived a lifetime since the river invaded her home.

Esther picked up the spoon she'd dropped on the brown tiled floor. "She's worked over twenty-four hours. Her manager, Warren Safford, has them working through the disaster. Nellie's tired, but wants to serve the town. We're cooking to give the other ladies a break." She gestured at the steaming pots on the stove. "Where are Willy and Harvey? The oatmeal's hot."

Lottie's mouth watered at the smell of oatmeal and a heaping plate of bacon. "Save them a bowl and a few slices of bacon. They're taking the next rescue mission. Frank and Henry are hungry, though. And Joe and Pete need a hot meal."

"Aren't they dreamy?" Esther tilted her head with a smile. "Real-life heroes."

Shoulders tensing, Lottie realized she didn't have a chance for a relationship with Joe if he caught her beautiful sister's eye. She had a knack of attracting male attention.

"Breakfast is ready." Susannah spooned oatmeal into a bowl. "Call

Nellie."

As Lottie stepped to the kitchen door, Joe and Pete came inside. Joe's dry pants were too short for his long legs, making white socks stand out starkly on his shoeless feet.

He followed her gaze. "Our boots are drying beside a heat stove."

She smiled approvingly. "Good."

"The heavenly aroma led us here." Pete snatched a piece of bacon from the platter.

"Hey." Esther laughed. "It's ready for the tables in the next room. You can help."

"Glad to." He smiled and winked. "As long as there's another slice of bacon in it for me."

She laughed. "We'll get this, Lottie. The phone's in the hall outside the pastor's office."

Now that the men were here, Lottie hesitated. "Give Henry a healthy portion. He's frail under normal circumstances."

Susannah filled another bowl. "Frank will keep a close eye on him. We're in this together. Do what you need to do."

4

"Lottie? Where are you?" Nellie's anxiety came through the phone line in tense tones.

"I'm in Troy, at the First Presbyterian Church." Lottie spoke quickly. "Everyone's fine. How about you? And Augusta?"

"Augusta's got her second wind. She's asked me to pass on any significant events to her at the *Troy Record*." Nellie sighed. "There's been a little too much news to pass on."

Lottie tensed at the sadness in her voice. "What's happened?"

"It will break your heart. Do you remember Harriet Pearson?"

"The older lady who lives on West Market?"

"Yes. She ... she drowned in her home."

Lottie gasped.

"When the house flooded, she had no place to go."

She leaned her forehead against the wallpapered wall. That could have been her family. They'd had a close brush with danger. An urgent desire to do whatever she could for her neighbors welled up inside her.

"It's been terrible." Nellie sighed again. "You have no idea. So much bad news and everyone's calling us for information."

"When will you get off?" Nellie needed rest.

"Who knows?" She yawned. "We'll serve the community by keeping the phone lines open."

Troy Telephone Company wasn't more than a ten-minute walk away.

90

"Did you eat breakfast?"

"Not yet." Nellie sighed.

That sigh decided her. "I'll bring food for you and your co-workers. If you show me how to operate the switchboard, you can rest while I'm there."

"You're a peach! I'm starving."

She smiled at the relief in her friend's voice. "I'll be there soon."

Joe carried a heavy pot of oatmeal and Lottie toted a basket of bowls, utensils, and a small sack of coffee for the coffee pot kept on the phone company's premises.

As Lottie stepped over a puddle, she told him about Harriet Pearson's death.

"Hate hearing that." He shook his head, his gaze on the horizon. "Gene Tilman, Wilbur Curtis, and Billy Quick rescued a family and were on their way back when the current changed. It took hold of the boat and forced them down West Market Street toward the Big Four Railroad. They grabbed onto a fruit tree and tied the boat to it. The tree snapped. The family, Aaron and Gertrude Smock and their one-year-old son, Franklin, fell in the water when the boat capsized."

"Did they drown?" She held her breath.

"I'm afraid so." He shifted the heavy pot to his other arm. "Gene held onto a rooftop that happened to be floating by. Wilbur swam. Those two were rescued by Frank Sharits. Poor Billy somehow got hold of a honey locust tree. Said it snowed some while he was up in that tree."

"How awful." What if Willy's boat capsized? What about Joe and Pete? They all risked their lives. "Please be careful."

Joe smiled at her. "I will."

His smile dazzled her. What a strange way for them to meet after all these years. Might it lead to something more? Lottie stumbled into a big puddle. He grasped the basket's handle, brushing against her hand in the process.

Her cheeks burned. "Thanks. Sorry I'm so clumsy."

"You're not clumsy." He halted in front of the phone company. "We've arrived at our destination. Want me to carry this up for you?"

"No." Lottie smiled her thanks. "You have to get back. Tell Esther I'll call the church before leaving."

"Sure thing." He gave her the heavy pot and opened the door.

Before entering, Lottie turned back. "Joe?"

"Yes?" His serious gaze searched hers.

"Please watch over Willy."

He tipped his hat. "I'll do my best. He's a good kid."

Drawing a deep breath, Lottie stepped inside. She wasn't alone.

Nellie had been asleep for three hours. Lottie relaxed at the switchboard after answering several calls. As her friend predicted, most folks didn't ask to be connected to another party. They simply requested news. Lottie kept adding new information to a running list on Nellie's desk.

She answered another call. "Yes, Mrs. Wyckham. I understand the fire bells rang numerous times to warn Troy families about the flood... You're right. Church bells rang, too. But there's no water on the street in front or back of your house? ... Good. You should be safe then... No, feel free to call and ask for the police station if you're afraid. You're welcome." She disconnected the call.

Suddenly the power went out. Hand on her throat, she stared at the dark board. Oh, no. What had she done? With the overhead light extinguished, only dim gray light seeped in through the window.

"What's happened?" Mr. Safford rushed behind her, casting a feverish glance at every dark switchboard. "The community requires that we be fully functional."

"The Troy City Power plant must be flooded." A stranger in the back of the room hurried to the window.

Stomach churning, Lottie stood and met anxious glances.

Nellie hurried to the chair Lottie vacated. "How about battery power?"

As the others discussed what to do, Nellie hugged Lottie. "Thanks for the lovely nap. It refreshed me."

"I don't know how to help now that the power failed," Lottie whispered.

"Don't worry." Nellie's tense shoulders relaxed. "We'll figure out something. Go back to the church and see if someone else needs help."

Lottie left with her basket in the rain on Tuesday afternoon, dazed from the swift turn of events, much of it too tragic for expression. Saturday had been such a lovely day. She stepped in a puddle, grimacing when icy water seeped into her shoe.

The church, previously lit by light bulbs, now contained lanterns and candlesticks strategically placed around the room. Lottie scanned the main room, but found none of her family. She made her way to the kitchen. A pleasant aroma of potato soup tempted her appetite.

Two other ladies had joined Susannah and Esther.

After greeting them, Lottie set the empty pot and basket on the table.

"Why, if you ain't a sight for sore eyes." Susannah gave her a motherly hug, which to Lottie's surprise was exactly what she needed. "How's Nellie?"

"Better. She slept three hours."

"Good." Susannah patted her arm and then sat on a high-backed chair. "Eat a bowl of soup."

A wave of unexpected exhaustion struck Lottie as she sat to eat the steaming soup Esther placed in front of her.

"It's a good feeling to help others, isn't it? But then, you already know all about that." Susannah reached for a potato.

Lottie frowned. "What do you mean?"

Susannah focused on the potato she peeled. "You take care of everyone in your home every day. We all love you for it."

Lottie shook her head as she ate a bite of delicious soup. Did she do that? "Did Willy help anyone?"

"A family in a single floor home cut a hole in their ceiling. They waited on their roof until Willy and Harvey rescued them." Esther glanced at her as she stirred a pot of soup on the stove. "A boy in that family needed a doctor, so Willy escorted the whole family to Edwards School on West Main. It's now an emergency hospital and shelter. He stayed to help with patients. Pete and Joe took the boat out when Harvey returned."

Lottie blinked rapidly. "What does Willy know about doctoring?"

"Sometimes what's needed most is a willing heart." Susannah patted Lottie's hand. "Runs in the family."

Lottie rubbed her hand over her forehead, stunned at this new side to Willy.

Esther selected a potato from the pile and sat at the work table next to Susannah. "He'll be fine."

"Where is Harvey? I didn't see any of our crew."

"Talking to the sheriff." Esther sliced the potato into cubes. "Rescue teams are needed so badly, they're releasing men from jail to help. Harvey plans to work with one of them."

Lottie blinked. "Are you joking?"

Susannah shook her head. "Folks shout for help from their rooftops in this cold rain. The sheriff needs everyone he can get."

Dire straits, indeed. Lottie hardly knew what to think.

"Henry and Frank found a quiet place to nap." Susannah peeled another potato. "Frank's sticking pretty close to Henry until we know he didn't catch a cold — or worse — this morning."

Lottie's shoulders slumped. The poor man. Henry's health was fragile at best.

Her meal eaten, she looked around. Everyone was busy except her. Should she remain here where she wasn't needed or find another place to serve? A couple of blocks further from the public square at the center of town, Forest School had been set up as a shelter.

Perhaps they needed her. Time to find out.

5

The ladies at the church loaded a large basket with sandwiches, corn muffins, cheese, and crackers for those at the Forest School shelter. Lottie's long afternoon operating phone lines gave her locations of shelters. If the school didn't need volunteers, she'd walk to the Methodist Church — as long as floodwaters remained below her knees. She didn't want to risk getting swept away by the current.

The power was still out. Lottie pushed the door open to the dark two-story brick school, blinking at the noise. Shouting children chased each other down a long hallway. Sporadically placed lanterns dimly lit the indoor hall on the gloomy afternoon. Several men stared at a door.

"The women are back here with my wife." A harried man grabbed her arm and propelled her toward the closed door. "Her name is Mrs. Johnson. I mean, Ermalene Johnson. None of the women have ever delivered a baby. You've got to help."

"Me?" Lottie's heart skipped a beat. Did she look old enough to be a doctor? "Mr. Johnson, I've never delivered a baby either —"

"You're a woman, ain't you? Women have that intuition thing, right? You've got to help. Just go on in, that's a good girl." He knocked on the door.

"All right. I'll do what I can." Anything to calm the frazzled man. "I brought food from the church," she gave him the well-laden basket, "to share with everyone."

The door opened a crack. "Lottie Stevens? Have you delivered any of your farm animals?" Dahlia Thomson, a former classmate, pulled her inside the room and shut the door behind her. The auburn-haired Dahlia had been married over a year, but had no children.

Gulping, Lottie gazed at the writhing young woman lying on a bed of blankets. Her labored breathing told even the inexperienced Lottie that the time for the baby drew near. "My brother takes care of our animals. I've always been there during the births, but he did everything."

"Close enough." She recognized the gray-haired woman as Mrs. Bradley from her church. "My only child is twenty-five."

"But … the children in the hall … None of you are the mothers?" Lottie shrugged out of her coat and laid it on a desk.

Mrs. Bradley shook her head. "I know it sounds like more, but it's just three families with children right now. Those moms are cooking at the church."

Ermalene moaned.

Lottie's hands covered her suddenly burning cheeks. "And you?"

Her voice sounded faint in her own ears as she turned to a tall woman in her late thirties.

"Hettie Campbell." She shrugged. "Spinster. I lived too far away to help my sister when her babies were born."

A wave of dizziness struck and Lottie grabbed the back of a student's desk. "Did someone send for a doctor?"

Worry shadowed Mrs. Bradley's eyes. "Two hours ago. The phones went out about that time. We have three lanterns. Will that be enough for you?"

The rain brought premature darkness. Three lanterns didn't cast much light. "Arrange them around Ermalene."

The ladies quickly complied. The concentrated lighting helped.

Lottie's heart raced. Could she do this?

"Please. Can you help me?" Ermalene's pleading eyes met hers.

Why did none of the older women step forward?

Lottie lifted her chin. She had to try. She dropped to her knees and grasped Ermalene's hand. "We'll take care of you until the doctor arrives. You'll be fine."

Tension left the young woman's face. "I've asked God to send someone to help my baby. Now she can be born."

Lottie's jaw slackened. Ermalene saw *her* as an answered prayer?

Ermalene's radiant smile renewed Lottie's fighting spirit. "She's strong, too. I've been talking to her. I believe she listens."

Lottie patted her shoulder. "I'm sure she does." Though not at all sure about the delivery, she'd do everything she knew to prepare for the baby. She stood and faced the others. "Scissors?"

Dahlia held up a sturdy pair for her inspection.

"Are there towels, blankets, diapers, a baby gown?"

"I brought baby clothes with me." Ermalene breathed harder.

Mrs. Bradley pointed to a stack of blankets, towels, and clothes on a nearby desk.

What else? Lottie fought to remain calm as her thoughts swirled chaotically.

Mrs. Bradley grabbed her hand. "Let's pray for Ermalene and the little life about to be born." They bowed their heads. Mrs. Bradley said a quick prayer for guidance, strength, and protection of mother and child.

Ermalene's gasp interrupted the prayer. They scurried to her side. "She's coming! Lord, help me!"

Lord, help me. Lottie repeated the prayer silently when the crown of a tiny head appeared. "Fetch me a couple of towels. I see her head."

The doctor arrived as Ermalene cradled her precious newborn in her arms. He finished the job and examined mother and child.

Dr. Francis turned to the women anxiously awaiting his approval. "Who delivered this child?"

Dahlia pointed to Lottie, who tried to hide behind Hettie.

"Have you ever delivered a baby before?" He stared at her.

Lottie lost the power of speech.

"She's there when her brother delivers farm animals." Mrs. Bradley patted Lottie's arm.

She cringed and closed her eyes. She'd done it all wrong.

Dr. Francis chuckled. "I reckon it came in handy today. The baby's fine. So is the mother." He picked up his black leather bag. "I expect you ladies will make certain they both eat and rest. I'll talk with Mr. Johnson and see to anyone else requiring medical attention while I'm here."

After he left, Lottie's body began to shake.

"You did well, my dear." Mrs. Bradley put an arm around her and led her over to one of the children's desks. "Why, look at you. You're trim enough to fit in a child's desk."

The comment jolted Lottie and she laughed. Relief washed over her now the ordeal had ended. Both mother and baby were fine. The doctor said so. *Thank You, God. Thank You.*

Ermalene smiled as the baby ate her first meal. "I've decided on a name."

Mrs. Bradley titled her head with a smile. "What is it?"

"Carlotta." She stared at her beautiful baby. "We'll call her Lottie."

The gesture touched Lottie, but she felt it was too high an honor. "Are you sure?"

"Yes." Ermalene's gaze returned to her baby. "I prayed for help. The doctor couldn't be here in time, so God sent you."

"I'm honored." Tears blurred her vision. "I need some fresh air."

Mrs. Bradley nodded. "You've earned a rest, my dear. Take your time."

Mr. Johnson grabbed her hand and pumped it as she exited the room. "Doc told me. Thank you. I knew you'd take care of my Ermalene."

"My pleasure." She gave him a trembling smile. "Ready to meet your baby girl?"

Sheer joy lit his face. He ran inside, closing the door behind him.

Tears spilled over. She escaped through the nearest exit, gulping in the night air.

ʊ ʊ ʊ

Joe, urged by Esther, took a short break from boat rescues and found Lottie leaning against a lamp post outside of Forest School.

"Lottie." Brow wrinkling, he set his lantern on the sidewalk and touched her shoulder. "Why are you standing out here without a coat? It's freezing."

She turned a bewildered gaze to her less than pristine white blouse. "I didn't realize."

That same shocked look had been in the eyes of too many flood victims today. "Lottie." He lifted her cold hands and sandwiched them between his. "What happened?"

"I … delivered a baby." She raised dazed eyes to his. "Dr. Francis said both are doing well."

Relief exploded into laughter. He'd have sworn someone died. "That's wonderful."

She shook her head. "But how did I do it? I've never even delivered a colt or a calf. That's Willy's job."

"The doctor didn't make it in time?"

"No." Her gaze fell to their clasped hands. "The other women were afraid, but they prayed for me. Someone had to help."

"Sounds like you rose to the occasion. God guided your hands." He thrust his chest out, thankful this tragedy had drawn them together. "I'm proud of you. You amaze me."

The breeze picked up. She shivered. "Me? Why?"

He put his arm around her to lead her back inside the school. "We'll discuss it another time. Let's get your coat and then I'll take you back to your sister. She's worried. I'll walk you to church where you can sleep. Tomorrow will be another long day."

Her brow wrinkled. "I haven't slept since Sunday night. No wonder I feel drained. How's Willy?"

"Great. He's still at the temporary hospital." He stopped at the door. "Wait here. I'll gather your belongings before you fall asleep standing up."

"Fall asleep where I stand?" Her eyes glazed. "What a marvelous idea."

6

Lottie awoke the next morning in a crowded room set aside for women and small children. Esther's blanket lay folded along the wall with several items of unused clothing and linen. Susannah slept near children who had begun to call her 'Grandma.'

Lottie peeked outside. The rain had stopped. Her heart lightened. How long before the river receded?

She had slept in a borrowed nightgown. Her blouse was hopelessly stained. She scrubbed stains on her white blouse and held it up with a sigh. It needed a good soaking. Leaving donated clothing for rescued victims, she donned her rumpled black skirt and damp white blouse. She combed her hair into her customary side swirls. Patting her hair, she wondered if Joe would have found her pretty in her new lilac Easter dress worn just three days ago.

A lifetime ago.

She joined Esther in the kitchen. The delicious aroma of hot biscuits reminded her she hadn't eaten since yesterday afternoon. Today, four women volunteered at the church kitchen with Esther. They didn't need Lottie or Susannah, who had appeared uncommonly fatigued last night.

Esther ate with her in the almost empty dining area.

Lottie had been too tired to speak last evening. She vaguely remembered holding Joe's arm on the stroll back to the church and the warm glow in his eyes. "Tell me about yesterday."

Esther's eyes widened. "We were busy. The market house over in the City Hall is now a food distribution center. Once we fed folks here, we cooked and baked for hours to send meals over there. I love cooking for lots of people." She frowned. "I don't want people flooded from their homes, but this is fun. I'd love to work in a restaurant."

"I understand." Lottie laughed. "You inherited our mother's skills in the kitchen." Her appetite rivaled Willy's this morning. She plowed through a plate of biscuits and gravy.

"What happened at the school?" Esther sipped her coffee. "Joe said it was your news."

She set down her fork. "You'll never believe it. I delivered Ermalene Johnson's baby."

Esther gasped. "Tell me." Her eyes widened as she listened to the details. "Lottie, I think you can do about anything you put your mind to. You're amazing." Unshed tears brightened her eyes as she hugged Lottie's arm. "I'm proud of you."

"You'd have done the same thing. I'm no one special." Gazing at her plate, she changed the subject. "Joe said Willy was still at Edwards School last night."

"I believe so." Esther rubbed a finger around the rim of her cup. "Pete told me Willy's following the doctor's orders. He's impressed the doctor and Pete said that's not easy."

"I wonder if the fellows slept at their homes last night." Lottie bent over her plate for another bite of gravy-smothered biscuit.

"I'm afraid not." Esther sighed. "With folks still stranded, they took the boat out again. They stopped long enough to eat supper with us. After that, Joe looked for you."

Heat flooded her face. Last night, Joe made it sound as if Esther sent him. Could her little sister be playing matchmaker? "Um … How's Henry?"

"Not sick or complaining." Esther smiled.

"That's not like him." Lottie smiled. "Heard anything from Nellie or Augusta?"

Esther gazed out the window. "The phones were running on batteries yesterday. Nellie's still answering calls. Augusta checks with her for news."

"Good." That eliminated two worries. "And Harvey?"

"He's on a rescue team," Esther clutched Lottie's arm, "with a guy from jail. They've rescued lots of folks. Susannah thinks the convicts might get reduced sentences for this dangerous service. People have died trying to save others."

Lottie shuddered as worries for Joe, Pete, and Harvey surfaced. "Who'd have guessed a week ago we'd all be scattered in different directions?"

An hour later, Lottie carried a basket filled with biscuits, bacon, and hard-boiled eggs one block to the large City Hall building on West Franklin Street. The absence of loud locomotive engines and whistles made Troy a different place. It might be weeks before trains ran on schedule again.

Would Joe remain in her life after the flood waters receded?

Such questions seemed selfish with dozens of townsfolk requiring nourishment. Most people she met remained in their homes, though they had no food.

Many congregated at City Hall to swap stories with volunteers. She laughed when hearing about a chicken house caught in a current on Race Street. Three chickens squawked with fright, doing a strange dance on the roof. Boys dove for them unsuccessfully as they sailed by.

A couple of farmers brought wagonloads of food—chickens, hams, and potatoes that fed the hungry crowd that came and went all day. Women from unflooded homes donated platters of meats and mashed potatoes.

In mid-afternoon, Joe and Pete, clothing and boots muddied, greeted her with tired smiles at City Hall.

Joe was safe. Just seeing him put a glow in her heart as she showed them where to wash their hands and faces. She took her first break to share a meal with them.

Lottie studied the slump of Joe's shoulders, the fatigue on his face, and encouraged them to sleep at least three hours.

"Folks are still stranded. Can't afford a nap." Joe's tired eyes fought with his set jaw. "Others sacrifice just as much."

Lottie pulled a deep breath. "I can't convince you to rest?"

He mustered a smile. "We'll stop when we have to. I promise."

"If you'd seen what we've seen ..." Pete shook his head.

Dead bodies? Lottie's gaze flew to Joe, who avoided her eyes. Her head lowered. They'd endured a lifetime in just three days.

"There are several rescue teams." Joe patted her hand. "We'll stop by when we can. You sleeping at the church tonight?"

The concern in his eyes warmed her. "If I'm not needed here."

He frowned and then smiled ruefully. "Reckon you don't want me asking you to do what I can't promise. Just ... don't wear yourself out."

Folding her arms, she laughed.

He laughed with her. "Okay. I'm leaving." He turned to follow Pete out the door.

"Joe?"

He turned back, eyebrows raised.

"Be careful."

He tipped his soggy hat at her. "You too, Lottie Stevens."

The memory of his concern lifted her spirits as she worked well past dark.

7

Lottie and Esther walked to Edwards School to visit Willy the next morning. A whole season seemed to have passed since the family ate Easter dinner together.

Perhaps it had.

Willy's hug in the otherwise empty hallway gave Lottie a welcome she hadn't dared hope for. She held his shoulders, clucking her tongue at dark shadows under his eyes. "When did you last sleep?"

Esther uncovered a ham sandwich in the basket she held. "When did you last *eat*?"

Grinning, Willy snatched the sandwich. "Can't remember." A third of the sandwich disappeared with one huge bite.

Esther's mouth dropped open. "I brought another sandwich. No need to devour it."

"Got milk in there?" He squinted at the basket.

She shook her head. "I can make coffee."

"No, thanks." He sighed. "That's what I've been living on."

"Is there food here?" Lottie peered into a classroom where people lay on blankets.

He nodded. "Neighbors bring meals. Can't do much for the really ill. We have blankets and coffee for everyone. Some downtown businesses made sure of that."

Lottie smiled. "Everyone has pulled together. Makes me proud of our town."

He nodded. "It's been amazing."

"How many are seriously ill?" Esther peered over his shoulder into an occupied room.

Sighing deeply, Willy glanced into the room behind him. "Three men came in with bad cases of pneumonia."

Esther covered her face with her hands.

Swallowing hard, Lottie put an arm around her sister, thoughts flying to her beloved Papa, who had died of that illness.

Willy's face turned grim. "See why I'm worried?"

"Want me to stay?" Lottie knew his answer as soon as she offered.

His face fell. "I love you, Sis, so don't take this the wrong way. If you've got someplace else to volunteer, go there. I feel like I'd rely on you too much if you stay. Comes a time when a man has to stand on his own two feet."

Tears burned her eyes. He'd matured a year during the four-day crisis. "I'm proud of you, Willy."

"It's okay to leave the food basket." He grinned.

They laughed.

"And bring more tomorrow." He enveloped his sisters in the same hug.

🍂 🍂 🍂

When Lottie and Esther returned to the church, they found that Joe and Pete had eaten a huge breakfast and were now asleep in the room set aside for men.

"They told Frank to wake them up in two hours." Susannah tapped a wooden spoon on the table. "But I told Frank if he sets foot in there before two o'clock, I'd have his hide."

They laughed. Susannah didn't give commands to anyone except her husband, and even that was rare.

Her heart lighter, Lottie turned to Esther. "Have a hot meal waiting." They were true heroes in her book.

Esther saluted. "Already planning it, big sister."

She frowned. "Am I too bossy?"

Esther laughed. "Not usually *too* bossy. You have your moments, but we all love you. And your ideas are usually good, so don't worry."

Heat rose in Lottie's face. Maybe she was too overbearing.

She sure hoped Joe liked bossy women.

Susannah set down her mixing spoon and placed her hands on Lottie's shoulders. "You've had a hard row to hoe since your mother passed. You took on the role of a parent. You care for boarders with varying health concerns." She patted Lottie's back before returning to her batter. "You've done an admirable job. Never doubt it. We're all proof." She looked at Esther.

"You held the family together." Tears shone in Esther's eyes. "I couldn't have handled the responsibility at sixteen the way you did." She stacked bread loaves in a basket. "Why not take a break after two and eat with us? See for yourself that the guys slept at least five hours."

"I'll try." It was a chance to see Joe again.

The morning flew as many flocked to the market house. It was after two before Lottie noticed hunger pains. She told another volunteer to expect her within the hour and rushed to the church.

They had started the meal without her as she requested. Joe smiled and beckoned her over to a place already set. Beside him. As if he had been watching the door. Seating herself, she returned his smile.

Frank, Susanna, and Henry were among those around the table with Esther.

Lottie greeted everyone before her gaze fell on the filled plate before her. "You prepared for me to be here." Laughing, she glanced at Esther.

"We hoped." Joe gulped his coffee. "As you pointed out, everyone needs a good meal to keep going."

She frowned. "Did I say that?"

"Not in words." He grinned. "But that's how I heard it."

A smile crossed her lips. Hoping no one noticed her flaming cheeks, she bowed her head to ask a blessing. There might be more to be thankful for than the meal. Joe wanted her there. Did his words hold a deeper meaning?

"We baked bread to take back with you." Esther sat beside Pete across the table. "Still warm, so slice it at City Hall."

"Thanks. We need biscuits and corn muffins, too." Was Esther interested in Pete? Her cheeks were flushed and she laughed at all his jokes. "You men look rested."

Joe glanced at his friend. "I feel like a new man."

Pete laughed. "Yeah, we ought to be set for another forty-eight hours."

Esther's eyes widened. "You don't think ..."

"Hard to say." Pet shrugged as he buttered a slice of bread.

"You men—and other rescuers—are saving many lives. Your community appreciates your efforts." Frank settled back in his chair beside Susannah, his hand resting on his coffee cup. "Remember that."

Joe flushed. His gaze swept the table. "It takes all kinds of volunteers to get the job done."

"True." Susannah nodded, her gaze settling on the horizon.

Lottie wondered if Susannah remembered another disaster when neighbors helped neighbors and made it through.

"I'm proud of all of you." Henry's voice sounded stronger than it had since the flood started. "And I thank you for watching over an old man who ain't got nobody else to do it."

Susannah patted his hand. "We all love you, Henry."

Tears sprang to the frail man's eyes.

Lottie walked around the table and put an arm around him. She pressed her cheek to his whiskered face. "Remember what I told you Monday? You're family, Henry. You've got a home with us as long as you want it."

He shifted in his chair. She returned to her seat while he swiped at his wet cheeks. "My own kin done give up on me. I got no money to pay my board. Why do you do it?"

Esther smiled. "Hasn't this horrible week given you the answer?"

A smile lit his face. "I reckon it has, at that."

The fork fell from Lottie's hand. It was the first time she'd seen him smile since his wife died.

8

On Friday evening, Joe walked to City Hall around supper time. His whole body ached from the most difficult week of his life. Three times, he and Peter had battled driving rain, strong currents, and a wind that sliced right through him, only to reach a home too late to save the family. The memories of their drowned, lifeless bodies haunted him.

Lottie's smile when he finally caught her eye rewarded him for walking to see her.

"The crowd's dying down. Will you leave soon?" He wanted to escort her back to the church, but was dead on his feet. He eyed a section of a brick wall. It invited him to lounge there. Who was he kidding? If he fell asleep now he'd sleep two days.

"Five minutes." She poured a cup of hot coffee for a man at the table beside Joe. "Can you wait?"

"Sure thing." She wanted him to walk with her. Some of his exhaustion slipped away. "Might there be a cup back there for a weary rowboat sailor?"

She laughed. "After all the people you saved?" Her eyes glowed up at him. "It's the least a grateful community can do."

And ten others we didn't save. Joe forced a smile. "Much obliged." At least Lottie hadn't seen those terrible images. He hadn't described finding the victims to anyone but the sheriff. Maybe someday he'd share the burden.

Her compassionate eyes searched his. She squeezed his hand. He hadn't realized how cold his hand was until her soft, warm hand slipped inside his. "Five minutes. We can talk then if you want."

A stranger cleared his throat.

Lottie blushed and removed her hand.

Joe glanced at the bedraggled man and realized he probably appeared the same way to the stranger. "Good evening." He extended a calloused hand.

"Evening." The stranger shook Joe's hand. "Looks like we weathered the storm."

Joe blinked. He nodded and left the serving table to sit with his back against a wall. He hadn't thought about recent events in just that way.

More like the storm had weathered him.

Though people still needed fresh food, Lottie hoped the tragic loss of lives was behind them. Everyone had been affected directly or indirectly through death of a family member, neighbor, or friend.

Joe leaned against a brick wall, his face an exhausted mask. A hero. Her hero. He rescued her family and at least fifty others.

She had tried to do her part as well. This day had been the easiest for Lottie.

Joe escorted her back to the church where her family planned to spend one more night. "Think the worst is over."

Lottie stifled a yawn. "Last night, Nellie slept at the church. The poor girl was completely worn out. Thankfully the telephone company was able to run on battery power, sharing a generator with the *Miami Union* newspaper."

"Telephone calls made it possible to save lots of folks." He stopped about a half block from the church. "Look, I wanted to talk to you. Pete and I will sleep in our own beds tonight."

Lottie's smile slipped. Their shared adventure was ending. "Your parents will be glad to see you."

He shuffled his feet on the damp sidewalk. "We've stopped in to make sure our families had everything they needed. Fortunately, neither of our homes flooded."

This was goodbye. Her spirits sagged. "Frank will stay with Henry while the rest of us inspect the damage to our house tomorrow. If the water's out of the first floor, we'll begin cleaning. If not, we'll return on Monday."

"Hate that you have to deal with that mess." Compassion filled his green eyes. "Your house has a secure foundation. Not everyone was as fortunate." He brushed her hair back from her forehead. "You're alive. It could have been so much worse."

Her breath caught in her throat at his gentle touch. "Despite all we've lost, there's much to be thankful for."

He nodded and began a slow stroll. He tucked her hand on the inside of his arm.

Her hand fit, warm and snug. Safe. She didn't want this stroll to end. A pile of debris, remnants of the storm, loomed in the distance. "So much heartache. So much destruction."

"I'll say." He gazed past the lamplights to the horizon. "The Dayton & Troy Electric Railway is hiring men to repair tracks south of Troy, offering forty cents an hour. Pete and I will work for them a few days. Do our parts to put our town back together. Then we'll return to our regular jobs at Troy Wagon Works."

Her spirits brightened that he'd repair tracks for the trolley that ran between Troy and Dayton—and that he had a job in Troy. College must be behind him. "I like that, especially the part about putting Troy together again. Good money, too." They both had plans for days ahead, but what about the future? She hadn't seen him for years since she left school. It might be years before they talked again. "We'll return to our normal lives."

They stopped next under a lamplight. His green eyes sought hers. "Maybe not."

"What do you mean?" She held her breath.

"After I've finished helping with town repairs and return to my job, I want to come one evening and help clean your house." The breeze picked up. He adjusted her coat more securely over her shoulders. "If you want me to come."

This wasn't goodbye. Joy bubbled inside her. "Please do."

Smiling, he caressed her face. "The best thing that happened this week was getting reacquainted with a sweet girl from my school days."

They continued walking to the church. This time, Joe tucked her hand inside his.

Lottie's heart sang. Her knight in shining armor held her hand.

On Saturday, Lottie, Esther, and Susannah cooked one last breakfast for a dwindling crowd. Then Harvey, Frank, and Henry joined them for a leisurely stroll to Edwards School. Rusty, their family pet, licked their hands when they picked him up from the family who had cared for him.

Rays of sunshine broke through gray clouds. Muddy terrain barred Henry from going home, so Frank, who suffered from his own health problems, planned to stay with him at the school while the rest inspected the damage.

At the school, Rusty lunged into Willy's arms. Their reunion brought tears to Lottie's eyes, reminding her of their animals left behind in the barn. Had they survived?

Unlikely. A weight descended on Lottie's shoulders. She depended on the fresh milk, butter, and eggs to feed her household. Now that they had all survived, financial worries pushed to the forefront of her mind.

Lumber, old trunks, and dishes haphazardly lined the way home. A chicken coop lay smashed on its side. A barn, swept from its foundation, rested in the middle of someone's yard.

A line of mud on all the buildings marked the flood level. Lottie's leather shoes squelched in soggy grass, her spirits sinking into the mud also with her shoes.

No one spoke.

A smashed table lay on its side. Ruined clothing lay in heaps.

Lottie picked up a child's boot. The filthy shoe would fit a boy of five or six. She pushed caked mud off the shoe for the little boy who'd need it. Heart aching, she placed it on top of a destroyed picket fence.

Puddles soon ran together and they walked in stagnant, ankle-deep water. Longing to hold her nose, Lottie raised her dark skirt instead to mid-calf to keep it dry.

When their muddy brick house came into sight, Willy ran ahead, splashing brown droplets on his blue pants. He halted at the barn.

Esther and Harvey ran after him. Lottie dropped her skirt hem and ran.

The stench struck her in the face before she stepped inside.

Tears drenched Willy's face. "Bert didn't make it." Multiple hoof prints scarred the wall.

Lottie hugged his arm, her heart broken. "Where's Ben?" There was no sign of the other horse. "And Belle and Bernice?"

Willy's face blanched. "Not here. Maybe they escaped before the flood."

Harvey waded through the barn. "Stall doors are open. If Ben left, the cows probably followed him."

"And some farmer's been caring for them ever since."

Lottie's throat ached at the loss. "Possible."

Hens clucked in the loft.

Willy pumped his fist in the air. "The chickens survived. I'll get them."

A ladder laid upside down in the corner. He propped it against the loft and tested his weight on a rung. "Still holds. Hey, there's feed left. Wonder if they rationed themselves." He disappeared. The sound of wings flapping echoed with loud clucking overhead. "They're fighting me.

Harvey, can you take her from me?"

Between them, they got all the chickens down. "There are at least two dozen eggs up here. Maybe three. Did you bring a basket?""

Fresh eggs. Lottie closed her eyes at their first bit of good news. "There are baskets on the second floor. Time to inspect the house. Then we'll ask our neighbors about the rest of our livestock."

The river no longer hugged the brick house. Lottie led the way up filthy porch steps that hadn't fared any better than the barn. She pulled a face at mud caked on the wooden porch in a disgusting mess. A layer of grime clung to the once-white swing. Would they have to rebuild the wooden porch? She longed to wash the front door free of nauseating slime.

She peeked inside an opening in the curtains. Her heart plummeted. Water. Nasty water. "Hope the door isn't locked since the key's upstairs." Taking a deep breath—then wishing she hadn't—Lottie twisted the slick knob. It turned easily. She pushed the door open. Water, smelling like sulfur, swished over her shoes, wetting the filthy skirt she had tried so hard to keep dry. "Ugh. The smell's overpowering."

Brown water seeped onto the porch. Everyone shifted to the side of the stream. "That answers one question." Esther peered into the window. "The river's still on the first floor."

Tempted to cover her nose to block the offensive odor, Lottie rested her hand on the door jamb. "Can't clean, but let's inspect the damage."

Susannah nodded. "May as well see what we're up against."

Lottie stepped inside. Muddy water covered her ankles. That was the extent of the good news in the sitting room—ankle deep water. "Oh, my word." Her heart plummeted.

Esther nudged her. "Go inside so we can."

"You don't want to." Lottie stepped gingerly into the horribly muddy room. Never had her sitting room been in such disarray.

Esther gasped and then covered her mouth.

Lottie lifted the edge of repulsive brown curtains. "Can these be saved, Susannah?"

Face grim, the gray-haired woman shrugged. "A good soaking in lye soap may bring them back to life or destroy them completely." Her nose wrinkled. "I imagine all the cushioned furniture is ruined."

Harvey righted a tan-colored armchair that had been sky blue a week ago. "Let's carry everything beyond repair outside."

"Good idea. And open every window." Susannah pulled her dress collar around her mouth and nose. "Air out that awful smell."

Willy pushed a window open to the highest point.

The ruined grandfather clock lay on its side. Lottie fought tears—the heirloom had stood in the same spot her entire life.

Esther squeezed her hand.

"My hands are grimy." Lottie turned to hide her tears.

"And bound to get dirtier." Esther held on. "Let's face it together."

Tears spilled down her cheeks. A houseful of loved ones faced this burden with her.

9

Lottie grimaced at mud and grime smearing formerly yellow wallpaper. Kitchens should never smell like this.

"Watch your step." Susannah spoke from behind her and Esther.

Furniture scraped against the sitting room rug as Willy and Harvey carried the ruined chairs and sofa onto the lawn next to other debris left there by the storm.

Lottie took a deep breath. "Let's see the dining room."

The three women stepped into the room off the kitchen. "Mama's china cupboard!"

Lottie seconded the sorrow in Esther's voice. The overturned cupboard turned her stomach. No glass or dish inside could have survived. Why hadn't they emptied it?

The grimy wooden table and chairs lay in haphazard array, warped beyond repair. It seemed as if a heavy weight descended on Lottie's shoulders. She only had fifty dollars in the bank ... not nearly enough to make the repairs. If her boarders had no place to eat or sit, they'd find somewhere else to live. How was she to care for her family?

Susannah patted Esther's shoulder. "Thank the Good Lord we survived."

The stench and destruction in Henry's room was even worse. "Bed's ruined." Susannah whispered. "Doubt the furniture is salvageable, but we'll try."

Esther picked up a picture frame floating on the top of the water. "This photograph of Henry and Luella used to hang on the wall."

"Their wedding day. Let's take it to him." Lottie studied the mud-smeared frame. "Needs cleaning. There must be dry towels upstairs."

"This will mean more than you realize." Tears trickled down Susannah's face.

Lottie peeked inside the bathroom and then slammed the door shut. Her stomach lurched, threatening to make her lose her breakfast. "On Monday, we clean here first."

They agreed.

"Are we brave enough to look upstairs?" Did Lottie want to know how far the water rose?

Esther's brow furrowed. "We must."

Harvey stopped them at the stairs. "Salvageable pieces on the porch to air out?"

Lottie shuddered at the condition of the porch. "Not today. Let's give fresh breezes a chance to work."

He and Willy led them upstairs. Lottie's heart lightened that the waterline stopped about four inches from the floor. All beds and bedding survived. The food not on the floor, which was most of it, had not touched the dirty water. All three ladies felt hopeful about saving the rugs.

"Finally, some good news." Susannah beamed.

"Thank You, God." The prayer of gratitude came from Lottie's soul.

They cleaned the old photograph and retrieved an egg basket. Back downstairs, Lottie examined the water covering the ruined sitting room rug with a heavy heart. How was she to replace all this?

"I can't wait." Willy rubbed his hands through his hair. "If our neighbors don't have our animals, they need us badly."

"Let's go." Lottie's footsteps dragged.

Susannah complained of fatigue. Esther decided to accompany her to town with Henry's picture and the eggs.

Lottie, Harvey, and Willy walked to the closest farms. No one had found the cows and remaining horse.

Her spirits sank lower. What should she do? Beyond the heart-wrenching loss, missing cows meant new expenses for milk and butter.

Her brother's miserable face convinced her to keep the new burdens to herself.

Joy and grief mingled together inside Lottie at church services the next morning. She hugged friends and acquaintances, grateful they'd survived the storm. Sadness nudged in all too soon—too many had lost loved ones and homes not to grieve. Worshipping with her church family consoled Lottie in a way nothing had since the rain started.

Had it only been a week since Easter? Her exhausted body swore it had been a month.

The next day, with Esther, Susannah, and Willy, she toted lime for cleaning the house. The Board of Health had given cleaning guidelines. Lottie sighed—they'd need temporary shelters a while longer. She longed for her own bed.

Rusty barked a welcome as they walked up. Because they'd be at the house daily, Rusty stayed on their property.

Harvey had promised to bring them supper after work and then help clean. Lottie reflected that he had been a rock for the whole family throughout the tragedy, especially for Willy. According to Joe, Harvey and his partner rescued over one hundred stranded people.

She left Willy outside to repair the barn and then scour the neighborhood for their missing animals.

The ladies cheered to find only muddy residue—no water—on the first floor.

They tackled the bathroom first, which took most of the day. After that, Lottie found a foot of water remained in the cellar. Mud caked the stairs and stone walls and probably clogged the single drain.

Turning up her nose at the idea of trudging through the foul-smelling water didn't get the job done—someone must clear the drain.

She stood on the cellar step just above the water line. "Esther, will you find a ruined cloth that has dried? We won't want it after I'm through with it."

Chills wracked her as she waited. This day was filled with unsavory jobs.

Esther brought her a broom with a rag wrapped around the top. "Susannah says if you can't reach the drain with the handle, let it go. There are diseases in standing water."

The older woman had a point. Susannah had confessed to living through the flood of 1866. Lottie leaned on her knowledge. "I have a fair idea of the drain's location."

It took several tries to move the drain cover. Water levels ebbed.

As she returned upstairs, Harvey carried a loaded box into the kitchen where Esther and Susannah scrubbed. He glanced at the slimy walls. "A fine evening for a picnic on the porch."

Though there was no electricity or running water, the clean bathroom beckoned Lottie. All of them had washed all week from a basin and pitcher. She imagined everyone wanted to feel clean from head to toe. At her suggestion, they abandoned all cleaning for the evening.

No one complained about toting water from the pump in the yard to heat on the stove and fireplace—the reward was worth it.

They took turns taking a bath. Even the men perked up at the prospect of bathing and wearing clean clothes from upstairs. Each cleaned the room after themselves, a job that normally fell to Lottie. She asked everyone to drop soiled clothes on the dirty laundry room floor, wondering if she could bear to touch the filthy clothing on washing day.

Yes, she could, for she needed every nickel she could make.

She waited until last. What heaven to soak aching muscles in the warm water until it cooled. Donning clean clothing, she felt like a new woman.

Joe had already seen her looking her worst. He'd promised to come when done with his temporary job. She hoped to be clean and wearing a pretty dress the next time they met.

If only he found her attractive. He'd held her hand. Maybe dreams did come true.

10

On Wednesday, Augusta, whom Lottie hadn't seen since the flooding started, took a day away from her news reporter job to clean. She slept at another female reporter's home until the boarding house reopened. Lottie, missing her, hugged her somewhat bossy friend

At Augusta's suggestion, they concentrated on the second-floor bedrooms. Augusta helped Lottie roll up a rug from her room and tote it to hang on freshly cleaned porch rails.

Lottie's back ached from washing the floors while the rest washed water-stained wallpaper sections with slacked lime. Four pairs of shoes, stockings, and items in three bottom drawers were discarded.

She wondered again how she'd replace ruined furniture from the first floor. And that awful smell stayed, no matter how much they cleaned, deepening her despair.

Nellie brought a newspaper to the school the next morning. In a daze, Lottie read Augusta's article about cleaning their home, citing examples of how valuable items might be saved. She praised their efforts and hoped for a speedy return home.

"Reckon we're famous." Frank's eyes twinkled. "Did she spell my name right?"

Everyone laughed as Susannah slapped his arm playfully. "You weren't there, remember? But she mentioned you anyway, you old tease."

Lottie tilted her head. "The article's really a compliment to your experience and guidance, Susannah. Both here and during the disaster."

Her eyes shone, but she waved off the tribute. "It's what any able-bodied person would do."

Folding the newspaper, Lottie reflected that Susannah summed up the whole experience in a nutshell. Her chin lifted. They'd all stepped up and made a difference.

Joe and Pete arrived at the boarding house after supper on Thursday evening.

"Heard you folks know how to clean a house." Hands in his coat pockets, Pete grinned after everyone exchanged greetings. "It's even in the newspaper!"

Lottie joined the laughter. "That's what comes of having a reporter live with you." As much as her insides tingled to see Joe again, she wished he'd come when her hair was combed and styled and her dress freshly

111

pressed. Instead she wore a faded print dress with a scarf tied over her hair. At this rate, he'd never see her dressed for an evening out.

"We're here to learn a thing or two about cleaning." Pete grinned at Esther.

Blushing, she laughed.

"Willy and I were just about to tackle a tough job." Harvey raised his eyebrows.

"No." Not the smelly, slimy cellar. Mortified, Lottie shook her head. Harvey and Willy planned to remove the worst of the mud. While she had been all for *that* suggestion, everything changed when it included two potential beaus.

Esther looked as if her supper suddenly disagreed with her.

"Why not? It's the job you most dreaded." Harvey frowned. "With help, we'll make lots of headway."

"But ... it smells so badly from the standing water." Gazing at her feet, Lottie wrung her hands. "We can't ask it of you."

Willy frowned. "But it's okay for me and Harvey?"

"Uh ..." Put that way, what could she say?

"After what we've been through? It'll be a piece of cake." Joe looked at Pete.

"Let me at it." Pete rubbed his hands together.

Joe turned back to Lottie. "See? By the way, the tracks are repaired on The Dayton & Troy Electric Railway. The trolley's running again. It leaves Troy on the half hour for Dayton."

The news comforted Lottie. "Our town's recovering."

"That it is." Joe squeezed her shoulder and then followed Willy to the cellar.

Lottie cringed when the cellar door creaked open. The awful smell wafted into the sitting room where the women had greeted the guests.

Susannah grimaced and then laughed. "I have a feeling we'll see those fellows often." Still chuckling, she led the way to the disastrous amount of mud awaiting them in Henry's room.

Frank insisted on coming with them again two days later, the first Saturday in April. Uncertain health for eight years made him cautious. Around his sixtieth birthday, he had suffered a lung complaint that eventually put him in the hospital. He'd never completely recovered his strength.

Since they'd ride the trolley, Henry wanted to come, too. Knowing the sad state of his room, Lottie talked him into staying in town. He didn't realize the extent of the damage to his room, which wasn't refurnished yet. Her spirits drooped at his disappointment.

Nellie and Harvey accompanied them today—Augusta was visiting her in-laws, who couldn't rest easy until seeing her.

Lottie boarded the trolley and sat on one end by herself to think. The cost of replacing the ruined furnishings overwhelmed her. The dining room table, matching chairs, cupboard, china, and all sitting room furniture had to be replaced. She felt encouraged about the kitchen, which had been sanitized. As soon as the ice man began making his rounds again, the icebox would be functional. That room had the least amount of damage.

Lottie rubbed her throbbing temples. She'd move Mama's bed to Henry's room, but his furniture—every article of clothing—had been beyond saving.

That fifty dollars in the Troy National Bank was not nearly enough. Then she remembered a little safe she got from the bank four years ago to prepare for a rainy day. For at least three years, she put in all the change left over at the end of the month. The safe had particular slots for each type of coin. Once it was nearly full, she put the safe on her bedroom closet shelf and forgot it.

A day didn't get much rainier than what they had just gone through. Anything helped when losses threatened to cripple them.

The sight of furniture in the yard and lining the porch jolted her from the daydream. A thousand dollars couldn't replace all this. How was she to care for her brother, sister, and boarders now? She clasped her hands together. *Please help me, God. I don't know what to do.*

Frank stopped at the mess in the yard. He pressed his hand against a mud-stained cushion. He turned a chair over and examined it. Then he set it aside and studied the next chair.

Mystified, Lottie glanced at Susannah, who watched her husband with hands clasped in a prayerful pose.

"This one is fixable." Frank pointed to a cushioned chair. "It'll take work. The cushions must be replaced. It'll need new fabric." He met Lottie's wide-eyed gaze. "But it's a far sight cheaper than replacing it. Willy, please carry this to the porch. Let's keep it out of the rain."

Esther's hands covered her cheeks. "Anything else?"

He ripped the seams of another armchair to the framework. "This one."

Harvey carried it to the porch.

Frank poked and prodded on the sofa. "I believe this is salvageable."

Tears rolled down Lottie's cheeks.

Susannah hugged her. "I guess we never told you Frank spent ten years in the upholstery business." She beamed at her husband. "He'll need help with the heavier jobs."

"No problem." Lottie's voice squeaked. She dashed tears away. "Thank you, Frank. There wasn't enough money to replace all this."

Willy rubbed his hand on the sofa. "I'll help. I like learning new trades, though I found my life's work."

Blinking rapidly, Lottie turned to him. "What's that?"

He straightened and met her gaze squarely. "Doctoring. I want to become a doctor."

She stumbled backward, mind racing to the stories he'd told of families at the temporary hospital. How had he come so far in two weeks without her noticing? She hugged him fiercely. "Then we'll have to figure a way to pay for college." She smiled, though inwardly she cringed — this, on top of home repairs? "I'm proud of you. The way you went beyond what anyone asked of you during the storm ... Mama and Papa would be proud."

He sniffed and picked up a chair. "These chairs won't move themselves."

Misty-eyed, Esther smiled at Lottie. "A day of happy surprises. Reckon we ought to get started on Henry's room? Maybe there's good news there, too."

11

For the next two hours Lottie and Esther tore grimy wallpaper from Henry's room while the rest worked on other parts of the home. They had almost finished removing all wallpaper within reach when a friendly voice called out from the porch.

"Hello, Lottie? Esther?"

"Come on back, Joe." Lottie answered. "We're in Henry's room."

Joe and Pete entered with an older gentleman, each wearing work clothes. Joe introduced the man as his father.

As they exchanged pleasantries, Lottie glanced at Mr. Bosworth. With his salt and pepper hair, he looked like an older version of Joe.

"Joe's mentioned your flood damage." Mr. Bosworth's green gaze swept across the bedroom. "Hope you'll allow me to help."

"Thank you." Lottie tried unsuccessfully to remove the sticky wallpaper glue from her hands with her apron. She smiled at them. "I'm not turning away any help."

Joe glanced at his father. "The flood destroyed the chicken coop."

"Won't take long to rebuild." Mr. Bosworth studied her. "We brought wood."

"How wonderful." Lottie met Joe's questioning gaze. "Thanks. Willy will be glad. Our chickens shelter in the barn at the moment."

Mr. Bosworth rubbed his hands together. "Our pleasure. Well, fellows, what do you say we begin?"

Pete looked at the torn strip of wallpaper Esther's hand. "Let's remove the rest of the wallpaper first."

"Excellent idea." Mr. Bosworth tore at a long strip. "Apparently the water did the hard work. I'll build a frame. Join me when these pretty ladies don't need you anymore."

Lottie didn't think that day would come. Her cheeks flushed.

After his father left, Joe peered at the walls. "Looks easier than the cellar." He grinned.

Lottie laughed and they set to work. The fellows' easy banter made the job fun. They talked about cleanup at Troy Wagon Works, where they both worked. Pete recounted several stories about odd sights around town after the flood, such as a sewing machine standing alone in the midst of an empty field or a stack of wood that appeared to have been picked up by rising waters and gently stacked again less than a mile away. Pete had a knack for making a simple story comical. The four of them laughed for the next hour. Amazingly, they made headway on the room. Finally, the walls were cleared of wallpaper.

Knowing she and Esther could wash walls but not carry Mama's bed downstairs, Lottie asked the men to return after lunch to do this. They agreed with a smile and went to the yard to build the henhouse.

She and Esther employed the ladder to wash down the walls with lime, thrilled that the last of the unpleasant smell in this room dissipated with the final cleaning.

Two applications of wax didn't return the hardwood floor to its former glory, though it was sturdy. Lottie rubbed her aching back. She couldn't replace the damaged floor, but the rug in her room might help. "Esther, I'll ask the fellows to bring down my rug before the bed is put together."

Esther made a face at the discolored wood floor. "That will help."

"Don't mention where the rug came from. Besides, he may not even notice it's a different rug." Maybe she could afford a new rug for her room in a few years. "I have coins I've saved for a rainy day. It might buy him three or four complete sets of clothing, including underclothes."

Esther squealed and hugged her. "Don't tell him or he'll never agree to it."

Lottie frowned. "Good point." They had to save his pride. "I'll ask Frank and Susannah to shop for him."

"I have an idea." Her eyes lit up. "Let's tell Henry the new clothes were donated by friends from Troy. We're from Troy, so it's the truth. Frank and Susannah will keep the secret."

Tension eased out of Lottie's shoulders. "That's perfect." She patted her sister's arm, thoughts swirling. "Hope the cash covers everything."

ᗜ ᗜ ᗜ

Joe hadn't intended to eavesdrop on the sisters' conversation. He hadn't deemed it necessary to knock when he reentered the house to ask about lunch, but the girls were oblivious to his presence in the sitting room, even with damaged, creaking floorboards.

A smile broadened. They were quite something, both of them. The more time he spent with the family, the more he liked them. Lottie, in particular, had captivated his interest. It sure had been a stroke of luck to rescue them. Or maybe it was Providence. If he hadn't recognized her name and volunteered to rescue the family, their paths probably wouldn't have crossed. As it happened, they had been together almost every minute he could spare.

Of course, there were other shelters giving hot meals. He had managed to go where Lottie happened to be. She sure had a way of making him chase her around.

He shook his head. He wasn't certain she even realized how hard he had worked to see her and make sure she was all right.

His heart felt full that so much good had sprung from tragedy.

Hard times sometimes brought out the best in people. Individuals who lost everything jumped in to help others. Maybe hard times *always* brought out the best in good people.

Lottie and her family were good people. Her inner light of strength had blazed during the disaster. She'd certainly snatched his attention.

He'd soon extend an invitation for an evening out to Lottie — after she got her home in order.

He tiptoed out the front door and closed it gently. Susannah, who ripped padding from a chair, looked up from the yard with a puzzled expression as he stood there idly.

Joe wasn't free to explain. He gave the sisters time to finish their conversation and then stomped his feet noisily against the wood as if scraping dirt off his shoes. Then he went inside. "Lottie? You in here?"

ᗜ ᗜ ᗜ

A simple lunch of roasted turkey sandwiches was a lighthearted meal. From the porch, Lottie spotted the frame of a chicken coop near the barn. Who knew a henhouse could be beautiful? Heart full of gratitude, she thanked the men.

"It'll take all afternoon to finish." Joe gulped his coffee.

"Lottie, both sofas are salvageable." Frank's gaze traveled to the wood furniture now stripped of cushioned seats. "And four armchairs."

"Thank you." Her heart sang. They lost only two of the fancy sitting

116

room chairs.

"The padding and fabric will have to be purchased." Frank sank back into the hard-backed dining chair with faded wood. "Since the wallpaper has to come down, you can change the color."

She met Esther's hopeful gaze. "I never considered that."

Esther smiled. "Pink?"

Willy groaned. "Green's my favorite color."

Lottie laughed. Purple was her preference. Maybe she'd poll everyone for ideas. After all, everyone had worked hard to repair and clean their home.

"I'll measure and let you know what we'll need." Frank sank back in a warped chair. "Do you know when we'll move back?"

"Well, I—" Was that farmer on a horse leading two cows toward their home?

Willy leaped to his feet. "Ben!"

12

Lottie unlocked the door to her home and turned to face her family and their boarders on Tuesday, April 8. "Welcome home, everyone." Joy radiated through her.

Willy cheered. Esther cried. There were hugs all around.

Lottie wheeled Henry into his room.

"Where's the new mattress from?" Henry wheeled himself closer.

"It's from my parents' room." Lottie clasped her hands together. They'd worked so hard, sacrificed so much, that any complaints would be a blow.

"And this is a new bureau." Frank opened a drawer filled with new clothes.

Henry gasped. "New clothes?"

"Friends from Troy heard you lost your clothing," Frank patted his shoulder, "and donated these."

Tears ran down Henry's cheeks. "Two weeks ago, I thought no one cared." He covered his face with a handkerchief. "I don't deserve such kindness."

Susannah covered his hand with hers. "There are good-hearted folks in this world."

"There sure are." He touched the crisp cotton. "I might not ever know who done this. I'll pray that God blesses them in some special way."

Susannah gazed at the ground. "Everyone I know could use such a prayer."

"I need to bake a cake," Lottie said past the lump her throat. She sped from the room with Esther at her heels.

117

Lottie hummed later as she walked through the home. All bedrooms, the bathroom, and the kitchen were ready. Fabric still needed to be purchased for the sitting room furniture. The cellar had been scoured with lime. The dining room was empty. There was no money for replacements, yet no one mentioned finding another place to live.

Esther cooked a celebratory supper of fried chicken. She supplemented the meal with a few canned vegetables. They ate on the porch on the pleasant, though chilly, spring evening.

Lottie dashed away tears, because a smiling Henry wore a new set of clothes for their first supper.

🌳 🌳 🌳

Lottie and Esther had just finished washing supper dishes two nights later when Harvey entered the kitchen.

"Evenin', Miss Lottie. Miss Esther."

The plate in Lottie's hand clanked onto the stack below. "Harvey. What can we do for you?" She raised her eyebrows at Esther, who shrugged.

He shook his head. "It ain't like that. Can we all take a walk? I'll fetch Willy."

Mystified, Lottie met Esther's wide-eyed gaze. She hoped Harvey hadn't found other lodging. She'd come to depend upon his steady strength and wisdom, especially with her brother.

He returned with Willy. They exited the back door as the sun sank to the western sky. Rusty ran over to them and licked Willy's hand.

They silently walked to the river. His request was so unprecedented that Lottie felt it must be important.

"Look at that." Willy pointed to a beautifully-crafted green park bench, large enough for five people, that faced the river. He raced ahead to stand in front of it. Color ebbed from his face.

Lottie ran to his side. A rectangular plaque on the top wooden slat read '*In honor and memory of Olivia Stevens.*' Her hand covered her mouth to stifle a cry.

Esther gripped her hand. "Mama."

A wave of loneliness struck Lottie as she stared at her mother's memorial plaque. She'd lost so many of her parents' possessions that her chest ached. "Harvey, did you do this?" Her voice shook.

He nodded. "Frank supervised me." His brown eyes turned smoky. "I did it for Olivia."

Lottie gasped. Her growing love for Joe had created a sensitivity to recognize those feelings in others. "Did you ... are you saying ...?"

"That I loved your mama?" The broad-shouldered man appeared taller than his six-foot frame. "Oh, yes, Miss Lottie. A finer woman never

118

lived." He closed his eyes. "It feels good to finally speak of it. I didn't know if there'd come a day when I'd tell you. Frank and Susanna agreed that the time is right."

"*They* knew?" Lottie's breath caught in her throat. "But why didn't …"

"It's a shock." He gestured to the bench. "Won't you sit?"

Lottie sat in between her siblings with Rusty at her feet. She stared at Harvey as if she'd never seen the quiet man with salt and pepper hair and a shy smile. She hadn't suspected her mother loved any man after her father's death. She'd always seemed so caught up in her children's lives and running a boarding house that Lottie never worried about her suffering from loneliness.

"I moved into your attic bedroom in 1905—about a month after Frank and Susannah." His gaze settled on the house behind them. "I've always been a bit backward, but your mother insisted I eat with the family. She included me in activities. She was so sweet and pretty. I loved her right away, but knew there wasn't any chance of her loving a big oaf like me."

Lottie drew a deep breath, hoping her mother loved this good, kind man.

"Two years went by." Harvey paced back and forth in front of the sturdy bench. "One fine spring day, your mother asked me to go shopping with her. Said she needed someone to tote heavy boxes of groceries back to the house because the store delivery boy had broken his leg." His eyes softened. "I was on cloud nine. Anything was more fun with Olivia. Anyway, we talked about ourselves that day, something we'd never done before. Her pretty eyes sparkled up at me. I treated her to lunch at the diner, just like it was a date. We went into Troy every Saturday until the delivery boy recovered. When I offered to continue our arrangement, she agreed."

Lottie met Esther's excited gaze. This was better than a novel—and it was about their mother.

"We took picnics to the park, strolled by the river, and even took the trolley to Piqua." He turned to face the river. "I proposed to her on this spot one summer's evening. She said yes."

Lottie's jaw sagged.

"You were engaged to Mama?" Esther's brow wrinkled. "Why didn't we know?"

"She wanted time to prepare you." He kicked at a tuft of grass with his boot. "You were all busy with schoolwork and your friends. Olivia waited for the right time. Months passed. Then she got sick."

Lottie closed her eyes. That nightmarish time hurt to recall.

"She ignored it for three months. Lottie, you noticed her fatigue and quit school to help. You studied with your teacher in the evening." Harvey shoved his hands in his pockets and turned to the river. "I finally convinced her to see the doctor, drove her in the wagon."

He paused so long Lottie wondered if he was done talking. She tensed.

"Cancer. Felt like a death sentence." His breath came in shudders. "This is the part that most concerns you." He stared at the river.

Tears ran down Lottie's cheeks. She grasped her siblings' hands.

"We knew she didn't have long. The doctor guessed three to six months." His mouth worked. "God gave us two. Olivia felt it unfair to give you a new stepfather right before she died. She ... decided not to marry me."

"Why?" Willy cried openly. "We needed somebody to love us."

Harvey turned back. The gathering dusk cast shadows on his heartbroken face. "Willy, you never lost it. I promised your mother I'd remain in your lives as long as you wanted me. It's a promise I aim to keep."

Rusty licked Harvey's hand.

"You have one more year of high school, Willy." He swiped his wet cheeks. "I told you that story so you'll let me help with the cost of college."

Willy's gasp mingled with Lottie's.

"I have enough saved to pay for the first year and maybe the second. Had I married your mother, I'd be paying for it anyway." He held out his hand imploringly. "Please. Let me do this in your mother's memory."

The big-hearted man finally ran out of words. Lottie leaped to her feet and stepped toward him. "I can't believe you'd have been my stepfather."

"Yep." A tear rolled down his face.

"Can we adopt you now?" Esther reached for Harvey's hand.

He grasped her hand and began to sob. They hugged him, crying with him. Lottie was surprised that happy tears wracked her body with sobs the same way sad tears did.

Willy recovered first. "I will accept. Now you'll always be part of us." He stuck out his hand manfully.

Harvey smiled and gripped Willy's hand. "I always have been. You just didn't know until today."

🌣 🌣 🌣

The change in Harvey amazed Lottie. He joined conversations. He laughed often and had long talks with Willy.

As for Lottie, she had gained a stepfather. Looking back, she wondered how she missed the signs. As a schoolgirl, she'd been too absorbed in her own life to notice the blossoming relationship that she now saw clearly.

Frank had purchased new fabric and cushions with money left over from Henry's clothes. He and Susannah worked on upholstering the furniture for the next two weeks. After the school reopened, Willy worked with them in the evenings. Both Joe and Pete came every Saturday and free weeknights. They cheerfully joined the continued cleaning.

Lottie never had time alone with Joe, but he didn't seem to mind. On the other hand, she was chomping at the bit to spend time alone with him, to talk the way they did the last night she worked at City Hall.

She sighed as Joe left. What was the man waiting for?

Joe invited Lottie to supper in Dayton for the last Saturday in April.

Thrilled that she was finally going to ride the trolley on a date — with Joe! — she could hardly wait the five days until Saturday. Esther helped her decorate her wide-brimmed black hat with wide lilac hair ribbon to match her Easter dress.

Joe visited her two evenings that week. One evening was pleasant enough to sit outside. Breathing in fresh spring air, she sat with Joe on the new bench and watched the sun set over the river. This was her first private conversation with him in a while, so she told him about Harvey's surprising engagement to her mother.

"Had she lived, he'd have been my stepfather. Breaks my heart they didn't marry." She gazed at the gold, pink, and purple sunset.

Joe whistled. "Bet a feather would have knocked you off your feet when he delivered that news." He slid his arm over the back of the bench.

"My heart aches for him." Her shoulder tingled where his arm brushed against her. "It's romantic to talk about when love ends tragically, but not so nice to live it. I wish they had married. It's sometimes a burden to take care of everyone in the house. Sharing the responsibility with my stepfather might have made all the difference in the world."

"You're a strong person, Lottie, with a strong faith." His hand caressed her shoulder. "I admire you so much."

His words, his touch, put a warm glow in her heart. "When I think of all the people you and Pete —"

He put his fingers on her lips. "We only did what everyone else also did." Dusk created shadows around them. He brushed her lips with his.

Heart racing, Lottie smiled up at him and his warm mouth covered hers again.

He raised his head reluctantly. "I hate to go," his fingertips touched her cheek, "but I have to be at work early tomorrow."

Their evening had flown. Dazed from his kisses, Lottie walked with him to the porch.

"Please tell everyone goodbye from me." He gathered her close. "I enjoyed our talk."

She fit perfectly inside his strong arms. So warm. So right. But it was time for him to go. She stepped back.

"I'll be by on Friday evening, if that's convenient." His gaze searched hers in the dim light.

Lottie smiled. "It is." She watched him walk to the trolley that ran about a hundred yards in front of her home, already missing the warmth of his arms. Who knew a simple hug could make a girl's heart sing?

13

Lottie hummed when Joe strode to her porch on Friday evening. They walked to Troy. Though she half-heartedly invited Nellie and Esther to go along, their refusal brought a smile to her face.

As they strolled, he tucked her hand onto his arm and talked about his college experience at the University of Tennessee. He had concentrated on literary studies and worked on the student newspaper, the *Orange and White*. He grinned. "I wore those two colors together often while in Knoxville."

She laughed. "I'd love to see one of your shirts." She paused to return a friendly greeting of a neighbor. "But why did you go all the way to Tennessee for college?"

"My uncle teaches there." He nodded cordially to a couple exiting a store. "I played on the basketball team and was a member of Chi Delta, one of the literary societies."

"If your greatest interest is the literary field, why work for Troy Wagon Works?" This side of him fascinated her. She smiled at him and loved the way his green eyes crinkled when he smiled back.

"I increased my class load and graduated in December. With my writing experiences, I hoped to start a journalism career right away. A week later, the editor of the *Troy Daily News*," his shoulders hunched, "told me to get some life experience and return in a year."

Her heart shrank at his disappointment.

His jaw tightened. "Don't worry. I'll try again."

She squeezed his arm. "You'll get that job."

She described her days running the boarding house. The topic didn't seem as boring with his interested questions. The evening passed all too quickly.

It was dark when they made it back to the porch. Joe kissed her goodnight, his lips lingering on hers. Her heart beat so wildly she thought she'd die of happiness.

Lottie dreamed of marrying Joe that night. The vision stayed with her the next day as she donned her prettiest dress, a lilac one that her sister declared enhanced her brown eyes and hair. Esther fussed over her until Joe, handsome in a navy blue suit, arrived at two o'clock.

He complimented her beautiful dress. Her heart skipped a beat at the warm look in his eyes.

Lottie pinched herself while riding the trolley for their date, as she had dreamed of doing. She laughed at his gentle teasing. The wonderful day exceeded her dreams. Even commonplace activities were more fun with Joe.

Holding hands, they strolled through Dayton. Prettier girls passed them—Joe didn't glance their way. His smiling green gaze remained on her, on pleasing her.

She couldn't keep a smile from her face, from her heart. She was falling in love.

He took her to a nice restaurant for supper where the tablecloths and linen napkins were pristine white and the waiter attentive. Lottie had never been to a place so fancy, but the prices weren't exorbitant. As Joe directed, she ordered what she wanted—baked ham. Bread, warm from the oven, and chocolate cake with a scoop of vanilla ice cream finished the perfect meal.

They talked of school days and discovered they both had a crush on each other in younger years. Her head reeled at the news.

The first stars were out when they arrived back in Troy.

"Want to get off in town and walk back to your house?" He bent his head, his gaze on hers.

"What a lovely idea." She laughed. "I need exercise after that cake." And an extra half hour with him.

He grinned. "Me, too."

They exited the trolley near the public square and strolled toward her home, greeting folks who smiled indulgently.

All too soon they were at her porch. Raising her face, she thanked him for the wonderful day. He bent and kissed her. The gentle kiss lasted longer this time and Lottie stared breathlessly at him when it ended.

She loved him. The dim light of the lantern someone thoughtfully left for them shadowed his features. Could he really care for her?

He kissed her once more, then left the porch swiftly. Filled with joy, she watched him walk away. Might her dream of marrying Joe be within her grasp?

After that special day, he planned fun activities every weekend. They strolled beside a peaceful river firmly back within its banks in Troy. He took her on picnics in the picturesque countryside on either end of town. They took the trolley into Piqua to eat supper there.

Sometimes Pete and Esther joined them. The two of them enjoyed a more casual relationship that seemed to suit them. For now. After the difficulties they'd all suffered, how wonderful to enjoy life again.

Joe invited Lottie to a play in Dayton at the end of June. "To celebrate the beginning of summer."

Lottie took extra care when pinning her hair. She wore her lilac dress and arranged a lilac ribbon on her black hat. A glance in the mirror showed she looked her best. Excitement bubbled. Did he plan something special?

Everyone who lived in the home sat on the porch when Joe arrived — except Lottie. Pulse racing, she waited for Esther to fetch her.

He looked so tall and handsome in a brown suit that her heart skipped a beat. She smiled when he complimented her beauty.

Lottie's face heated when Willy snickered. The rest wore indulgent smiles.

They strolled to Troy to pick up the trolley at the station. She rested her hand on his arm.

Expecting to go directly to the station, Lottie raised an eyebrow when he stopped at Forest School. "I haven't been here since the week of the flood."

Joe turned to her. "I found you after you delivered Ermalene's baby. Remember?"

Gazing at the brick building, she smiled. "I'll never forget how God answered my cries for help that night. That's the only explanation I have."

He clasped her hand. "It was a special night for me."

She frowned, trying to remember their conversation. She had been so drained by the time Joe came. "Why?"

His green gaze intensified. "Because that's when I fell in love."

Her left hand flew to her throat. He loved her?

"I fell in love with you during the flood, Lottie." He sandwiched the hand he held between his.

"But I looked terrible." Her voice rose. *That's* when he fell in love with her? "I hadn't slept in two days. My clothes were filthy —"

He put his fingers over her lips. "I didn't care. I already knew you were beautiful."

Her stomach fluttered. "That awful night was when you fell in love with me?"

He tugged at his collar. "Am I wrong? I hoped you felt the same way ..."

Bubbles swelled inside her chest. "Oh, Joe, it seems I loved you always. I'm not sure when it started. I only know it's here to stay."

Joe swept her into his arms and kissed her. Right there on the street corner. This kiss held a promise of love and a future together. Heart singing, Lottie joyfully returned his kiss.

A man behind them cleared his throat.

They broke apart. Heat flooded Lottie's cheeks as she met the glance of an older woman who tossed her head and declared, "Well! I never."

"Ahem." Joe met her disapproving look. "Perhaps we should make this official."

Lottie gasped as he got down on one knee.

The couple who had just passed turned back.

"Carlotta Stevens," Joe's serious gaze held hers, "will you marry me?"

"I will." Happy tears rolled down her cheeks. "Yes, Joseph Bosworth, I will be your wife."

Leaping to his feet, he enveloped her in a hug and kissed her soundly.

Several people clapped, including the earlier disapproving couple.

Joe then reached into his pocket and gave her a small jeweler's box.

Her hands trembled as she took it from him. The small round diamond on a gold band took her breath away. "Joe, it's perfect." She threw her arms around his neck.

Joe turned her within the circle of his arms, to the knowing glances around them. "She said 'yes.'"

"We noticed." A gray-haired gentleman chuckled. "Congratulations." The crowd broke up after wishing them well.

Joe held Lottie's hand as they strolled to the station. "Lottie, I should ask Willy for permission to marry you."

Lottie considered. "Will you ask Harvey *and* Willy?"

He grinned. "Seems appropriate."

She hugged his arm, loving him for understanding her need to include Harvey.

In spite of the heartache and loss caused by the flood, something very good had happened. Her city had endured.

And in her world where nothing much ever happened, love had surprised her. The storm brought Joe back into her life ... 'til death did them part.

Acknowledgements

The author wishes to thank Bob Patten, curator of Overfield Tavern Museum and Doug Tremblay, President of the Board of Museum of Troy History. They introduced her to the rich history of Troy, Ohio, as she walked through their museums.

The flood of 1913 affected various towns and cities. The main characters in this story, though fictional, are set against a backdrop of real people who courageously stepped forward to meet the challenges presented by a horrific event. Heroes are born at such a time.

Award-winning and Amazon bestselling author **Sandra Merville Hart** loves to uncover little-known yet fascinating facts about our American history to include in her stories. She is Assistant Editor for DevoKids.com. She has written for several publications and many blogs including: *The Secret Place, Harpstring, Splickety Magazine, Pockets Magazine,* Afictionado, ChristianDevotions.us, and DevoKids.com. Her debut Civil War Romance, *A Stranger On My Land,* was IRCA Finalist 2015. *A Rebel in My House*, set during the historic Battle of Gettysburg, won the 2018 Silver Illumination Award and is 2018 Faith, Hope, and Love finalist. *A Musket in My Hands*, where two sisters join the Confederate army with the men they love, releases November of 2018. Watch for her novellas, *Trail's End*, in "Smitten Novella Collection: The Cowboys" releasing in August of 2019.

Connect with Sandra on her blog, Historical Nibbles: *https://sandramervillehart.wordpress.com/*

Facebook: *https://www.facebook.com/sandra.m.hart.7*

Twitter: *https://twitter.com/Sandra_M_Hart*

Pinterest: *http://www.pinterest.com/sandramhart7/*

COLD READ

by Sharyn Kopf

To my sister, Susie Kopf Jarvis,
who gave this single woman a sense of family
by letting me be a part of hers.

Note: For those unfamiliar with the language, a glossary of theatre terms appears on the last page.

1
Stephie

... because it is not always that the hopes of deserving, loving human beings are blessed ...
~N. Richard Nash, "The Rainmaker"

It is, quite possibly, the first time I've ever seen anyone mosey, other than John Wayne. So, the first time in real life. But mosey he does, right through the double doors of the Holland Theatre and straight into my heart, dragging a chill rush of autumn air in his wake. All six-foot-four of him, with his bald head and smirky swagger.

Please God. Please let him be here for the auditions.

Auditions always make me nervous, whether I'm posturing for a part onstage or casting from the seats below. This time it's the latter—my first directing job at the old, historic theatre in downtown Bellefontaine, Ohio. We had just started auditions, and I was already swiping sweat from my forehead at the lack of men showing up. Leave it to me to choose a play that requires six of them. Everyone knows you have to beg, borrow, and steal to get more than a handful of guys to audition for community theatre. So far, eleven women have read for the one female part compared to three men for the six male roles. And of those three, two were teens and the third is perfect for H.C., the main character's dad.

Which means I still haven't found my over-the-top leading man, Starbuck.

And now, here he is, standing in front of me, grinning and handing me his slightly wrinkled audition form. How it got wrinkled from the lobby to here, I ... well, maybe he's nervous too. I stick out my hand. "I'm the director, Stephie Graham, and this is my assistant, Merle Borscht."

He takes my fingers in a firm grip. "Andy Tremont. Is this a cold read?"

"Yes." And if that isn't confirmation enough, I nod so hard my blue-green beret tips forward, knocking lavender-highlighted bangs into my eyes. I brush my vision clear.

"But if you have something ready," I say, "we'd love to see it."

"Uh, nope." He scuffs a shoe on the floor and looks toward the door he just walked through. "I just found out about this today, so I'm not too prepared."

"Oh, that's okay!" I say, tossing out a hand breezily and accidentally smacking Merle in the chest. Which jolts the elderly man out of his reverie long enough to say,

"You have any experience, son?"

Good old Merle. He shuffles everywhere and has thick, white hair and warm eyes and doesn't think anything interesting has happened since the Rat Pack broke up. I mentioned once I felt the same way about the Brat Pack and he looked at me with such disappointment, I imagine he went home that night and wept for my generation.

But he knows theatre like Sinatra knew Vegas, so I'm lucky to have him on my team. Such as it is.

Andy hooks a thumb into his belt loop, Duke-style, and says, "Oh, sure." He leans over the table I'm perched at and points to the "previous experience" section of his form. "When I lived in Columbus I did a bunch of stuff. Motel in *Fiddler*, the Stage Manager in *Our Town*, and Porthos in an outdoor production of *The Three Musketeers*. That was fun."

I'll bet.

He stands up and his head seems to brush against the star-studded theatre ceiling. His green eyes light into mine. I take a deep breath and catch a whiff of soap and leather. I almost sigh.

Trouble, thy name is Andy.

I stare. I blink. My, but he is tall.

He clears his throat.

Say something, Stephie, before he moseys out of your life.

I finally exhale and whisper, "You sing?" Because that is the most important information necessary for someone who *isn't* auditioning for a musical. I almost smack myself.

He doesn't seem to mind, though. "I do okay."

"Because we're doing a musical in the spring." *Good grief, Stephie.*

"I'll keep that in mind."

"Well," I say, trying to regain control of what I'd momentarily lost sight of, "we, um, don't have any other women here at the moment so would you mind reading for Starbuck with, uh, me?"

"Sure."

I hand him the sides for the scene I want him to read and follow him up the ramp and onto the stage.

And he nails it. I have my Starbuck. He's so perfect, I fight the urge to just play Lizzie myself. My youthful fantasy of falling in love with my co-star during a show calls out to me. But how could I? We have plenty of talent in Bellefontaine and, well, I don't really look the part.

Darn it.

Merle grins and gives me a thumbs-up. As I make my way back down the ramp, something crashes to the floor backstage. Andy jumps.

I laugh. "Don't worry. It's just Juniper."

"Juniper?" Andy glances behind him. "Is she auditioning?"

"Oh no," I say, and waggle my eyebrows at him. "She's our resident ghost."

Merle nods. "Every decent theatre has one."

Now Andy smiles. "I'll have to take your word on that."

And then two more women arrive to audition and the moment is over. I don't see him leave but I have his number.

"Andy's perfect," Merle tells me later. "He even reminds me a bit of Peter Lawford."

"I thought Burt Lancaster played Starbuck in the movie."

Merle frowns and sighs, gaping at me like I'm a high school girl speaking in hashtags.

Shoot. I might have just said something else that will make him weep.

Later that night, I let myself into my small, one-bedroom apartment. My cat, Cozy, meets me at the door, purring and weaving around my ankles. I pick her up and carry her to my only seating area, a ragged, but clean, red-plaid couch. It isn't much of an apartment—old, ugly, and it somehow always smells like bacon—but they let me have a cat for a reasonable price so it's home enough for me.

"Home is where the heart is, right, Cozy?" The cat looks at me, meows, and bats a paw at my arm. She jumps down and meows again, teeth bared. I sigh. "Oh, all right."

I follow her into the kitchen and refill her food dish, then grab a bottle of cream soda from the fridge. Taking a seat at the kitchen table, which also serves as my work desk, I open my laptop.

First thing I do is Google search for "Peter Lawford." A Rat-Packer, of course. Tall, handsome but with a full head of hair. So, for the most part, Merle was right. Personally, though, Andy reminds me more of a bald Jeff Goldblum.

All in all, he's a nice combination of wonderfulness and swagger and just the guy I need to play Starbuck.

Couldn't ask for more than that.

After turning on a 50s Pandora station, I open the marketing packet I started yesterday for a Marysville dermatologist and get to work.

I finally crawl into bed around two a.m., which is actually pretty early for me. But I toss around all night, messing up the carefully tucked sheets and dreaming about the tall, bald actor who seems destined to break my heart.

2
Juniper
September 1933

Juniper Remington waited in the wings of the Holland Theatre, her nerves twisting from her stomach to her throat. How would she ever be able to sing like this?

Maybe I could turn off a few lights. If no one could see me...

That would never work. Not that it mattered anyway. The one person she wanted to see smiling at her from the audience wasn't there. William was gone, and he wouldn't be back. For all she knew, he was already in New York, meeting important people and forgetting all about silly old spinsters with too much love and not enough money.

The pianist, Frederick, came to wait beside her. She glanced at him, then whispered, "I want to sing 'What'll I Do'."

He didn't turn his gaze from the brother and sister juggling act onstage, but his heavy black mustache twitched in the corners. Perhaps he was trying not to laugh. Or he was about to sneeze. "Why would you want to do that? We've been rehearsing 'Someone to Watch Over Me' for three weeks."

Juniper shrugged. "I've changed my mind."

"Whatever you want." And he shrugged too.

She took a deep breath as the Master of Ceremonies, Mr. Van Meer, strode onto the stage to introduce her. It would be over soon. She could sing "What'll I Do" in less than three minutes, and still put in enough heart and soul to bring every feminine eye in the room to tears. Short and effective suited her mood much better tonight.

And perhaps, with that song, she could put William behind her. Still, she knew it would take all her fortitude to get through the last line:

When I'm alone with only dreams of you, that won't come true.
What'll I do?

3
Stephie

We hit the stage full force at our first read-through the following Monday. I had to hunt down actors to play the sheriff and his deputy but Ron Morris and Brad Forrester both owe me for helping them put together successful marketing campaigns for their businesses. Besides, they love acting so it wasn't too hard to convince them.

The part of Deputy File is just as important as Starbuck, at least for what I have in mind, and Brad could bring the right amount of pathos and anger and hope to it. Though not as tall as Andy, he is, in several ways, better looking. Mostly because of his full head of thick, black hair and the laugh lines around his soft brown eyes. The contrasts between Andy and Brad are exactly what I need.

I settled on Willa Barnes as Lizzie. Since she typically grabs the lead in most Holland productions, I hesitated, not wanting to perpetuate the cliquish casting I've seen so often in community theatre. I would love to give someone new a chance, but Willa is the best one for the part. She's petite and vulnerable and, though certainly attractive, we could make her come across as plain—like Lizzie is described in the play—with the right makeup and coloring. But though Lizzie is initially considered unattractive, there needs to be a beauty in her that Starbuck sees first, followed by File and, hopefully, the audience.

Best of all, Willa pulls in a crowd. Everybody loves her.

So, cast in place, we sit in a circle and introduce ourselves. As much as we need to anyway. Andy is the only new guy; everyone else has been a Holland regular for years. Next to Andy, I'm the most recent addition and even I've been involved at the theatre since I moved to Bellefontaine three years ago and snagged a chorus part in *The Music Man*.

When I ask how many are familiar with the play, only Willa and Andy raise their hands.

"Well," I say, "my experience with the show has always been that the audience feels disappointed when Lizzie chooses File over Starbuck. With Starbuck portrayed as her soul mate, how could it be any other way?"

I glance at Willa, the only other woman in our circle, and she smiles and nods. Encouraged, I continue. "I want to change that. I would like to perform this in a way that makes the audience happy when she chooses File."

Glancing around at my talented circle of actors, I grin. "But you know what might be even better? If half of the audience wants her with File, but the other half prefers Starbuck. And they leave the show talking about it, even arguing over who they think she should have ended up with."

Turning to Brad, I say, "This puts a lot on you. Even though you seem to reject her in act two, there has to be something in the way you look at her. We can get a lot of this across in blocking, but it has to be there in your performance too."

Brad bobs his head, and I can tell he's considering his character and how to pull that off. Knowing what a committed actor Brad is, I'm confident he's more than capable of making it happen. And he'll probably surprise me in the process.

Then I turn to Andy. "And all you have to be is charismatic and larger than life, but as fleeting as a hummingbird. Think you can handle that?"

He chuckles. "I'll do my best."

By the end of our first reading, I have chills. *The Rainmaker* has been one of my favorite plays for years and now, finally, I have a chance to bring it to life. To add my own flair. To watch a great cast offer new flavors and nuances and attitudes. And, over time, to see that cast become a family. An eight-week, one-time-only family.

It's not a real family, but you take what you can get.

I hand out rehearsal schedules, and we wrap things up. I barely get out, "See you tomorrow," and Andy is out the door. And it occurs to me he might be married. With kids. Why hadn't I thought of that before? He has to be close to forty, if not over it. Good looking. Tall. Dare I use the word "virile"? Someone must have snatched him up by now. Just because I hadn't noticed a ring…

And, just like that, I'm sad enough to sob into my now-flat cream soda. No, wait. In Ohio they call it "pop." Still trying to get used to that one. I wander around the theatre, putting chairs back and turning off lights. I don't even have Merle shuffling around with me; the school board meets the first Monday of the month and, as the middle school principal, he kind of has to be there.

So it's just me, feeling abandoned and morose and thinking about so many other things that, when I flick off the last stage light, it takes me a second to realize one of the lights is, in fact, still on.

Must have missed it.

I try all of the switches—and there are plenty—yet that one light, stage right, hovering over the grand piano they'll let us move after the upcoming Gershwin tribute concert, doesn't even flicker. It has to be one of the switches on the main breaker. I test them all again, three times in fact, and nothing.

That's when a chill crawls up my spine and trickles through my hair.

I whisper, "Juniper?"

And the light switches off.

I grab my things and race out of the building, grateful for the string of floor security lights that show me the way.

By the end of week two, I have all three acts blocked. Everyone knows his—or her—exit and entrance and every move in between has been mapped out. It looks great.

On the downside, Jim Hessington, who plays Lizzie's dad, H.C., can't quite seem to get his lines down and asks for a hint every ten seconds, and our sheriff, Ron, has missed half the rehearsals. But he knows finding a replacement at this time would be near-impossible. All I can do is beg him to commit to the show—for my sake and for the sake of the rest of the cast.

I suppose I should be glad that at least Ron calls to let me know. Most of the time. Still, it's beyond frustrating. I consider siccing Juniper on him, but that freaks me out. Instead, I give myself my director pep talk, focusing on the one truth of theatre I've seen happen again and again: The show will go on and it will all come together in the end. I don't know how. But it just will. It's silly for me to worry that this production might somehow break that cardinal rule.

On the other hand, it might. Because that's my life right now.

Besides, these are small things. I have a Starbuck and Lizzie a Broadway director would kill for. Their chemistry sends steam off the stage, and I can't take my eyes off of them. Okay, I can't keep my eyes off of him. Andy brings an enthusiastic, almost boyish, sexiness to his character.

Willa, of course, plays her part with polished professionalism. Which is great, except … it's almost too polished. I want her to relax and even mess up. Lizzie is a lonely woman, destined for a life of spinsterhood, living at home with no hope of anything more. Then this gregarious, charming hunk of a man knocks on her door. Not only that, but he sees something in her. He wants her.

It's not the kind of upheaval just anyone can pull off. Even someone as talented as Willa. I try to believe she understands what it might be like. But then we come to the scene where Starbuck kisses Lizzie, and I know she doesn't get it. She moves into the kiss like a seasoned actress, not a timid spinster with low self-esteem. I almost hop up onstage to show her how it's done.

But I don't.

I'm not that good of an actress. It's taken about three rehearsals for my attraction to Andy to turn into a full-blown crush. Adding to my struggle: I still don't know if he's married. No ring and he hasn't said a word about a wife or kids, but I've learned the hard way not to take too much stock in what a guy doesn't say … or wear. He always hurries out the door as soon as I dismiss them.

We've only really talked a few times, but it was enough to know he is witty and smart and nice. And not "what-a-nice-guy" nice. Good-nice. He encourages everyone, offers advice, and spends much of his limited down-time helping Ron learn his lines.

But the clincher happened right before our third rehearsal started, when Andy asked if we could say a quick prayer. A few cast members politely declined while the rest of us stood in a circle and held hands as Andy thanked God for the fun opportunity and the great cast and wrapped it up by asking Him to bless our endeavors.

That's when I fell. Crashed to the ground like a chopped tree.

In most respects, though, Andy is still a mystery. What he does for a living, how he spends his weekends, who he hangs out with, where he stands on deeper spiritual matters like church and biblical authority—I don't have a clue. And if things don't change soon, the show will be over, he'll go his way and I'll go mine and that will be that.

I so don't want that to be that.

But what can I do? I can't just walk up to him and ask if he's married.

As we finish our second Thursday night rehearsal, I remind everyone I expect them to be off-book by Monday and we all say good night. Then Merle takes off, mumbling something about how he promised his wife he'd be home by nine and it was already five after. Everyone's leaving and the lights are still on. It's the first time I've been alone in the theatre since the light incident almost two weeks before.

What can I say? I panic like a high school girl in a horror movie.

"Andy!"

He turns around, almost to the lobby doors. "Yeah?"

"I, um. Could you … stay while I turn off the lights and lock up?"

He starts toward me. Moseying, of course. Then he grins. "You're not scared, are you?"

"No." *Yes.* "But what if I am?"

"No one could blame you."

"It's an eerie place."

"With a ghost."

"Yes." I grin at him. "It has a ghost."

We walk backstage and turn off the lights. The darkness settles around us. He feels so close. He smells so good. Not like cologne but a nice, crisp, clean laundry kind of smell. I want to rub my nose in his shirt.

"So," I say, "I feel like I hardly know anything about you."

Andy follows me back onstage and helps me change the set from the act-three arrangement to the act-one set-up we need for Monday. He says,

"What do you want to know?"

"Well, for instance, what do you do for a living?"

"I'm a real estate agent. What about you?"

"Me?" I have a hard time reconciling such an unromantic occupation with the impressive specimen of a man standing in front of me. It's a good career. I was just hoping for something a little more exciting. Like an architect or a U.S. marshal.

Right, Stephie. U.S. marshals always end up performing in community theatre in Bellefontaine, Ohio.

"Yes, you," he says. "You do have a day job, don't you?"

I put my hands on my hips. And wish I was smaller than a size twelve. Wish I was cuter. Wonder if he likes purple-streaked hair. "Of course I have a … well, sort of. I'm a freelance marketing specialist."

Andy quirks an eyebrow at me. "Did you just make that up?"

He looks so seriously unserious I have to laugh. "It's a real job, I promise." *Just not a very secure one.* "I also substitute teach and take on other short-term jobs as they come along. I mean, I make decent money, most of the time—"

Stop talking.

"But I have to be careful, money-wise, and I'm glad they're paying me for this, though it's not really all that—"

Please stop talking.

And, finally, I do.

Which makes Andy ask, "It's not what?"

"It doesn't pay a whole lot." I sling my purse over my shoulder and pick up my script and notebook. We head toward the exit. I don't have any more excuses to draw the evening out. Besides, he probably wants to get home to his wife.

I sigh, just as a stage light flicks on.

Oh bother. Not again.

We both stop and look at the stage.

Andy says, "Didn't we turn all the lights off?"

"Pretty sure."

"We must have missed one." He heads back to the front. "You wait here. I'll get it."

He's halfway there when the light snaps off again.

Andy glances back at me. "That was weird."

"Uh huh."

He starts toward me, pauses when he sees what I'm sure isn't the most nonchalant expression on my face, and his eyes widen. "Oh, wait. You think it's your ghost, Juniper."

"She's not *my* ghost."

"But that's why you wanted me to stay."

"Well—"

"And here I thought it was because you had a thing for me."

135

This, of course, immediately causes my heart to stop beating. He stares down at me, grinning like a cat with a mouse.

That's when half of the security lights click off. I can still see him, caught in the dim glow coming from the entrance hall behind me. So close. Close and cute and full-on Starbuck. I almost expect him to tell me to admit I'm pretty, just like in the play.

But he does say, his voice low and a little hoarse, "I think she likes me."

"Who?"

He laughs. "Your ghost."

"She's not my —"

And he kisses me. He grabs me by the shoulders and plants one. Firm but soft and completely awkward.

It's so unexpected and perfect and too soon but too late that I can barely take it in. I don't have a chance to kiss him back before he lifts his head. One second and it's over. I stumble a bit and grasp his arm. All I can think to say is,

"Are you married?" Apparently, I *can* just up and ask him.

He chuckles. Deep and teasing. "No. Are you?"

"Definitely not." Though I try to keep the regret and hurt out of my voice, I suspect he hears both.

For several seconds — a lifetime, if not longer — we stare at each other. As I watch, his expression changes, from open and interested to closed and uncertain. His hands drop from my shoulders, and he takes a step back and says,

"Stephie, I'm … sorry about that. I'm not really sure why I kissed you."

"That's okay."

"No, it's not. I mean, I don't want you to get the wrong idea."

Well, here we go.

He says, "I'm not —"

"I know."

"I just don't think we should —"

"It's all right, Andy. I … don't expect anything. Sometimes these things just happen."

Always. Not sometimes. These things just happen to me *always*.

4
Juniper

The Wellesleys offered to drive Juniper home so her parents could leave early. Juniper needed to stay and mingle and Mrs. Wellesley needed to wax eloquent over every act of the night and admire every evening gown of every woman she knew. And as the wife of beloved Bellefontaine physician Dr. Horace Wellesley, Anna Wellesley knew every woman in town. This meant they were at the theatre until the manager locked the door behind them.

But Juniper was, at last, seated in the backseat of the Wellesleys' Chevrolet as they motored toward her house. Normally, she'd be sitting and chatting with the Wellesley's daughter—and her dearest friend—Coraletta, but Cora was home with a fever. Tonight, though, Juniper was almost glad she didn't have to say a word.

She clutched a stunning bouquet of red roses to her chest, aware of the thorn on one of the stems that scratched at her skin just above the neckline of her dress, but too weary to do anything about it. As it was, she was trying her best to pay attention to Mrs. Wellesley's effervescent gushing over Juniper's performance. The pricking thorn, in point of fact, helped her stay focused on what the good-hearted, if rather flighty, woman was saying.

"Delightful, my dear," Mrs. Wellesley declared for the hundredth time. "And so heartfelt!" The older woman looked back over her shoulder from where she sat next to her husband in their new Ford. "How do you know so much about lost loves, dear?"

Juniper was grateful for the ride, but she longed for silence. Fortunately, Mrs. Wellesley never expected an answer. She only stopped talking long enough to draw a breath and, every once in a while, to let her husband insert a quip or question of his own. He had a biting sense of humor, and his wife always had a quick response. If her mood had been better, Juniper would have enjoyed the ride and their banter so much more.

As it was, she'd basically forgotten most of what was said five minutes after getting home. Once the Wellesleys dropped her off at her parents' house, all she wanted to do was go to bed. But her mother met her at the door, grabbed her by the hand, and pulled her into the back parlor.

"I've already received almost half a dozen phone calls about your performance, dear, and the Methodist Ladies' Aid Society wants you to sing at their Christmas benefit."

"They do?"

"Now, we'll want to start putting together your repertoire right away."

"Oh, not tonight, Mother. Please. I'm exhausted."

Mrs. Remington clicked her tongue much like she did when feeding the chickens and held up Juniper's arms to her sides like a cross, examining the silky, backless white sheath she wore. "This dress is perfectly lovely, but we should do something different with your hair."

Juniper held back a groan. "But that's months away. Can't we talk about it in the morning so I can go to bed now? Please?" She tried to give her mother an "aren't-I-cute?" look but suspected she just looked pinched and pained.

Her mother stepped back and studied her face. She didn't smile. "Junie, you need to stop acting like bad things happen *to* you."

"But … they do."

Martha Remington smoothed a hand over Juniper's softly waving brown hair. "No, dear. Bad things just happen. To everyone. You're only a victim if you make yourself one."

"William's gone, Mother, and I'll never see him again. That happened *to* me. And because of me."

"Don't be ridiculous. It's not your fault."

Juniper turned away. "Yes, it is," she whispered. She'd never been able to tell her mother the whole story of why William left. Martha thought he simply wasn't in love with her. And he wasn't. Not enough anyway. But there was more to it: William believed her family was beneath him. If only Juniper had been clever enough or alluring enough to convince him she was worth it.

So here she was. An old maid at twenty-two. Living with her parents. Singing at ladies' society meetings. Could it be enough? Could she be happy?

She should pray and seek God's guidance. It would help.

Maybe. Or maybe not.

Instead she went to bed and cried herself to sleep.

5

Stephie

Because we're both so used to acting, Andy and I are able to pretend nothing has happened to change our director-actor relationship. I try not to think about how strong his lips felt against mine or wonder why he tasted like Pepsi when I've never seen him drink anything at rehearsals other than Tim Horton's coffee or bottled water.

But I put all that behind me and concentrate on getting *The Rainmaker* ready for opening night.

Then, the Monday after Halloween, less than three weeks before the show is to start, I get a call from Geoffrey Barnes, Willa's husband. Geoffrey, not Geoff. Willa insists everyone call him Geoffrey. Maybe he prefers it too. Who knows? I doubt Willa ever asked him.

Anyway, he calls me at nine that morning while I'm looking for costume pieces at Goodwill and, with barely a "hello," blurts out the news that Willa was in an accident the day before. Which immediately causes me to have a minor breakdown next to piles of belts and shelves of shoes.

"What happened? Is she okay?"

"We were hiking the caves at Hocking Hills and, well, she tripped on a tree root and broke her foot."

"Oh, ouch. How is she?"

A breath that sounds rather frustrated vibrates the airwaves. "The doctor says she'll be fine eventually but … I'm sorry, Stephie. She can't walk. She's supposed to stay off her foot as much as possible."

I sure wish men would stop apologizing to me for stuff they can't — or won't — change.

"If she needs to miss a few rehearsals or wear a cast, I understand."

"Actually, she asked me to let you know she's going to have to drop out of the play."

"Wait. What? She can't do it at all?"

"I'm afraid not. She might need surgery."

I take a deep breath and try to calm myself down. "Lizzie could have a cast. We could just make it part of the show."

He laughs. "Willa actually suggested that but the doctor said he didn't even want her standing up long enough to do the dishes. Lucky me."

"But … what am I supposed to do? Where am I going to find someone who can pick up the part in three weeks?"

Even as I speak, though, I know exactly who can and will play Lizzie. But Geoffrey and Willa — especially Willa — don't need to know that.

"Sorry, Stephie," he says again, only this time I don't mind. "I hope everything works out."

And the line drops dead.

So. I'll have to do it, of course. Who else could jump in at such a late date? I would be Lizzie. I swallow down a giggle. No one should rejoice in another person's pain.

But I do let myself smile a little. Then I turn toward Goodwill's hat section to see if they have a 1930s-era straw bonnet that happens to fit me.

🌙 🌙 🌙

That night, I bring a card for everyone to sign to include with the flowers I plan to send Willa. But I'm in a room full of men, and they don't seem all that concerned about needing a new actress. Still, someone does ask who I plan to replace Willa with.

I say, "I thought that, maybe — since we don't have many options at such a late date — I could play Lizzie. Would you all be okay with that?"

They shrug and nod and Andy says, "Sure, why not?"

They don't exactly lift me up on their shoulders and carry me triumphantly onto the stage, but they don't dump all over the idea either. One of the benefits of a mostly male cast. I put Merle in charge as we jump right into act one, scene one, and run through the whole thing, beginning to end. It flows much more smoothly than I expected. And I only need Merle to throw me a handful of lines.

But when the time comes for Starbuck to kiss Lizzie, Andy brushes the corner of my mouth with his lips in what I would label "brotherly" at best. It will never do, and we don't have time for him to be shy. He hadn't had that problem with Willa. Besides, the man can kiss.

Can he ever. And I still have the goose bumps to prove it.

I don't know how to bring it up, though, so I let it go, figuring it can wait. If things don't improve, I'll have to say something. Which causes me to spend the twenty-four hours before the next rehearsal hashing it out and hoping and praying he'll man up and get it done.

Because all I can come up with is, "Remember how you kissed me the other night? Yeah, do that again." Which wouldn't be awkward at all.

Turns out, I fretted for nothing. Our second rehearsal as Lizzie and Starbuck is pure magic. He falls into his part so completely, in that moment I'm not Stephie and he's not Andy and the kiss is perfect and passionate. I ask Merle later how it looked to him and he says,

"Well, the two of you have chemistry all right."

"So, it works?"

"Like Bogie and Bacall."

If that had come from someone else, I would have worried he was just being nice or I'd have pushed for more feedback. But coming from Merle, that's high praise and I know we're on the right track.

At Thursday's rehearsal, I bring homemade chocolate chip cookies and creamy vanilla ice cream. It's supposed to be our last run-through before we start full-blown dress and set and lighting and sound rehearsals on Monday. I'm ready to celebrate.

Then, of course, everything falls apart. People miss entrances, forget lines, and phone in their performances. Even the characterizations we've been working on for seven weeks are off. Not just off. The whole show is a dozen shades of blah. Everyone just seems bored. So before Merle even gets to the rehearsal notes, I announce my intention to have an extra rehearsal on Saturday or Sunday.

"I don't care what time or which day," I say. "We need it."

After some discussion, we settle on Saturday morning at ten. The men file out but, to my surprise, Andy lags behind. Since the night I'd asked him to stay and we had our little moment, he hasn't raced out the door as quickly but seems to wait to see if Merle is staying to help me lock up. Most of the time, Merle does and Andy leaves. But this night, Andy strolls to the back to take care of the lights while I set the stage for Saturday.

Once we're done, without any interference from lights or troublesome spirits, he starts toward the exit while I gather all my stuff together. Then he stops, turns, and comes back.

"Are you hungry?"

"Hungry?"

"Yeah, I was thinking I might go get something to eat. And some company would be nice."

I smile. "Don't you have to work tomorrow?"

He grins back, hooking his thumbs in his belt buckles, reminding me of John Wayne and the first time he swaggered into my life almost two months ago. "Fridays are a bit more flexible at my office and I don't have any appointments until ten."

"What did you have in mind?"

"Pizza at Six Hundred? We could just walk over."

"Sounds good."

We step outside, and the November chill slices through me in an icy blast. I run across the street to put everything but my purse in my ancient red Subaru. Andy meets me on the sidewalk and I pull my scarf tighter around my ears as we take the short stroll to the downtown restaurant. Stars and a half-moon light the night sky. It's only eight-thirty, yet the streets are practically deserted. After years of living in Chicago, I'm still not used to the slower pace of small-town Ohio life.

I like it, but I'm not used to it.

We don't say much as we walk; it's possible Andy is as cold as I am. He hunches over in his leather jacket, his hands stuffed in his pockets. Our breaths come out in wisps of frosty air. I would have been more excited about finally arriving at the restaurant if not for the fact we'll have to walk back to our cars later. When it will be that much colder. Good thing we chose a place barely a block from the theatre.

Andy opens the door, and we hurry inside the renowned pizzeria, called Six Hundred because that's the temperature at which they bake pizzas in their old-fashioned brick oven. The appealing scent of sauce and cheese and baked dough surrounds me, igniting my taste buds, and my stomach responds. I guess I am hungry. Though I can always eat pizza. So I gratefully let Andy hang up my coat and lead me to a booth in the corner. He settles in across from me.

Though it's not quite Thanksgiving yet, the restaurant is draped in Christmas colors and soft twinkle lights. I clear my throat to stop myself from saying something silly about how incredibly romantic it is.

A petite waitress with thick, curly, dark hair and Chinese letters tattooed on her wrist bounces over.

"Welcome to Six Hundred," she says with enough enthusiasm for all of us. "I'm Emily. Can I get you something to drink?"

She hands us menus as we both ask for water, sans ice. I would have preferred hot chocolate to warm me from the inside, but it's not on the menu. They don't have cream soda either. So water it is. Emily returns with our drinks, and we order a large chicken barbecue pizza.

Then we sit there in silence, sipping water and staring at the pictures on the walls. I run through my lines from the play in my head and wish someone would write a script for my life. For this moment anyway. That way I'd have something brilliant and delightful to say, and he would laugh and fall heels over head for me. You can write any two people in love in a story. It's not so easy in real life. Even when that real life includes a tall, sweet man who can make you forget your own name with one kiss.

If only that moment made things easier now. But here we sit, pretending it never happened and that we actually want to be lounging in a restaurant sharing a friendly silence because we don't need words.

Yeah, right.

Finally, he breaks the quiet with some questions about the show. It's all pretty theatre-related until he asks, "Do you live here in Bellefontaine?"

"Yes, I have a little apartment a few blocks down the street from the hospital. You?"

"My family has a farm near Indian Lake."

I take a sip of water. "You live with your family?"

"Near them. My parents are in the main house, but I have my own place on the other side of the hill. And my sister and her family live just down the road."

"Sounds nice."

"It is. We're pretty close." He tugs on his earlobe, then, "What about your family? Are they around here?"

"My family?" Shoot. I'm about to out-and-out lie when Emily saves the day by showing up with our pizza, setting the pie on an empty restaurant-sized tomato sauce can in the middle of the table.

I gnaw down a few bites, swallow politely, and, just in case he wants to return to the subject, throw in, "I have a cat."

"Oh yeah?"

"Yeah." I scoop a piece of cheese from my plate and lick it off my finger. "Wait, don't tell me—you're allergic. Seems like everyone is nowadays."

"No. We have four or five at the farm."

"You're not sure?"

"Well, they come and go." He laughs. "It's more like we belong to them than the other way around."

"I know what you mean. Cozy likes to let me know who's in charge."

"Cozy?"

"Short for Cosette, from Les Mis."

"Cute."

I snag a second slice, relieved. I have successfully changed the subject. I can eat in peace. Which of course is when he says, "So, you were going to tell me about your family."

Gulp. "I was?"

"You weren't?"

"Well … there's not much to tell."

He waits. Chews. Smiles.

"I … um … don't technically have one."

He leans back. "You don't have one? How do you not have a family?"

"A woman found me when I was a newborn, screaming in an alley behind a high school in Chicago. I grew up in the foster system." I shrug, like that's a life history people tell all the time. I don't mention the years of wondering why no one wanted me. "So, no parents, no siblings, no aunts or uncles."

For what seems like hours, he sits there like a statue, staring at me. Okay, I don't look like an orphan. Then again, what does an orphan look like? Annie? Pollyanna? Even Pollyanna eventually grew up. It's obvious Andy doesn't have a clue how to respond to this revelation. Poor fellow. I should at least try to make it easy on him.

"It's not as traumatic as it sounds. I had several decent foster parents and one really good one and, well, God has taken care of me. Besides, don't they say what doesn't kill you makes you stronger?"

"You seem strong."

"You bet I am. Most of the time." At his look I continue, "Holidays can be rough, but I've had thirty-seven years to figure out how to make it work."

"Did you grow up in Chicago?"

Since I now have a mouth full of pizza, I hold up a pause finger and he nods, taking a bite himself while he waits. It's so tasty, I savor it a bit before saying, "I did. Lived there until I moved here three years ago."

"Really." He seems genuinely intrigued. What an unusual man. "How on earth did you end up in Bellefontaine?"

"Hmm, well, that's a long story and it's getting late." I take out my wallet and set a twenty percent tip on the table. Deciding it's worth a shot, I grin as casually as possible and ask, "Rain check?"

He scowls at me. Tilts his head. "I hate rain checks. Don't have the patience for them."

Ha. "I know what you mean. But seriously, I'd kind of like you to get used to the whole idea of me being an orphan before getting into the rest of my story. Besides, my journey to Bellefontaine isn't nearly so interesting. Trust me. One why-I'm-so-messed-up revelation at a time is enough."

More than enough.

Then Andy says, "Would you want to get together for lunch after rehearsal Saturday? You could tell me then."

I don't even pause for a micro-second. "Yeah, that would be great. But you have to tell me one of your issues too. If we're going to be friends, you have to be at least a little messed up."

He seems surprised and amused. "Okay. I think I can meet that criteria. So ... Saturday?"

"Sounds good."

Saturday. Just two nights without sleep.

I can manage.

6
Juniper

Later the next day, Peter Billings came to call. Juniper couldn't remember a time when they weren't friends. She couldn't possibly take him seriously, though; he lived for baseball and goofing around with his friends at the jelly joint, drinking root beer and throwing peanut shells on the floor. Still, he had a knack for lightening the day, and her mood.

"Hiya, sweetheart," he said, chucking her under the chin. "I heard you were aces at the show last night."

All she could do was smile and invite him in. "I did all right."

"Ah, don't kid a kidder." Then he grinned. "After all, I was there."

"What? Now who's kidding?" She led him into the parlor. "I didn't see you."

Peter almost fell onto the sofa, crossed his legs at the ankles and leaned back like he owned the place. "I didn't want you to see me."

"Congratulations. I didn't." Juniper settled into a wingback chair near the fireplace and crossed her own ankles in a more acceptable and genteel fashion. She didn't look at him. Sometimes Peter's silly games seemed nothing more than tiresome and childish. Why couldn't he just grow up?

"Well?" he said. "Aren't you going to ask me?"

Juniper sighed. "Ask you what, Peter?"

"Why I didn't want you to see me."

"What difference does it make?"

"Oh, uh ..." He suddenly seemed uncertain, like he hadn't expected such a reaction. But he said, "I thought it would make things easier for you."

"Really?" Juniper smoothed her hands down her navy-blue pencil skirt. He was like a boy offering her a lollipop. How could he possibly know what would make things easier for her? Could he go to New York and bring William back?

"Sure. I didn't want to make you nervous when you saw me out there."

Which only made her laugh. "Oh, Peter, when have you ever made me nervous?"

He lowered his voice to almost a whisper. "I could make you nervous."

She took a breath that probably sounded as frustrated as she felt. "Why did you come over?"

"To see you."

"Peter."

"What? You know how I feel."

As if on cue, her mother chose that moment to flounce into the room. Few people could flounce like Martha Remington. "Ah, there you are, dear." She turned to their guest. "Peter. Lovely to see you. How is your father?"

"He's getting along. The doctor told him to take it easy for a few weeks."

"I'd say, at the very least." Mother shook her head, her eyes sad. "A heart attack is nothing to take lightly."

Peter smiled. "No, ma'am."

"Tell your mother I'll come by tomorrow with fresh bread and some of last year's tomato jam. It's my best to date." At Peter's nod, Martha turned to Juniper. "Your father and I are supping with the Wellesleys tonight. You can heat up the rest of the macaroni casserole for dinner. And there's plenty for Peter, if he wants to join you. I'm sure he's hungry after a hard day's labor."

"I sure am, Mrs. Remington. Though it wasn't that hard of a day." With a grin, Peter looked at Juniper, his sky-blue eyes lit with hope. "If it's okay with Junie, I'd be keen to stay."

"Of course," Juniper said. "Don't be dingy."

Martha shook her head. "Well, I take it that means 'yes.' I don't know why you kids have to be constantly making up new words when we already have more than we need, but I'll leave you to it."

After she had gone, Peter followed Juniper into the kitchen, where she put the casserole in the oven. She leaned against the counter and watched him for a moment. He really was ridiculously cute, with his shaggy hair and ready smile. When he wasn't being so off the cob, anyway.

So she said, "I just can't take you seriously, Peter."

"Why not?"

"Because you don't take anything seriously. You have no ambition."

He crossed his arms on his chest and tried to harrumph, though it wasn't as effective as one of her father's growls. "For your information, I have a great job with plenty of potential."

"You're a shoe salesman."

"I'm in retail with an eye on a management position."

Juniper tilted her head and pursed her lips. She didn't like word games. "Don't give yourself airs. You're still just a shoe salesman."

"And a snazzy one at that."

He grinned and Juniper groaned inwardly. This wasn't getting them anywhere. Maybe she just needed to be blunt.

After about an hour of honesty and arguing, Peter finally stomped away, taking his broken heart with him. He slammed the door on his way out, making Juniper jump half out of her skin. She hadn't handled that well at all but knew he'd get over it eventually.

"I guess everyone's disappointed in love," she whispered. Maybe that's just the way things were.

With her stomach still growling, Juniper turned toward the casserole she'd pulled out of the oven half an hour before. The once-bubbly cheese sauce was now lukewarm and had congealed on the top.

But she ate some anyway. After a few bites on a suddenly sour stomach, though, she discovered her appetite was sorely wanting. With nothing else to distract her, she cleaned up the kitchen and went to bed.

7

Stephie

Everyone shows up for Saturday's rehearsal in costume, as I had requested, and we fly through it. The improvement over Thursday night is so phenomenal, I can't stop smiling. Until Andy comes up to me afterward and tells me he forgot his fourteen-year-old nephew has a basketball tournament at one this afternoon and he promised to be there. I barely have time to be disappointed when he adds,

"So, do you want to come? It's in Marysville. We could grab subs on the way."

"Um, yeah. Sure."

"We probably won't get back until, like, eight or so. Is that okay?"

It briefly occurs to me to hesitate. To say I have plans tonight. To not be that girl without a social life. But what's the chance he'd believe that?

So I say, "That's not a problem."

I follow Andy out to his mud-encrusted, black Jeep and hop in. We stop for subs—chipotle steak for Andy, turkey and provolone for me— then head east on 33. I almost ordered tuna but decided it wasn't a good idea when eating in a confined space. I sometimes wish I'd stop worrying about making a good impression and just relax and enjoy myself. A psychiatrist, I'm sure, would have something to say about that.

But, really, I'm with a man I'm attracted to, and I don't want to turn him off with strong odors. Is that so wrong?

We eat in relative silence as Andy steers the Jeep toward Marysville. I consider a dozen things to ask him on the way but swallow each question down for one reason or another. Worst of all, I feel a gnawing desperation for him to like me. This happens a lot when I'm interested in someone and usually means I will, in the end, push him away. So I dig down deep for some measure of normality, say a quick prayer, and remind myself that even if things don't work out with Andy, I'll still be fine.

Alone, but fine. Like always.

When we arrive at the high school where the tournament is being held, I realize it's quite the event. The place swarms with kids and adults, yet Andy makes a beeline for a far corner of the gym, where about twenty people immediately surround him.

A woman, not much older than me, grabs his arm. "It's about time! Jordan's second game is about to start."

Andy glances around the gym, then waves at a gangly, red-haired kid who grins and waves back. Andy asks the woman, "How did the first game go?"

"It was close but they eked out a win." She smiles at me, looks at Andy, and tilts her head. In that moment, I definitely see the resemblance. She asks how our rehearsal went.

"Fine," he says, his eyes on the basketball court.

With a grunt, the woman sticks out her hand toward me. "Well, if my brother can't take care of introductions, I'll do it. I'm Brenda."

"Oh, sorry." His tone tells me he really isn't. "Brenda, this is Stephie, our director. Stephie, meet my pushy, older sister."

"Pushy!" Brenda laughs. "The correct word is 'assertive.' And somebody has to be around here." We shake hands and she says, "Brothers. Do you have any, Stephie?"

Andy clears his throat, and a line of red splotches up the side of his neck.

"No," I say. "No brothers."

Brenda chuckles again. "Lucky. You want mine?"

I'm not sure how she misses it but, somehow, Brenda doesn't catch the tension radiating off of said brother. Poor guy. He hasn't a clue how to handle this. So I say,

"Oh, I couldn't do that to you. We all have to accept our lot in life."

Laughing, Brenda introduces me to more of Andy's family: his parents, of course, and Brenda's husband, Tom, along with the rest of their children. I count at least half a dozen. I might have missed a few. Then we take our seats on the bleachers, eat popcorn, drink ice cold cans of cola, and watch Jordan's team win three more games, making it to the final four before being taken out by a team that, to me, looked decidedly older. Definitely taller. Still, the grins sported by Jordan and his friends tell me they consider it a successful day.

Throughout the series of games, I spend more time chatting with Brenda than Andy, in between cheers. Someone that easy to talk to doesn't come along every day. She has a great sense of humor and we talk so much I barely have a chance to catch my breath. By the time Jordan's last game ends, I know most of her life story and she even knows quite a bit about me. Which is why, with very little prying, I relent and tell her my family history. Or lack of one.

She leans her chin on her hand and stares at me with the same intense expression Andy had when he heard the story. Again, I notice the family resemblance. Especially in the deep green of their eyes.

Finally, she says, "Oh, so that's why Andy was all sweaty when I asked if you had brothers."

"That's why."

A smile lifts the corner of her mouth. "Are you sure you don't want him?"

I chew on a fingernail and glance over at where Andy stands on the sidelines, talking with his dad and ruffling Jordan's spiky hair. "I might."

"Yeah, I thought so."

When I look at her grinning face, she shrugs. "It had to happen eventually. Even for a giant schlub like my brother."

"Schlub?"

"Oh, he's a schlub. Trust me."

"Okay." Now it's my turn to laugh. "I don't know what that is."

148

Her dad—I already forgot his name—calls up to us from the front of the bleachers, "Brenda! Steph! Come on. We're taking the kids to Benny's for pizza."

Pizza? Twice in three days? Well ... why not?

I turn to join them and Brenda puts a hand on my arm. "He likes you too, Stephie."

"Hmm." I look at her. I glance around the gym. I do not look at him. "I'm not so sure about that." My voice cracks, despite every effort to sound easy-going. *Not even close to breezy, Stephie.*

"Well, I could be wrong." She wiggles her eyebrows like we're co-conspirators. "But I'm not."

Can I believe her? I want to. But I have a history and great guys like Andy wanting to share my life never seem to become a part of it.

This, however, doesn't stop me from letting hope bubble and spread its heat through the center of my chest. If Starbuck can fall for Lizzie, why can't Andy fall for me? So I push aside the reminder that *The Rainmaker* is a work of fiction. All fiction has some basis in fact, right?

Eventually, I believe, things can change. So I ride with Andy to Benny's, cozy up to him as much as possible at the crowded table, laugh at his liberal use of red pepper flakes, and let myself imagine what it might be like to be a part of the Tremont family.

All the way home, we talk and laugh and I know, if nothing else, we're friends. I say, "So, do you think you'll participate in future Holland Theatre productions?"

"You bet."

"But if you've lived here all your life, why is this your first show?"

"Well, I grew up here, but I moved to Columbus for college. It's when I was at Ohio State that I really caught the acting bug."

"Oh, right. You told us about your performances there at auditions."

"Yep. I've only been back here for a few years and this is the first time I've been able to audition." He glances at me with an easy smile. "And I really wanted to play Starbuck."

"I'm glad you did."

"By the way ..." He pauses so long I wonder if he forgot what he wanted to say. Then, "You wanted to know my ... issue."

"No. That's okay. I was just kidding around."

"Yeah? Well, I'm gonna tell you anyway."

I brace myself. Reach up and grab the handle over the door. Then I realize how awkward that looks and rub my hand on my jeans. "If you want."

"All right." He takes a deep breath. "I haven't been in a serious relationship since college."

I find that hard to believe.

He continues, "That's surprising, I guess—"

Mind reader.

"—but I had a bad relationship and I've been pretty jumpy about the whole thing ever since."

"What happ—" Then I hold up my hand. "No. You don't have to tell me." We're back in Bellefontaine and he pulls up next to where I left my car at the theatre.

Andy puts the Jeep in park and turns to me. "She broke my heart. In a nutshell."

"I'm sorry."

"I suppose it's not that unusual."

"No, it's not." I shift sideways and lean my head against the seat as I study him. It's so quiet; I don't even hear cars on Main Street. Of course, it's after ten. But it's also a Saturday night. A nearby streetlight flickers off and I wonder, for a moment, if Juniper has access to that switch too.

Who cares? I want to feel closer to him. Emotionally and spiritually, if not physically. Again, I catch his clean, masculine scent.

"I like your hair that way." He whispers it, as if he, too, likes the intimacy of the moment.

"You do?" I smooth my bangs from my forehead. I dyed it back to my natural, dirty blonde color. Lizzie couldn't very well have lavender-streaked hair back in the 1930s. "I thought it looked kind of bland."

"Stephie, the last thing you will ever be is bland."

We sit there for a few moments longer. I'm aware of his breathing and how the sound competes with the strong winter winds whipping around us outside. I'm not looking forward to having to leave the warmth of his truck for my cold car. Finally, I say,

"Well, I guess I should go."

"All right. Good night."

I sigh but don't move. "Good night."

Then he chuckles. "Do you want to stay?"

"No." But I nod.

"So stay."

So I do. We talk for another hour about life and movies and dreams and theatre. I honestly don't remember anything specific. But when I finally scurry to my car, I'm happy.

8
Juniper

Three months after Peter stormed out of her house, Juniper stood in the Holland Theatre's dressing room, preparing for her latest performance, a holiday benefit arranged by the Ladies' Aid Society. She hadn't talked with him since that night and, even more remarkable, had actually convinced herself that was a good thing. Now, as she painted her lips cherry red and scrolled through her song repertoire in her head, she mentally stopped herself at least half a dozen times from slipping upstairs and searching the audience.

For Peter.

Mercy. Why was she still thinking about him? He was just a boy. A cute and funny and ambitionless boy. He couldn't fulfill her dreams. Nothing about Bellefontaine, Ohio, could make her dreams come true.

She needed to leave this town. That had become crystal clear over the last few months. If she could just get to New York. To Broadway.

To William. Surely he would take her back. He would see her and recognize her unstoppable ambition and want her again. She could picture them together in New York, taking over the big city with charm and finesse. William had the skill to revive Wall Street; Juniper would shine on the stage. Tucking a curl into place on her forehead, she sighed.

You can't build a life on a dream, Junie.

Still, as she primped it occurred to her that the dream had lost some of its charm. Did she really want to chase after a man who had rejected her so coldly? Did she want to chase after a man at all? What if she showed up on his doorstep, only to have him turn her away? The thought sent a chill through her.

Footsteps on the stairs broke Juniper's reverie. Martha Remington came through the door, grinning and carrying a corsage box.

"Dear, you look stunning," she said. "Are you about ready?"

"Yes, Mother, I think so."

"Wonderful!" Her mother pulled a white gardenia corsage out of the box. It was lovely. She carefully pinned it to Juniper's sleek, red gown. "Your father and I decided you needed something special and so I ordered this. Isn't it perfectly beautiful?"

Catching a whiff of the flower's delicate scent, Juniper breathed it in. It soothed her spirit. "Yes," she whispered. "It's perfect."

Mother fussed over Juniper's dress and hair, smoothing and curling and patting things into place. Then she said, "I saw Peter in the lobby," and Juniper's heart momentarily stilled.

Gathering her thoughts from where they had suddenly scattered throughout the room, she said, "Peter's here? He came to the show?"

"Of course, dear. Why wouldn't he? I've never seen a boy so smitten."

"Oh, Mother." She took another deep breath. What difference did it make? It was too late for anything now.

But when she stepped on to the stage, she chose not to think about—

or sing for — William.

9

Stephie

I love Tech Week. It's always been my favorite part of a production. Seeing all of our hard work finally come together with costumes and lights and sound never fails to thrill me. And this show couldn't be more exciting. When Andy first walks into his scene in his suspenders and rakishly tilted straw hat, the swig of cream soda I've just taken attacks my throat and I cough and sputter for a good five minutes. Merle, always on-hand to help out, slaps me on the back, which shakes me up and hurts a little but doesn't make things better. So I suffer 'til my eyes water.

Once I can talk again, I ask the actors to take their places. After going over announcements and notes and whatever else is on my mind, I join them onstage.

The hardest part is being under the lights instead of enjoying the magic from the audience. Something I didn't take into consideration when I leaped like a trout into the role. Oh well. It just means I can never stop moving. Every time I'm offstage, I run to the back of the auditorium to check with Kelvin, our sound guy, and Janeane, who does lights, or slip into the wings backstage to chat with our stage manager, Trish, about props and curtains and any tiny costume pieces we might still need. Merle, meanwhile, keeps his eyes on everything taking place in the scene.

We wrap up late Monday night. With only three more rehearsals until we open, I can feel the pressure, like hands on my shoulders, pushing me down. I am reassuring myself with deep breaths after almost everyone has left, when Merle turns to me and says,

"I'm just not sure it's enough."

"Enough what?" I clear my throat, hoping and praying that scratchy taste is damage from the cream soda incident, not an indication I have a virus that will rise up on angry hind legs and mutilate my dream of a smooth performance.

"Enough income to keep things going."

I turn to him. "What are you talking about?"

Once again Merle looks at me as if he has serious doubts as to my intelligence level. Then he sighs. "I'm talking about the buy-out. Come on, Stephanie."

Now it's my turn to give the look. "Merle, I haven't heard about any buy-out. Could you just tell me what's going on?"

"All right." He adjusts in his chair so he can face me directly. Merle doesn't like to turn his head. "If we don't make enough with this show, the board is considering selling the theatre to a developer."

152

I lean back, so thrown off I'm glad I'm sitting. A developer means one thing: no more theatre. They'll tear it down and put in a parking lot or another Speedway or a cheap apartment complex. I swallow my frustration with Merle and realize the feeling in my throat is worse. If I don't get some immune support drugs in me soon, I won't have a voice by opening night. I say,

"Why didn't you tell me? I would have done something else, like *My Fair Lady* or *Scrooge*. Musicals are always better money-makers than straight plays."

Merle shrugs. "To be honest, I don't think it would have mattered. A few of the board members think upkeeping the place costs more money than it's worth."

"How could anyone think that?" I stand and stride up onto the stage. Raising my arms, I turn in a slow circle, studying my home away from home. "This can't possibly be anything but a theatre. And it should be treated as a vital part of the community."

With a sigh, I glance around, trying to imagine it gone. The Holland truly is an amazing, historic structure. To add to its charm, the theatre's massive, two-story walls are painted to look like a 17th-century Dutch cityscape. The buildings are mostly two-dimensional but dimly lit from within. Two large, moving windmills add just the right touch. When I glance up, a twinkling of stars wink back from the ceiling. The Holland Theatre is a one-of-a-kind piece of history that should not be torn down. Which is exactly what I tell Merle.

"I know," he says. "I have many fond memories of hanging out here with friends back in the 50s, watching William Holden and John Wayne fight the Nazis." He rubs the back of his neck and looks around the building, much like I had just done. "There's a lot of history here. Would be a shame to see it torn down."

"So? Can we do anything about it?"

"Like what?"

"I don't know, but we have to try." I pace in front of the stage. The lights in one of the fake Dutch buildings flicker and I wonder if Juniper agrees with me. "What about a fundraiser?"

"It's a great idea, Stephanie. But, to be honest, I think it's too late."

The whole thing is starting to chafe my hide a bit. "That's the plan, isn't it? Keep it on the down-low until it's too late for the community to do anything about it." I stop pacing, trying to ignore my now-sandpaper throat and the pure dread icing through my veins. I need to go home. I need a good night's sleep. I need the show to be so phenomenal this weekend that there will be a town-wide uprising at the thought of shutting the place down.

I need a miracle. But I don't believe in miracles.

Finally, I sit down and sigh. "This stinks."

Merle nods, his thick, white hair moving with the kind of sheen a runway model would envy. "There's a lot of history in this old girl. Juniper would be heartbroken at the thought. She used to sing here, you know."

No, I didn't know. "Really? You mean there actually was a Juniper connected to the Holland?"

"Oh, sure. Juniper Remington. I even heard her sing once. I was five and they had a talent show." He takes a deep breath. "She had the voice of an angel. Looked like one too."

"Wow. So … what happened to her?"

"Hmm." He closes his eyes, as if looking through a photo album of memories. "I don't rightly remember. I think she died young in some kind of accident. Although—"

Merle pauses and I lean toward him. "Although —?"

"Well, there were some who insisted she died of a broken heart. Others said she took her own life. But, as far as I could tell, it was never anything more than gossip. Everyone likes a tragedy."

"True, but it's still sad. I wonder what really happened to her."

"Disappointed in love, I imagine. That's usually the story."

"I suppose." Doesn't make it any less heartbreaking. "Poor Juniper. No wonder she can't let go."

Merle glances at me, concern etching his face, so I add, "No, I don't believe in ghosts. But sometimes you hear a story and you can—almost— understand why a soul would have trouble leaving such great sorrow behind."

"I suppose. Well, if you're really curious, you should ask Cora Wellesley-Jones. Her family and the Remingtons go way back. I imagine she knew Juniper's beau as well."

"The one who broke her heart?"

"Now, that I can't rightly tell you. But Cora could."

Of course, I don't have time to talk to Cora this week. Because not only do I get a nasty cold, I have to throw all my energy into the play and several projects clients keep pestering me to complete. In the rush of things, I forget all about Juniper and her sorrows.

I chew on vitamin supplements like they're M&Ms and run warm saline water through my sinuses several times a day. I drink warm lemon and honey tea and pray God will heal me before opening night. But even as I say the words, I doubt the probability. Colds typically hang onto me for weeks at a time, kind of like a hurtful comment.

The night before the show is to open I can't sleep or breathe, so I swallow cold pills and sleep aids and gulp down almost half a bottle of Nyquil. I know it's foolish but all I want is a good night's rest.

When a chilly November sun finally peers through the curtains and nudges me awake, I feel drained. With effort, I crawl out of bed and stumble into the shower, hoping some cool water will wake me up. Halfway through it, a wave of heat and exhaustion washes over me and I have to sit down or pass out. I huddle there, water raining over me until, slowly, a bit of strength returns. Finally, I'm able to step out of the shower and look in the mirror. My face is as white as the snow drifting past my bedroom window.

Apparently, the Holland won't need a ghost over the weekend. It will have me.

Not being the kind of person to ignore illness and hope it will go away, I get dressed, then hurry to my doctor's office for an antibiotic. Yes, it's unlikely they will take effect before the performance tonight but it's a step in the direction of better health. And surely I can fake it for four performances.

I have to. They're counting on me. I don't have a choice.

When I walk into the theatre just before our six o'clock call time that night, every pair of eyes takes on an expression of horror. Andy's the first to speak.

"What happened to you?"

I clear my throat, attempting to lessen the raspy quality of it. "I have a bit of a cold."

"A bit? You look like Typhoid Mary!"

"For your information, Typhoid Mary didn't have typhoid. She just carried the virus."

Andy grunts. He couldn't look more annoyed.

I continue, "So she was never actually sick."

He raises an eyebrow. I've never seen a condescending eyebrow before. Kids these days. Nobody cares about history anymore.

"Besides," I say, "it's not that bad." At least, that's what I try to say. The effort to speak causes me to collapse into a coughing fit that lasts a good minute. I pop in a heavy-duty zinc cough drop, then smile at my cast through watery eyes. "I'll be fine."

Andy moves a step closer, then rethinks it and backs up again. "Um, no. I don't think you will. You shouldn't do this."

I lift my hands. "I have to. It's opening night. We can't cancel the show because of a little cold." Attempting to throw a bit of lightheartedness on the situation, I add, "You know what they say: The show must go on. And it will."

After I take a few steps toward the stage, I turn back to my cast. "But if you're praying people, a few words on my behalf would be appreciated. And please take care of yourselves. One phlegm monster per show is plenty."

They laugh, and I get to work. So much to do to get everything ready and that doesn't include turning me into spinster Lizzie Curry. Fortunately, my friend Ginger is coming by to do my hair so I can save time by applying my makeup then.

But first, I need to find Trish and go over —

Andy taps me on the shoulder, then his hand slides down my arm. That gets my attention.

"Steph, I'm worried about you."

"I appreciate that, Andy, really I do." I put my hand on his arm. Wow. This real estate agent works out. Nice. I hide a sigh behind a breath. "I'll be fine."

"You say that, but I still want to help. So ..." He bends his head to gaze right into my eyes. His sparkle like frosty green Christmas lights. Mine probably look more like gray, drippy rain clouds.

But he smiles anyway and asks, "Do you trust me?"

"Trust you? Andy, I don't have time—"

"Just answer the question, Stephie. Do you trust me?"

"Well, yes." I look closer and see my answer reflected in his eyes. "Yes, I trust you."

"Then let me be your director tonight."

Wow. I wish he'd stop being so sweet. "Andy, I can't ask you to do that, you have enough to focus on. You know, playing the lead and all?"

"You're right. I'm onstage a lot." He shrugs. "But I'm a great delegator. I've been watching you keep this show running for eight weeks and I know what needs to be done. So does the rest of the crew, for that matter."

Yes, they could do it. But do I want them to?

"The only real question," Andy says, reading my mind again, "is can you relinquish control of your show?"

No, of course not. It's mine. My work and sweat and ideas. I sneeze and sway a bit, almost knocked over by a wave of dizziness.

He grips my arm to steady me. "Just let it go, Steph. It's all going to be just fine."

And a great sandbag of stress falls from my shoulders and lands with a thud behind me. Then I turn to see Ginger strolling down the right-side aisle toward us. "All right," I tell Andy. "I officially hand the reins to you."

He grins and moseys off. "You won't regret it," he calls over his shoulder.

I turn to Ginger. "I'm all yours, honey."

She shifts her equipment bag from one shoulder to the other and follows me down to "the green room." In reality, it's a damp, cold, creepy, cement-walled room at the bottom of a steep flight of stairs. I refuse to go down there alone but, at the moment, it contains the rest of the cast members, sans Andy. My fellow thespians joke around as they slap on suspenders and apply makeup.

I snatch up my personal makeup bag from the table where I left it earlier and take a seat in an old metal chair in front of a cheap, full-length mirror leaning against the wall. Ginger gets right to work, pulling and tugging and twisting my hair. Since it's barely chin-length, she'll have to add a fake hair piece. I've just started on my foundation when my friend says,

"So, who was that tall drink of water you were talking with?"

The chatter in the room immediately switches off while I turn several shades of red. I catch her eyes in the mirror and mouth, "Thanks a lot." She grimaces and whispers back, "Sorry."

I glance around the room and say, as breezily as possible, "That's Andy. He's the lead."

Ginger sighs. "I'll say."

Good grief. "How's your husband?" I stress the last word with as innocent a smile as I can muster.

She tugs at my hair and I catch her snarky grin in the mirror. "Jake is fine. I mean, it's football season so I never see him."

"Well, you did marry a coach."

She shrugs and the conversation lapses. I've only known Ginger since I started attending her church a few months ago and we aren't super close yet. Besides, she's married with a two-year-old boy who tears through her life like the Looney Tunes Tasmanian Devil. So I'm not entirely ready to tell her about my crush on my leading man—a crush that may or may not be reciprocated.

What is there to say? Besides, I need to save my throat as much as possible until performance time.

I remain glued to that chair long after Ginger has finished and left to find her husband and seats, where they can enjoy the show thanks to the comp tickets I gave her.

While I sit there, sucking on cough drops and zinc tablets and going over my lines in my head, I see Andy come down to the green room several times, asking the other actors to help with various tasks. He's right. He's a good delegator with natural leadership skills. Finally, thirty minutes before curtain, he stays long enough to apply makeup and finish getting into his costume.

Actually, he asks me to do his makeup. Of course I say yes. After I wash the germs off my hands with a wet wipe, I pick up the foundation. Leaning in close, I smooth a bit over his forehead and his cheeks and his bristly chin. He chews a piece of cinnamon gum and takes deep breaths. We don't talk. I'm not sure how he feels about it, but I've decided it's best not to blow my illness into his face.

Being so close feels so strange and, while applying foundation around his lips, I remember the kiss, and feel heat slide up my neck and into my face. I can't hide it. I can't leave. What can I do but hold my breath and press on? Some cheek rouge, face powder, and a bit of eyeliner and mascara, and I'm done. Except for a light, manly (or so I promise him) lip color, but I hand that over to Andy, perfectly confident he can handle it on his own.

This time, I don't blush.

He looks in the mirror as he takes care of his task. Then he steps back. "It looks good. From a distance, you can't even tell I have makeup on." He must have noticed the expression on my face because he laughs. "Yes, I know that's the whole idea. But when you don't normally wear the stuff, it can feel like you've been painted up like a clown."

I just grin.

Then he says, "I'm proud of you, Stephie. I know this is hard, especially the being quiet part."

You have no idea.

Trish comes down the stairs and shouts, "Five minutes, everyone! Five minutes!"

Andy takes my hand and pulls me to my feet. "You're going to be great."

I whisper, "So are you."

🦋 🦋 🦋

And I'm right. The show comes together like peppermint and hot chocolate. The crowd loves Andy and gives him a standing ovation. Even my cold stays out of the way. Well, for the most part.

Halfway through the play, after I exit following an intense scene, Kelvin forgets to turn off my mic right away and my coughing fit echoes across the stage and over the auditorium for a good five seconds. But, by the grace of God, I don't find out about that until the show is over.

As soon as we take our bows, I race down to the green room, slipping a bit on the cement stairs as I run, then change from costume to street clothes before the rest of the cast—who are still schmoozing the audience—can catch me *in flagrante delicto*. Since Andy has promised the cast and crew will take care of everything, all I want to do is get home and collapse onto my bed. I can't think of anything else, I'm that miserable.

158

It takes me less than fifteen minutes to go from theatre to apartment to bed.

I then proceed to sleep fourteen hours, waking up once for a bathroom visit and a couple of times to take an antibiotic and guzzle from a jug of water on my nightstand, trying to relieve my dry throat.

The blaring of a police siren as it streaks by my house, along with the purring of my cat right in my face, finally stir me awake. I stretch. I drink some more water and run a few vocal tests to see if I'm any better. The aches are gone. My throat still feels a bit scratchy and my sinuses are a little stuffed up. But, overall, I'm about seventy-five percent better. I pull Cozy close and say,

"So, what do you think, kitty? Can I handle another performance tonight?"

She purrs and meows and leaps to the floor, looking back at me with her, "Where's-my-lunch" face. I clear my throat. Definitely better. I flop back down on my bed, relieved, and proceed to sleep another hour … until a gnawing hunger pushes me toward the kitchen. A bowl of hot chicken noodle soup and a glass of orange juice later, and I know the worst is over.

What a relief.

Once I've taken care of Cozy, I head back to bed, this time setting my alarm for four p.m. That should give me plenty of time to shower and get to the theatre by five-fifteen.

Our second performance is even better — better audience, better timing, healthier director. It just clicks. The magic of theatre, once again, thrills and surprises me. The only time I stop smiling is when it doesn't suit the scene.

In fact, it's looking to be a near-perfect performance until we're smack dab in the middle of act two. I'm standing backstage when a horrendous crash mars what was the relative quiet of a normal scene. I freeze for a second, then dash for the side curtain. An old mirror hanging on the back wall of the set has dropped, shattering into a thousand pieces, and the shock of it sends a silent panic echoing through the auditorium.

No one moves, including this fearless director who finds herself completely clueless as to what to do about this disaster. But I'm certain I don't want my actors crunching over broken glass until the next intermission. I also don't want the audience over-distracted by something that's clearly not part of the show. Like it or not, I have to fix it. Handling unexpected stage bugaboos is part of my job.

Gritting my teeth, I glance around. "Juniper, that better not be you."

Kyle, who plays Lizzie's youngest brother, Jim, is standing next to me. He must have heard me muttering because he says, "What?"

I lean toward him and whisper, "Can you get a broom and dustpan and clean up that glass?"

He stares at me, his eyes wide. "Now?"

"Well, it's as good a time as any."

With an expression that lets me know he thinks I'm crazy, Kyle shrugs and says, "Okay."

But as he walks away, I add, "Just stay in character!"

He nods and does just as I ask.

It works out even better than I imagined, actually. The other actors onstage play along, adlibbing a side joke or two and looking very much like a roomful of men who don't know what to do about a mess when a woman isn't around. The audience laughs — partly out of relief, I'm sure — and a few people even applaud the improvisation.

After the show, while I'm taking down my hair, Andy approaches me with a grin. "Was that your idea?"

"What?"

"To have the guys sweep up the glass."

"Well, yeah. I couldn't just leave it there."

"I guess not." He studies me and I would give my last cream soda to know what he's thinking. "Pretty clever."

I continue pulling bobby pins out of my hair and flinch when I yank on one a little too hard. "You don't have to seem so surprised."

"I like it when you surprise me."

Then he walks away.

Just like that.

Men.

We breeze through Saturday's matinee without a hitch and barely have time to munch on chips and apples and sandwiches some friends of the theatre have brought for us before we're setting up for our final performance. I can't believe it's almost over. I savor every moment, knowing each show is a once-in-a-lifetime blessing. Sometime tomorrow afternoon, while enjoying the lifted weight of it being good and done, I will cry for thirty or forty or one-hundred-and-two minutes because it will have moved to nothing more than a happy blip on my memory meter in less than twenty-four hours.

At the beginning of act three, one of the few scenes when I'm not onstage, I have to, again, get from stage right to stage left. The best way to do that is to squeeze through a dark, narrow passageway behind a scrim and curtain at the very back of the stage. I usually try to take a small flashlight, but this time I forget. The journey requires slow, quiet steps and finesse if you don't want to trip on the many wires and cords and ropes criss-crossing the floor.

I'm halfway to the other side when a tall figure looms ahead of me. Even without his height I would have known it was Andy. Despite my slightly stuffed-up nose, I can easily discern the wonderfully clean scent of him.

We come face-to-face. I move left; he moves right. Then we both scoot the other way, a classic case of two people trying to coordinate their way around each other in the dark. Finally, Andy takes me by the shoulders and pushes me around him. We're so close, his body brushes against mine. I glance up and catch the glint of his eyes in the dark.

Then his hands tighten and he pulls me up and kisses me. This one is even more sudden … and so much longer. He tilts his head and deepens the kiss as I wrap my arms around his neck. I can barely breathe through my still-damaged sinuses, but I don't care. Emotions rattle through me like an old locomotive. I'm not sure how long it lasts, but it's long enough for my fingers to explore every bump and curve on the top of his head.

Finally, the realization that we have a scene coming up brings me to my senses, and I push him away. I gulp down pillows of air to still my racing heart. I can't very well go onstage flushed and wheezing.

Andy's hands slide all the way down my arms. A simple yet intoxicating caress. He squeezes my fingers and whispers, "Thanks."

With that, he turns and slips away, while I stare at his retreating back, dumbfounded.

Thanks? What in the name of Ding Dongs is he thanking me for? But I don't have time to wonder because, in the next instant, I hear my cue and realize I'm late. Sending a quick prayer that the other actors will cover for me, I hurry to the wing, stage left, from where I make my entrance.

And proceed to perform the scene with the sweaty awkwardness of a chubby kid in gym shorts, slowly stewing at kiss-'em-and-thank-'em Andy the whole time.

ꙨꙨꙨ

And, just like that, we're done. I haven't talked to Andy since the behind-the-curtain incident, not sure what to say. I still don't have a clue what he's thinking, so I suppose there's nothing to do but wait it out. Chances are good we'll say good-bye after the cast party and I won't see him again until next spring … *if* he auditions for the summer musical.

But before we can celebrate our success with pizza and fun moments and stories about all the things that could have gone wrong but, miraculously, didn't, we need to strike the set.

Men and women, including several who've volunteered to stay after the show and help, crowd the stage, pulling out nails and stacking scenery flats. My main job is to tell people who the various items belong to or show them where theatre-owned pieces need to go.

While going through the props with Trish, I see a well-dressed businessman greet Andy with a handshake. A platinum-blonde Jean Harlow wannabe, draped in red chiffon and white cashmere with ruby and gold jewelry cascading from her ears and throat, stands at the businessman's side, sliding her hand down Andy's arm and sizing him up like he's a French silk pie.

I don't like her.

When Andy glances my way and frowns, I like her even less. Our eyes meet, briefly, before he turns away. I huff a breath into my bangs, which don't budge thanks to layers of gel and hairspray. I'm sure I look lovely, with my dripping, stage-makeup raccoon eyes, after-performance jeans and T-shirt, and worked-over theatre hair. Right. I know without even glancing in the mirror that I'm wilting. Jean Harlow, on the other hand, seems more than ready for her close-up.

Yet even though I realize it will be like a sick duck approaching an elegant swan, I can't help myself. Until Andy tells me otherwise, I choose to believe there's a chance for us. I sneeze three times on the way over, which I'm sure does wonderful things for my nose and eyes, but I don't care. If Andy prefers someone like her then he doesn't want someone like me.

Still, I strut over there like I just stepped out of a fashion magazine. Let them scoff at my —

And I trip over a bump in the floor, catching myself before I sprawl across the stage by doing a sloppy two-step with a skip and a jump. Then I grin, sneeze once more, and say,

"Did you get all your costume pieces from the green room yet, Andy?"

Brilliant, Stephie. The blonde smirks at me with all the confidence of a woman who has never had a rival in her life. But then I notice the smile on Andy's face.

Unless I'm completely mistaken—always a possibility—he might actually like me. His eyes dart to my lips for a tap of a second, and heat crawls up my neck. Jean Harlow's face tightens slightly as she glances between us.

Let her wonder.

"Not yet," Andy says, then frowns again, clears his throat, and indicates the businessman. "Stephie Graham, this is Pat Hansen. We, uh, work together. And his date, Jessica Withers."

Jessica. Joan. Jean. Whatever. I shake their hands. Their cold, better-than-me hands.

Hansen laughs. "Don't be so modest, Andrew." Then Mr. Business slaps a hand on Andy's back and turns to me. "This young man is going to help me buy this place."

"Buy this place?" I look at Andy. "Are you kidding me?"

His spreads his hands wide, trying to look innocent. "Stephie, it's just—"

"I couldn't be less interested in your excuses." Surprise fills his eyes and I add, "Apparently, you're an even better actor than I thought."

He grabs my arm but I jerk away and race toward the backstage area. Without giving it much thought, I take the stairs toward the green room at a run, realizing too late I'll be trapped down there if Andy comes after me.

As if he would.

But my foot hits the top step on a skid before I have time to change my mind and the next thing I know I'm flying, horizontal, and heading straight toward the unforgiving cement floor below.

10
Juniper

She stood behind the curtain, stage right, biting her lip as she waited for Mr. Van Meer to invite her onstage to take her bows ... and to accept the large bouquet of red roses he held in his arms. But the distinguished gentleman was feeling especially verbose this night. Juniper wasn't sure what he was talking about, but she did know he'd mentioned "during this festive season" at least a handful of times.

Not that she minded. In fact, she appreciated the time to decide what she should say to the audience. It was one thing to sing in front of hundreds of people; it was quite another to stand before them and try to find her own words—the right words—to express how she felt.

The next moment, though, Mr. Van Meer swung his arm her way and called her name and decision time was ended. So she smiled as she swept onto the stage, surprised and humbled to see the crowd surge to their feet once more. Mr. Van Meer handed her the bouquet. She thanked him, then turned to the audience.

The stage lights blared into her eyes, blinding her until they dimmed and the house lights came up. She smiled at the faces she recognized—her mother and father, several women from the Ladies' Aid Society, the Wellesleys.

And William. Her heart studded against her ribs. He stood in the front row, clapping, his face passive and proud. Juniper gulped down her shock, and curtsied, to him more than anyone else. She smiled, murmured a thank you, then froze as a stunning woman with jet black hair looped her hand around Will's arm. The ring on her left hand shimmered in the light.

Juniper felt the color drain from her face. She took one final bow and hurried to the relative sanctuary behind the heavy stage curtain. Her heart trembled.

Could it be possible? Had he really found someone else so quickly? Someone … permanent? Vaguely aware of the audience milling around the auditorium and the prick of rose thorns in her arms, Juniper wondered if she'd ever felt so lost.

He didn't want her. It was over. The words "spinster" and "brokenhearted" thudded through her brain.

"Juniper! Juniper, look who's here!"

Her mother. Her sweet, clueless mother. Now what?

I have to get away. The light to the basement dressing room beckoned to her, and she started for the stairs. But a movement toward the stage grabbed her attention. Peter Billings stood near the curtain, caught in the glow of what few lights still lit the theatre. He wore a new, blue, double-breasted suit and he looked handsome, grown-up. Determined. Even with the flop of hair across his forehead, something was different. Juniper glanced back at the stairs, wondering if she should run *away* from whatever beckoned to her in his eyes … or *to* it.

Her mother's words from September come back to her:
You're only a victim if you make yourself one.

Peter took a step closer. She whispered the name her heart ached for.

It wasn't *William*. The thought frightened her more than she had ever expected. She turned … and rushed for the stairs.

11
Stephie

I stand at the bottom of the stairs, stunned. What just happened? Did I fall? I was falling; I'm sure of it. The next thing I knew I … wasn't. Andy yells my name and I glance up.

He hurries toward me. "Are you okay?"

"Uh, yeah. Why wouldn't I be?"

"You screamed."

"I did?"

"Yeah." He studies me, head to foot and back. "A blood-curdling scream. Like someone just stabbed you in the stomach."

"Oh. I don't remember that."

I glance around. Seriously, what just happened? "I slipped on the stairs and fell. Or I didn't. I don't know."

"You seem fine."

"I feel fine."

"Though, you *are* trembling."

He's right. My hands are shaking more than they do when I drink too much caffeine.

Andy smiles and shakes his head. "I guess you have an angel watching over you."

Do I really? I've always felt so alone. It would be nice to have real, physical evidence that I'm not. Except I don't have physical evidence. Just a weird case of a few seconds of my life that have disappeared without explanation. Seconds that might mean everything.

Or nothing. Except, perhaps, I'm losing my mind.

And yet … something on Andy's face tells me I'm going to be just fine. He grins again, looking all hopeful and cute, like the hero in a Hallmark Christmas movie. And I want him to kiss me already, until I remember he plans to cash in on my theatre.

So, instead of putting my hand on his and smiling back, I say, "Why would you do this?"

The smile fades. "It's not what you think, Stephie."

"It's not? Because it would seem you want to make money on seeing the Holland turned into a parking lot. Or a Dollar General."

He grabs me by the shoulders and—I'm not kidding—shakes me like a broken gumball dispenser. "Honey, you have got to stop jumping to conclusions or you're gonna hurt yourself."

There he goes again, trying to make me fall in love with him. Forget tumbling down a flight of stairs; this is a fall I might never recover from. So I back away. "Explain then. You don't have to rattle my teeth loose."

"Yes, Hansen and a group of investors want to buy the Holland …" He holds up a hand to halt my interruption. "But not to tear it down. They want to restore it. Bring it back to its original glory."

Oh, poo. "Really?"

"I swear. I love this old theatre. I want to be in more shows." Then he flicks his eyebrows at me. "But only if you're the director, of course."

Now I can smile. "Of course."

Two hours later, with the set cleared, the pizza gone, and most of the cast and crew having hugged their good-byes before heading home, Merle and I still sit slouched in theatre seats, sipping on sodas and talking about what went right and what we need to do different next time.

"Overall," he says, "it was a fair success."

"I agree."

"And you were an excellent Lizzie."

Sweet man. "Thanks, Merle."

I glance around the darkened theatre. "Other than the mirror, we didn't have any serious problems during the performances. Maybe Juniper approved after all."

"Maybe."

"Shoot. I still haven't had a chance to talk to Cora. Hopefully, I can visit her next week."

"Coraletta Jones?"

"Yeah." Why does he sound so confused? "You said she could tell me about Juniper."

"Oh, right." He rakes a hand over his hair, his eyes apologetic. "Well, not anymore. She had a stroke last week. Coraletta's not talking to anyone. Besides, she's in her nineties. I'm not sure how much she'd remember anyway."

Too late. Sadness for Coraletta and sadness because of the story she can't tell me now makes me want to cry. I don't, but I want to. "I'm so sorry to hear that."

"I'm sorry too, Stephanie."

"Even just knowing what Juniper looked like would be nice."

He shifts in his seat. "Oh, well, there's a picture of her in the back." Merle stands, a little more slowly than usual. "Come on, then. I'll show you."

Andy appears out of the backstage area. I hadn't realized he was still around and, for a moment, wonder what he's been up to. I say, "Merle's going to show me a photo of Juniper if you're interested."

His eyes widen, sending twinkling green sparks my way. "Try and stop me."

We follow Merle to a tall, old filing cabinet in the back. After rustling through a few drawers, he finally pulls out a framed photo and hands it to me.

Of course it's old and in black and white but the picture shows two rows of women; some smiling, some not. Merle points to the saddest one in the group.

She's beautiful, with deep, wide eyes and smooth hair that sweeps across her forehead in a thick wave. Her dress is sleek and satin and she has on white, elbow-length gloves. Her hands are folded serenely in front of her.

Andy says, "She's pretty, but she's not happy."

Merle nods and clears his throat. "Well, I'm beat. Can you two lock up if I head home?"

"Sure we can." I put a hand on his arm. "Thanks for all your help, Merle."

"Any time."

He shuffles away. Andy and I just stand there, brooding. Well, I am, anyway. Poor, sad Juniper. Would my story have an ending just as depressing? I glance up at the man next to me. No reason to think it won't.

"Thanks for staying," I say as we switch off the lights.

"Sure."

Various other topics scroll through my brain and I finally land on one. "What are your Thanksgiving plans?"

"Oh, you know. Family stuff."

The only brilliant thing I can think to say to that is, "Oh, nice."

We head back to the auditorium, and I load up my arms with bags of costumes and scripts and whatever else I need to take home. Without my having to say anything, Andy picks up the empty pizza boxes and a large garbage bag stuffed with trash and follows me out the side entrance.

"So," he says, "how will you spend the holiday?"

"A family from church invited me over."

"That's cool."

"Yeah, it's nice. I have a standing invitation with them for any holiday when I don't have somewhere to go."

He drops the garbage in a dumpster. "Is it hard?"

"What?"

"Not having a family."

"Well, no. I mean, it's just the way it is." Not that I haven't fantasized as to what it would be like to be part of a family. But dreams are cheap and only hurt for a moment. Then I move on.

I always move on.

He says, "I really enjoyed working with you, Stephie."

I smile. The end is near. "Me too. I hope you'll participate in future productions. The summer musical is always a lot of fun."

"Yeah, I'm planning on it."

He walks me to my car, slow, hesitant. "So, I'll call you. We'll get together."

"That sounds great."

He just stands there for a month of moments, staring at me, and I wonder what he's mulling over. But whatever he wanted to say comes out as, "Well, I'll see ya."

Then I watch him mosey out of my life, much like he moseyed into it two months before.

He doesn't call.

A month later, I shuffle around my cold apartment, setting a different kind of stage. A Christmas-y one.

To save money, I've put the thermostat at a crisp sixty-four degrees, and compensate for the chill by layering on an aqua turtleneck, a cream sweater, and a deep blue-and-cream-striped hoodie, completing the look by draping a purple Sherpa throw across my shoulders. The calendar declares it's Christmas Eve, and I've decided to celebrate by roasting a small turkey breast with all the trimmings. I'll have enough leftovers to last me until the New Year.

I turn on the twinkle lights on my plastic, three-foot Christmas tree as well as the strands draped around the room and across the useless but homey white-brick fireplace.

Happiness is all about the mood lighting.

After firing up an evergreen-scented candle, because that's part of my happy place too, and sticking my copy of *Chitty Chitty Bang Bang* in the DVD player, I settle on the couch with Cozy on my lap. Not having a family of my own, I've created my own traditions, and a little Dick Van Dyke zipping around in a flying car is a big part of that.

Right in the middle of "Toot Sweets," the doorbell rings. My heart jumps because no one ever comes to visit. And who would show up after five p.m. on Christmas Eve?

I pause the movie, then tiptoe over to the door. Peering through the peephole, I almost drop to the floor. But I don't. Instead, I glance in the coat rack mirror to make sure I look presentable, and quietly thank God for nudging me to take a shower earlier. No makeup but clean hair. I open the door.

Andy stands there, smiling, with his hands behind his back. "Hey. Merry Christmas."

"Merry Christmas." He looks great. Cold and scruffy and huggable. In two seconds I've managed to push the fact that I haven't heard from him for over a month to the back of my brain, I'm that happy to see him.

So I step aside and swing my hand to indicate the living room. "Come on in."

And he does. He glances around, taking in my sparse but snug furnishings and the strings of Christmas lights. "Smells good in here."

"Thanks. I'm making a turkey."

He steps back, suddenly flustered. "Oh, sorry. I didn't know you were expecting company."

"I'm not. Can't a single gal make a Christmas bird?"

"Sure." He grins again. Then we just stand there, happy to be together. Well, I am, anyway. And he certainly seems happy.

"So," Andy says, "I was doing a little research on the Holland and found something I thought might interest you." He hands me a piece of paper.

It's a copy of a *Bellefontaine Examiner* article from September 1948. The headline reads "Local Singing Star Returns Home for Benefit." And there's a picture of a beautiful woman with the name "Juniper Remington-Billings" printed underneath.

I murmur, "You found her."

"Yes, I did."

I glance up, smiling. "I guess she didn't die."

"Nope. Well, eventually, but not until years later, when she was in her eighties, according to the records I found."

"Which means the Holland doesn't have a ghost. At least, not a brokenhearted one." Though I never really believed the theatre was haunted, I'm still a little surprised by my disappointment. I hold up the article. "Where did you get this?"

"It took a little digging." He tilts his head, his eyes blazing into mine. "But it was worth it."

Oh. "You did this for me?" I seem to be having trouble speaking louder than a whisper.

He takes my hand. The Sherpa throw slides to the floor. "I missed you, Stephie. I'm sorry I didn't call."

"It's a busy time of year." Not that I consider that an excuse but I'm just so glad to see him I really don't care. "Still, why did you come by tonight? On Christmas Eve?"

"Oh, well, long story." He points to the couch and I nod. He takes a seat; I pick up Cozy and drop down next to him. "I was at my sister's, eating caramel corn and watching the kids beg to open presents and—" He glances toward the TV. "Is that *Chitty Chitty Bang Bang*?"

I follow his gaze. I'd paused the DVD right in the middle of an impressive kick line by the dancers. "Um, yeah."

"Love that movie."

"You do?"

"I always wanted to be an inventor like Caractacus Potts when I was a kid."

Cute. He stares at the screen for a second and I come this close to asking if he wants to watch the movie with me. Instead I say,

"Andy, why are you here?"

"Oh, right." He takes a deep breath, facing me again. "Brenda made me come over."

Well, that's flattering. "She did? Why?"

He scrunches up his nose and scratches his chin. "Her exact words were, 'Stop moping around and go get your woman.'"

"She said that?"

"Yep."

I remind myself to breathe and whisper, "Is it true?"

He puts his hand along the side of my face, brushing my hair back by drawing a line from my forehead to my neck with his fingertips. "Yes." Then his lips follow the same line his fingers had.

And now I might never breathe normally again.

"I really like you, Stephie. If how much I've missed you this last month is any indication, it's a bit more than 'like.'" He leans back, and I miss his warmth. Then he says,

"I want you to come home with me."

Home.

I say, "Okay," and hear a bell ding, like I just answered a question right on a quiz show. I pull back, confused. Then,

"Oh, the turkey's done."

He laughs and I laugh. Something needs to be done about it, but I'm fuzzy as to what that might be.

Then he says, "Well, are you going to get it?"

"Get it? Oh, right." Skipping into the kitchen, I pull out the turkey. It looks good—golden and juicy. Definitely edible. If the man of my dreams wasn't sitting on my couch, I'd be nibbling on it already. Instead, I set it on the counter and turn off the oven, then skitter back to Andy and plop down next to him. I say,

"So, you really do like me."

"Yeah, I guess I do."

I shake my head. "Why?" Because it can't possibly be true.

"Why?" He looks at the ceiling, like he has to think about it. I almost hit him. He chuckles and says, "Maybe it's because you're so clever." And he kisses my forehead.

"Well, I can't deny that."

"Or it's your sense of humor." This kiss lands on my nose. "Or because you're so talented." His lips slide across my cheek. "And sweet."

Okay, that's enough of that. I put both hands on either side of his face and kiss him. But only for a second, because he pulls away.

"Wait a minute … why do you like me?"

I shrug. "Honestly, I wouldn't know where to start."

"Well, at least try."

"All right." I tilt my head, just like he always does. "You're very nice-looking. And strong. And you have good teeth."

He rolls his eyes. "I'm not a horse, Stephie."

I giggle. "Fair enough. I guess … it's mostly … I mean the main reason—"

"Spit it out, hon."

"Fine. You make me feel … safe." Then, praying it isn't too soon, I add, "Like I'm part of something."

"Something?"

"Yes."

"Like a family?"

Biting my thumbnail, I give my attention to everything but him. "Maybe."

"It's okay."

I look into his eyes. Those warm, Christmas-green eyes. "Really? It's not too weird?"

He smiles. "If that's weird, we're all weird."

So I grab him by his wonderfully bald head once again and make out with my weird, mosey-through-life, realtor boyfriend. Until he pushes me away and clears his throat and invites me to his sister's for Christmas dinner. Because, well, that's just the kind of man he is.

That night, I dream about Juniper. She looks like she did in the picture I saw at the Holland Theatre — young and beautiful and sad. Then, like a spark landing on dry twigs, she alights with a smile and skips away, daring me to follow. She leads me to a sun-draped field where flowers droop in the browns and tears of fall. A boy waits for her there — cute but strong with shaggy hair and grown-up eyes. Juniper jumps into his arms; they laugh and kiss and fade into the trees and sky. Then I wake up.

My mouth and throat are desert-dry but waves of happy endings wash over me. Maybe Juniper's life wasn't so sad.

Maybe we both have a story to tell.

Early-morning sunlight glistens off snow-covered trees and filters through my curtains, calling me to the day. I slide out of bed, smiling.

Today, for the first time in years, I won't spend Christmas on my own but with Andy and his family.

Maybe, someday soon, *my* family.

I need to get ready.

Theatre Terms

Acts – a division of a script, usually made up of *scenes*. Intermissions are often taken between acts.

Blocking – stage movements and positions worked out by the director so actors know where they have to be without bumping into each other.

Cold Read – reading aloud/performing a script without prior preparation, usually for an audition.

Cues – a prearranged line or action that indicates to actors, crew members, or stage technicians what the next line or action is.

Flat – a *flat* piece of scenery usually consisting of a wooden frame covered with stretched fabric or lauan, a thin plywood with a smooth surface that's easy to paint.

Read-through – a first rehearsal of a play during which the actors read their lines from scripts.

Scenes – shorter sections that make up the play's *acts*.

Scrim – a plain or painted gauzy curtain that can be opaque or translucent, depending on the lighting.

Sides – a few pages containing a specific set of lines handed out at an audition.

Strike the Set – the process of disassembling a set once a production has ended.

Tech Week – the last week of rehearsals before a performance during which all of the technical elements are present for the first time.

Wings – the backstage areas on each side of the stage, which the audience typically can't see.

Sharyn Kopf didn't find her voice until she found a way to turn grief into hope. For her, that meant realizing it was okay to be sad about her singleness. In doing so, she was finally able to move past her grief and find hope in God.

It also meant writing about the heartaches and hopes in being an older single woman. She published her first novel, *Spinstered*, in 2014, and a companion nonfiction version titled *Spinstered: Surviving Singleness After 40* in 2015. The sequel to the novel, *Inconceived*, released in September 2016 and, one year later, she finished the series with *Altared*. Her current project is a novel about a lonely girl with a knack for matchmaking.

Besides writing and speaking, Sharyn is a freelance ghostwriter, editor and marketing professional. In her spare time, she enjoys goofing off with her nieces and nephews, making—and eating!—the best fudge ever, long walks on the beach or through the woods, and playing the piano.

DEBT TO PAY

By JPC Allen

A stick snapped. I jumped, like I was six instead of sixteen. And I was the one who had stepped on it.

What was the matter with me? Tightening my grip on the chainsaw, I glanced around the twilight woods of the Wayne National Forest. Nothing had spooked me when we walked through here two hours ago. Soaked in November sunshine, the bare trees and bright cover of fallen leaves had seemed cheerful, friendly. But now … I flipped up the collar of my jeans jacket. With the sunset just a bloody cut on the horizon, the woods wore the growing shadows like a Halloween costume. A creepy Halloween costume.

"C'mon." My brother David dropped the handle of a wagon loaded with split logs and turned to me. "No matter when we get home, you still gotta finish your geometry."

He almost blended with the skinny trunks of the oaks and maples, except for the bill of his Cincinnati Reds baseball cap sticking out.

"You're only twenty-two," I switched the chainsaw to my less sore hand, "and you're way bossier than Grandma ever was, and she was sixty-six when she died."

"Sixty-seven. Maybe I'm bossier because you don't mind me like you did her."

There was more truth to that than I was going to admit. I squinted at the sunset bleeding over the edge of the hills. Almost two years now, since she'd passed away.

"Come on." David spun back around, grabbed the handle, and marched even faster, the soaked leaves squishing under his beat-up boots and the rickety wagon wheels. "We ain't eatin' until we stack —"

A moan rose out of the dark.

I dropped the chainsaw. Where'd it come from? No animal could make a sound like that. That was all these spooky woods needed.

"Knock it off, Jay."

"It – it ain't me." I took a couple steps in the direction of the moan, then stopped. Did I want to find the source?

Another moan, ending in a gurgling cough. Goosebumps sprouted like well-watered melons.

"It's comin' from over there." David took off, dodging through the trees.

I picked up the chainsaw and holding it with both hands in front of me, trailed behind.

A breeze caught at the bare branches, black fingers scratching at the darkening sky. Their creaking was the only sound accompanying our squishy footsteps.

More moans, crawling over the dead leaves. David's speeding shadow passed through still ones. My muscles wound tighter.

"Over here! By the crick!"

Peering through the gloom, I spotted the outline of my brother kneeling beside a lump at the bottom of a steep slope, where the creek skirted it.

"It's okay." David rested a hand on the lump as I dropped down beside him.

A tall man, even taller than David, lay half in the creek. The dying light didn't reveal much, but his right leg was wrapped in some kind of homemade splint.

"Help … me!" The words fought through a cough that contracted his body. "I can pay you anything – anything!"

Setting down the chainsaw, I scanned his head. Guy must have had a concussion to say a weird thing like that. Or maybe a fever.

"Thanks for the offer." David shrugged out his jacket and spread it over the man. "But we're the good Samaritan types. We'll help you for free. Don't guarantee our work, though. Jay, sit down."

I did what I was told, my jeans soaking up the water from the soggy ground as soon as they touched.

David lifted the man by his shoulders and laid him in my lap.

"I'll run home and make a stretcher. We'll carry him back home, then I can drive to where I can get reception and call 911."

"No." The man grabbed David's arm with a blood-covered hand.

Jumping, I tried to scoot out from under him.

"Jay! Be careful!"

I couldn't help it. It was like a zombie reaching up from his grave.

The man raised his head, streaked with blood, into a beam of red sunlight. Deep-set dark eyes pleaded from a face with a high forehead and a jaw carved from a cinder block.

"It's him!" I shouted loud enough to knock off the few remaining leaves on the oak towering above us. "It's – it's that millionaire-zillionaire guy who crashed his plane! Adam Everett!"

"But they found the wreck six, seven miles from here." David patted the man on the arm. "That's some hike, buddy. But don't worry. You're safe now. We'll call --"

174

"NO!" With a haunted-house groan, Mr. Everett pushed himself up on his elbows. "No paramedics. No … police. Somebody tampered with my plane." He fell back onto my lap.

A gust of wind pushed against us as my eyebrows took a hike up my forehead, and my brother's mouth fell open.

David said, "You mean somebody tried to kill you?"

Mr. Adam Everett nodded. "I don't know who. I can't let them … try … again." He broke off for a spasm of coughing.

"But, sir," David said, "if you're hurt bad, and we don't take you to a hospital, you could die."

Mr. Everett gulped. "I know. But I can't lay in a hospital bed, wondering, waiting …" His eyes flew open, and he clutched at my brother's arm, pulling himself up. "I promise I'll make it worth your while. Name your price. Help me!"

ᘐ ᘐ ᘐ

The advantage of a long, unpaved drive was that we could hear anybody coming up to our house long before they came into view. When the tires first ground into the gravel, I ducked under the beams of the crawl space and waddled to the small hole cut in the ceiling over the kitchen table. I placed the old camcorder's lens on the hole and peered through the viewfinder.

Our combined living room-kitchen-dining room was wrapped in shadows, the only light coming from the fire snapping in the fireplace and a small lamp glowing by the front door.

Standing by the kitchen table, David stared directly at the hole, giving me thumbs up.

I thumped my foot to signal I was ready. He nodded, and then bouncing on the balls of his feet, walked out of my view. The front door creaked open.

He was so psyched for this. In the three weeks since we'd found millionaire-extraordinaire Adam Everett and worked on this scheme, David had never had a single doubt we could pull this off.

Me? I blew out my cheeks and repositioned the camcorder over the peep hole. A thousand and one things could go wrong. But if we were going to play the good Samaritans, we had to do it even if it got dangerous.

The engine quit, and a door slammed.

Our front door creaked again, and David said, "Come on in."

My brother walked back into sight, stopping at the table with a man not much older than he was. Throwing light upwards, the lamp by the door gave David and the stranger a secretive look, like they were about to unfold a map and plot to blow something up.

The man brushed snow off his coat, sweeping the room with light-colored eyes. "Nice shack. Decorate it from garage sales? Or are you just squatting here?"

"It was our grandma's." David held out a mug. "Coffee?"

"I don't drink with blackmailers."

After his visit to the airport, David had told me the guy was smooth, and there was no better description. Smooth, pale face, smoothed down blond hair, smooth leather jacket. Even his jeans appeared smooth, as if he wore them for style instead of work.

Lowering himself into a cracked chair, David said, "I never said anything about blackmail, Mr. Conley, when I came to see you."

"Let's get to the point." Conley slapped his gloves in his hands. "I'm not one of your druggie, redneck friends. I can read you like a headline. You know I was the mechanic who worked on Everett's plane just before he took off. You claim you've got proof I tampered with it so it would crash. And you wanted me to come here and talk it over. That's blackmail."

"I haven't said anything about money."

Conley smirked. "You will." He loomed over my brother. "Where's your proof?"

Footsteps. I swiveled my head to pinpoint the noise. Behind me, at the back of the house. Only about an inch of snow, but that still should have muffled a person's steps pretty well. Whoever was out there had no idea how to sneak in snow.

A smile pushed back my cheeks. Our bait had lured in the big fish.

"Here." David unfolded a sheet of paper lying on the faded tablecloth. "Ever hear of a death-bed statement?"

Conley snatched the paper from David's hand.

The person in the snow stopped.

"My brother and me found Mr. Everett after he drug himself seven miles from his plane." David poured coffee into a mug. "With a broken leg, that took a long time, long enough for him to figure out that only you could have drained half his gas from his tank and then monkeyed with the gauge so it read full."

Hurling the paper away, Conley said, "The handwriting is terrible. Not even an expert could confirm Everett wrote it."

There. The person was on the move again, slow but shuffling loud enough for even David, occupied as he was, to hear.

"We can let the cops decide." David scratched at his sparse, blond beard. "I believe a death-bed statement carries a lot of weight with cops."

"Oh, I didn't realize you'd been to law school." His fake respect slid under my skin and stung. "Or did you learn this from your court-appointed attorney?" He planted both hands on the table. "You picked the wrong guy to blackmail. I'm only a mechanic and sometime pilot."

"Oh, I know you don't have much money." David grinned up at him. "But whoever hired you does."

The fire crackled, making the shadows waver. Mr. Smooth straightened and glanced at the front door.

Leaning back, my brother said, "I know the person who bought you off is here. I don't reckon you kept my visit to the airport to yourself. And I don't reckon your boss wanted you to come here alone."

Twisting his black gloves, Conley frowned at my brother, then at the door.

"And," David took a long sip from his cup, "somebody's trompin' around outside. I need to talk to whoever's responsible for the crash."

The front door flew open, cracking against the hooks on the wall behind it.

My whole body started, kicking the boards under my legs. Tightening up, I put my eye back to the viewfinder, and the air died in my lungs.

Conley, gun in hand, was watching the ceiling, not even glancing at the fashion model who stalked over to the table.

"I heard something." He pointed with his gun. "Up there."

Idiot, idiot, idiot. How could I have been so surprised when I had heard someone prowling around outside? And Fashion Model—we'd expected a mastermind, but not her.

"Probably raccoons." My brother hadn't even jostled his coffee. "You know how us rednecks are." With all the speed of me pulling out my geometry homework, he began to rise from his chair.

Fashion Model waved a shiny gun that looked like she had picked it as an accessory for her black boots and knee-length coat. "Sit down."

"My grandma taught me," David finished standing, "to get off my backside when a lady enters the room."

"How eighteenth century." She flipped long, red hair over her shoulder. "I don't hear anything, Ryan."

"What do we do?" Conley's eyes shifted from the woman to the ceiling and back again.

In and out of my view, the woman click-clacked around the room on her skinny heels. "What's his proof?"

Pointing to the sheet on the table, David said, "It's all there, Mrs. Everett." He took two steps, putting him almost under my spy hole, blocking Mr. Smooth's searching gaze.

She snatched up the paper, read it, and stuffed it into a huge pocket of her coat. A smile curved her dark lips, and it chilled me more than seeing the guns. "Adam doesn't name me in this. Only Ryan."

"He didn't know. Never suspected." David centered himself beneath me. "He just knew Mr. Conley had no reason to kill him on his own. So he must have been paid to do it."

"And you two good Samaritans decided to cash in, rather than go to the police. That decision is going to cost you more than you — Ryan, there's nobody here." Her voice was as sharp as the diamonds glittering in her rings and bracelet.

Conley was staring up again.

Every muscle tightened to snapping point as I scrunched over the camcorder.

"I watched that boy leave almost an hour ago," she said. "And I've walked all around the house. There's nobody here."

So she had cased our place. I let out a long, quivering breath, almost grinning. But she hadn't seen me slip back in.

"I could see if there's an attic," Conley said. "Something made a noise. I know it."

Mrs. Everett shrugged her thin shoulders. "Go ahead. We're going to have to kill time until the brother gets back." She turned to David. "But first, where'd you bury the body? I don't want somebody stumbling over it."

As Conley walked past him, David said, "I didn't."

"What?" Mr. Smooth whipped around, like he was afraid he'd step on it.

David shook his head. "You people hear only what you believe. I say I know something about Mr. Everett's crash, and you think 'blackmail,' I say death-bed statement, and you think 'body.'"

Except for extending her gun hand, Mrs. Everett stood as still as ice. "What do you mean?"

"He means," said a voice, rasping like a crow's, "I was on my death bed, but I got off it."

Out of David's bedroom, Mr. Adam Everett limped in on a homemade crutch, holding my .22 rifle, a few feet from David. "And I'm the one you heard, Conley. I don't move so gracefully on a broken leg."

Conley screamed, almost dropping his gun, but Mrs. Everett only stuttered back a few steps.

Not good, not good. Because of my dumb reaction, David and Mr. Everett were in a stand-off, instead of in control.

"Why, Natalie?" Mr. Everett sagged against the door frame. "Of all the people I could think of, I never thought of you. Even when David suggested it, I dismissed it. Why?"

The diamond-edged voice spoke. "Why be married to an ATM when

178

you can own one?"

Mr. Everett slid a few inches down the frame, but the .22 stayed level.

"Ryan, stop breaking your neck and cover them." Still holding her gun, Mrs. Everett wiggled off every ring and unclasped her bracelet. Dumping them on the table, she aimed her emerald eyes at David. "I'll give you all of these and double anything Adam's paid you, if you help us kill him."

Since I was flat on my belly, my jaw could fall only a few inches, instead of to my feet.

David pulled back, drawing closer to Mr. Everett.

And Mr. Everett laughed. Not a good-natured laugh, but the laugh of someone so worn out that he finds the weirdest things funny.

"You couldn't pick a worse person to bribe, Natalie." Mr. Everett held his chest with his free hand. "Double what I've paid them? I haven't had a dime since I crawled out of that wreck. You know how I hate to drive with things in my pockets. I left my wallet and phone on the passenger seat."

He gasped. "I've promised them all kinds of payment. And they have very politely turned me down every time. Being a well-mannered kid, he'll turn you down the same way."

His laugh reached a scary, high note, and I winced.

"You've made nothing for all your trouble?" Mrs. Everett waved her gun above the jewelry. "This is yours for the taking. Right here, right now. That's a lot better than any promises."

Mr. Everett's laugh died away, and his rifle barrel swung toward David, covering my brother as well as Fashion Model and Mr. Smooth.

"No," I mouthed.

My brother swiveled his head to face him. "Are you worried, Mr. Everett?"

He shouldn't be. And he should know that. When you are with someone almost continuously for three weeks, with only the radio and some downloaded game apps for entertainment, you get to know each other real well.

Fashion Model leaned over the table. "You've never had money. You don't know what it can do for you."

David's gaze never moved from Mr. Everett. "Are you, sir?"

The rifle still held David and the other two in its range.

I had to get down there. David was the only person who didn't have a gun, and if Mr. Everett was turning paranoid, David would need me.

But I'd have to leave the camera, leave my only line of sight. I slid my feet under me, inch by inch, still bent over the view finder.

The four people below me stood so still I wasn't sure anyone was breathing. A log split and dropped lower on the grate in the fireplace.

Setting his jaw, Mr. Everett shifted the barrel away from my brother. "No. I'm not worried."

A long stream of air escaped my lips. I hadn't been breathing, either.

"Good. Because my feelings would have been fatally wounded if you were." David's voice held a smile as he turned to Fashion Model. "Ma'am, you're right on the first part—I've never had much money. But I do know what it can do for me—get me smashed into a hillside or caught in a stand-off with my wife. Thanks anyway, but I'll stick to being a dirt-poor redneck."

He coughed, loud and long. "Sorry. I need a drink."

My cue to leave and call the cops. But with Conley suspicious I couldn't leave fast. I straightened my back and lifted the camcorder from the hole in the ceiling.

Mrs. Everett: "We're not going to—where did the boy go?"

Mr. Everett: "To get the police. They'll be here—"

Mr. Smooth: "There's a hole! By the light fixture!"

A bullet jetted up where the camcorder, and my face, had been.

A crash like a herd of moose charging through the front door exploded beneath my feet.

This was my fault, my fault. Clutching the camcorder, I duck-ran to the back of the house under the ridge of the roof, kicked in the trap door, and dropped into the bathroom. I skittered down the ladder we had set up, scraping my tail-bone on the rungs, and hit the tile floor with a thud.

More thuds came from outside the closed door, shots punctuating between them.

I crawled to the door. Forget running down the road to call the cops. I had to fix my mess. The fight sounded like it was to the right of the bathroom door, in front of the bedroom where Mr. Everett was standing. If I came out of the bathroom fast enough, I might be able to surprise Fashion Model or Mr. Smooth.

Two bullets exploded through the door, slamming into the wall under the window.

Okay, that way was blocked. And I needed a gun. I darted back to the window, hand on the sill, and waited for more shots. Three deep breaths, and I had to go. I shoved up the window and threw myself out.

Falling on my gut, all the air clogged in me. Fat flakes floated down, gilded silver in the full moon light, melting on my sweaty face.

Sitting up, I reached for the 30.06 rifle David had stashed under the window, beneath a camouflaging white sheet, for protection on my trip to make the call.

Mrs. Everett rounded the corner of the bedroom.

My eyes zeroed in on her like a rifle scope.

180

Outlined in the weird silver light, she drew her lips back from her teeth, like an animal, and with both hands, raised her gun.

The rifle. I lunged for —

The bedroom wall exploded, like an ice dam bursting in the spring, and a dark figure leaped out.

Mrs. Everett wheeled and fired as the figure carried her into the ground.

What just ... who ...?

No sound. All the crashing and thudding had stopped. So had the shots. Just my harsh breath scraped in and out, its cloud mingling with the snow.

I grabbed the covered rifle, whipped off the sheet, and scrambled to where Mrs. Everett and David or Mr. Everett lay stone still. My stomach balled up so tight, I could barely run.

With a groan, the figure rolled off Fashion Model.

"She didn't hurt you, did she?" Mr. Everett whispered.

I gulped an apple-sized lump and wiped at my eyes. "No, sir."

"Get her gun."

Embedded in the snow, arms outstretched, Mrs. Everett lay like a bug that was smashed with a fly swatter. Scraps of condensed air drifted from her bloody lips, the only sign of life

My hands shook as I pulled the gun from her limp fingers.

"Jay! Mr. Everett!" David staggered into the hole where the bedroom window once belonged.

"You're okay!" Stupid tears made the silhouette of my brother blurry.

"Except for a hole in my leg. Conley's unconscious. Are you all right?"

"Yeah. I'm the only one who is."

"Mr. Everett, how 'bout you?"

Mr. Everett stared up at the swirling snow. "I ... can't tell."

A dark spot was staining his tan shirt below his collar bone. "Your shoulder. David, he's shot in the shoulder!" I snatched up the sheet to tear it.

My brother limped away from the opening and then threw out a bundle of sheets and blankets. "Wrap his shoulder tight. I'll tie up my leg and bring the truck around. You'd better drive." He hobbled out of sight.

"Gotcha." I wadded the strip of sheet into a compress, pressed it against the wound, and then wound another strip as gently as I could around it. "Why didn't you use my rifle, Mr. Everett?"

"Conley fell into me when David jumped him, and I dropped it. When I saw Natalie run out the door, I knew she was after you. I had to stop her. Somehow."

More stupid tears. I brushed them off as I tucked a blanket around him.

"It's all my fault. Lettin' Conley hear me. I am really, really sorry. I owe you. Big time."

"You owe me?" Mr. Everett's dark eyes met mine. "I'm glad I had a chance to repay you."

"Mr. Everett, me and David told you a thousand times—you don't owe us nothing."

"I know. That's why I had to repay you." He laughed, a real laugh with real humor in it, and his good arm moved beneath the blanket to hold his ribs. "And I didn't need a penny to do it."

JPC Allen began her writing career in second grade with an homage to Scooby Doo. She is a 2016 semi-finalist for her YA crime novel, *The Truth and Other Strangers,* in the American Christian Fiction Writers' Genesis contest. A former children's librarian, she loves to introduce tweens and teens to the adventure of writing through her workshops. She offers writing tips and prompts for beginning writers at *JPCAllenWrites.com* and *Facebook.com/JPCAllenWrites.* A lifelong Buckeye, JPC Allen has deep roots in the Mountain State.

SOLDIER'S HEART

By Tamera Lynn Kraft

1

Friday, July 8, 1864, Ravenna, Ohio

Noah Andrews' heart raced faster than the Ravenna Locomotive roaring along the C&P railroad tracks. It had been so long. He wondered if the bride still looked the same. Still smelled the same. Like gardenias. Like home.

When he'd joined the Ohio Seventh Volunteer Infantry Regiment the cars were filled with recruits going to war. A roar of anticipation filled the train the day they left. Over a hundred young men, in clean starched uniforms, whooped and hooted with each other about how they were going to teach those rebs a lesson they wouldn't forget. They'd be home by Christmas.

Today, the chatter was more subdued. Less than thirty men from his hometown returned with him, their uniforms faded, tattered, and stained with blood. Most of the soldiers from Company G had been wounded, taken prisoner, or killed on a battlefield. The men's faces beamed with excitement, but they couldn't bring themselves to let out the merriment they felt inside. Somehow letting out a cheer would seem disloyal to their comrades who didn't return.

Noah stared out the window, trying to spot familiar sights. Trees and foliage blocked the view, but occasionally wooded areas thinned out where a house stood next to a corn or wheat field. He couldn't wait to be a farmer again, to grow crops and raise pigs on the farm his father left to him before the war. To put the horror behind him.

Even on the trip home, tragedy followed the Ohio Seventh when Oliver Trembly from Company C slipped and fell off the train. A captain had alerted the engineer, and the train had come to a slow stop as the wheels squealed on the tracks.

Soldiers jumped out and ran back to where the man fell, but it was too late. He'd already drowned in the Ohio River. Sergeant Trembly had fought in every major battle they'd faced without a scratch on him, but he still didn't make it home.

Noah pressed against the window and squinted to catch the first glimpse of the town. It looked the same. Portage County Courthouse, a brick building with six columns and a bell tower, all painted white, stood in the center of town with the two-story, brick jailhouse beside it. It'd been there since before he was born. The Immaculate Conception Catholic Church was new with its massive stone walls and clock tower, but not much else. Ravenna never really changed, and he was glad of it.

A few soldiers in the Seventh had re-enlisted or were mustered into the Ohio Fifth for the remainder of the war and were already marching to the sea with General Sherman, but after Ringgold Gap, after what happened there, Noah would have none of it.

It was a bright day, and a slight breeze blew through the open windows. He heard birds chirping, a dog barking, band music. It grew louder the closer they got to the Sycamore Street Station. Brakes squealed, and a whistle blew as the train came to a stop.

He grabbed his pack and Springfield rifle and made his way through the soldiers pushing against him, all trying to depart the train in one clump, as if, in one accord, they'd determined never to move in a single line formation again. They were civilians now.

Scanning the area, he stepped off the railroad car, but he couldn't see Molly among the masses crowded in front of the brick depot to greet them. Apparently, the whole town had come out.

A banner, "Welcome Home Company G," was strung over the door. The din of the mob blended with fifes, drums, trumpets, and trombones playing *When Johnny Comes Marching Home Again*. Men and women he'd known all his life thrust in on him like a regiment of rebel troops as they patted him on the back and shook his hand, but after three years away, they were strangers.

He needed to find Molly, to get away from this rabble.

Mrs. Thompson, a plump lady in her forties, grabbed hold of him and hugged him almost too tightly. "I'm so glad you made it home."

A wave of nausea swept through Noah. Her son would never return. He'd died on the battlefield in Georgia.

Making his apologies, he pulled himself from Mrs. Thompson's grasp and marched further into the fray. His stomach knotted as the throng pressed in tighter. He had to get away.

"Molly!" His voice trailed off to the music of *Battle Hymn of the Republic*.

He squeezed through more well-wishers until he saw Aaron Billings, his brother-in-law and best friend. Aaron stood on his crutch and wooden leg, sandy brown hair blowing in his face, delivering the same winsome grin Noah remembered. He pulled Aaron into a bear hug.

Aaron saluted. "Welcome home, Sergeant Noah."

Noah didn't return the salute. "I'm not a sergeant anymore. Have you seen Molly?"

"Sure have. She fetched me to get you, wanted your meeting to be a little more private. She's inside the depot."

Noah pushed through the throng until he managed to open the door of the small brick building. He spotted her, and his stomach fluttered. She was even prettier than he remembered, with blond hair curled and pinned in ringlets and big blue eyes twinkling at him. She wore her wedding dress, cream colored satin with little roses on it and a pink ruffled bonnet. His mouth watered. She wasn't the girl of sixteen he'd married. She'd matured in all the right places.

She smiled and held her arms out. He ran to her, picked her up, spun her around, and kissed her, not caring who saw it.

"Whoo hoo." A group of onlookers applauded. He bristled, noticing for the first time there were others waiting inside the station.

"Let's go home," Noah whispered in her ear.

Molly chuckled. "We can't go home now, silly. The whole town came out to give you a hero's welcome. Everyone's meeting at the courthouse lawn, and Mayor Brown's even planning on making a speech."

"I'm not a hero!" It came out sharper than he intended.

Her eyes widened, and she took a step back.

"Please." He cringed at the pleading in his voice. "I want to go home, alone, with you."

Molly nodded and made their apologies as they made their way to their buggy parked across Main Street in front of the Ravenna Book Store. It was a bowl coal box carriage with red cloth seats, Noah's prize possession.

The Mertz and Riddle Carriage Manufactory located on the corner of Main and Chestnut made the finest carriages in the world. When Noah decided to court Molly, he didn't want to subject her to riding in the wagon, so he sold one of his horses to buy the coach. The truth was, he wanted to impress her. It worked. They would ride to church together and sometimes drive to Brady Lake in comfort.

They rode the carriage home on their wedding day. The next day, they rode it to the train station where he joined his company. He brushed his hand across the mane of their sorrel, Sam. The horse had only been a colt when he left. He helped Molly inside, and they rode toward his father's farm, his farm.

Willow, elm, oak, and a few apple trees lined the road along with farm houses and barns. He'd forgotten how much bluer the sky was than in Tennessee or Virginia. He used to find shapes in the white fluffy clouds when he was a boy. Not many clouds in Tennessee.

Not a mountain in sight. A heaviness rested on his chest. He never again wanted to see a hill larger than the one near his farm. Too many men had died on the mountainsides he'd climbed.

"I'm fixing fried chicken, mashed potatoes, and cornbread for supper tonight." Molly intertwined her arm in his. "I heard how hard it is for you soldiers to get a decent meal. You're too skinny, husband. I plan to fatten you up."

"Sweetheart, you're making my mouth water. I never want to see another hardtack cracker again." He gazed at her, and another hunger rose inside of him. "Your cooking isn't the only thing I'm looking forward to tonight."

Molly blushed, but her coy smile had a hint of desire.

She placed her head on his shoulder, and they rode in silence. They didn't need to say anything. Just being together was enough.

Noah pulled off Cleveland Road and headed down the lane leading to their farm. After they crossed the creek, he flicked the reins to urge Sam to go faster. They'd be there soon. When he reached the apple tree on the edge of the field, he stopped the buggy.

Acres of the most beautiful golden stalks of corn stood knee-high. "How did you manage this?" He helped Molly down and swung her around. "I thought we'd have to make do with a small garden, my soldier's pay, and what I managed to hunt. I didn't expect you to have a crop this size ready for me to tend."

She giggled. "I worked my fingers to the bone."

Noah clasped her hands in his. They weren't the soft hands touching his face as they said good-bye at the train station years ago. They were rough and had callouses, a farm wife's hands. He drew them to his face and kissed them. "Mighty fine fingers they are too, but you couldn't have done all this on your own."

"Father and Aaron helped with the planting. I didn't want you to have to wait a whole year to harvest a crop. I wanted to surprise you."

"You certainly did." He placed his hands on his hips. "I suppose we'll need to buy some hogs."

Molly chuckled. "We have enough pork to last. I cured some and sold the rest to Hackenwald's Butcher Shop. I figured you could buy more, next Spring."

Noah's voice cracked. "I... You did..." He wiped his hand across his beard. "You are a treasure."

"Nonsense. I did what was needed." Molly placed her hand in his. "I am relieved to be done with it. Now I can lay the burden of running a farm and making ends meet on my husband's shoulders where it belongs. From now on, I plan to devote my time to my herb garden and my chickens."

"Sounds like you'll have too much time on your hands." He raised his eyebrow. "Maybe you need a few babies to raise. You know, just to keep you busy."

She gave him a mock scowl. "Noah Andrews, just what are your intentions?"

He grabbed her and kissed her, long and hard. He couldn't get enough of the taste of her lips. "Let's go home, wife."

A warmth welled up inside of him until he had to blink to keep his eyes from tearing up. The war wasn't over yet, but it was over for him. It wouldn't follow him here.

♡ ♡ ♡

The rooster crowed. Molly pried her eyes open. Noah had already dressed in his Union blues and was pulling on his boots. He'd lost too much weight while he was gone. The clothes he'd left behind were too big for him. Even his uniform hung on him.

In a few days, after she shared their accounts with him, she'd ask him about buying material for new clothes, maybe even a ready-made shirt and trousers to tide him over until she could sew more.

He sat on the edge of the rope bed, gazing at her with those piercing blue eyes of his. The hard muscles in his arms flexed as he wrapped her up in them and kissed her. Heat flushed her face. It was a hungry kiss, taking her breath away.

The night before, his kisses had been tender, his touch gentle, more like the last time, their first night together. He left for war the day after their wedding.

Her father wanted her to wait to marry him until he returned, but she loved him all of her life and wouldn't hear of it. Noah was meant to be her husband no matter how long they had together. She couldn't have borne it if something had happened to him and she hadn't had a chance to be his wife.

After several seconds, she pulled away. "Why didn't you wake me?"

"I wanted to have Sam and the chickens fed and the cow milked before you woke."

She blinked her eyes to keep tears from forming. It'd been so long since she could depend on his strength. She'd longed to be able to feel like a woman again without having to work so hard planting, harvesting, tending the animals -- doing man's work.

That wasn't the only heavy load she had carried while he was gone. She'd lived with a fear so deep, it rested on her chest from morning 'til night. Whenever she made a trip into town, she could scarcely breathe until she checked the casualty list posted at the courthouse. She would tremble as she read off the names, but that was over now. Noah was home.

187

She eased out from under the red and blue log cabin quilt she had helped her mother make when she was a little girl and stepped onto the rug covering the wooden floor. After pouring some water from the pitcher into a basin, she splashed her face.

Their bedroom was larger than most, with plenty of room for a cradle when the time came. The rope bed in the center of the back wall was the largest piece of furniture, but she also had a dressing table with a mirror, an armoire, and a chest of drawers. She'd made the blue curtains for the window to match the print in the blue-flowered wallpaper.

She'd moved into the two-story farmhouse when she'd married Noah. Her folks wanted her to stay with them until her husband returned, but she insisted. This was her home now, and it was her responsibility to look after it while Noah was away.

She grabbed her forest green day dress from the armoire on the wall next to the door. "I'll have pancakes and coffee waiting for you when you get back."

He drew her close and kissed her neck with a low growl coming from his lips. "Don't get dressed yet."

Chills traveled up her spine. She giggled and pulled away."We can't do that. It's daytime."

He leaned against the doorpost and perused her hungrily, causing her heart to race. "I missed three years of making love to my wife. I plan to do some catching up."

He scooted out the door before she could dispute what he said. Heat scorched her face. What would her mother say? Was it really that improper? After all, he was her husband, and he'd just come home from the war.

Walking barefoot into the kitchen, Molly felt the warmth from the fire Noah must have already started in the cook stove. She pulled a tin off the shelf labeled flour and measured out some in a bowl sitting on the roughhewn table in the middle of the room. They would need more soon.

She remembered the last time she bought supplies, and a shiver went through her.

ᗐ ᗐ ᗐ

Last November, she had ridden into town to buy supplies at Sutherland's Groceries. It had started to snow, and a breeze blew through and chilled her. Mr. Green and Mr. Talbot, both farmers around her father's age, huddled around the stove talking to Mr. Sutherland about three battles that had just taken place outside of Chattanooga and how the Ohio Seventh was a part of them. A lump lodged in her throat.

When Mr. Sutherland saw her, he shushed the other men. After she placed her order, he asked if she wanted one of them to go with her while she checked the casualty list.

Molly's stomach churned. "Yes, please."

"I'll go," Mr. Talbot said. He escorted her across Main Street. The lawn in front of the Portage County Courthouse had oak and elm trees planted along the edge in an effort to beautify the town, but today, they were barren. Her throat ached. She loosened the collar on her blouse. Dead trees, dead soldiers. Was her husband dead too?

They climbed the stairs, and entered the courthouse through the large wooden doors. They reached the foyer, and her knees weakened. Mr. Talbot grasped her arm to steady her. A group of women she'd known for years pressed in around a list tacked to the wall.

Mr. Talbot's voice was soft and low. "Would you like to wait here while I check the list?"

She shook her head and scooted in behind them. This was something she needed to do. Her husband had made it through every other battle, including Cedar Mountain and Gettysburg, unscathed. His name wouldn't be there. She pressed her eyes closed. It couldn't be.

Sobs rose from the group huddled around the list. Mrs. Thompson held her hands over her face. A gasp rose, and a cry, "No, not my Tommy."

The ladies surrounded the distraught mother. Molly slipped in front of them and checked the list. The Battle of Ringgold Gap. Ringgold Gap? She'd never heard of it. Noah had written they were waiting for a battle at Lookout Mountain near Chattanooga, but he'd never mentioned Ringgold.

The first row listed soldiers who had been killed. So many. She ran her finger along the names and blew a sigh of relief. Noah wasn't among them. He wouldn't be on the wounded list either. She was sure of it.

She blinked to clear her vision. Noah Andrews was the first name. She didn't remember much after that, only Mr. Talbot coaxing her from the floor where she must have fainted.

She had spent the winter at her parents' home. Two agonizing months, waiting. Finally, a letter arrived from Noah. It had only been a flesh wound, and he would be fine.

Her hand shook as she poured water and coffee grounds in the tin pot and placed it on the stove. Last night, when she'd seen the scar on his shoulder, she knew it had been worse than he'd let on. He flinched when she touched it. At least he didn't lose a limb like Aaron.

It wouldn't take long to do the morning chores, so she pulled plates from the hutch her father had made. He was the only furniture maker in town, and he'd outdone himself with the cabinet.

Father might need to make a cradle soon since Noah was home. She imagined her children would all have blond hair and blue eyes since both she and Noah were fair. Her brother, Aaron, had sandy brown hair and hazel eyes like her mother. Maybe one of them would take after him.

She allowed herself to daydream some more as she mixed the flour, milk, and eggs, and warmed the maple syrup she'd drawn from the tree at the edge of the creek. The coffee brewed and the syrup warmed, but Noah hadn't returned. She looked at the clock on the wall and bit her lip. He was taking too long.

She didn't want to start the pancakes until he got back, or they might grow cold before he had a chance to eat them. She sat at the table, tapping her fingers against it and trying not to worry. Maybe the cow had gotten into the field somehow. Surely Noah wouldn't have started raking out the barn before breakfast.

After another ten minutes watching the clock, she couldn't sit and fret any longer without seeing what the delay was. She hurried to the bedroom and slipped into her green cotton day dress. Her fingers fumbled on the large bone-colored buttons up the front. She slipped her boots on and didn't bother to lace them up before rushing outside.

Standing on the porch, she scanned the area for any sign of her husband. He wasn't in the corral or the fields. The outhouse door was open. No sign of him there.

Scolding herself for making such a fuss, she ran to the big gray barn out back. He probably was checking out where the walls needed repaired. A storm last month had blown away a few of the boards.

She opened the door and stepped inside. The cow stood in the stall with a bucket and stool beside her, but Noah wasn't anywhere around.

Molly swallowed hard. She headed toward where the chickens perched. A man from behind the stall grabbed her arm and pulled her down. She started to scream when he placed a hand over her mouth.

"Shhh, they'll hear you." It was Noah. His jaw clenched, and sweat beaded his forehead. He took his hand away from her mouth but didn't let go of her. "We need to stay low or they'll find us."

Molly's heart raced. She kept her voice at a whisper. "Who? Who will find us?"

"Them." He pointed to the cow. "The enemy soldiers over there."

Molly tried to pull away, but his grasp tightened. "Noah, you're hurting me."

"We have to hide." He swiped at his long hair. His blue eyes, normally calm as the sea, darted all over.

"You're scaring me." She pushed at his chest. "There's nobody there." Tears filled her eyes. "Please, let go of me."

"There's nobody there?" He said it as if in a daze. "There's nobody there. There's nobody there." He let go of her arm and sank against the side of the stall. "I saw them. At least I thought I saw them. Graybacks. They were there."

Molly backed up against the barn wall and rubbed the sore spot where he'd grabbed her wrist. A bruise was starting to form. She'd never been afraid of him before, but she couldn't stop trembling.

He stood, stepped toward her.

"Get away from me." She grabbed a rake and held it in front of her.

"Oh, Molly." He held his hands up as if trying to calm a scared child. "I'm so sorry. Did I hurt you?"

She dropped the rake. "What's wrong with you?"

Noah turned and stared at the bucket on the ground near the cow. "I thought once I got home, was with you, this would go away."

She wiped her eyes. "What do you mean? What would go away?"

He wouldn't look at her. "Soldier's heart."

Molly gasped. "But you can't... You're a war hero."

Noah stepped toward her. His steel blue gaze turned her to stone. "I'm not a hero, Molly. You might as well know that right now. The men in my squad..." His voice thickened. "The men who died at Ringgold Gap, they're the heroes."

The lump in Molly's throat threatened to choke her. "I don't want to talk about it. You hear me? You just got home yesterday. You need time to get used to things being normal again. Everything will be fine in a few days. You'll see. It will be all right."

He nodded and took her in his arms. "I'll be fine. No need to fret."

She couldn't hold back the sobs lodged in her throat any longer. A torrent of tears threatened to drown her as she cried on his shoulder.

"Shhh, it's all right." He stroked her back as she tried to get hold of herself. "I'm home now. I just need a few days, and I'll be right as rain."

She wiped her eyes and tried to smile at him as if nothing had happened. He had to be okay. Please, Lord.

2

Noah parked the buggy outside the large red brick church on Prospect Street, with a white steeple taller than any building in Ravenna. He helped Molly step down. Before the war, this place was his second home, but he tensed at the thought of stepping through the tall wooden door leading to a large sanctuary. Being around all those people asking him questions. Calling him a hero. He swallowed down the lump in his throat. He'd tried to convince his wife he wasn't ready, but she gave him a pleading gaze, and he had melted. After all she'd been through waiting for him to come home and then having him scare her, how could he refuse her?

He wrapped her arm in his, stepped into the building, and climbed the stairs to the sanctuary. Ravenna Methodist Episcopal Church was more crowded than he remembered. Almost every cushioned pew was filled. The church didn't believe in assigning pews according to donations, and the only seats left were in the front two rows. A light shone in his eyes from the stained-glass windows, and he squinted as he glanced up at the balcony. He let out a silent groan. Molly would never agree to sit there. She always insisted they sit as close to the front as possible.

He decided to try one last time. "Maybe we should come back another day."

Molly pulled away and delivered a glare that would win the war if he could find a way to turn it on rebel troops. "What is wrong with you? You never missed a day of church in your life. Don't tell me you've learned heathen ways in the army."

"Of course not." Noah swiped his hand across the back of his neck. "There are just so many people. I'm not ready for this."

"Pfft, you, not ready to socialize? My husband?" She marched to the pew closest to the front and scooted in.

Noah stood dumbfounded for a moment. There was no way around it. He scrunched in beside her. She didn't understand how hard this was. He might have enjoyed polite conversation in the past, but that was before, when there were things he wanted to talk about. What would he say if the mother, or sister, or wife of one of the men in his squad asked him questions? How would he explain? He'd watched his men die and did nothing to stop it. His stomach knotted as he scrunched in his seat to make himself smaller. Maybe nobody would see him.

"Noah, my dear boy." Mrs. Thompson stood at the end of the pew and, since there was no means of escape, Noah nodded a greeting toward her. "Is there room here for us?"

"Of course." Molly slid over while grabbing Noah's arm to pull him closer. "Plenty of room."

Mrs. Thompson sat, followed by her three younger daughters and her husband. She patted Noah's hand. "I'm so glad you're back. I've prayed for you every day since my Tommy... Well, my prayers were answered."

Noah wasn't sure what to say since he suspected if she could have had her son home safe instead of him, she would gladly have had him die in Tom's stead. "Thank you, ma'am."

"We wanted to invite you and Molly over for supper. Maybe next Sunday?"

Noah's voice caught in his throat.

"We'd love to come," Molly said. "Wouldn't we, Noah?"

"Well, ah…" was all Noah could get out.

"Splendid," Mrs. Thompson said. "I so want to hear more about Tommy."

The pipes covering the wall at the front of the church vibrated as the organ played *Abide With Me,* Noah's favorite hymn. He stood and opened his hymnal, never more relieved for a church service to begin.

The words reached into his heart as he sang it as a prayer. He needed God to abide with him as he never had before. When he sang, "I need thy presence every passing hour," his voice thickened. Somehow, if he could sing those words a few more times, God could heal his soldier's heart. The song ended too soon.

After the congregation sang a few more songs, Reverend Obadiah Haskell, garbed in his white robe, stood, and welcomed everyone. A tall man in his early forties, he had been Noah's pastor since Reverend Clark had retired in '57. Before that, he taught boys ages ten through sixteen and discipled them in the Bible. Noah had been one of those boys. So had every soldier of Company G who attended the Methodist Episcopal Church, including every man under his command.

"Today, we have reason to praise our Lord." Reverend Haskell's voice boomed. "For today, the members of the Seventh Ohio Volunteer Infantry have returned home."

Heat rushed to Noah's face. He scrunched down in the pew, hoping he wouldn't be noticed. He couldn't see how to avoid it, considering he was wearing his uniform.

"Could all who have served in the Ohio Seventh stand?"

Noah considered staying seated, but when both Molly and Mrs. Thompson elbowed him, he reluctantly rose to his feet. He didn't bother to see who else was standing. The congregation applauded, and after a moment of wishing the floor could swallow him up, he sat back down. Fortunately, Reverend Haskell didn't decide to say any more to embarrass him and went on with the service.

Noah had always enjoyed Reverend Haskell's sermons, but after the humiliation of being forced to stand when his squad didn't make it home, he couldn't keep his mind on the message. All he wanted to do was find a way to escape this crowd, no matter how good their intentions were and how glad they were to have him back.

If they knew, if they understood, they would tar and feather him and run him out of town.

Molly let out a slow breath. First Noah kicked up a fuss about going to church. Then he whisked her away from the church service so fast, Reverend and Mrs. Haskell didn't even have a chance to welcome him home. Now he didn't want to go to her parents' for Sunday dinner. He wasn't acting like the man she married.

Noah finally agreed to it, but as they sat around the wooden table her father had made, he barely spoke. The man who used to monopolize every conversation before the war acted as if he'd lost his voice in battle.

"It's good to have you back." Mother filled Noah's coffee cup. "We had a fretful time after we found out you were wounded at Ringgold Gap. Especially after what happened to..."

A smirk crossed Aaron's face as he patted Mother's hand. "What she's trying to say is she's glad you didn't lose your leg like me."

Mother smacked his hand. "Aaron, you know that's not what I meant. So many didn't make it back, and more will die before this tragic war is over. I just..." She blushed. "I don't know what I mean. I'm glad you're home safe."

"Thank you, ma'am." Noah took a large bite of his chicken leg.

Nobody said anything as an awkwardness filled the air. Molly nudged Noah with her elbow, but after giving her a 'what?' look, he ignored her.

"So Noah," Father said. "It looks like you'll have a good crop this year."

"Yes, sir." Noah took a sip of coffee. "Thank you for helping Molly during planting season. I never expected acres of the prettiest golden corn stalks I ever did see waiting for me when I got home."

"Aaron and I were glad to do it. Should make you a fine profit."

"I agree." Leave it to Father to know talking about the farm would loosen Noah's tongue. "From what I hear, the army is buying up all the corn they can get. At a handsome price, too."

Father leaned back. "It's sad it took a war to get us out of the recession of '58."

"How's the carpentry trade going?" Noah asked.

"Doing fine. Especially since Aaron returned to help me. Billings Furniture Store doesn't make furniture anymore, at least not until the war is over. We're assembling wagons for the army. After you get the crops harvested, this fall, we could use your help."

Noah rubbed his beard the way he used to when he was pondering some deep thought. "I might just do that." He ate the last bite of his bread.

"Molly," Mother said. "Pass Noah some more bread."

Molly reached for the bread basket.

Her father grabbed her hand. "What's that?" He pointed to the bruises around her wrist.

She pulled her arm back and covered her wrist with her sleeve. "Nothing, I must have hit it on something."

Father glared at her and then at Noah. "It doesn't look like you bumped it. It looks like somebody grabbed you hard."

Molly's stomach tightened. "Really, Father, it's nothing."

"Let me see." Father's request sounded more like an order.

Tears threatened to form in Molly's eyes. Why didn't she wear her green dress instead of the brown one? It had longer sleeves.

"Molly," Noah said softly. "Show him your arm." When she glanced over at him, he nodded and gave her a slight grin.

She pulled up her sleeve and stretched her arm across the table. The ugly purple bruises from fingers pressed into her flesh were clearly visible.

Father directed his glower toward Noah. "Who did this, Molly?"

"I did." Noah's voice barely sounded through a whisper. "I grabbed her arm to pull her back. I was trying to protect her."

"From what?" Controlled anger came through Father's tone.

"I saw..." Noah's Adam's apple bulged. "Graybacks."

Father stood. "This far north? Where?"

"They weren't there." Noah glanced down and then looked directly into Father's eyes. "I saw them." He wiped his hand across the back of his neck. "But they weren't there." Knocking over his chair, he got up and stormed out the door.

A tear dropped down Molly's cheek. Why did he have to tell them what happened? Everything would have been all right if he hadn't told them.

Aaron's wooden leg and crutch thumped on the floor as he chased after Noah. Mother sat beside Molly and hugged her. Molly glanced up at her father.

He sank into his chair. "Molly, tell me everything that happened from the beginning."

3

Noah stood outside, leaning against a buckeye tree, and gasped in the fresh air. He couldn't get enough to fill his lungs. The sun shone through white fluffy clouds dotting the sky. A blue jay sang on the limb above him. The scent of hydrangea bushes swept past him. Somewhere in the distance, the rumble of a train sounded. All of it mocking him, as if he could find peace here. Anywhere.

A thumping noise sounded behind him. Aaron's wooden leg.

"Soldier's heart?" Aaron always could sum things up with as few words as possible.

Noah hunched his shoulders and lowered his head. He nodded but didn't turn around. He couldn't face him. Not yet.

"When I got back, I wouldn't leave the house for months." Aaron circled around until Noah could see the toe of his boot. "Lots of soldiers have a hard time of it."

Noah studied the buckeyes on the ground in front of him. They didn't have the strange looking nuts in Tennessee. "You lost a leg."

"Yeah, I did, but I made it home safe. Sarge, you lost your whole squad. That's got to stick in your craw some."

Noah managed to lift his gaze. "Molly thinks once I'm home for a while things will get better." He shrugged. "Maybe she's right. They did for you."

"I wish I could say it were true. I still have times I want to wallow in it."

Noah kneaded the back of his neck. "I never thought of myself as a coward, but lately..."

"You, a coward? Balderdash." Aaron crossed his arms and glared at Noah. Yellow specks flickered in his hazel eyes. "You saved my life and the life of every man in your squad when you drew the rebels' fire at Cedar Mountain. If it hadn't been for you, I would have lost more than a leg."

Noah picked a buckeye off the ground and threw it as far as he could. "And you're the only one still alive." His jaw twitched. "They all died because of me."

"What happened in Ringgold?"

"I don't want to talk about it. Molly's right. I need to get on with my life and forget about the war."

"Good luck with that." Aaron placed a hand on Noah's shoulder. "If you don't get it out into the open, it will haunt you. When you're ready, I'm here."

A weight rested in Noah's gut. "I can't." It came out as a raspy whisper.

"If you don't want to talk to me, you could see Reverend Haskell. He helped me a lot."

Noah swallowed. He knew Aaron was only trying to help, but it was different with him. "Thanks." Aaron lost a leg, but he lost every man in his squad. "We better get back inside. I expect your father's waiting to have a few words with me."

Aaron grinned. "Would you like me to scout things out first?"

The muscle in Noah's cheek twitched. "Nah, better to get it over with."

They walked back to the house and stepped inside. Molly and her folks sat around the table eating blueberry pie. Molly had stopped crying.

A good sign.

"Sit," Mrs. Billings said. "I'll cut you both a slice."

Noah slid in beside Molly and stared at his hands folded in front of him. He let out a deep breath and faced Mr. Billings. "I expect you have something to say to me. I'm ready to hear it."

"Noah, son." Mr. Billings' tone was gentle. He started to reach out to touch Noah's arm, but pulled his hand back before he did. "I know things were rough there. Aaron's told me some of it. It takes time to get back to normal." He pointed his finger in Noah's face, and his voice grew stern. "But if you hurt my Molly again, you'll wish you were only facing the rebs again."

Noah nodded. "I won't hurt her. I'd never hurt her." If he wasn't able to put this behind him, he would leave Ravenna before he'd cause her any more pain.

🌿 🌿 🌿

Molly scooted closer as Noah drove the wagon to Sutherland's Grocery Store across from the courthouse. With her husband home, they needed supplies. When she asked him, he told her to make a list and they'd go the next day.

It had been a couple of weeks since Noah came home, and nothing bad had happened since the incident in the barn. She didn't want to tell him, but she was relieved. If he had another crazy spell, she didn't know what she'd do.

She had packed a picnic basket, and suggested they ride up to Brady Lake after their shopping. They could make it a special day, like when he used to court her.

Noah parked the wagon outside the store and helped Molly down. They entered together, arm in arm.

Mr. Sutherland stepped to the counter. "Noah Andrews, so good to see you. I wanted to say howdy when you got home, but you skedaddled out of the train depot so fast, the mayor didn't even get a chance to shake your hand."

"I wanted to spend some time with my wife. Hadn't seen her in three years."

"I don't blame you, 'specially with a wife as pretty as Molly. It's good to have you back. How can I help you today?"

Molly handed him her paper. "I have a list."

Mr. Sutherland looked it over. "I have all this in stock, but it'll be about an hour. There's some customers ahead of you."

"Thank you," Molly said.

The bell above the door rang, and Mr. Green entered the store. "Well, well, if it isn't the returning hero." He patted Noah on the back, but the gesture didn't seem friendly. "I figured you'd re-enlist, at least until the war was over. I didn't figure you for a quitter."

Noah stuck his hands in his pockets. "My three-year enlistment was up, Mr. Green."

Molly's stomach tightened as she tugged at Noah's arm. "Husband, let's check out Poe and Brother Store. You need some clothes."

Noah nodded. "If you'll excuse me, I have errands."

He escorted Molly outside, and they strolled down Main Street to the fabric and clothing store. The bell rang as they entered, and Molly nudged Noah toward the bolts of material on the table under the window.

The bell rang again, and Mrs. Thompson entered and strode toward them. "Noah, Molly, so good to see you. I'm sorry you couldn't make it, last week, but I insist you have supper at my place, this Sunday."

Molly shot a glower toward her husband. They'd had words when he cancelled, last Sunday. Turning to Mrs. Thompson, she delivered her warmest smile. "It's so good of you to invite us. We'd love to come."

Noah gripped Molly's arm tighter. "I don't know. Molly's folks might want us over for supper with them."

"Nonsense," Mrs. Thompson said. "They had you over two Sundays in a row since you got back. I won't take no for an answer."

Noah stroked his beard. "I really think we should visit the Billings."

Molly touched his arm. "This is the second time Mrs. Thompson invited us. My parents will understand."

Noah's gaze darted toward the door.

"Please, Noah, it would be a kindness," Mrs. Thompson said. "It's been hard for us since Tommy died. It would help hearing about... knowing what happened."

"I'm sorry, Mrs. Thompson." His voice was stern. "We can't make it."

Mrs. Thompson's face turned red. "I'm sorry for troubling you." She blinked several times and pulled out her hankie. "Perhaps another time." She rushed out of the store.

Heat rushed to Molly's face. She grabbed a bolt of blue calico. "You need a couple of shirts and some work pants." She couldn't keep the irritation out of her tone. "You can't keep wearing that uniform."

Noah gawked around the store and pulled on the collar of his blue jacket. He looked like a skittish calf trying to escape the branding iron.

She set the calico down, drew in a deep breath, and started looking through the rack of men's shirts. Maybe if she ignored him, he'd calm down. "If you think we can afford it, I'd like to buy you a ready-made shirt and trousers to wear until I can get some clothes sewn." She pulled a plaid shirt off the rack. "And I'd like to buy enough material to make you a Sunday shirt and me a new day dress."

Noah stroked his beard and stared at a spool of thread.

"Husband, did you hear a word I said?" She turned away and hung the shirt back on the rack. She didn't want him to see her watery eyes.

He didn't answer.

She'd had enough of this. Why couldn't he just answer her? She blinked a few times to clear the tears and spun around. "Well, is there enough money?"

Taking a step toward the door, he bumped his leg on a crate. "I don't know. I… I don't know. I… um…"

Molly rubbed her temples. "Do you want me to wait? I could just buy the ready-made shirt and trousers for now."

"Trousers?" Noah glanced at his uniform. "I'm not sure."

She let out a deep breath and tried to calm her tone. "If you're worried about the money, I can wait. I need to know what you want me to do."

"Please." Noah pulled his hand away. "I need to get out of here. Please." He ran out the door, knocking over a display of dresses.

Her chin trembled as she looked around. Mr. Poe and the ladies in the shop stared at her. They must have seen it all. Avoiding looking in their direction, she grabbed the dresses off the floor and hung them on the rack. "I'll be back later for the goods I need."

She hurried outside and found the wagon still parked in front of Sutherlands' where they left it, but Noah was nowhere around. She gazed up and down the road, trying to get a glimpse of him. Nothing. Her heart pounded louder than army drums. Where could he be?

Loping next door, she glanced in the window to make sure he hadn't gone back to Sutherlands'. She held her stomach, trying to squelch the panic rising in her. Noah always loved to read. Maybe he decided to buy a new book. She hurried past Poe's and the *Ravenna Democrat* newspaper office toward the bookstore. He wasn't there.

She squeezed her nose. She wouldn't cry. Maybe he'd decided to sit on the benches for a spell. She headed to the courthouse and scurried to the back yard where the bandstand and benches were, but he wasn't there either.

Her thoughts raced faster than the train through town. There had to be a reason he took off like that. Of course. The bank. If they were going to buy all those wares, he would need to draw money out of their savings. That's where he'd be. Hurrying past the firehouse and the jail, she headed to the First National Bank of Ravenna. With each step, she tried to convince herself she'd find him there. She walked into the brick building. Mr. Potter, the bank clerk, sat at his desk eating an apple. He was the only person in the bank she could see.

Mr. Potter glanced up and wiped his hands on a napkin. "Can I help you?"

Dread travelled down her back into the pit of her stomach. She shook her head and pushed through the door. Standing on the wooden sidewalk, she glanced both ways. She didn't know where else to look. What if he had another attack? She had to find him.

Hurrying her steps, she walked a few more blocks up Main Street and then traveled the other way, stopping in front of Grier's Tavern. He was nowhere in sight. She bit her lip. No lady would ever enter the pub, but Noah had never set foot in there, either. She was sure of that. He called whiskey the devil's drink and never allowed it to touch his lips.

Molly suspected Noah was so strongly against drink because his father had been enslaved to it. Regardless of the reason, she knew in her heart he wasn't there.

Tears leaked from her eyes. She didn't know what to do. Ambling back to the wagon, she climbed into the seat. It was too far to walk home. She pulled out her handkerchief and sobbed into it. Wherever he was, he had to make it back here eventually.

4

Noah found himself in front of the Methodist Episcopal Church. He wasn't sure how he got here. He remembered wandering out of Poe's store, but not much else. The look on Molly's face, bewilderment, fear. He never wanted to hurt her. His father had caused his mother pain so often. He'd sworn he'd never be like that. He had to get hold of himself.

He stood in front of the parsonage, set his jaw, and knocked.

Reverend Haskell, a tall man with an infectious smile and a compassionate gleam in his brown eyes, opened the door. "Noah, come in."

"I don't mean to bother you." Noah stroked his beard. "Aaron seemed to think you could help me."

"Come in, son. Come in." Reverend Haskell shook his hand with enthusiasm. "Sit. Mrs. Haskell is out visiting, but I can make you a cup of coffee. I can't guarantee how good it will be."

Noah took a seat across from his pastor. "No, thanks."

Reverend Haskell gazed at him without saying a word.

Noah's jaw twitched. It was so hard to admit the truth to this man who had mentored him in the faith. If it hadn't been for Reverend Haskell and his weekly Bible studies, Noah might have strayed into drink like his father. In a way, the reverend was more of a father to him than his own was.

"You can trust me." The look of concern in Reverend Haskell's eyes confirmed what he was saying. "Now, what's bothering you?"

Noah let out the breath he was holding, and the words poured out. "The last big battle the Ohio Seventh fought was at Ringgold Gap. As sergeant, I was in charge of about ten men, my squad. Used to be thirty, but after almost three years of war..."

"It must have been hard."

The lump in Noah's throat threatened to choke him. "Yeah. It was a nightmare. We went after the rebs crowing like roosters, sure of another victory after we whipped them good at Lookout Mountain and Missionary Ridge. They were on the run, and all we had to do was catch up with them.

"We marched into the gap and found out..." Noah's voice thickened. "It was an ambush. Lieutenant-Colonel Crane fell first. When Colonel Creighton ran after him, he was killed too. The smoke from the gunfire and cannons was so dense I could barely see my men. I yelled out for them to follow me and let out the rooster call, hoping if we stayed together, we could make it through."

He blinked to keep the tears from falling. "I'm sorry. I never used to cry like this, didn't think it was manly."

"Nonsense," Reverend Haskell said. "After what you've been through..."

Noah wiped his face. "Anyway, the men under me, they trusted me. I led them into the fray." He cleared his throat. "That's where they died. All of them strung together like a bucket of night crawlers covered in blood. Somehow I managed to stay unscathed, but I stopped. I couldn't bring myself to move another inch even when I saw a reb aim his bayonet at me. When it stabbed through my arm and blood steeped through my sleeve, all I could think to do was throw myself on the ground, face down in the mud, and beg God for my miserable life."

Reverend Haskell drew his hand to his mouth, obviously disgusted by his behavior.

Noah let out a sigh and stood. "So now you know. I'm no hero the way everyone's spouting off. After I led my men to their deaths, I got scared and wallowed in the mud like a coward."

The reverend stepped in front of him and placed a hand on his shoulder. "This is a good first step. Now, I might be able to help you."

Noah sank back in his seat. "Help me with what?"

"Soldier's heart." The reverend sat beside him. "That's what you came to me about, isn't it?"

Noah grunted and couldn't help but offer a lopsided grin. "How do you do that? Ever since I was a kid, you always knew what was on my mind before I ever said anything."

Reverend Haskell shrugged. "Aaron suffered from it too. When he sent you to me, it didn't take much to figure it out."

"He said you helped him through it."

"The Lord helped him. I just gave him wise counsel from the Word of God."

"I need some of that counsel. Ever since Ringgold Gap, I have nightmares, I can't sleep, I can't make decisions. And I blow up over nothing. It's like my confidence is gone. The worst part is the nightmares I have when I'm awake. Everything around me fades, and I'm in battle again. I can't control myself. I feel, see, even hear, and smell everything like I'm going through it all over again."

"Does Molly know?"

Noah placed his face in his hands. "She does now. I had a spell the day after I came home. Reverend, I grabbed her wrist and threw her on the ground. I left a bruise."

Reverend Haskell lifted his eyebrow.

"I would never hurt her if I was in my right mind. I love her."

"I know, son."

"Why is God letting this happen?" Noah's jaw twitched. "He's punishing me for being a coward."

The reverend placed his hand on Noah's shoulder. "You're not a coward. You charged into the heat of battle and didn't falter until your men were already dead."

"I'd always heard God wouldn't put more on us than we could take, but I can't handle this."

"You didn't hear that from me." Reverend Haskell cleared his throat. "Son, God never said we wouldn't go through the fire, but He did promise He'd go through the trials with us."

"I don't know what to do. Reverend, can you help me?"

"I'll pray for you, and I can give you some ideas that might help."

"I'd sure appreciate it."

"Don't try to hide what you're going through. You can talk to me about it. Aaron would understand, too, since he's been through the same thing." Reverend Haskell stood and grabbed a book off the shelf. "When David was running from Saul, one way he got through the hard times was to write down what he was feeling. That's where most of the Psalms came from." He handed Noah a book.

Noah looked through it. It was bound with blank pages.

"It's a journal. Write down your thoughts and feelings. When you have these episodes, try to figure out what caused them."

"That's it? Just talk to you and write down what I'm feeling. That sounds too easy."

Reverend Haskell leaned back in his chair. "Trust me, son. It's not easy. It'll take time. And there's more."

"What else?"

"You have a lot of memories needing reconciled, hurts only God can heal. Whenever you have a nightmare, or remember something, or when one of these bouts comes on you, ask God to heal your hurt."

"I got my men killed. How can God heal that?"

"Jesus died for your sins. He'll provide the forgiveness you need."

Noah nodded. He knew God forgave him, but he wasn't sure he'd be able to let it go. "I'll try."

"One more thing, son." Reverend Haskell steepled his fingers in front of his mouth. "Talk to Molly about what happened. She needs to understand."

"I don't know if I can ever tell Molly how cowardly I was."

"Pray about it. God will give you the courage when it's time."

"Thank you, Reverend Haskell." Noah stood and headed to the door.

"Why don't you stay for supper? I know Mrs. Haskell would love to see you."

"Some other time. I need to get back to the store. I walked out on Molly without letting her know where I was going." He swallowed. "If you're praying for me, Reverend, you might want to start now. She's gonna be fit to be tied."

5

The sun beat down on Molly's face as she tried to adjust her bonnet to block the rays. If she'd known her husband would desert her, right here on Main Street, she would have insisted they take the buggy. It wasn't as big as the wagon, but at least it would provide shade.

She wiped the tears off her face and blew her nose in her handkerchief, determined to get herself together before Noah returned. If he came back. She thought when he came home, her weeping would end.

Maybe she should get the provisions they had ordered and go home. Let him walk the five miles. He should be used to that after all the time he spent marching. It would do him good.

She marched inside the store and asked Mr. Sutherland to load her groceries.

The storekeeper raised an eyebrow. "Mrs. Andrews, where's your husband?"

Molly bit her lip. As angry as she was with Noah, she didn't want others to think poorly of him. He was her husband after all. "He had some errands to run. He'll be back soon. He asked if I could have you load the wagon, and he'll be over later to pay."

"This is rather odd." Mr. Sutherland motioned to his clerk, a redheaded boy, barely twelve. "Load up Mrs. Andrews' wagon." Turning to Molly, he said, "After the heroism your husband has displayed, this wagonload is on me. No charge."

Molly flustered. "No, Mr. Sutherland. You've got it all wrong. We have the money to pay for this. It's just... Aaron needed his help, and he rushed off in a hurry and, well..."

"Don't matter." Mr. Sutherland wiped his hands on his apron. "Mr. Andrews is a hero in my book, and I'm not about to charge you. Next load, you can pay me full price if you want."

Molly tried to object, but Mr. Sutherland took her by the arm and escorted her to the door.

"Now, you just wait in the wagon. My boy will have it loaded in no time."

She didn't know how to get out of it, so she climbed into the wagon. Checking the street once again, she hoped she'd see Noah, but she didn't.

The boy finished up and tipped his hat before going back inside.

There was nothing left to do. She untied the hitch and led the horse into the dusty road. Noah walked in her direction as if he were out for a stroll.

Heat rushed through her. She marched to the middle of Main Street where she met up with him. "Where were you?"

A wagon drove by, stirring up dust. Noah stared at the dirt swirling around his feet. At least he had the decency to look ashamed. "Not here. Let's get the supplies, and I'll explain everything on the way home."

Her shoulders tensed. "I already got them."

Noah glanced at the wagon. "Then I'll go pay."

"He said 'no charge' because you're such a hero."

His mouth twisted. He brushed past her on the way to the grocers'. She ran after him to catch up.

Noah marched over to the counter. "Mr. Sutherland, I pay my own way. How much do I owe?"

Mr. Sutherland glanced up with a grin. "This is on me. I want to do something for the brave men fighting for our country."

Noah's hand fisted, and Molly let out a prayer he wouldn't do anything foolish. "I'll tell you what." His Adam's apple bulged. "I'll pay you full price, and you can deliver supplies to Mrs. Jefferson. I imagine she's had it rough since her husband died at Ringgold Gap."

Mr. Sutherland furrowed his brow, then grinned and shook Noah's hand. "I'll do it. Twenty dollars will take care of it."

Molly let out the breath she was holding.

"Deal," Noah said as he pulled two ten dollar coins out of his pocket and laid them on the counter. He didn't wait for the grocer to respond, just grabbed Molly by the hand and marched back out onto the street.

Molly pulled away.

Noah stopped and stared at her with those blue eyes of his as if he was begging her to understand. "Please, Molly, I'm sorry. Can't we just go to the lake like we planned? I need to get out of here."

Molly nodded and let him help her into the wagon, but she couldn't look at him. He was breaking her heart, and she didn't know what to do.

Noah wanted to explain what happened while they rode to Brady Lake, but every time he was about to, he glanced over at Molly. She stared at the trees and road with red swollen eyes, anywhere but his direction, reminding him how much he hurt her. He couldn't bring himself to say a word.

He parked the wagon next to the lake and wrapped her hand in his. "I'm sorry about what happened."

Molly nodded but didn't look his way.

"Molly, look at me."

She did.

"When Mrs. Thompson came in the store, I had to get away. I'm not ready to talk with her yet."

"Why?" Molly pulled her hand away. "You've been friends with her son since you were a boy."

Noah stroked his beard. "I watched Tom die. All the men in my squad were killed, and I couldn't do a thing to stop it. I can't take sitting down with their wives and mothers and telling what happened. Not yet. Please, try to understand."

Molly started to get down from the wagon, and Noah rushed around to help her. She strode to the back where the picnic basket and blanket sat and paused. "All you had to do was tell me the reason."

"I should have."

"Noah, you were rude to her. I've never known you to be cruel before."

That struck Noah as if Molly had slapped him. He didn't want to bring Tom's mother more grief. "You're right. I'll apologize the next time I see her. I'll make things right."

"You didn't have to run off like that." She glared at him. "Everyone was staring at me. And when you left, I didn't know what to do. Mr. Sutherland asked where you were. I didn't know what to tell him. You could have... You might have had another... incident, and I didn't know where you were or when you'd be back."

He wrapped his arms around her, and she sobbed in his shoulder. "Shhh. It's all right."

She pulled back. "No, it's not all right. Where did you go?"

"I went to see Reverend Haskell."

Molly grabbed the basket and strode to the edge of the lake.

Noah followed her with the blanket and spread it out on the grass.

She set the basket down and gazed at the lake. "I'm glad you went to see him, but why didn't you tell me instead of letting me fret like that?"

He swallowed. "I didn't know I'd end up there."

Her lower lip quivered, and for a moment, he was afraid the tears would return, but she jutted her chin, sat on the blanket, and pulled a tin pail of chicken and some cornbread wrapped in a cloth out of the basket. "Did he help?"

He sat beside her and grabbed a chicken leg. "Yes, some. He gave me a journal to write down my thoughts, and he told me to ask God to heal me."

She spread butter on a piece of cornbread. "Prayer always helps. It got me through these last three years, but I can't figure how writing things down is going to do anything. You should try to put it all behind you."

"I have tried, but I can't do it. I need to get out what's bothering me." Noah watched a flock of geese head toward them and threw out a few crumbs of bread. "He said I should tell you what happened."

Molly stood and strode closer to the lake. "I don't want to hear it. It's over."

He walked to her side.

She wrapped her arms around him. "Husband, you're the strongest man I know. You can do this. You just need to get hold of yourself."

As Noah held her, a heaviness pressed upon him, the same weight sinking him to the ground at Ringgold Gap. "I'll try, Molly. I'll try."

ᗢ ᗢ ᗢ

The deafening sounds of musket fire caused Noah's ears to ring. His legs were numb as he moved through the smoke and sparks of gunpowder. A cannonball whizzed past his head and knocked down a soldier. Colonel Creighton was just ahead.

Noah waved to his men to follow. If he could get to the colonel... A blast of a rifle, and Creighton's body jerked and fell like a rag doll.

He turned to make sure his men were close. "Tom!" he yelled, knowing they wouldn't hear him above the gunfire. Tom lay on the ground covered in blood, a cannonball lodged in his gut.

"Run, men! Stay close." He started back toward them when rapid shots, one after another, hit each of them. He couldn't get to them.

A rebel rushed him with a rage he'd seen on the battlefield before, but it still startled him when the bayonet sliced through his shoulder. Blood everywhere.

Noah woke with a start. Sweat drench his nightshirt. He was at home, safe, with Molly sleeping at his side.

He wanted to wake her, to tell her he had a bad dream, to hold her until his heart didn't pound through his chest, but he didn't. She didn't want to know his struggle.

Getting out of bed slowly so he wouldn't wake her, Noah made his way into the kitchen and poured some water from the pitcher over a rag. He wet his face and the back of his neck.

It was a hot night, but a shiver still went through him.

He spotted the journal Reverend Haskell gave him, grabbed a fountain pen and a bottle of ink, and sat at the table. He wrote everything in his journal, the words bleeding onto the page.

God, heal me. Give me peace.

6

A perusal of her handiwork brought a smile to Molly's face. Noah's three-piece, charcoal gray sack suit was the last of his old clothes she'd taken in. She'd altered the work shirts and trousers first but hated him wearing his uniform to church.

She left wide seams for his waist to expand. In the couple of months since he'd been home, Noah had filled out some. With the way he devoured her cooking, she wasn't surprised.

It was a relief things were finally getting back to normal. Noah had taken over the hard work of running a farm, and he hadn't had any spells since the day they went shopping.

He was still avoiding Mrs. Thompson, but that was to be expected. After all, seeing her reminded him of Tom's death and all the unpleasantness he'd gone through.

Noah attached the red checkered cravat onto the collar of his bleached muslin shirt and ran a comb through his hair and beard. "What do you think?"

"You look handsome, husband. I'll be the envy of every single girl at church."

He grunted and enveloped her in his arms as he charged her with his lips. "I love you so much."

Tingles coursed through Molly. She pulled back and tried to regain her composure. "I love you too, but we need to get going."

Noah let out a heavy sigh and nodded.

They went out to where the box coach buggy was already hitched.

Even though it was the middle of September, it was another hot day. The sun beat down hard with no clouds in sight. If it didn't rain soon, the crops would suffer.

Noah helped her into the carriage, and scooted in beside her. "After church today, I want to teach you how to ride a horse and shoot my rifle." He flicked the reins, and Sam trotted toward town.

Molly's chest tightened. "I promised my folks we'd be over for supper."

His eyebrow rose as he threw a glance her way. "We have time to do both. You should learn to ride and shoot. Something might happen where you need those skills."

"Nothing ever happens in Ravenna." She fanned herself, flustered he would even consider such a thing. "I managed take care of myself and the farm for three years without ever having to shoot a gun or ride a horse."

He took out his handkerchief and wiped the sweat off his brow. "If there's anything I learned in the army, you should prepare for the worst."

"It's not ladylike." Molly crossed her arms. "I won't do it."

Noah pulled up on the reins. "Why are you being so stubborn?" His voice had a harsh edge.

"Aaron tried to teach me how to ride when I was little." Her shoulders slumped. "I fell off and broke my arm."

He didn't say anything, but she didn't dare look at him. She couldn't believe he would be angry with her about this, about something no lady was expected to learn.

"I'm afraid," she admitted.

"I didn't know." He grabbed her hand. "Molly, darling, look at me."

She swallowed and turned toward him, but she couldn't bring herself to meet his gaze.

He rubbed her hand. "I'm sorry I was harsh. I just want you to be safe."

"I have you. You'll protect me."

"We'll hold off on this for now." His reassuring smile allowed her to relax.

"Thank you." She rested her head on his shoulder as he jerked the reins and continued toward the church.

"But not for long." Instead of looking her way, he stared straight ahead. "I am going to teach you… and soon."

Molly stiffened and fanned herself. She had to find a way to get him to change his mind.

ひ ひ ひ

Noah leaned against the apple tree in front of the church and waited for Molly to finish conversing with the women. He suspected she was avoiding him.

He would try to reason with her later. It was true most ladies never learned to shoot or ride, but he knew she could do it. She had to. If something bad happened, he wasn't sure she could count on him to protect her, not after what happened in Ringgold Gap.

That wasn't what worried him the most. In the last couple of months, the bouts with soldier's heart had happened a few more times, always when he was in the fields, so he could keep from her how bad it was. If he were to lose his wits when she was around, maybe seeing enemy soldiers that weren't there, what if he attacked her? He had to make sure she was safe, even if the danger came from him.

Writing in his journal every day and talking to Aaron and Reverend Haskell had helped, but the dreams still haunted him, nightmares about his men being killed in front of him while he just stood and watched. Delusions that sometimes came upon him when he was awake.

A group of men stopped near him. One of them, Horace Green, flailed his hands as if he were trying to take flight. "I'm telling you, if they bring that infernal draft to Ravenna, my boy's not going. He's only eighteen."

"Horace, calm down," Mr. Sutherland said. "You're not going to go against the United States government, and you know it."

"Besides, it might not come to that," Mr. Talbot, another farmer, said. "They're only going to have the draft if we don't meet our quota. Men are signing up every day."

Mr. Green's face turned red. "The government has no right to draft my boy. It goes against the United States Constitution. If Mr. Lincoln keeps it up, he'll have a fight on his hands in the North as well as the South."

Mr. Talbot pulled at his collar. "The Supreme Court says President Lincoln has the right."

"Well, that's one more reason Mr. Lincoln should be run out of office. Why don't he just let the rebels go? No use sending our boys to get killed over states that don't want to be a part of us anyhow."

"Horace, you're talking like a copperhead," Mr. Sutherland said. "You need to calm down."

"Just stating my opinion is all. Last I heard this was a free country, but with the draft and that infernal new income tax, and all, who knows how long it will stay that way?"

"You don't make enough to pay the tax, anyhow," Mr. Talbot said. "None of us do."

Mr. Green cracked his knuckles. "The only reason we're fighting with our own countrymen is Lincoln's friends with all them abolitionists, and you know it. Why, I've even heard he's had a fugitive slave at the White House. It's just not right for a president to consort with their kind."

Noah tried to mind his own business, but Mr. Green's opinions caused his heart rate to quicken. Noah had been one of the first to sign up to hold the Union together. His men had given their lives for it, and he'd always hoped the war would end slavery, even in the South.

"And you." At this point, Mr. Green decided to bring Noah into it when he pointed his finger in Noah's face. "You're part of the bloody Seventh. Why didn't you re-enlist like some of the others and finish the job?"

Noah's muscles tensed as they did whenever he had marched into battle, but he tried to control his tone. "I did my part for the Union. My three-year enlistment was up."

"You mustered out, but you want my boy to go and fight, and maybe die, in your place. You're a yellow belly."

A fog clouded Noah's vision as he lunged at Green, determined to beat the man into the ground. The cackle of a rooster, his regiment's battle cry, escaped from his lips. He pounded his fists into Green's face and stomach with a vague awareness of men holding his arms and shouting.

"Stop!"

"Green, get away from here."

"Calm down, Noah!"

"Get a hold of yourself!"

Green backed away, blood seeping from his nose and lips.

Noah slumped. The men restraining him let go, and he collapsed to the ground. His sight cleared.

Talbot and Sutherland were seeing to Green. Most of the congregation fixed their eyes on Noah. Aaron and Mr. Billings' disapproving looks choked the air from his lungs.

Molly sobbed in her mother's arms.

Reverend Haskell delivered a scorching glare. "Mr. Sutherland, maybe you'd better get the law."

Mr. Sutherland headed toward the jail.

"Mr. Billings, why don't you take Molly to your house?" the reverend said. "I'll send word after we settle this."

Molly's mother and father helped her into a carriage. Aaron patted Noah's shoulder before joining them.

"As for you..." Reverend Haskell crossed his arms, glaring down at Noah. "Wait in my office."

Noah nodded and pulled himself to his feet. Every muscle in his body shook, and he worried his knees would not hold as he headed toward the church. He didn't mind the scolding he was sure to receive from his pastor, or even a few nights in jail. He deserved it for losing control like that. He'd never hit anyone before in his life, except in battle.

What scared him more than anything was the horror on Molly's face as she cowered with her hand over her mouth. She was afraid of him.

He couldn't lose her.

7

Noah sat in the wooden chair in front of Reverend Haskell's desk. He felt like a boy waiting for his father to meet him in the woodshed. Father was always fair when he was sober, but when he was drunk... Noah didn't like to think about that.

The door opened and Reverend Haskell entered with the town marshal, Emmitt Collins. Marshal Emmitt was in his late thirties, square jaw, tall, built like a mountain man. Not a man to cross.

Noah stood at attention, prepared to accept the consequences.

"You're a lucky man," Marshal Emmitt said. "Green isn't pressing charges."

Noah released a sigh.

"Until now, I've never known you to cause trouble, but the acorn doesn't fall far from the tree." The marshal jabbed a finger into Noah's chest. "I ought to throw you in jail for the night anyway. Fighting on the church lawn. And on a Sunday to boot. See to it you don't start picking up your father's ways, or the next time, I'll haul you off and throw away the key. You cotton my meaning?"

Noah's jaw twitched. "Yes, sir." He'd spent his whole life proving he wasn't his father, and had destroyed the reputation he'd built in one day.

"Good." Marshal Emmitt stormed out.

Noah caught the look in Reverend Haskell's eyes and stayed at attention. When the man who'd been closer to him than his father got through, he might wish Marshal Emmitt had arrested him.

"Sit down." The reverend sat and propped his arms on his desk.

Noah sat across from him but didn't say anything. There was nothing to say, no defense excusing what he had done.

"What happened?"

"Green was spouting his copperhead views about the war and the draft." Noah ran his fingers along the edge of the desk. "He said I should have re-enlisted, that I wanted his son to die in my place. He called me a yellow belly."

"And since when do you pay attention to anything Horace Green says?"

Noah looked at the floor. He didn't have an answer for that.

Reverend Haskell leaned back in his chair. "You think your men died because of you. That's why he got to you."

He stroked his beard, unable to dispute what his pastor said. "I've asked God to heal me and forgive me like you said, and I've been writing in my journal every day, but I still have nightmares, almost every night, and I've had a few more bouts where I've seen graybacks that weren't there. It's not working."

The reverend stood and circled his desk. "Have faith, son." He placed his hand on Noah's shoulder. "Things don't just go away all at once. It takes time."

Noah placed his face in his hands. "I'm trying."

"Stop trying." Reverend Haskell grabbed the Bible off his desk and flipped through the pages. "Isaiah 41:10 says 'Fear thou not; for I am with thee: be not dismayed; for I am thy God: I will strengthen thee; yea, I will help thee; yea, I will uphold thee with the right hand of my righteousness.' Trust God. He'll help you through this."

"I know the verse, Reverend. I quoted it enough. How am I supposed to not be dismayed when I'm fighting off all these memories tormenting my mind? This battle's harder than any I faced in the war."

"I have some Scriptures for that, too." Reverend Haskell flipped through a few more pages. "Do you want to hear them, or are you too busy wallowing in self-pity."

Noah winced. The words hurt as much as a trip to the woodshed, but he needed to hear the rest. "Go ahead."

A slight grin crossed the reverend's mouth. "2 Corinthians 10:3-6. 'For though we walk in the flesh, we do not war after the flesh. For the weapons of our warfare are not carnal, but mighty through God to the pulling down of strong holds; Casting down imaginations, and every high thing that exalteth itself against the knowledge of God, and bringing into captivity every thought to the obedience of Christ.'"

For the first time in months, hope crept into Noah's heart. "Do you think it's possible? To bring my thoughts into captivity to the obedience of Christ?"

"Yes, I do." The reverend sat on the edge of his desk. "If it weren't, God wouldn't have commanded it, but it won't be easy. And it won't happen all at once. The question is if you are willing to obey God and surrender this to Him."

"I want to." Noah swiped at the moisture forming in his eyes. "Would you pray with me?"

ロ ロ ロ

Molly sat at the table with her mother, staring at her cup of tea. She drank a sip to wash down the lump in her throat. After shedding many tears, she had wiped her eyes and determined to make the best of this.

Noah was the gentlest man she'd ever known. If he attacked Mr. Green, he had to have a good reason.

Unless he had lost his wits again.

It was terrifying seeing Noah like that, pounding Mr. Green with his fists until he had to be pulled away. Her stomach quivered. She couldn't help being startled by it.

Molly had pleaded with Aaron and Father to go see what had happened. She couldn't take not knowing. What if Mr. Green had been hurt worse than she thought? What if the marshal took Noah to jail?

Mother placed an arm around her. "Maybe you should stay here tonight, just to make sure you're safe."

"Safe? From Noah?" Molly stood and paced to the door and back. "Mr. Green has spouted off his venom since I was a little girl. He's a copperhead and a bully, Mother, and you know it."

"Maybe, but Noah never would have reacted that way before."

Molly wrapped her arms around herself. She wanted to deny it, but all the ways her husband had changed flashed through her mind.

Mother poured some more tea. "You should have waited until he came back to marry him. We tried to warn you. War does things to men."

Molly's chin quivered. "Aaron's different, too, but you weren't about to throw him out. And he's doing fine now. Noah needs time to put everything behind him."

"I'm not suggesting you leave him. He's your husband, lawfully wedded in the sight of God, but I'm worried about you."

The door flew open, and Aaron and Father came inside.

Molly ran to her father. "What happened? Is he in jail?"

Father put his arms around her. "I'll tell you everything. Give me a chance." He motioned for them to sit around the table.

"I talked to Mr. Sutherland," Father said. "Green provoked Noah."

"If he'd said that balderdash in front of me," Aaron said, "I would have knocked him clean into next Sunday."

Father chuckled. "At least Green had the good sense not to press charges. Sutherland told him if he didn't let it drop, the whole town would be in an uproar about the things he said."

Molly let out a sigh of relief. "Then why isn't my husband home?"

"Reverend Haskell was still talking to him when we left." Aaron wiped a hand over his mouth. "I wouldn't want to be him right now."

A few minutes later, Noah arrived with his hands in his pockets and his eyes downcast.

"You look like you've been whipped worse than Green," Aaron said. "What did the reverend say to you?"

Noah delivered a half grin. "Nothing I didn't deserve." He placed his hands on Molly's shoulders. "I'm sorry I scared you."

"You're sorry!" Heat traveled up her back, and she pulled away. "It's not enough, you hear me? I don't even know you anymore."

Noah stepped toward her and held out his hand. "Molly--."

She brushed it aside. "You attacked a man on the church lawn where the whole town could see. If they hadn't pulled you away, you might have killed him. What's wrong with you?"

"Molly, please." He glanced at her father. "Can't this wait 'til we get home?"

"No, it can't. What happened out there that changed you into this? How many men did you kill?"

"Molly!" Her stomach tightened at the sound of her father's voice. "That's enough."

"Father, please." Molly glanced at Noah who seemed fascinated by his boots. "You don't understand what he's put me through."

Her father grabbed hold of her hands. "I told you to wait to marry him, but you wouldn't listen. Did you expect this to be easy? Noah has gone through the mill. Maybe he suffered different from Aaron, but he had it rough just the same."

"But Father…"

"He could have died out there. I taught you better than to treat your husband with disrespect, especially in public."

Her cheeks burned, and she wished she could crawl under the floorboards.

Noah stepped forward. "Mr. Billings, that's uncalled for. It hasn't been easy for her, me suffering from soldier's heart and then having a row on the church lawn."

"It doesn't matter. She married you for better or worse." Father turned to Molly. "You're his wife. Start acting like it."

Her bottom lip quivered as she looked into Noah's eyes. What she saw scared her more than his soldier's heart or getting into a fight. She'd never known him to be afraid.

Noah's jaw twitched. "Let's go home."

8

Noah hadn't talked to Molly on the way home, while they were eating supper, or as they sat on the porch that evening staring at the stars. He didn't know what to say. Despite what her father said, she had a right to be angry with him. He was useless as a husband.

He mulled over what Reverend Haskell had said to him earlier that day and took captive the thoughts tormenting him. He could do all things through Christ who strengthened him, even discuss things with his wife. "Molly, we need to talk."

Molly nodded as a tear rolled down her cheek. "I'm still angry with you, but I was wrong to disrespect you in public. I'm sorry."

"I forgive you." Noah grabbed hold of her hand. "I'm sorry, too. I never should have hit Mr. Green or scared you like that."

She wiped her face. "Husband, I love you, and I want our marriage to be a happy one."

"I do, too," Noah said.

"I don't know what to do. I prayed for three years that you would come home safe. I never thought you would change like this."

"I haven't changed toward you." He kissed her, but when she didn't respond, he drew back. "Reverend Haskell helped me to see what I need to do to get through this, but I need time."

"So do I," Molly said. "I promise I'll do my duty as your wife, but I can't act like everything's all right. When you attacked Mr. Green like that, it scared me. What do I do if you lose your wits again and assault me?"

"A fair question." Noah swallowed the lump in his throat. *Fear thou not, for I am with thee.* "I believe God will help us both, but that doesn't mean we shouldn't take precautions. That's why you need to learn to ride a horse and shoot."

"I'm not going to shoot a gun." Molly bit her lower lip. "I wouldn't fire it at you even if you did lose your wits."

Noah placed his arm around her. "If you learned to ride, you could at least get help."

He felt her tremble.

"I'll try. Promise you won't let me fall."

He kissed her forehead, knowing that was one promise he would keep, no matter what.

〇 〇 〇

Molly stroked Sam's mane, hoping the action would calm the horse. The sorrel had never looked so tall. "Shouldn't I learn to ride side-saddle?"

"I don't think so." Noah strapped on the saddle. "It's easier to ride astride."

"It's unladylike to ride that way."

"We live out here in the country. Nobody will see you." He tightened the cinch. "If you want to learn side-saddle later, I'll buy you one."

Sweat beaded Molly's forehead. "What do I do first?"

"Nothing too scary. I'll ride with you until you get used to handling the reins."

She nodded, and Noah helped her mount the horse. She adjusted her skirt to cover her legs. He hoisted himself behind her and placed his arms around her.

Working to steady her breathing, she leaned back against him. She remembered the first time she rode a horse, but he wasn't there then. This time she felt safe, protected.

He flicked the reins, and Sam trotted at a slow pace. The hoofs hit the ground with a slow steady rhythm, and she started to relax into it.

"You need to work on your form," Noah said. "You can't ride a horse leaning back."

She giggled. "I like leaning against you."

He chuckled in her ear. "Squeeze your knees together, and let your body rise and fall to the movement of the horse."

She did what he said. "Like this?"

"That's good. Now lean forward a little, and I'll let you take the reins."

They rode all afternoon, and he even helped her urge Sam into a full gallop, but he never let go of her. A warmth flooded her. She loved him so much. If only this solder's heart would go away, they could go back to the way things used to be between them.

He stopped the horse and helped her down. "Are you still afraid?"

"No, not with you helping me."

"I won't be there if something happens. You need to ride alone."

Molly nodded. "I know, and I will. Maybe tomorrow."

Noah handed her the reins. "Not tomorrow. Now."

"No!" Molly placed her arm on her roiling stomach. "I'm not feeling so well. It must be the heat. I need to lie down."

Noah stroked his beard. "I can't let you get out of it, sweetheart. You need to face this fear. Don't worry. You'll be fine."

She tried to swallow, but her mouth was too dry. "Please, let's wait until tomorrow."

He wrapped her in his arms and kissed her. "You can do this. I'll be right here."

Molly bit her lip. Sam looked back at her and whinnied. Even the horse was urging her on. She let out the breath she was holding and mounted.

"Good girl," Noah said. "Just like I showed you, flick the reins."

After a day of riding, it did feel comfortable in the saddle. Maybe it wasn't that hard after all. She flicked a little too hard, and Sam started into a gallop. She clenched the reins. "Help! Noah."

"You're all right." Noah called out. "Pull back."

She did, and the horse slowed, then stopped.

Noah ran to her and helped her down. "You did great, sweetheart. I'm so proud of you. We'll try again in a few days."

"That soon?" She thought she might be sick.

He leaned into her and kissed her. She surrendered to his kisses, but she still wasn't sure she could trust him to protect her.

Noah stood in the middle of the corn stalks reaching his shoulders and took a scoop of dirt in his hand. He let the dry sand seep through his fingers. They needed rain.

He glanced up at the dark clouds forming in the western sky. If they produced the storm they promised, it might be enough to save the crops. Otherwise, starting tomorrow, he'd carry buckets of water from the creek to pour on each stalk. Back-breaking work, but if it saved his harvest, it would be worth it. It would only be a couple of weeks before the corn would be ready to harvest.

Things had been better between him and Molly. The passion they had for each other returned since the horse riding lesson. She'd only been fourteen when they started courting, and he was four years older. He loved her so much it was hard to wait until her sixteenth birthday to take her as his wife. It was even harder when he learned he would have to catch the train to Cleveland to join up the day after the wedding, but her father had insisted they wait.

He had dreaded attending church with Molly that morning. After what had happened the week before, some might think he'd taken to his father's ways. He wouldn't blame them if they did, but if he wanted his wife to confront her fear of horses, he had to show the example.

It hadn't been as bad as he thought it would be. Mr. Sutherland greeted him at the door and patted him on the back. Mr. Talbot told him Green deserved it. Everyone else, including Reverend Haskell, acted as if nothing had happened. By the time the service began, Noah's trepidation had eased.

That was until he'd escorted Molly outside. Mr. Green stood beside his buggy with a swollen lip and black eye. He squeezed Molly's hand, knowing what he had to do. "Stay here." Uneasiness crossed her features, but he couldn't let that stop him.

He strode to the man and extended his hand. "Mr. Green, I'm sorry for attacking you like I did. Will you forgive me?"

Mr. Green scowled. "Well, ain't that something. You hit me and the whole town's on your side. Well, no sir, I do not accept your apology. And the next time you accost me, I'll see you rot in jail."

A lump had formed in Noah's throat. He'd nodded and walked away. He hadn't blamed Mr. Green for being angry.

I deserve it. I let my men die.

The back of his throat ached. "No! I won't think that. There's nothing I could have done to save my men. I've confessed my sins to God, including my cowardice and my violence toward Green. God is faithful and just to forgive me of my sins."

Fear thou not; for I am with thee: be not dismayed; for I am thy God: I will strengthen thee; yea, I will help thee; yea, I will uphold thee with the right hand of my righteousness.

He let out a slow breath as the anxiety left his body. Ever since he'd talked to Reverend Haskell, when this foreboding would infiltrate like a dark cloud surrounding his thoughts, he worked at taking it captive like the Scripture said. He'd also spent time every day praying for God to heal him, memorizing verses, and writing in his journal. It had only been a week, but it seemed to be working.

A strong wind whipped through the field, and the clouds opened and released a torrential downpour. Noah started toward the house as he uttered a "thank you" for the rain.

Since the horse riding lesson, Molly's attitude toward him had changed. If only she'd let him talk to her about what happened in Ringgold, or at least read his journal. She still wanted to forget the war ever happened, but his men's faces were etched in his memory. He didn't want to forget them.

Water soaked his shirt and pants and dripped off his hat. He gazed up toward the sky. It had a greenish cast to it. and the dark clouds swirled in a circular motion. This kind of dangerous weather produced hail, winds, maybe even a cyclone.

He had to get to Molly in time.

9

Molly kneaded the bread dough for supper, but her mind wasn't on her work. She kept mulling over Reverend Haskell's sermon, this morning. Things were better between Noah and her, but she realized she still had been in the wrong.

Her father was right. She expected it to be easy. Noah would come home as the conquering hero, swoop in, and handle all the problems she'd dealt with while he was gone. It would be as if he'd never left. She hadn't considered what he'd suffered, that he would need time and an understanding wife to help him through it.

She bit her lower lip and laid the bread aside to rise. Aaron had a hard time of it when he returned. Mother had told her he had nightmares and suffered with bouts of anger.

Molly remembered one day when she decided to stay with him and prepare his meals while her parents traveled to Cleveland for a carpentry job. She figured he would enjoy the company, but he wouldn't say more than two words to her. She read him the reports about the Seventh OVI's heroic feats at Gettysburg, hoping it would cheer him up.

Aaron threw his crutch across the room, shattering her mother's vase. Then he pounded his wooden leg into the floor until his stub became bruised and bloody. She tried to stop him, but wasn't strong enough. Finally, he collapsed on the floor, heaving and wincing in pain.

She had knelt beside him and held his hand until he was able to tell her why he'd become so angry. He'd let his unit down. They had to fight those battles without his help, all because of losing a leg.

Aaron had gazed up at her with an intensity in his hazel eyes that scared her. "Don't you see, Sis? Without my leg, I'm useless. I can't even help myself."

Molly had done everything she could to reassure him and help him until he learned to cope with it. Why didn't she do the same for her husband?

She opened the Bible to the passage Reverend Haskell used as his text, 2 Corinthians 1:3-4, and read aloud. "Blessed be God, even the Father of our Lord Jesus Christ, the Father of mercies, and the God of all comfort; Who comforteth us in all our tribulation, that we may be able to comfort them which are in any trouble, by the comfort wherewith we ourselves are comforted of God."

She remembered all the comfort that she'd received when Noah was away, and her heart broke. She wiped a tear off her cheek. She had the opportunity to comfort him the way she'd been comforted, but instead, she demanded he forget about the war and get over it.

Lord, forgive me.

Thunder crashed in the distance, and Molly glanced out the window. The sky grew dark. She lit the lantern and prayed Noah would make it inside before the rain started. A few moments later, torrents crashed into the window, and the wind howled through the trees.

Noah banged the door open. "It's a bad one, Molly. We need to get to the root cellar."

Her stomach churned. She grabbed the lamp and followed him into the tempest. A branch broke and fell on the path in front of them. Noah grabbed her hand and pulled her close just in time.

When they came to the root cellar, he yanked open the wooden trap door and ushered her inside. He followed and latched the door.

She made her way to the back and sat in the corner on the dirt floor beside a bin of potatoes. Noah sat beside her, wrapped his arms around her, and leaned against the stone wall. The cellar where they stored vegetables and cured meat was barely tall enough for Molly to stand.

Thunder crashed, closer this time, and the wind roared in fury. Noah sat beside her and wrapped his strong arms around her, comforting her, as she should have been comforting him.

The wood beams above them rattled as water poured into the dugout and drained into the ditch Noah had dug.

Molly leaned her head against her husband's chest and thought about telling him how sorry she was for the way she'd acted, but the storm was so loud she doubted he'd be able to hear her. There was plenty of time for apologies later.

After a while, the wind died down, and the rain slowed to a patter.

Molly lifted her head. "Looks like it's about over." She stood and headed to the ladder leading to the hatch.

Noah grabbed her, pulled her back. "No, don't." His eyes darted in the lantern light. "They're out there."

Her chest tightened. "Who's out there?"

"The rebels. Don't you hear the cannons? We need to stay hidden."

For the first time, she understood. He was never a danger to her. All this time, he wanted to protect her. "It's all right, husband." She led him back toward the wall. Even when he was afraid, and the war crashed through his thoughts, he considered her safety above his own. "We'll stay here until you feel safe."

Noah nodded and sat beside her, and she held his hand. *Lord, help him through this.*

🦶 🦶 🦶

Noah's heart raced. He'd done it again, found himself in the middle of a battle that wasn't there. Molly sat beside him, her head on his shoulder, acting as if nothing was wrong. Probably hiding how scared she was. "I'm so sorry. Did I hurt you? I didn't mean to…" The words choked in his throat.

Molly clasped his hand. "No, you didn't hurt me. You were trying to keep me safe."

Noah pulled away.

"Everything's all right." She held her hands up as if he was a wounded animal she was trying to calm. "Every time this happened, you only wanted to protect me. I can see that now. Let's go inside. I'll fix us some tea, and we can talk about it."

He backed against the ladder. His heart sank to his stomach. Any chance he had of proving himself to her, of getting her to trust him again, blew away with the storm. "I can't. I need to get out of here."

"Where are you going?" She stepped toward him, placed her hand on his arm. "I'll go with you."

His stomach tightened. Now she thought he was crazy, that he couldn't be trusted to go anywhere alone. "No! Stay here."

Climbing the ladder, he rushed into the house and grabbed his Springfield rifle off the hooks over the mantle. Making his way to the bedroom, he rummaged through the trunk until he found where Molly had put away his uniform. He pulled it out and hurried outside, leaving the trunk open.

The light rain trickled on his face. He squished through the mud, stepping into a puddle as he pulled open the barn doors. He led Sam out of his stall and saddled the horse as quickly as he could. He needed to get away before she came after him.

He cinched the saddle and swallowed the lump in his throat. It wouldn't be easy, but if he loved Molly, he had to leave her. He mounted Sam and rode off through the woods.

He galloped toward the edge of town. He'd leave a note for Molly with Aaron. His brother-in-law could return the horse to her. Then he'd march to the recruiting office and reenlist. The army was still looking for men to join Sherman's march to the sea or to help Grant with the siege in Petersburg.

Reaching Main Street, he rode past Black Horse Tavern. The old, log cabin pub used to be a stagecoach stop, but its only use since the train came to town was to serve whiskey to men who wanted to get drunk. Noah's father had spent more time there than he did at home.

Noah hadn't been in the tavern since he was a boy. His mother had often sent him to fetch his father. He'd sworn that he would never allow whiskey to touch his lips, but he had also promised he'd would never hurt his wife the way his father hurt his mother.

He'd broken one promise, so why not break the other? He turned his horse toward the tavern and hitched him to the post. A drink would fortify him for what he had determined to do. He needed it. He couldn't face going back to war without it.

When he marched inside, the stench of liquor, body odor, and sawdust hit him. He stood by the door and allowed his eyes to adjust to the low light. There was only one lantern, and no windows to cast light. The men here didn't want to be seen.

He strode to the bar. "Whiskey."

The bartender was a skinny man with a missing tooth, making him slur his words. "Glasssss or bottle?"

"Glass." If he ordered the bottle, he might not make it to the recruiting office.

The bartender slammed a tin cup on the counter and poured some whiskey.

Noah sat at one of the tables and set the cup in front of him. He could smell it and wondered how it would feel traveling down his throat.

A rumpled older man at the table beside him was passed out with his head in his arms, drooling. His father often looked like that.

Noah remembered once when his father had decided to head to the tavern. He was only about twelve at the time, and somehow, he found the courage to ask, "Father, why do you have to go off drinking when you know how much it hurts Mother? Don't you care about her?"

He had flinched, expecting his father to hit him. Instead, Father set his hand on his shoulder. "Son, I'd give anything to stop. I do love you and your mother, but ever since I took that first drink, the whiskey got hold of me, and it won't let go. I wish it were different."

His father died a few months later, not knowing the freedom he sought could be found in Christ.

Noah stared at the brown liquid. If he took this drink, he might not be able to stop with one. He'd become that old man. He'd become his father.

He slid the cup aside and strode outside. *Lord, forgive me. Help me finish this, for Molly's sake.*

Noah decided to make a stop at the parsonage. Reverend Haskell would understand why he had to do this even if Molly or Aaron didn't, and he owed it to the man to explain why he had to leave. He hitched his horse and knocked on Reverend Haskell's door.

His pastor's face lit up. "Noah, my boy. Come on in. I'm surprised to see you out on a day like this."

Noah stepped inside. "I can't stay. I stopped to say good-bye."

Reverend Haskell's lips pressed together. "What do you mean? Are you going somewhere?"

Noah wiped his hand over his face. "I did good taking my thoughts captive over the last week, until today. When we took refuge in the root cellar, I had another attack."

"I'm sorry, my boy, but this takes time. You can't stop because of one failure."

Noah's jaw twitched. "I can't put Molly through this. I'm re-enlisting. I never should have come home before the war was over. Like Mr. Green said, I should have finished what I started."

Reverend Haskell delivered a glower. "What does Molly think about this?"

Noah glanced at his feet. "She doesn't know. I'll leave her a note with Aaron explaining it all."

The vein in Reverend Haskell's neck pulsed. "So you're running away. When you told me you were a coward, I thought you were being too hard on yourself. It turns out you were right. You're a yellow belly who can't even face his wife and tell her the truth, that you've given up on her and your marriage."

Heat shot up Noah's back as he grabbed Reverend Haskell by the collar. "I love my wife!" He let go, stepped back, held up his hands. "Oh, Reverend, I'm sorry. I'm..." He slumped into a nearby chair, mortified he would do such a thing.

Reverend Haskell sat beside him. "If you love Molly as much as you say, don't you at least owe it to her to tell her why you're leaving?"

Noah stroked his beard. Reverend Haskell was right, but how could he face Molly? How could he tell her he was leaving?

10

Molly's stomach quivered as she watched Noah ride away. She wanted to help him, to make him understand that she'd support him through this. She didn't blame him for wanting to get away after the way she'd treated him since he got home. Of course, he expected the worst.

There was nothing she could do for him now. Whenever he needed to talk, he would ride into town to see Aaron or Reverend Haskell. That's where he'd be headed now. When he returned in a few hours, she could let him know how sorry she was and how she would make it up to him.

In the meantime, she had work to do. Other than a few tree limbs in the yard, she didn't see any damage from the storm, but she needed to check everything to make sure.

She sloshed through the mud and looked inside the barn. No loose timbers, and the cow mooed, indignant at being cooped up in the barn. The chickens and rooster were all accounted for. A light shower sprinkled her face as she strode toward the cornstalks. They looked greener than they had in weeks. The rain had done them good. Being careful to avoid the puddles, she walked around the outside of the house. No damage.

She went inside, removed her muddy boots, and tried to decide what to do next. How could she reassure Noah she would be there for him?

Her mother always said that food was the way to a man's heart. If that were true, having supper ready with blueberry pie, his favorite dessert, would help. She scooped flour out of the sack and made the pie crust.

The kitchen door banged open, and two men with pistols drawn stormed inside. She let out a scream, and one of them, a man in his early twenties with pox marks on his face, grabbed her. "Don't worry, ma'am. We're not going to hurt you." He grinned in an ugly way. "Unless you do something foolish."

Molly could barely rasp out the words. "What do you want?"

The second man, a little older and taller than the first, stroked his full brown beard. "We need some food and a dry place to sleep tonight. Do what we say, and we'll be on our way soon."

Molly pulled away from the poxed man. "You won't find anything to steal here. We keep our money in the bank."

"We don't want your money," the bearded man said."

"Then why are you doing this?"

"There's a wagon and a carriage in the barn, but we didn't see no horses," the bearded man said. "How soon before your man gets here?"

Molly stepped back, her stomach churning from fear. "He won't. He's a soldier."

"You hear that?" The poxed man who had grabbed her earlier pressed her shoulders against the wall. "Her husband's a soldier. Went off and enlisted without even leaving her a horse."

She could smell the tobacco on his breath and turned her head away.

"Joe, we're not here for that," the bearded man said. "Ma'am, we're not planning to hurt anyone, but for your husband's sake, you need to tell us when you're expecting him."

Shaking her head no, she pressed her lips tight.

Joe took hold of her chin and made her face him. "Is that what he did? Leave you without a horse?"

Molly's stomach hardened until it felt like it was made of stone while she tried to figure out a lie they would believe. "He took the horse with him. Said my brother would bring it back, next week."

"Joe," the bearded man said. "Hide the horses in the barn just in case." After Joe left, the bearded man turned back to Molly. "Don't you worry, ma'am. If we have our way, the war will be over, and your husband will be home soon."

Molly let out a whimper. "What do you want with me?"

He placed a hand on the wall beside her and leaned close. "Just a place to hide out from the law."

Molly gasped. "You're outlaws?"

He stepped away and lit his cigar. "No, we're not outlaws. We're the Sons of Liberty. All we want is to stop this war, but Governor Brough didn't see it that way."

"I don't understand." She stepped to the side, determined to get away from this madman.

"He ordered his men to arrest us."

She inched another step. "Then you're traitors?"

The vein in the man's neck throbbed as he hit the wall with his fist. "We're patriots!"

The pounding of her heartbeat throbbed in her ears as she dashed to the door.

He grabbed her arm, jerked her around, and slapped her.

Startled by the noise and pain, she drew her hand to her cheek.

He dragged her to a chair and pushed her shoulders until she sat. He pulled out a handkerchief and wiped his face. "Don't do that again." His tone calmed. "If you're good, we'll leave in a couple of days, and you can spend the rest of the war pining for your husband. You know he probably won't make it back alive."

She blinked, determined not to let him see her cry.

"If you try that again…" He pressed the barrel of his revolver against her head. "I'd hate to have to shoot a woman, but I will."

Noah pulled up on Sam's reins at the edge of the cornfield. The corn stalks had come alive after the heavy rain. In a couple of weeks, his fields would be ready to harvest, but he wouldn't be here. He'd be in some battlefield in Georgia setting fire to stores and homes or raiding towns and villages near Richmond.

He considered going ahead with his original plan and leaving without having to face Molly, despite what Reverend Haskell said, but he couldn't. It would make things easier for him, but it would devastate her. He was doing this to make things better for her, not to avoid the pain it would cause him.

Setting his jaw, he rode to the barn. He dismounted and led his sorrel inside. Two horses stood in the stalls, one a bay gelding, the other a roan. He'd never seen them in town before.

His stomach knotted as he searched the barn and the loft. Their farm was so far outside of town that nobody ever came by, at least anyone whose horse Noah wouldn't recognize.

No reason to fret. His soldier's heart was making him see danger where none existed, just as it did during the storm. His jaw set. Grabbing his rifle, he loaded the gunpowder and musket ball and headed to the house.

Inching his way closer, he stayed low. His gaze travelled from the corn fields to the corral. He made it to the kitchen window and let out a breath before peering inside.

A young man with pox marks sat at the table and pointed a Colt army revolver at Molly while she cooked eggs in a skillet. She had a red mark on her cheek.

Noah's fist clenched. Since the man was facing away from the window, Noah took a chance and looked around to see if there was anyone else. If there was anyone else, he was in another room.

Noah squatted under the window. He needed a plan. He only had a one-shot musket rifle against a six-shot .44 caliber cylinder revolver. Even if he could get off a shot before the man fired, he wouldn't be able to load again in time if another culprit ran in with a gun. Maybe he should go for the sheriff.

No. He wouldn't leave his wife alone with a man who struck her and was holding her at gunpoint.

As much as he wanted to believe there was only one gunman in the house, the two saddled horses told him differently.

So, two men and two guns.

He leaned against the side of the house and stroked his beard, trying to come up with a tactic to rescue his wife.

There was only one way. The rifle would be useless, so he'd do a frontal attack. Hopefully he would surprise pox man enough so he couldn't shoot him right away. All he wanted was to keep him busy long enough for Molly to get away. If there was another man, he'd worry about that when the time came.

Sam was saddled and ready for Molly to ride to town to get help. He sent up a prayer she would get hold of her fear of riding. The culprits' horses were also saddled. If the men subdued him, they'd ride after her.

He made his way back to the barn, unsaddled the roan and the bay, and led them out back. He slapped them both on the rumps and winced at the noise it made when they galloped off. Glancing at the house, he didn't see anyone. They must not have heard.

Okay, then.

He slunk up to the house, let out a rooster crow, and charged into the kitchen. The man turned. Noah lunged into him and knocked him to the ground. "Molly, run!"

The man tried to point his gun.

Noah jerked the man's hand away and tried to push it to the floor. "Ride Sam to town."

The pistol drew closer to Noah's face. "Get help."

He struggled to pull the revolver from the man's hand. Molly dashed out the door and slammed it.

A sharp pain hit the back of Noah's head. Everything went black.

11

Molly's lungs burned. She ran to the barn as fast as her legs would carry her. She glanced back to see if they were following. Nobody there. Maybe she should try to help Noah instead of getting away. What if they shot him?

There wasn't anything she could do. She had to ride to town, get the marshal.

Opening the barn door, her jaw clenched. Their sorrel stood saddled and ready for her to ride. Sam strode toward her, oblivious to the terror he caused. She had to do this.

She swallowed, pulled up her skirt, and hoisted herself onto the horse. It was so high off the ground, everything around her swirled. She placed her hand on her stomach and tried to think of another way to help Noah. Before she could come up with one, the men shouted and ran toward the barn. She squeezed her knees, flicked the reins hard, and rode toward town.

The wind whipped through her hair as she leaned forward in the saddle the way Noah had taught her. She was tempted to stop, but she didn't dare. Those men would be after her soon. Besides, Noah needed her.

When she reached the train tracks, she chanced a look back, but nobody was in pursuit. She crossed the tracks and steered the horse to follow them. It would be faster than staying on the road. It was only a five mile ride to the train depot, but it seemed longer. She slowed the horse to a trot and turned onto Sycamore, then Main, and hitched the horse in front of the jail. Taking a moment to steady her breathing, she dismounted and hurried into the marshal's office.

Marshal Emmitt stood. "Is something wrong? Did somebody attack you?"

She splayed her hand over her sore cheek. It was starting to burn. "Noah's in trouble."

The marshal furrowed his brow. "What did he do?"

"Not him. Two no accounts pushed their way into our home. Noah tried to save me. Marshal, he's still with them. Please, hurry."

"Wyatt." Marshal Emmitt called to his deputy as he grabbed his Henry rifle. "Get some men together and meet me at the Andrews' farm." He turned to Molly. "Are you sure there were only two?"

"Yes, sir."

"What did they look like?"

Molly tried not to panic while she described the men and their horses. This was taking too long. They needed to hurry, or it might be too late.

"Don't worry. We'll get them." Marshal Emmitt strode out the door.

Molly's knees buckled, and she slipped into a nearby chair, but she couldn't stay seated. Praying they would get there in time, she left the marshal's office and strode to her father's house. He would give her a ride home so she could check on her husband.

Noah had to be all right.

Father pulled the buggy next to the house. Molly didn't wait for him to stop. She jumped down and ran into the front door. "Noah! Husband!"

"In here," Noah called from their bedroom.

She hurried to his side. He lay face-down on the rope bed with Doctor Griffith beside him, threading a needle. Blood from a gash on the back of his head soaked through a bandage.

"Even with the Laudanum, this is gonna hurt," the doctor said.

Molly grabbed hold of Noah's hand. He winced every time the needle went into his flesh and squeezed her hand, but he didn't make any sound.

Doctor Griffith tied off the stitch and threaded the needle again. Molly's stomach turned when he pushed it into the wound again, but she wouldn't turn away. Noah risked his life for hers, and she wanted to be brave for him.

After meticulously finishing off five stiches, the doctor said, "That should do it."

"Is he all right?" Molly asked.

"He will be." The doctor had Noah sit up and wrapped a fresh bandage around his crown. "Good thing his head is as hard as it is. He could have been killed, rushing them like that."

Noah groaned. "How long before the headache goes away?"

"A week, maybe two. I'll be back to take the stitches out then." Doctor Griffith gathered his tools into his black bag. He turned to Molly. "See to it he doesn't get out of this bed for at least a couple of days."

"I have crops to harvest, Doc." Noah started to stand, let out a heavy breath, and sank back into the bed.

Molly placed a hand on his shoulder to make sure he didn't try that again. "They'll keep. Doctor, I'll see to it he rests if I have to hogtie him."

"And you, young lady…" The doctor held onto her chin and turned the side of her face toward him. "Make sure you keep cold cloths on that cheek. It looks pretty swollen."

"I will," Molly said.

"Nothing more I can do around here." The doctor headed to the door. "Let me know if he has any dizziness or nausea, or if he becomes confused."

"Wait," Molly said. "Do you know what happened to those men?"

Doctor Griffith turned. "The marshal and his posse went after them. That's all I know."

Molly nodded, and the doctor left as her father entered the room.

"Glad to see you're all right, Noah." Father's voice thickened. "Thanks for keeping my girl safe."

Noah shrugged. "I'd never let any harm come to her if I could help it."

Father headed to the door. "I'll leave you two alone."

As the door clicked behind them, silence shrouded the room. Molly knew what she wanted to say, but she wasn't sure how to start.

Noah touched her cheek. "I'm sorry I left you like that. If I'd stayed, they might not have hurt you."

"Or they might have killed us both." Molly leaned forward and kissed him gently. "You saved my life. Even when you were suffering from those bouts, you tried to protect me. I can see that now."

He cleared his throat. "About that, it's going to take time to get over what happened to me in the war. I don't want to hurt you, so I've made a decision. I'm going to reenlist for another year. That will give us both the time we need."

Heat rushed to Molly's neck. She placed her hands on her hips and glared at him. "You aren't reenlisting, so get that thought out of your head."

"But Molly—"

"I'm the one who's in the wrong here. I should have been more understanding. Even when you weren't yourself and saw enemy soldiers that weren't there, you tried to keep me from harm's way. That's why you grabbed me like you did."

"But what if I hurt you?"

"You won't. I trust you, husband. I'm sorry I didn't help you through this, but that's going to change. I'm your wife, and I'm going to be by your side for better or worse, no matter how long it takes."

Noah pulled her by his side and kissed her as if he never wanted to let her go, but he didn't have to worry. She was right where she wanted to be. By his side where she belonged.

12

Noah parked the wagon outside of Sutherland's Grocery Store and helped Molly down. Dried leaves crunched underfoot It had been a couple of months since the men had invaded their home and held Molly prisoner. Marshal Emmitt and his posse had caught up with the men and arrested them.

The marshal told Noah the Sons of Liberty had plans to break into the prison at Johnson Island in Lake Erie and arm the Confederate soldiers with rifles. Fortunately, they were found out before they could carry out their plan. One of their leaders had already been hung for his part.

Since the traitors had invaded their home, Molly had been supportive as Noah fought the battle of guarding his mind, and although he still had nightmares and times of agitation, he hadn't seen any more rebels who weren't there.

After they placed their order for supplies to get them through the winter months, Noah suggested they stop at Poe's. Once the snows started, Molly would have plenty of time for sewing. And now with a baby on the way...

They stepped into the store. Mrs. Thompson stood at the table, spreading out a bolt of fabric. Noah's stomach tightened when he thought about how he treated her when he first got home. She had avoided him ever since, but it was time to change that.

"Mrs. Thompson," Noah said. "A few months back, you asked Molly and me for supper so I could talk to you about Tom. I'm sorry I acted like I did."

Mrs. Thompson furrowed her brow. "I guess I shouldn't have pressed you."

"No, it's my fault. Please, forgive me."

"Of course."

Noah wiped his hand across his mouth. "If the invitation still stands, we'd love to come this Sunday, before the weather gets too bad."

Her eyes watered. "Are you sure?"

"I want to tell you how brave and honorably your son served."

"I'd like that." Mrs. Thompson excused herself and left.

Molly placed her arm through his. "Husband, how much material can I afford to buy?"

"With the bumper crop we had, get everything you need plus enough to make you a new dress after the baby is born."

Molly smiled and went about purchasing the fabric she wanted.

Afterwards, they walked back to Sutherland's, and Noah loaded the groceries on the wagon. They rode home for a little ways before Molly spoke. "Husband, I was thinking, if you still want to show it to me, I'd like to read your journal."

Noah smiled. "I still want you to."

Throughout the journal, Noah had written down all the events wounding his heart and mind. It would take time to win this war, but God was healing his soldier's heart.

Tamera Lynn Kraft has always loved adventures. She loves to write historical fiction set in the United States because there are so many stories in American history. There are strong elements of faith, romance, suspense and adventure in her stories. She has received 2nd place in the NOCW contest, 3rd place TARA writer's contest, and is a finalist in the Frasier Writing Contest. Her newest novel, *Red Sky Over America* is Book 1 of the *Ladies of Oberlin* series. *Alice's Notions* is a historical romantic suspense set shortly after World War II. She also has novellas published in eBook and print.

Tamera been married for thirty-nine years to the love of her life, Rick, and has two married adult children and three grandchildren. She has been a children's pastor for over twenty years. She is the leader of a ministry called Revival Fire for Kids, where she mentors other children's leaders, teaches workshops, and is a children's ministry consultant and children's evangelist, and has written children's church curriculum. She is a recipient of the 2007 National Children's Leaders Association Shepherd's Cup for lifetime achievement in children's ministry.

You can contact Tamera online at these sites.

Website: *http://tameralynnkraft.net*

Newsletter: *http://eepurl.com/cdybpb*

Goodreads:

https://www.goodreads.com/author/show/7334438.Tamera_Lynn_Kraft

Word Sharpeners Blog: *http://tameralynnkraft.com*

Facebook: *http://facebook.com/tameralynnkraft*

Twitter: *http://twitter.com/tamerakraft*

SUMMER SONG

A Tabor Heights novella; sequel to **FIRESONG.**

By Michelle L. Levigne

December -- Tabor Heights, Ohio

Firesong's final Christmas concert took place at the Tabor High School auditorium. It was appropriate, because Dani Paul, her brother, and their three Gibson cousins had won their first talent competition there. Jason had still been in high school, and Dani had been in middle school. A lot of growth and change and loss had occurred in the years between then and now.

Dani moved off the stage after the final encore, followed by Bruno, the newest member of the band, and third keyboard player since her brother had been murdered. She picked up her pace, remembering how Bruno had been eyeing the mistletoe in the dressing room doorway. Now was not the time to have it out with him. She liked Bruno, but not like he seemed to want her to.

"Merry Christmas." Kurt Green filled the doorway. He laughed, dark eyes sparkling, when Dani stumbled, sure she was imagining him.

"You jerk!" She laughed and flung her arms around him.

Kurt spun her into the room and kissed her like she had been dreaming of for the past three months.

"Excuse me." Bruno stomped to the other side of the room.

Perfect timing. Dani's face felt scorched, but at least now she knew Bruno would believe her when she said, yet again, she had a boyfriend. Much more than a boyfriend, judging by that kiss.

Jason, Jim, and Tom Gibson let out whoops and other teasing noises and surged through the doorway. She reluctantly stepped out of the curve of Kurt's arm so he could greet her cousins. Her gaze landed on Bruno, jamming his arms into his jacket. His face was redder than the poinsettias that had lined the front of the stage.

"We can clean up tomorrow, right?" He directed his words to Tom.

"Uh -- yeah." Tom took a step back and frowned, watching Bruno stomp out of the dressing room.

"Was that --" Kurt began.

"Yeah, Bruno, the new keyboard." Jim shook his head and stepped into the doorway, leaning out to look down the hall after him. "Guess he finally got the message."

"Message?" Tom dropped into the nearest chair and started unbuttoning his Christmas red vest. He glanced between Dani and Kurt and a light seemed to dawn. "Oh yeah, that message."

Dani was just tired enough, she didn't care about her cousins' juvenile reactions. She leaned into Kurt as he wrapped his arm around her waist, rested her head on his shoulder, and sighed as several tight bands inside her loosened for the first time in months.

She loved working for the Allen Michaels Evangelistic Association, but traveling with Firesong as the face of the youth ministry required sacrifices. Such as being on the road three-quarters of the year. She had anticipated the sacrifices that came with ministry. However, she hadn't anticipated falling in love with a man high in the ranks of AMEA. Thank goodness for the unlimited plan on her phone and data contract. She and Kurt had drastically conflicting schedules so they were never in the same town at the same time. They emailed every other day, texted several times a day, and sent photos and video clips. Constant contact didn't make up for being close enough to share his warmth, smell his subtly spicy-clean aftershave, and savor that slight zing in her lips from his kiss.

"What message?" Kurt said, as he and Dani settled into folding chairs.

"Hey, we've done our best, but why should the guy believe Dani is taken when you're nothing but a picture on our phones and a name in emails?" Jason shrugged.

"Taken?" Kurt grinned. "Well, not official enough for me." His gaze locked with hers, and his smile slowly faded. "How bad has it been?"

"If Bruno was a little more pushy, maybe there wouldn't be a problem. You know, big confrontation, yelling, hurt feelings, then it finally gets through his thick skull." Tom shrugged.

Jim gestured at the mistletoe in the doorway. "Hopefully that finally did the trick."

Dani hoped so, too. She glanced down at her hand clasped in Kurt's. It was on the tip of her tongue to say that if she was wearing a ring, none of them would have to worry about things like that. How could they really get close enough to be sure they were a good match, the right match, when they hardly spent any face-to-face time together?

Despite that kiss he gave her just now, how could she be sure about his feelings, let alone hers? If he gave her a ring for Christmas, she didn't know if she had the courage to say yes.

The fact that she had been thinking about Kurt and rings and revising her road schedule to accommodate married life was a little frightening in and of itself.

♡ ♡ ♡

The incident after the concert lay heavy on Dani's mind all through

Christmas break. She and Kurt spent as much time together as they could. That meant time with his aunt and uncle. Their daughter had been married to Dani's brother for a few months, until she died of an inoperable brain tumor. Then he was murdered. The holidays always brought those bitter-sweet memories closer to the surface. This year seemed especially poignant.

Sometimes when she was especially tired and blue, Dani wondered if she and Kurt would only have a short time together before some tragedy separated them, some radical lunatic got through AMEA security and bombed a crusade where either of them was working. While dying in service to God sounded noble and romantic, she wanted to grow old with Kurt. She wanted to argue about stupid things like squeezing the toothpaste tube and socks on the floor and disciplining their children. How could they raise children if both of them were on the road most of the year -- and never together?

She knew better than to bring up questions like that, now, when a ring was nowhere in sight. The timing never seemed right for such discussions. Then they ran out of time. Kurt had to fly to Australia two days after Christmas. Firesong had a New Year's Eve fundraiser concert sponsored by the Arc Foundation, a philanthropic group that partnered regularly with AMEA. Not much down time for either of them.

ꙮ ꙮ ꙮ

Bruno announced his resignation from Firesong after the New Year's Eve concert. They were scrambling to take apart the sound system and pack up their instruments, and pile into the vans that would take them to Quarry Hall, the Arc Foundation's headquarters, for the countdown to midnight. Dani got out of the backstage area and let Tom handle this. He was their leader, after all. She busied herself with packing away their concert clothes to be washed and making a list of what they would pack for their first four-week tour of the new year. Not busy enough, though, to avoid thinking about Bruno. All of them had expected him to quit, just not so soon.

On the ride to Quarry Hall for the party, which Bruno elected to skip, Tom told Dani what they had agreed to. He would tour with them until their three-week break around college spring break. They had to find someone to take over at keyboard by the end of March. Then they would have the three weeks of downtime to bring the new keyboardist up to speed. Everything was nice and neat and amicable, but Dani had the niggling feeling some loose strings wouldn't be cleanly wrapped up.

ꙮ ꙮ ꙮ

By the third college stop on the tour, audition videos were arriving at

AMEA headquarters, and Conrad, Firesong's supervisor, told them more than dozen inquiries had come in already. Those who passed the first round of evaluations would be invited to meet with them for face-to-face interviews during the tour, and to see how they "clicked." Dani wondered if it mattered how well they got along with the candidates. Hadn't they gotten along well with Bruno from the start? Look how that "click" had turned to a "clank."

Bruno seemed in good spirits, although he avoided talking to Dani. She barely noticed. Firesong's days were full with traveling, arriving and setting up, interacting with students before and after concerts, collapsing in the guest quarters, having breakfast with music students and teachers, then hitting the road to the next college and concert. Their first break in the routine on their sixth stop, their half-day of freedom, included the first keyboard candidate interview.

Kurt caught up with them there. Dani didn't feel any guilt leaving her cousins to deal with the candidate, while she and Kurt had their first official date since Christmas. Listening to the Gibson brothers discuss the man later, before they all went to dinner, Dani was glad she hadn't been there. She wished the candidate hadn't either, because he started the meeting by listing all the "flaws," stylistic and theological, in their CDs. Tom asked why he hadn't mentioned that in his application. When he refused to answer, Tom skipped ahead in the interview, to the statement of faith and compliance with AMEA standards. The candidate refused to sign it. When pressed, he admitted that he intended to use Firesong to confront Dr. Allen Michaels about his "theological errors." Then he gave them a list of his demands before he would join. Tom had to tell him three times that they weren't offering him the job.

"Did you report this to Conrad?" Kurt said.

The five of them had met in the room Jim and Jason shared in the college guesthouse. Dani suspected they used that room because Tom shared a room with Bruno, who was notable by his absence.

"Didn't have to. We were Skyping the interview," Tom said. "Should have seen his face when he started threatening our reputation, what he would tell people about the interview, and we reminded him everything was being recorded. He signed a paper permitting it, too."

A knock on the door interrupted them before Dani could ask what Conrad said. Bruno had returned. They tried to laugh about the interview over dinner, and Dani was impressed that Bruno didn't seem at all smug. Just maybe he felt a little guilty about the trouble he was causing them? He really was a talented keyboard player, able to shift gears with little warning, and he got along so good with the teens. She was grateful he had only spent three months with them. Barely any pictures of him appeared on their website or blog. He would fade from memory quickly enough to leave no scars.

Bruno claimed he was tired and didn't join them in the guesthouse living room after dinner. He had stared at Kurt and Dani's joined hands too many times on the walk to and from the college cafeteria.

"That does it," Tom said, after a door slammed shut at the far end of the hall. "The next keyboard player has to be a girl."

"Yeah, and what do we do if she falls for one of us?" Jason fluttered his eyelashes. "Especially if she falls for you?"

They laughed. Tom calmly responded that his wife, Stephanie, would love to come on tour with them.

Later, Dani wondered who else remembered Jason's joke when they met Salem Tucker eight concerts later. Tiny, with coffee-and-cream skin and an incredible, low alto voice, she was a dynamo on the keyboard. Jason looked like he had when he was twelve, tried to jump four bicycles on his skateboard, and landed flat on his back. Wide-eyed, with a goofy grin, he quickly dominated the hour-long interview.

"Love at first sight," Dani reported to Kurt when they talked on the phone that evening. "For all of us, but triple that for Jason."

Kurt had called with an interesting proposition for the band. AMEA had several boot camps that trained teens for summer mission projects. The rest of the year, the campgrounds were available for retreats and training programs. Drew and Eve Leone, friends of Kurt's, ran Camp Sower, a music boot camp, in Coshocton. Would Firesong be interested in participating in boot camp this year? The plan would be to give aspiring Christian musicians guidance, with an eye to expanding AMEA's music ministry. As an added plus -- for Dani, at least -- Kurt would be there during the entire operation.

By the time they got off the road for spring break, and settled down to rehearse with Salem, Firesong had decided yes, they would participate. Dani almost felt sorry for Bruno when he said goodbye, because he sounded as interested in working boot camp as they did.

May -- Camp Sower -- Coshocton, Ohio

Firesong arrived in the middle of the first influx of staffers and delivery trucks dropping off supplies for the college-age boot camp. The organized chaos impressed Dani, until she turned around and saw Bruno wearing a fluorescent green t-shirt clearly labeled Staff. Just how had he been hired without anyone at AMEA making the connection and telling Firesong?

"If he didn't badmouth us to headquarters, and we didn't tell people he quit because you wouldn't be his girlfriend, why would anyone turn him down?" Tom said, when she told him. "It's his problem if he can't handle seeing you and Kurt together."

"He'd just better not make it mine."

They went to the administration building to report the possible problem to Drew Leone. Dani was only slightly relieved by his clear surprise. He was very sure that Bruno's application said nothing about touring with Firesong. He would have remembered a detail like that.

"We can't really make a fuss about it," he admitted. "You guys are basically working undercover. Nobody knows you're supposed to be here this first week, until the big reveal at the concert this weekend. Everybody's on a first-name basis. All church memberships and performance experiences are to be left at the camp gates. We want to put everyone on an even footing. The kids sort themselves out soon enough." He made a note on the notepad next to his computer. "I'm going to check into why he would leave that detail out. Kind of suspicious."

The next hour made up for the first shock. Dani met Eve Leone and her mother and stepfather, the Hansons. Eve had met Mr. Hanson when she came down to Coshocton three years ago to supervise building the camp on what had been half of the Hanson family farm. Her widowed mother came to visit, and as Eve confided to Dani later, the old farmer swept her off her feet. The Hansons and his son, Nathan, were in charge of maintenance and security for the campgrounds year-round. Dani and Eve hit it off immediately, and laughed when Eve confided in her that she had finagled Firesong's presence so she could check out Dani and make sure she and Kurt were right for each other. Kurt had been like a big brother to her during Eve's early years of training with AMEA.

🦫 🦫 🦫

Staffers and supplies were still arriving through the dinner hour. Eve, Dani and Salem went into town for dinner, to escape the dwindling chaos. Full dark had fallen by the time they returned. Eve had a meeting in administration, so Dani and Salem headed for the cabins they were to lead. Dani wondered how long Drew's plan for an even playing field and Firesong going incognito would last.

The solar lights on stakes, lining the paths through the camp, created interesting interwoven designs when seen from a distance. That triggered an idea for a new song, and Dani zoned out. Salem hummed snatches of a new tune she and Jason had been fiddling with on the bus and didn't even try to get a conversation going.

"Huh." Salem's single word brought Dani out of her mental wandering. Jim called it brain-trickling instead of brainstorming.

"What?" Dani looked around. They had stopped at an intersection in the women's side of the camp. The cabin directly to their right was

238

Salem's, while Dani's was two more down the path.

"A few lights are out." Salem pointed down the path. The lights were spaced maybe five feet apart, so the gap where some had died was obvious. "You got those numbers for whoever takes care of stuff?"

"Good idea." Dani pulled out her phone as they said good night. She found the grounds crew number Eve had given her, and pressed the button to call as she stepped into her cabin.

A quick glance around showed her co-leader, Shelby, had arrived and settled in. Her sleeping bag was spread out on the bunk on the other side of the door from Dani's. Suitcase and duffel bag neatly stowed underneath. A string of butterfly patio lights hung from the frame. Dani liked that whimsical touch.

An answering machine picked up on the other end of the line. Shelby came through the door right then, with a neon pink plastic basket of toiletries in one hand, clothes hung over her arm, and a towel around her neck. A good guess was that she had been to the bathhouse. She wore gray shorts and t-shirt, with the stylized Ohio State O, and a buckeye. She stowed her basket and hung up the towel on the end of the bunk, as Dani left a message why she was calling.

"Not good," Shelby said, after Dani hung up. "Dani, right?"

"If you're Shelby." She settled down on her bunk. Cabin co-leaders had been asked to take bunks next to the door. Drew joked that they were stationed there to prevent campers fleeing for their lives after they realized what they had gotten into.

"Did you hear the news at dinner? Firesong is spending boot camp with us, and they're looking to add to the band. You know, kind of like Broadway shows on the road, different teams. I mean, what are the chances of actually traveling with Firesong? But just knowing you kind of have their name, singing their songs, that'd be so cool."

She paused for breath, while Dani scrambled to think of something to say to shut down the torrent of words before it got awkward.

"Although that would kind of be dishonest, wouldn't it, saying we were Firesong, when we really weren't? But when you think about it, they work for Allen Michaels, so maybe they don't own their name?"

"Actually --"

"Gads, this is stupid. I'm kind of blitzed. Really long day. I'm just jabbering at you." She dropped down on her bunk, making the springs squeak in protest.

"Where did you hear that about Firesong?"

Dani wanted to laugh. How had Drew's plans been short-circuited before boot camp officially started? Was this trouble, or just crossed communications? Someone didn't get the word about the secrecy element?

She didn't hear half of Shelby's response.

"Cosmic mega-awesome and a whole gob of other stuff. This is my third year. I came the very first year and it was just so much fun, even though everything was so new and they were still working the bugs out. I was on Drew's road team. It was so cool. And so sweet, because he was just calling Eve every single chance he got."

She hopped up while she was still talking and scampered to the back corner of the cabin containing the half-bath, just a sink and toilet. A small refrigerator crouched in the shadows. She pulled the door open and reached in.

"Finally, they're cold. Want something?" She pulled out two bottles of peach tea before Dani could respond. "I love romance, but that summer was like the best romance novel ever, because it was real. Did you know they met in college, but they broke up and it took them like another twelve years to get back together? God brought them together. Isn't that cool? Drew says it was all his fault and Eve is a saint, but she just laughs. I hope I find somebody and can figure out how to love him and he loves me like those two love each other."

She twisted the tea bottle open with a loud pop for punctuation.

"So, anyway, about Firesong --" Dani began.

"You know, I found one of their first CDs on eBay. People want like fifty dollars for them."

"You're kidding!" Dani nearly fumbled her tea bottle.

"Makes it kind of hard to get hold of the early ones. Before they were professionally recording. Penniless college student and musician, y'know?"

"That's just so wrong. You didn't pay fifty dollars for it, did you?"

"Nope. Hoping my folks pick up on my hints and get it for me for Christmas."

"I can get it for you cheap." A small price to pay to fix the awkwardness Dani could see down the road.

"That would be awesome!" Her smile froze. "How cheap is cheap?"

"Cost." Dani shrugged. "What?" she said, when Shelby frowned and her torrent of words didn't resume.

"Okay, I said I was blitzed. Cabin leaders are returnees. We've proved ourselves. I know you've never been here before. How did you get in?"

"My boyfriend works for AME, and he's a friend of Eve. He kind of ..." Another shrug. "Vouched for me."

This was beyond awkward. The anonymity Drew had hoped for, keeping a wrap on Firesong's participation in the boot camp, had been trashed. Dani didn't care about that. The stories already going around worried her, though. How many campers would be hurt or even furious, when a big break chance they thought had been promised to them evaporated? She needed to go find Drew right now, but how could she leave when she and Shelby should be getting to know each other?

"Let's start over, okay?" Dani took a deep breath. "First of all, I'm Dani Paul."

Shelby just blinked. She shook her head a little. Dani sighed. This was not a good beginning.

"I write songs."

"Okay, makes sense. You're here to teach songwriting."

"For Firesong."

Shelby fumbled the tea bottle. The cap was off. She grappled at the bottle as maybe a third of the tea spilled on the wooden cabin floor. A hard rapping on the cabin door startled a squeak out of her.

"Dani?" A semi-familiar man's voice.

"Yeah?" Dani gladly broke free of Shelby's stare and got up to answer the door. Nathan Hanson stood on the deep doorstep, with two other men behind him.

"How many lights did you say were out?" He moved back, beckoning for her to come outside. Shelby followed.

"Uh … Not that many."

Entire curves of lights were now missing from the intersecting paths through the campground. Lights over the doors of three cabins were also missing. Dani knew they had all been lit when she walked down this path less than half an hour ago. She followed as the men went to investigate, with Shelby behind her.

Drew and Mr. Hanson came out to join them as they walked up and down all the paths, assessing the damage. The solar-powered path lights were all simple, individual units. No electrical cords, no master control. Dani still had her phone on her and offered to take some pictures of the damage, caught in the wide beams of the flashlights all the grounds crew carried. A little more than a third of the affected lights were missing, stakes and all. Half of the remainder had the light knocked off with the stake still sticking in the ground. Those were easy enough to find, still lit, sometimes ten feet away from the stake. The rest of the units had been smashed. In the morning, fragments of black plastic littered the pathway and grass like a weird kind of glistening snow.

"So," Shelby said, after Dani estimated that maybe a fifth of the lights had been out when she called. "So like whoever was doing this was still out there, doing it, when you called it in?"

Drew exchanged grim looks with Mr. Hanson. "How hard will it be to triple nighttime patrols?"

"Not too hard," Nathan said. "Lots of men at the partner churches would be glad to earn a little extra money. Thing is, we can't depend on the trouble to only happen at night."

Mr. Hanson shook his head. "Son, we're dealing with some local idiots, not terrorists."

"How much damage do they have to cause to be considered a hate crime or a threat? I know I'm not in the Marines anymore, but that doesn't make this problem any less serious."

"Okay." Drew sighed and looked around at the shadowy mounds of cabins. Now they struck Dani as somewhat sinister with all the gaping black holes where lights were missing. "We institute curfews, and lock doors at night, and everybody gets I.D.s on lanyards. For starters. We do a lot of heavy-duty praying. And hope we catch them fast, or they get bored, so we don't have to keep it up all summer."

Once the girls returned to their cabin, Shelby was as quiet as she had been bubbling over with words before. Dani was thankful for the tiny half-bathroom installed in the cabin, saving her from having to fight her hyper imagination when she needed to use the toilet in the middle of the night. She washed up, and when she came out of the bathroom, Shelby had the butterfly lights turned on and was lying on her back, legs up in the air, rolling a hacky sack between her feet.

"That's kind of cool. Sorry." Dani couldn't repress a giggle when her words startled Shelby into dropping the ball.

"You think I'm a total flake, don't you?" Shelby didn't look at her as she rolled over and nearly fell out of the bunk to retrieve the hacky sack.

"Considering some of the people I've run into on the road, you're not even in the top hundred."

That got a grin. Shelby finally looked Dani in the eyes.

"Don't worry about it." She hung her damp towel and washcloth on the crossbar of the bunk. "It's good to know what people are saying. Especially since it's pretty much all wrong. Gives Drew time to work on defusing it." She settled down on her bunk and glanced at the door.

"Don't worry. It's locked. I checked it three times already. Wonder if they're going to have to issue us keys." Shelby took a deep breath. "So, what's the scoop?"

"No auditions. We *will* meet up with and hold concerts with the teams on the road. We *will* be doing a lot of mentoring. Everything else, we're figuring out as we go along."

"Sounds cool."

"And we brought copies of our early CDs to sell."

"Awesome!" They shared a grin. "You know what would be cool, and totally cut the feet out from under those pirates making mega-bucks off your old stuff? Re-issue them. Re-master them, let people know this is the original stuff but in new wrappers."

"That's a good idea."

Shelby had lots of good ideas and a talent for a clever turn of phrase. She wanted to write songs and was constantly jotting down ideas for titles, or the subjects of songs, or rhyming words.

Once she calmed down, she was organized, upbeat, and kind, and displayed an amazing instinct for seeing people's personalities. She easily identified the troublemakers, the "we're all that" group, and the uncertain newbies with big dreams and wobbly confidence. She and Dani agreed to keep up the first-name-only policy, to reduce chances of people either being intimidated or sucking up. By the end of the first full, official day of camp, Dani and Shelby had formed a solid partnership. They laughed at the obliviousness of several girls in their cabin who claimed to be major fans of Firesong, yet didn't recognize Dani when she was five feet away from them.

"Gotta wonder if they would recognize you if you sang," Shelby remarked. The afternoon orientation meeting had ended, and nearly 100 college students headed for the dining hall.

Cameron and Tuli, two of the twelve girls in their cabin, were walking just a few steps ahead of them. Four young men caught up with them. The girls squealed about the classes they signed up for. The tallest boy, with a goatee gelled to a point, put his arm around Cameron. Another boy, who had to be his brother, sans the beard, put his arm around Tuli.

Something about their pale blond, slicked hair, and matching pastel shirts in different colors struck a chord of unpleasant recognition for Dani.

"Either they think they've already made it, or they're wannabes who think looking the part is all they need," she muttered.

"Oh, definitely," Shelby said, as the six picked up speed, moving away from them to the dining hall. "Those are the Shades."

"Like -- sunglasses, shades?" Dani muffled a chuckle. She gladly slowed her pace with Shelby. It wasn't like they had to find a seat. All the cabin leaders had been asked to sit together tonight.

"Shades like colors. Notice their shirts? They're like a freaking bleached out rainbow."

They passed through the door into the dining hall. The muted roar of campers pulling chairs out to sit down and the tramping of feet on the wooden floor surrounded them. She spotted Kurt, standing at the far end of the long table set aside for the cabin leaders. Dani picked up speed and wove through the people finding seats. Shelby fell behind several steps, giving them a few seconds of semi-privacy as Kurt caught her shoulders and bent down for a too-brief kiss. Only Shelby seemed to notice. She had a big grin when she caught up with them. Dani knew she blushed as she introduced her new friend to Kurt.

"I want all the juicy details," Shelby muttered as they followed Kurt to the end of the table. Dani saw enough empty chairs together that Shelby could sit with them.

Now she found Jim, Jason, Tom and Salem. They were talking with the people around them. Dani hoped they had been teamed with other people as easy to get along with as Shelby.

"Nothing juicy. Kurt and I have been dating since ..." Her throat closed up at the mere thought of saying, *since my brother was killed.* "Well, since we signed on with AME. We knew each other when we were kids."

The room fell silent in rippling waves as Drew waved one arm, standing on a platform maybe two feet high. He waited until total silence filled the room. Dani caught a few people mouthing silent communication across tables, or making gestures. Just because they were here for ministry training didn't guarantee maturity. Or politeness.

Finally the room was silent enough to suit Drew. He said a blessing over their meal and the weeks of preparation ahead of them. As the serving team brought platters and bowls to the tables, Eve and Drew took turns making announcements, giving final details and apparently answering questions that had come up since the opening meeting. Kurt had his first bite of chicken strip in his mouth when Eve called him up to the platform. He chewed quickly as he got to his feet.

"Be prepared," he whispered, before walking over to stand by Eve.

Dani had a suspicion what would happen next. While Eve introduced Kurt to the gathering, Dani looked down the table, but couldn't catch the gazes of the other band members to try to warn them. Kurt denied all the rumors, some worse than what Shelby had reported last night, and asked Firesong to stand.

Mutters and groans merged with squeals and laughter. Dani guessed that nobody had recognized her cousins, just like the girls in her cabin hadn't recognized her.

Dinner passed in relative comfort. The people sitting close enough for polite conversation were mature enough not to ask silly questions or keep saying how stupid they felt not recognizing Firesong. After dinner, Kurt gathered them all together, and invited their cabin co-leaders to come along. They went to the pavilion next to the retention basin pond for a short meeting. Because of the rumors, he and Drew had made some quick changes in the plans for the two weeks of camp. Possible projects included a live recording of the final concert and a photo album of the boot camp experience online at both the AMEA website and the Firesong website.

Then he asked them to try to track down the source of the rumors.

"Bruno, you think?" Tom said, when the meeting broke up.

"What about him?" Jim said.

"He's here."

From the reactions of Jim, Jason, Salem and Kurt, Dani guessed they had been too busy to spot Bruno, or maybe he just took some effort to stay out of their view.

Salem and her co-leader, Olivia, walked back to the girls' side of the camp with Shelby and Dani. They all laughed together as Shelby bemoaned all the fun they had missed out on, testing the perceptiveness of the girls in their cabins. The laughter and chatter faded into silence as they got within twenty feet of Salem and Olivia's cabin. Faces were visible in several windows and three girls stood in the doorway, watching them approach.

"The nice thing about the lions in Rome was that once they got their jaws on you, your suffering was over," Salem remarked. That got a snort from Shelby and snickers from Olivia.

"We who are about to die salute you?" Dani offered. That got more laughter, muffled. She gave Salem a sideways hug before Salem and Olivia headed for the door of their cabin. Dani strained her ears for any kind of outcry as she and Shelby walked away. Other than the creaking of the screen door and the thud as it closed, she heard nothing.

"Too late to get pepper spray?" Shelby muttered.

"It can't be that bad. Please, Lord, don't let it be that bad," Dani said, just as quietly. She took a deep breath as Shelby opened the door.

Squeals and an immediate babble of questions hit the moment she crossed the threshold. None of the faces surrounding her looked angry. Several girls laughed at themselves. Cameron gushed about Dani pulling a "Cinderella move" on them. From the confused frowns, nobody else understood that any better than Dani did. The excitement died down quickly enough, and most of the girls returned to getting ready for bed. Then Tuli asked if being assigned to the cabin with Dani meant they would spend the summer traveling with Firesong.

"Honestly?" Shelby stepped out of the bathroom where she had been washing her face, with the door open, and in just the right position to make faces at Dani during the worst of the hubbub. "Have you seen the size of their tour bus? It's more like the special kids' bus when we were in elementary school. Where are all of you going to ride? The roof?"

Most of them laughed. Tuli looked crestfallen rather than embarrassed or angry. Dani hoped she and Cameron were the worst of the silliness element in the cabin. Shelby then reminded them of what Kurt had said at dinner, denying all the rumors, starting with "winning" a chance to tour with Firesong.

"At least they're fun, nice ditzes. Harmless," she confided to Eve the next morning. They had met to change some schedule items, since the "big reveal" would no longer occur. It was the first team-building exercise period. That meant free time for cabin leaders.

"Except to your ears?" Eve guessed.

They were in Eve and Drew's cottage, rather than the administration building. She felt a little under the weather this morning, and he had told her to take it easy.

"Better that than having a bunch of Cordelias."

"Oh, please. Tell me that is not a Buffy reference." Eve laughed and put down the mug of murky-looking tea, her mother's newest idea for treating her recurring physical problems.

"Okay, I won't."

They laughed together, and Eve admitted with much eye rolling that she had all the high school years of *Buffy the Vampire Slayer* on DVD. She insisted the show declined once Angel left and Buffy went to college.

Dani wondered briefly what the guys in the Shades were like, if both girls were pretty much all fluff and sweetness. Then there was no time for speculations as boot camp officially swallowed her whole. She had two morning workshops, first songwriting, then band management and business practices. After lunch, Firesong had rehearsal time during more teambuilding exercises. Since the plan for Firesong to work boot camp incognito had failed, they could skip going to the Hansons' church, half an hour of driving away, to rehearse. Now they could walk ten minutes to the Shoe, the camp's outdoor performance venue.

Construction had taken advantage of a natural curve and dip in the landscape and formed it into a horseshoe-shaped amphitheater. A firepit sat in the bottom of the curve, and a simple wooden platform capped the open end to make a stage. A framework with a retractable roll of canvas provided shelter against sun or rain. A simple speaker system and two lighting towers turned it into a concert venue. The grassy seating area had been christened the Shoe in honor of the stadium at Ohio State University.

At rehearsal, Dani asked her cousins what they knew about the Shades. Cabin assignments grouped campers by focus. Vocals, tech support, or instruments. Aaron, the Shades' leader, was in Kurt's cabin for group managers or leaders. Aaron was dating Cameron, and his brother, Ethan, was dating Tuli. The two girls were vocals -- according to Shelby, "adoration corps." By clerical error, they ended up in Dani's cabin, which was supposed to be for songwriters and management. The boys of the Shades seemed all right so far. Kurt didn't say anything until Dani pressed him later for his impression of Aaron.

"The guy's a used car salesman. He'll be and do and say whatever it takes to make the sale."

"Meaning?"

"Meaning I have to wonder why they're 'slumming it,' doing Christian music and summer missions."

"Maybe the Shades see it as a stepping stone to bigger and better. As soon as they --" Dani muffled a gasp. "That's who they remind me of. That band you were babysitting at that youth leaders conference in Indiana."

"The White Knights?" Kurt nodded. "Spot on."

"Whatever happened to them?"

"They escaped the Christian music ghetto -- their words. Crashed and burned making their first secular album, then broke up. Not ashamed to say I don't feel one bit sorry for them." Kurt put his arm around her and glanced around.

Dani hoped he was just checking for privacy, rather than fearing what people would say. What was one more wild rumor among all the other ridiculous stories?

"He who puts his hand on the plow and turns back?"

"Makes me pray extra hard God keeps me on the straight and narrow." Kurt brushed a kiss against her forehead. "All of us."

🝰 🝰 🝰

Dani managed some alone time in the cabin the next afternoon. Everyone was out on the Green, around the central flagpole, having a water balloon fight. She had just jotted a few lines for a new song churning in her head when Eve rapped on the screen door. She entered with both hands pressed against her abdomen.

"Are you okay?" Dani knocked the notebook to the floor as she leaped up to meet her.

"Can I borrow a pad?" Eve looked more embarrassed than in pain. "A tampon will do, just to get me home."

"Borrow usually means you give it back." Dani pulled her smaller case from under her bunk. She was glad when her bad joke earned a snort and a smile from Eve.

"You are saving me much embarrassment," Eve said, when she came out of the bathroom. "Usually when I get this queasy-crampy feeling, I'm about to gush."

"Need help getting home?"

"The worst is over. Thanks. Actually, the worst part is there's no pattern."

"Not to get nosy. Especially since we're just getting to know each other..."

"Yes, I'm seeing a doctor." Eve pressed her knuckles into her hips and pushed inward, then made a visible effort to stand up straight. "Been dealing with this since college. I never really cared until Andy came back into my life. We really want kids but ... well, our getting back together was a major miracle. How many can we ask for from God before we look really greedy?"

When Dani ran into her again an hour later, Eve looked entirely back to normal, dealing with whatever new minor crises people kept bringing her. Dani said a quick prayer for her friend. Eve's comment about having children led to wondering, yet again, how she and Kurt would handle having children and a ministry on the road. If they ever had children. If they ever got married. If he ever asked her.

ᘒ ᘒ ᘒ

At lunch, Shelby and Salem snagged Dani and asked her to sit with them. They had an idea for a fun song they wanted to bounce off her. The working title was "Unsocial Media." It lamented the attempts of technologically challenged members of the congregation of Saints Fuddy and Duddy to reach out to the youth of the world. Dani loved it, despite some tortured rhyme schemes. She agreed to help with lyrics, so Salem could concentrate on the melody line, which kept changing key. They had fun at the far end of their table. Maybe too much fun, because Shelby reported later she got some snide comments along the lines of "forgetting the reason they're here." Meaning they thought Salem and Dani should be constantly available for consultation. The Shades and the Robinhoods, who specialized in acapella and torn jeans, led the gripers.

The hint of a sour note ringing through the summer increased when Firesong got to the Shoe for rehearsal and discovered vandalism.

One support pole for the canopy lay across the stage. Another was cracked in half. The canopy had partially unrolled across the stage, showing multiple slashes and smears of some dark substance that turned out to be manure.

Fortunately, the sound system components were still in storage. The shed behind the stage showed no sign of any attempts to break down the door. Firesong's instruments stayed in the tour bus, so they were safe.

The sheriff's investigators left before the teambuilding exercises finished. Kurt and Drew took care of the call to AMEA headquarters to report the incident. Dani and Salem went to report to Eve, while Tom, Jim and Jason joined the grounds crew to start repairs and cleaning up. Nathan was coldly furious, like a personal affront to him that the damage had happened.

"In a way, it is," Eve said, when Dani voiced her thoughts. "This land used to belong to his family. The vandals are most likely local."

Dani shared that idea with Kurt later, and he agreed. Since the Arc

Foundation partnered with AMEA, and mutual friends worked for Arc, he had asked for some research help. Specifically, investigating a socialism guru teaching at a nearby college who had been vocally, viciously opposed to the camp's presence in his metaphorical backyard.

"You think he's sending people over here?"

"I think he's too savvy to advocate anything that could be grounds for legal action. However, nothing stops his followers from acting on his hints." He seemed about to say something more, but stopped and gestured down the path to the dining hall. The afternoon had passed too quickly, and it was time for dinner.

"What are you thinking?"

Kurt sighed. "I also asked them to check the people in Bruno's background. I find it a little suspicious that no one who gave him glowing recommendations mentioned he toured with you guys. Something is up, and I'd rather know what, now, than later, after some nasty surprise."

Dani had to agree with him, and appreciated the caution, but that didn't mean she had to like it. He laughed a little sadly when she told him, and stole one more kiss.

The chatter over dinner revealed a new problem that had cropped up while they were dealing with the vandalism. The rehearsal scheduling sheets had all vanished from the sturdy plastic frames attached to each rehearsal room door. Rehearsal time was at a premium, with more groups than rehearsal rooms. Arguments flared immediately because there was no record of who signed up for what room. The Robinhoods, the Magnificats, and the Shades were chief suspects because they all had tried to sign up for multiple practice room sessions in a row. The dining hall divided into armed camps, taking sides.

The maneuvering and childishness kept going. Cameron and Tuli tried to nudge aside Shelby on the walk back to their cabin from the evening campfire. They nearly knocked Dani off her feet. She and Shelby had been walking arm-in-arm, chuckling over more ideas for "Unsocial Media." The two girls apologized quickly, then tried to get between Dani and Shelby again, and almost knocked each other over. The other girls in their cabin muffled giggles and hurried on ahead of them. More apologies devolved into a jumble of questions. Both girls wanted Dani to give them the inside scoop on how to appear on Firesong's next album.

Dani had to say something, even though she feared it would do no more good than any previous attempts to short-circuit the rumor mill.

"This is the last time I'm saying this," she announced, once she had the attention of everyone in her cabin. "We are not recruiting. No one from AME is coming to do interviews. Don't ask me about the album, because honestly, if people insist on believing lies, we won't do the album here at all. Don't ask me again. You'll just get the same answer. Got it?" She looked around the cabin. A few girls looked crestfallen. She wanted to punch whoever had filled their heads with false dreams.

Dani needed to get out of the cabin. For some alone time, if nothing else. She especially didn't want to be alone with the girls when Shelby headed for the bathhouse.

"Gotta get something from the bus," she said, and headed out the door. This was a good time to get that CD she had promised Shelby.

Dani took the long way around to the parking lot, avoiding the tall spotlights and staying in the shadows so no one could follow her. She tried to calculate how many CDs remained in the cargo compartment. Could she justify giving Shelby one, and not offering to the other girls? Her irritation insisted yes, she could. They hadn't earned such gifts. Especially if Firesong's old CDs were going for three and four times the original price on eBay. By the time she reached the parking lot, she decided to give the CD to Shelby when no one was around. Maybe she needed to repent of her attitude, too.

"Okay, Lord, we need some help here," Dani whispered, slowing her steps. "Someone is out to get us, to ruin this summer. Help?"

She stepped out of the shadows and came around the back of the bus, still gnawing on the rumor problem. The dull thud of a dark shape kicking at the front door of the bus startled her. She stumbled to a stop. Another figure came around the front of the bus. Both looked male. Their features were lost in the shadows. One had a crooked metal bar in his hand. The one kicking at the door had a bat.

Her first reaction was to shout and stop them. Common sense stopped her. But this was her bus. She was the business manager, she was responsible. She had to do something.

Facing two people with weapons of any kind wasn't smart.

Dani backed up, praying hard that they didn't turn to see her. She still moved cautiously after she put the bus between her and them. When her foot touched the grass strip between the parking lot and the asphalt path, she ran as hard as she could. A dark shape emerged from the clump of trees to the right, where the path split. She clenched her fists and raised her arms to protect her head and nearly stumbled as the figure stepped into the spotty moonlight.

Nathan Hanson.

"Hey, what's --"

"Parking lot. Someone breaking into our bus." She pointed back behind her, which was stupid, because -- duh -- Nathan was head of security. He knew where the parking lot was.

As evidenced by how fast he darted away from her, talking into his radio. She followed him, and nearly laughed at how breathless she was. How could she be out of shape? Everyone teased her about doing calisthenics on stage, running herself ragged with all the backstage work. She should have great lung capacity and breath control.

Two voices shouted. She heard feet running on gravel. Nathan called out, ordering someone to stop. Like that would do any good, since he didn't have a gun? The people trying to break into Firesong's bus didn't know that, though, did they?

A figure darted out from behind the bus, heading straight toward her. Nothing in his hand. She bent low, spread her arms, and put on speed. He skidded on the gravel, trying to change direction. She hit him hard, low in his ribs, and they went down, sliding. One of his flailing fists caught her on the cheekbone. He swore and struggled and shrieked like a tenor. Dani had lots of practice defending herself against her brother and cousins, growing up. She held on and wasn't ashamed to use her knees and wrap an arm around his neck as tight as she could.

Then suddenly she was surrounded by flashlights and security workers, and Nathan was there, his face twisted in something fierce and oddly stunned. She could see clearly enough now. Whoever she had tackled, he looked like he was college age, but nobody she recognized.

🗘 🗘 🗘

"Not one of ours," Drew reported an hour later, coming into the back office of the administration building where Eve sat with Dani. He gestured, and she lowered the makeshift ice pack on her cheek. "Not that I have much experience, but I don't think you'll have a black eye. Just one lovely rainbow of a bruise for a few days, max."

"You're sure?" Eve wrinkled up her nose at him. "The kid, not Dani. Positive he's not one of ours?"

"Oh, yeah. Nathan says he's not a local, as far as he can tell. Hal showed up to take him to the sheriff for processing. Went really white when he saw the uniform."

One hard thud on the office door, and Kurt burst in, out of breath, barefoot, and wearing a ragged t-shirt and gym shorts that Dani suspected he slept in. He went to his knees in front of her, his face red, his mouth flattening as he studied her face.

"She's fine," Eve said.

"How did you know?" Dani blurted.

"Shelby called me when you didn't come back to the cabin." He caught hold of her hands. "How do I keep you out of trouble?"

Dani shrugged. She knew better than to say what immediately popped into her head, prompted by Kurt on his knees in front of her: find a way for them to be together 24/7?

"What exactly did you hear?" Drew asked.

"Met up with a couple of the security guys and they were still laughing at how she took the guy down."

"Word of warning." Eve got up and gestured for Kurt to take her place on the sofa next to Dani. "She's made quite an impression on Nathan, which is kind of hard to do, with him being a Marine."

"Oh boy." Drew wrapped an arm around his wife's shoulders. "Better be careful. The guy doesn't exactly fight dirty, but ..." He winked and tipped his head, indicating Eve. "You do not want to go up against that guy if he sets his sights on your girl."

"Seriously?" Dani grinned. Kurt's hands tightened around hers almost to the point of pain.

"You know he's getting his degree in theology?" Drew continued.

"What does that --"

"Of course, you know it's a law that no seminary student is allowed to graduate without a wife."

Dani laughed. She thought of all the criticism dumped on her since she first stepped on stage to sing. She wasn't feminine enough, humble enough, a good enough Christian. She was self-righteous. The idea of her as a minister's wife was ridiculous.

Kurt wasn't amused. The wrinkles around his eyes and mouth got deeper, despite Eve's promise that she would have a talk with Nathan. He was her step-brother, after all.

🗭🗭🗭

"Don't worry," Eve told Dani the next morning, after another deputy came by to get more details of the "incident" for the report. "I warned Nathan that you and Kurt are as close to being official as you can get without a ring."

"I don't think ..." Dani pressed her hands against her hot cheeks. "Do you think?"

"Oh, yeah. There were a few girls who chased Kurt when we were working together at headquarters, and he never looked at any of them like he looks at you. All the time." Eve sighed when the muffled sound of the bell at the front desk drifted into her office. "I told Nathan Kurt is the big brother I never had, and I do not want to have to beat up on my step-brother, but I will if I have to."

🗭🗭🗭

The talk among the campers about the attempted break-in died down by lunchtime. Dani didn't know whether to be irritated or relieved. Glad the students were focused on their summer music ministry, or worried that they didn't take the threats more seriously? Or maybe she was just irked that no one in her own cabin, besides Shelby, showed any concern over the bruise across her cheekbone? She had done something at least slightly heroic, hadn't she?

Not that she would go out after dark by herself, even after the security team numbers increased and all those path lights had been replaced. Safety in numbers.

More irritation and a little concern came from learning the nineteen-year-old she had tackled came from West Virginia. He was a student at Ohio University, but on summer break, and had no reason to be anywhere near Coshocton. Dani caught Kurt and Drew exchanging telling looks when that information was shared at another small meeting. Neither of them elaborated on whatever silent communication they had just had. Kurt did mention he was calling Sophie, the resident Internet genius at the Arc Foundation, to do some specialized investigating for him. Just in case a theory, which he refused to divulge, panned out.

Dani decided to leave it at that.

On the positive side, Kurt held her hand whenever possible, and he got that steely look in his eyes whenever Nathan showed up. Dani believed Eve, that her step-brother had taken the warning, but obviously Kurt didn't. Maybe she was being silly, but the price she paid in a bruise and a little fear was small compared to what she got in return.

ᗡ ᗡ ᗡ

By Saturday, the end of the first full week, the heavy-duty prayers of the leadership team seemed to be having some effect and the rivalries and rumors settled down. Dani wished she could come up with a song lampooning the whole ridiculous situation, but there was nothing amusing about discord among people preparing for a summer of music ministry. All the cabin leaders and workshop teachers had stories of petty arguments and power struggles.

Dani tried to be optimistic. She was glad for the public reconciliations. However, she remembered other up-and-coming groups Firesong had encountered while working for their big break. She thought about the White Knights, who had abandoned Christian music when they were offered enough money. As someone at AMEA had pointed out during a training workshop, they were all performers. They had learned to wear a smile and clown for the audience so no one guessed they had had a bad day or didn't know if they had enough gas to get home after the concert. Skilled performers could convince their boot camp instructors that they were getting along -- and plot to destroy those they saw as rivals rather than fellow servants in ministry.

Dani volunteered to help with the mail distribution on Monday, when Eve came to breakfast looking like she needed to spend the day

253

curled up with a heating pad and a Buffy marathon. There wasn't much mail to hand out, only a week into boot camp. Four paper ream boxes came for the Shades. A small box, maybe three inches on each side, came for Kurt, from his parents, with a tracking code, overnight delivery, and insurance. She knew he was waiting for a new wireless hotspot that was stronger than his cell phone could generate. But wouldn't equipment come from headquarters, rather than his parents?

She loaded the Shades' boxes onto a wheeled cart and headed for the cabin assigned to Aaron and Kurt. Cameron and Tuli caught up with her, shrieking in delight, before she was twenty steps away from Administration. They babbled about the shipment. Aaron had decided the Shades needed more changes of costumes for tour. Dani knew none of the tour programs called for costumes. So what made Aaron think the Shades would be the exception to the plan? Despite the girls being so silly, Dani didn't want to hurt their feelings, so she said nothing. She let the girls take the cart, and took Kurt's box.

He wasn't in his cabin, so she left a note and returned his box to the office. She had a workshop to lead and another meeting with Shelby and Salem to work on their silly song. Someone had been going through their notebooks in their cabins. Salem thought some notes were missing. She couldn't be sure, because they had so many drafts of "Unsocial Media," she hadn't kept track of which ones they threw out. Neither girl seemed worried, but Dani mentioned it to Kurt when she finally caught up with him and they took a short walk, looking for a little privacy.

Kurt agreed that the issue was worth some concern, but he hoped it was only an overblown competitive spirit. The alternative was someone from outside getting past the security teams, sneaking into the cabins, looking for things to steal or destroy, some way to harm the camp. He and Drew and Nathan had just had another conference call with headquarters about increasing security.

"What if it's campers causing trouble?" she had to ask as they came into the amphitheater, which by some miracle was empty.

"Considering the arguments I keep walking in on ... yeah, it's possible. I try to stay out of it, not flaunt my authority, but they keep trying to drag me into it. Then when I offer advice, they say I'm interfering. I've gotten a lot of insinuations about keeping secrets, and a bigger agenda, and they can't trust me." He tipped his head slightly and studied her. "What kind of fallout have you gotten?"

"No matter how many times I tell them the truth, people want to believe that yes, we're recruiting, and someone is going to leave here an instant star." She snorted. "Thanks a lot, *American Idol*." Then a thought struck her.

"What?" He gripped her shoulders and his smile went crooked. "I know that look. You just got a brainstorm. Please don't tell me you're going to write a song about all this mess."

"You wish." She made as if to thump him in the stomach. Kurt laughed and wrapped an arm around her, nearly pulling her off balance. They settled on the front edge of the stage. "The rumors started the first night, so the creeps knew we were coming, and they think they have a reason to sabotage the whole boot camp. So what's their reason? Find that out, we might find them."

"That's an idea. Sounds like more research for Sophie. Thank goodness we have all the brainpower of the Arc Foundation helping us."

"Instead of *American Idol*, it feels more like *Survivor*. All the nastiness and plotting. A big, crazy reality show, with someone playing the mole, to cause us trouble and test us."

"I could almost hope so." Kurt brushed a kiss across her forehead. "Because, sweetheart, this is not what a ministry boot camp should be. What went wrong when these kids were picked?"

"One bad apple makes the whole barrel rotten?"

"I hope we're dealing with nasty locals, because the alternative is too painful. As it is, I had to move my equipment to Eve and Drew's for security yesterday. I still have work to do for headquarters while I'm here. The printed files have been moved, and I think someone tried to hack my computer."

"Nobody saw anything? Nothing suspicious?"

"Well, there are a few guys in my cabin ... but I've had enough run-ins with them and their enormous attitudes, I'm prejudiced." Kurt lifted their joined hands, so her fingers faced him. "They remind me of so many arrogant, I'm-all-that creeps ... can't really trust my judgment."

"I would always trust it."

"Yeah, well, you're biased." He managed to kiss three of her fingers before the tickling got enough to make her twist her hand free. "Dani ... you know I love you, don't you?"

A shout and several heads appearing over the top of the amphitheater hill interrupted before she could even take a breath to respond. Kurt groaned. Dani caught hold of his collar, drawing him down to her for a quick kiss. He grinned and held perfectly still as she scooted off the stage. Dani was relieved to learn the intruders were looking for Kurt, rather than her. For a change.

She kicked herself later for not asking if Kurt got his package. With the problems in his cabin, it was entirely believable someone would steal the note she had left.

Sometimes, Dani wondered if praying about concerns of any kind was like sending out a signal to the enemy for the heat to be turned up.

In the next morning's songwriting class, Shelby and Salem debuted "Unsocial Media." They only got past the first verse and three lines into the chorus when an argument erupted in the back of the room. When Dani moved over to investigate, it became very clear one side was trying to shut up the other. Then the argument turned into accusing Salem of stealing the song.

Other students added to it, and suddenly Salem hadn't just stolen the song, but her place in Firesong.

It took the rest of the day, asking questions and backtracking what everyone, accusers and accused, had heard and done and said, to find some resolution.

The girls who accused Salem of stealing her own song thought they were defending the creative rights of their friend, Chasity, one of Dani's most combative songwriting students. She had displayed a chip on her shoulder from day one. Chasity admitted she had found lyrics on a balled-up piece of paper someone tossed into her toiletry basket in the bathhouse. She figured someone threw them out and didn't want them, so that made the lyrics fair game, right?

Several times she thought someone was spying on her when she sat with her guitar and worked through the song. When she told her few friends, they acted as guards to protect her creative time. Chasity admitted when she heard Salem and Shelby singing the song, she first thought Shelby had set her up, trying to cause her trouble. Then she just wanted to leave, because she knew Shelby wasn't that kind of person. Her friends insisted she speak up. Chasity couldn't admit she had found the rough lyrics, so she tried to get them to shut up.

The charge that Salem stole her place in Firesong was based on a new rumor just starting to circulate. It began Sunday when someone overheard someone else insisting Bruno had been kicked out of Firesong to make room for Jason's new girlfriend. Salem was mortified because she and Jason had been trying to keep their blossoming romance quiet.

The question was where the rumor had started, because hours of backtracking who heard the accusation from whom revealed no one ever heard Bruno make that claim. No one remembered his name and face from the few PR pictures posted on Firesong's website or blog, until the rumor started. Once Bruno handed in his resignation, he hadn't been introduced at concerts and wasn't mentioned in the blog reports, so he had faded out quietly. No fuss, no wild stories, no questions. Until now, Dani and her cousins thought everyone had been satisfied.

Bruno's application materials to work boot camp ignored the months with Firesong. So if he didn't want the administration of Camp Sower to know he had been with Firesong, why tell the campers?

"I haven't checked with Sophie on that question," Kurt said, during a subdued lunch meeting, all of Firesong included, at Eve and Drew's cottage. They certainly couldn't eat and talk in the dining hall, with the entire camp in an uproar. "With the vandalism and security breaches, I told her investigating Bruno was low priority. Maybe not anymore."

Dani wasn't witness to Bruno's questioning, being busy backtracking Chasity's work on the stolen lyrics. She tried to encourage the girl, who had taken the song in a new direction, but Chasity declared she would never finish the song. It was tainted.

"But how did he get his position leading a cabin and maybe a road team, if he hid his time with us?" Tom wanted to know.

Drew revealed that Bruno's audition pieces were outstanding in their simplicity. He didn't try to hide failings with glitz and fancy backup recordings. It was just him and his piano and electric keyboard. Even more impressive were the many letters of reference and spiritual maturity assessments from his current and former ministers, attesting to his outreach activities and his work with the church youth.

"But none of these people mentioned his time singing with you," he said. "Feels like a conspiracy."

"Well, there is one … no, that really can't be an answer," Eve said.

"I think I know what you're thinking," Kurt said. "Those churches you've run into that think Dr. Michaels is another false prophet?"

"They didn't mention Firesong because they think Bruno is ashamed of being with them?" Drew nodded. "Yeah, for a few seconds, it sounds great, but why they would give him glowing recommendations to come here, if they're against everything *we're* doing."

"Exactly," Eve said.

"Unless they sent him here as sabotage?" Tom said.

"Ouch. Cynical." Jim smiled when he said it.

"Sophie has to have something by now." Kurt pulled out his phone and Dani glimpsed his email screen as he started tapping a message.

"The thing is," Dani said, "he knew we were going to be here. Maybe he asked them not to mention him being with us, and he didn't say anything, because he thought he wouldn't be accepted?"

"So sour grapes from us, instead of him?" Tom said. "Maybe he's still hoping to get you to dump Kurt, and take him."

His brothers laughed. Dani tried to laugh, but the attempted joke was too close to some doubts she had tried not to entertain lately.

She and Kurt went off by themselves when they left the cottage. She was glad just to walk in the dark and quiet and hold hands. Maybe Kurt had been having the same thoughts, regretting how little private time they had together. He led her to the Shoe and they settled on the middle of the horseshoe, directly in the center of one of the spotlight puddles. A good choice for a private talk without giving anyone grounds to accuse them of questionable behavior. Even if no one could see them, they were still in leadership positions and always representing AMEA.

"This summer sure isn't turning out like we hoped, is it?" Kurt kept hold of her hand.

"It's had its rough spots. At least I wake up in the same bed every morning and the food is good and I've made some new friends." She raised their joined hands. "And this is pretty nice."

"I keep thinking about those creeps who were breaking into your bus. What if they had seen you before you could go for help? With all the stuff that went on today, what if ..." Kurt sighed and leaned in so their foreheads touched. "You know how much I love you?"

"Enough to be really sick of being on the road all the time?" She caught her breath as Kurt tipped his head down for a slow kiss. The breath came out as a regretful sigh when he ended it far too soon.

"Dani."

Cloth rustled, then his hands shifted to catch her hand between them. He pressed a small cube, covered in cloth, into her palm.

She opened her eyes. It was a little box. Black with gold trim. It looked like a ring box. She nearly yanked her hand away. Kurt laughed, the sound ragged. He wrapped her hand around the bottom of the box, and with his other hand tipped up the top half.

The box was empty, but for the satin lining and the slit for the ring.

"It was there this morning. I swear!" Kurt jumped to his feet and turned, surveying the amphitheater. "I knew I should have left it with Eve. But I was going to propose this morning after breakfast, and we had that meeting and I didn't see you, so I hid it. To ask at lunch."

"Fat chance of that." She tried to smile, but she felt sick from the anguish on Kurt's face.

He was going to propose. He even had a ring.

Lord, when are we ever going to catch a break?

"I thought it was safe. I thought I was imagining ..." Kurt scowled, looking down into the darkness beyond the spotlights.

"Imagining what?"

"I thought the box had been turned, but I couldn't be sure. What if I moved it when I took it out for breakfast? Or put it back before lunch?"

"Somebody got into your stuff, like you were afraid. That's what came in the mail the other day, wasn't it?"

"When you tackled that guy, I wanted to carry you away somewhere safe." Kurt sat down and wrapped his arm around her. "Then Nathan ..."

He shrugged.

"So you thought you'd just put your mark on me, and scare away all rivals?"

"Kind of stupid, huh?"

"Kind of adorable, you being all chivalrous and --"

He stopped her with a kiss sweeter and longer than anything they had allowed themselves in far too long a time.

While Dani wanted to prolong the moment, they needed to deal with this new problem. That meant going back to Eve and Drew's cottage to report the theft and call the sheriff.

On the short walk, Kurt described the ring to her. To make matters worse, this was Grandmother Green's ring. It was made of braided silver threads, and the knot where the strands came together held three tiny diamonds, for her three sons. It had been a twentieth anniversary gift from her husband.

Mr. Hanson and Nathan were just leaving the cottage when Dani and Kurt returned. While Kurt and Nathan were going over the timeline of the ring's arrival in the mail and Mr. Hanson got on the phone to call the sheriff, Eve and Drew had a quick, whispered conversation. Dani's curiosity was aroused because they were both grinning. Drew hurried down the hall

"What's going on?" Dani asked, sitting down next to Eve.

Her friend just gave her a wide-eyed look of totally unbelievable innocence, and shrugged.

Mr. Hanson was already off the phone, having left a message for the sheriff, when Drew returned. Nathan and Kurt had a list of everyone who would have had access to his cabin, and the times when people could go in and out without running into one of the campers assigned there. Nathan believed one of the guys in Kurt's cabin had stolen the ring. Security patrolled the cabin areas when the campers were supposed to be in workshops or rehearsing or at meals.

Then the sheriff called back, and Nathan and Mr. Hanson went to the kitchen, so they could put the phone on speaker and both talk to him. Drew took Kurt aside for a moment. Dani knew something was up when Eve watched her husband and grinned, with a suspicious gleam of wetness in her eyes. Then Kurt laughed, and he shook hands with Drew.

"You might want to stand up for this," Eve said, nudging Dani. She nudged harder when Dani didn't move.

Dani was glad she stayed seated, when Kurt went down on one knee in front of her and took hold of her hand.

"You do know I love you, Dani?"

"Yes." Her voice cracked. She laughed and pressed the fingertips of her free hand against his lips. "I love you. Yes."

"Like -- yes?"

"They're worse than we were," Drew muttered, but he grinned and settled down on the arm of the couch next to Eve.

Kurt uncurled Dani's hand and slid a ring on her finger. A gumball machine ring, with a big square of blue glass, and the silver paint rubbed off, revealing the dark tin band.

"It's just a loaner," Eve said. "That's our second engagement ring. We figure it should be a good luck charm or something like that."

They were still exchanging hugs and shaking hands when Nathan and his father came out of the kitchen. The sheriff would come by in the morning to take the official report, but he would start inquiries tonight. It helped that Kurt had pictures of the ring, on his phone. His father had taken several for insurance purposes when he had it cleaned and then mailed it to Kurt. When Kurt emailed the photos to the sheriff, to help in the investigation, he copied Dani.

ᘓ ᘓ ᘓ

"What is that?" Shelby caught hold of Dani's wrist as she was reaching for the doorknob to leave the cabin the next morning.

"What's what?" Dani grinned at the flash of sunlight on the glass jewel in her ring. So what if it was a loaner? She loved it. Maybe she would raid every gumball machine she came across, to always have a reminder of the night Kurt proposed.

"That is not you." Shelby slid in between Dani and the door and gave her a shove to step backwards.

"Well, to be honest, no, it's not. This is actually Eve. Her engagement ring."

"Then why are you wearing it?"

The chatter of the other girls preparing to head to breakfast faded away. Dani felt the pressure of all those eyes focusing on her.

"It's kind of a place-holder. Kurt proposed last night."

The cabin rang with shrieks and congratulations and demands for explanations. Shelby just stood back and laughed while the other girls scrambled to get a look at the ring and demand all the "juicy details." Dani had to think for a moment what to say and not say, because so much camp-related business went on last night. She finally simplified the story to say Kurt took her for a walk, and when he opened the box, the ring was missing. When they went to Eve and Drew's cottage to report the theft, Drew loaned Kurt the ring he had used for his second engagement to Eve.

Of course, all the girls in the cabin thought the story was so romantic. Several made sounds of sympathy and horror when Dani told them the history of the stolen ring.

She pulled out her cell phone, to show them the pictures Kurt had sent her. Cameron let out a shriek. She staggered backwards, tripped over her own cosmetic bag, landed on her bunk, then burst into tears.

"That slimedog lied!" Tuli burst out, as she went down on her knees to hold Cameron.

"What slimedog?" Dani said.

"Bet you a million dollars, it's Aaron," Shelby said.

Cameron wailed louder and hid her face in Tuli's shoulder.

Aaron had given Kurt's ring to Cameron after a very subdued evening campfire singing time. He also gave her a convoluted story about finding it in an antique store when he was in high school and saving it for the perfect girl. He made her promise not to show it to anyone until they were home and could announce their engagement to their parents and their home church. It was nobody's business but theirs. Naturally, Cameron showed it to Tuli.

Cameron and Tuli turned state's witness against the boys of the Shades. Some things were more important than stardom. Boys who lied and stole other girls' engagement rings were the lowest of the low. What they didn't reveal, the investigation of Bruno's supporters did.

The report from the Arc Foundation completing the puzzle had come two days ago, but the email had been deleted. Aaron and his brother had matching criminal records, which the Arc Foundation had uncovered with the help of a friend in the FBI. Aaron distracted Kurt to let Ethan take his cell phone after he used it, before it timed out. The plan was to inconvenience Kurt by deleting emails that looked important. Aaron never read the email that revealed someone was investigating the music minister at his church. As he later snarled, if he had known that, the Shades would have turned in the man to make themselves look good, long before the ring was stolen.

Or maybe not. In Shelby's words, "The boy's got a 'tude."

The Shades were responsible for the rumors about touring with Firesong. They stirred up the rivalries and created competition where there should have been none. Along with stealing the rehearsal schedules, they sabotaged other people's cell phones, poured water into instrument cases, blocked the plumbing in some cabins, and let air out of the tires of the church vans sitting in the parking lot.

However, they didn't vandalize the Shoe, destroy the pathway lights, or attack Firesong's bus. The guilty parties were discovered by other means, and their identity had already been included in another report from the Arc Foundation that never reached Kurt.

All four boys in the Shades created the mess with Salem and Shelby's song. They stole the notes, planted them on Chasity, and then spied on her to make her nervous. The plan had originally been to embarrass her because Chasity wouldn't work with Cameron in songwriting class.

The Shades had come to boot camp armed for bear, and Firesong was their main target. They also had the help of two staffers from their home church, which explained how the false rumors about Firesong had started before the campers arrived. Their music minister was Bruno's former music minister, with a grudge against AMEA. When Bruno grumbled to him after quitting Firesong, he set out to punish them. He prejudiced the Shades against the band, and guided them in destroying Firesong's reputation.

"This is one guy with a very greasy grasp on reality," Drew commented, after looking through emails Sophie at Arc had accessed.

Emails between the music minister and Bruno proved Bruno's innocence in the whole scheme. Emails from the music minister to Aaron and the two staffers guided the sabotage of the boot camp. He had promised the Shades they would take Firesong's place working for AMEA. He had sent all sorts of false stories about Eve and Drew Leone to the two staffers, to turn them against the camp leaders. He had lied on his resume when he was asked to leave Bruno's church and found his new position at the Shades' church. Sophie followed her sense of trouble and backtracked him. He had a long history of rewriting his biography and presenting a pleasant, trustworthy face and manner so no one dug too far or asked any dangerous questions. The information the Arc Foundation had found had been sent to all the churches where he had worked, stirred up trouble, and fled. None of the congregations were entirely innocent victims. The departing music minister had enough dirt on them, they were intimidated into being kind and vague when contacted about his work history. So no one was warned.

Bruno had asked his other references not to mention the time he spent with Firesong. He wanted to be accepted at boot camp on his own merits. He was ashamed over how his time with Firesong had ended, and had hoped to stay in the background and avoid running into them. He hadn't realized until it was too late that they would be working directly with the campers.

Dani believed him. That was more like the Bruno she had come to know and even like, before his hurt feelings got in the way.

Sophie hadn't neglected the higher priority search, investigating the socialist professor who had specifically targeted Camp Sower as a "purveyor of mental illness" by using music to "infect malleable, inferior minds" with "dangerous religious thinking." The boy who was caught attacking Firesong's bus was one of his followers. Several mobile representatives of the Arc Foundation had come down to Coshocton to stake out the campgrounds and keep watch on who tried to get in and out, day and night. The professor's students made mistakes covering their tracks, allowing the Arc Foundation girls to collect a pile of mounting evidence. When they had a pattern, they looked backward to previous incidents of vandalism elsewhere.

Su-Ma, at the Arc Foundation, had a talent for puzzles. She found the professor used his daily blog to send coded messages to his students and give them new targets. They were very busy, attacking a different church or charity or private religious group every night. Once Arc knew what to look for, and passed on the information to the local authorities, the evidence came together with laughable, yet frightening ease.

Dani wasn't in the mood to be present when the Shades' parents and the pastoral staff from their church came to Camp Sower to take them and the two disgraced staffers home. Cameron and Tuli were a little too hysterical to be believed. The boys refused to apologize. The two staffers had been so furious over being manipulated, they gladly helped convict their music minister. On a more positive note, for once he didn't have enough ammunition to force the church to give him a kind reference. He was fired before he could quit.

ワ ワ ワ

The college-age boot camp ended on a low note, but not as low as it could have been if the saboteurs, inside and outside, hadn't been uncovered and dealt with. Most hurt feelings were soothed, arguments resolved, friendships repaired, and new ones forged, with a solid foundation built on hard lessons. Eve's report stated that she had high hopes for great things from the road teams, because they had all come through a fire of testing.

"I'm inclined to believe God lets the enemy take shots at us to toughen us up," Drew said. Those who would remain at Camp Sower for the high school session gathered for a lunch celebration after the last bus and van of college students rolled through the gates. "Some of those kids are going to do something great and surprise themselves."

Bruno stayed behind at camp to help set up for the high school session. While he wasn't guilty of anything more than hurt feelings, his distant relationship with the Shades had tainted him. The college-age touring groups didn't want him with them.

Those who had worked directly with Bruno over the last two weeks were willing to give him the benefit of the doubt. He had learned a painful and valuable lesson. He had a gift for identifying good voices and helping musicians tackle performance problems. He had refrained from adding to all the rumors. That indicated he could be trusted to model the right behavior among teens put under his care.

The meeting finished with a conference call to their immediate supervisors at AMEA headquarters.

"Sir, one more thing," Kurt said, after the business had been dealt with and the other leaders had left the meeting room. Only he and Dani remained with Eve and Drew. "I'm going to need that reassignment we talked about last year. Any chance of that long list of replacements being narrowed down enough to take over in the next ... well, we really didn't pick a date yet, did we?" he said, turning to Dani.

He caught hold of her hand, and like he did every time since finally recovering the ring, he raised her hand to kiss the finger with the ring.

"You've been kind of busy," Eve said.

Dani could only grin and shake her head. On the speaker phone, Conrad laughed and offered his congratulations. She felt a little odd knowing Kurt had been arranging for them to serve together, because that meant he had been planning on marrying her for some time now. Nathan's interest had only nudged Kurt to move sooner, rather than frightening him into acting. Tomorrow they would have to sit down and look at Firesong's schedule and Kurt's on-the-road duties and determine when they would have time together to plan, to dream, to pick a date.

Tomorrow. They could deal with new questions and plans tomorrow. Tonight it was enough to know she and Kurt were going to spend the rest of their lives together. If they spent most of it on the road, in ministry, that was all right. As long as they were together.

On the road to publication, **Michelle Levigne** fell into fandom in college (a recovering Trekker), and has 40+ stories in various SF and fantasy universes. She has a BA in theater/English from Northwestern College and a MA focused on film and writing from Regent University. She has published 80+ books and novellas with multiple small presses, in SF, fantasy, YA, and sub-genres of romance. *Summer Song* is a tie-in to her Inspirational Romance series, **Tabor Heights**. Her official launch into publishing came with winning first place in the Writers of the Future contest in 1990. Her most recent claim to fame is being a finalist in the SF category of the 2018 Realm Award competition, in conjunction with the Realm Makers convention. Her training includes the Institute for Children's Literature; proofreading at an advertising agency; and working at a community newspaper. She is a tea snob and freelance edits for a living, but only enough to give her time to write. You can find her at *www.Mlevigne.com*, *www.MichelleLevigne.blogspot.com*, and on Facebook,

Twitter, Pinterest, and Wattpad.

CHRISTMAS ANGELS

by Carole Brown

Dedicated to our real life Beth — one of the strongest women I know. Love to you!
...and in memory of the real Recie — my grandmother.

1943

Abigail tightened her grip on the crumpled paper in her fist. She didn't have to read it again to know what the message conveyed.

"...I may not come back..."

What did her husband mean? That he would be killed? Taken prisoner? Or that he didn't want to come home?

I may not come back. I may not come back. I may not come back.

The words revolved in her mind like a tornado funnel, driving her crazy with implications she didn't want to think about.

She'd known something was wrong. He'd sent no letters for the last two months, and there had been no communication, even after she'd called for some kind of word of him. All the Air Force authorities had given her was the runaround.

She'd always been so strong. Ready to take on the world. Unafraid of problems. Counted them as challenges. Patrick had said she was brave enough to face anything, but was it true? She smiled, but no mirth bubbled up inside her.

Her baby stirred in her lap, and she looked down, rocking and sing-songing. "Daddy's gonna buy her a..."

Her gaze refocused on the lazy snowflakes fluttering by her window. What on earth was she going to do? Christmas and no money to buy little Laura Beth anything at all.

And worst of all, a husband who'd indicated he wasn't coming home.

The few dollars Patrick had urged her to save were gone. Rent and food had taken it all. And the few measly dollars she'd earned — doing errands and tasks from the boarding house residents — had gone for a doctor bill when Laura Beth had gotten the croup.

The window pane reflected the seven-foot artificial evergreen tree with its ancient blown-glass ornaments. Elderly, rich and mysterious Willa Hanson, in the second floor back apartment, had insisted she use it.

Mrs. Hanson's jeweled fingers had flashed with color and light, her cultured voice modulated with tones of richness and depth. "Dear, I'm really getting much too old to be bothered with putting up a tree; take it.

I'm just so glad that there is someone young and pretty to enjoy it. Besides, your child needs a tree."

She'd taken it and decorated it with the things Mrs. Hanson had given her. Laura Beth laughed and clapped her tiny hands in glee at the beauty of the tree. Her big honey-brown eyes—so like Patrick's—grew round with wonder when Abigail had lifted her up so she could touch the silvery white angel sitting atop of the tree. Her ohs and ahs had warmed Abigail's heart.

But now, two weeks before Christmas, and nothing to put under the tree. The small stack of bills on the side table drew her attention, and she sighed.

It would have been better not to have even had a tree. What did a rich person like Mrs. Hanson know anyway? She never had family visit, but her friends were numerous, and she constantly went out for dinners and quiet parties. How could the elderly lady ever relate to a young wife and mother like her?

Maybe she should have forgotten all about Christmas this year and gone on pretending that it was just another day. Without Patrick here to...

"Abigail! Ab—i—gail! Can you hear me?"

The voice from downstairs interrupted her moody contemplation.

Abigail bent over Laura Beth's crib to lay her in it, covered her, then moved to the door. She propped it open with the old iron black dog doorstop so she could hear if her baby cried, and ran down the stairs to the first floor. Mrs. Owen, the landlady, stood at the bottom of the stairs, beaming. Her chubby round cheeks glowed with good humor. Her orange-red curls bounced as she bobbed her head to emphasize her words.

"Abigail, just come and look at what was delivered to my door. Come on, child. It'll knock your eyes out."

For a brief moment, Abigail forgot about her troubles and laughed at Florence Owen's slang. She moved with her into the ample five-room front apartment. Irene, one of Mrs. Owen's two big white cats, curled around her legs. She bent to pet her then looked for the shy male cat of the family. "Where's Ian?"

Mrs. Owen rolled her painted eyes. "He's pouting under the loveseat because he had liver this morning instead of the tuna he wanted."

"Poor baby."

Pointing at the two large red Poinsettias that took up the center of her table, Mrs. Owen crowed. "Won't you look at those things? Aren't they gorgeous? One from Carl and one from Evan."

Two sons who loved her enough to send flowers, but not enough to be there for Christmas.

"I told myself, 'Florence, where are you going to put two large plants like these? One will just fit my apartment, but two?' So I said to myself, 'That young Abigail and her daughter will enjoy one of these.' Now you help me decide where's the best place for my Poinsettia and the other one is yours."

Where on earth would Mrs. Owen put even one Poinsettia in the already knick-knacked-to-death apartment? Abigail listened as her elderly friend chattered on, and moved around the room rearranging pillows and dragging a small table to the other side of the room. Shoving a chair closer to the divan, she settled the poinsettia on the floor close to the front window and then stood back to look at her simple handiwork. Mrs. Owen's satisfaction was evident from the simper on her face, but she didn't have time to express it.

The phone on her hallway stand rang, and she waddled to it.

"Hello. Hello? Yes, this is Mrs. Owen. What? Who did you say? Yes, you're in luck. She's right here. Hold on." The woman turned and beckoned at Abigail. "It's long distance."

Patrick? Abigail's heart picked up its pace. If only.

"Hello, this is Abigail."

"This is your mother. Why haven't you been to see me? You don't work, so you have no excuse."

"No, but I have a —"

"A baby. That never stopped me from visiting my mother..."

But her mother had lived across town, not across two states, as Abigail did from hers, and glad for the distance.

"... and I can understand why it took you so long to get a man. You're much too independent. If you'd only listen..."

Listen to her mother who'd wanted her to date a guy whose parents had influence and had used that influence to pull every deceitful string possible to keep their son out of the service. A guy who was known to use girls and then toss them aside when a more interesting woman came along.

Hopefully, her mother didn't know about either of those two facts. Or maybe she just didn't care.

"I don't have the money right now to make that trip. If you want me to come that badly..."

"Are you suggesting I pay for your way? What makes you think I have that kind of dough? If you don't want to come, then I surely don't want you to put yourself out for my sake."

Abigail blocked out the voice. No matter what she said, no matter how much she explained, her mother would never listen.

So much for *her* advice. She *had* married a man. A wonderful one — or so she'd thought.

Later that night, the knock on her door was loud and insistent. Abigail hurried to open the door.

Molly Simmons taught music at the St. Imes Catholic School, and what a pianist she was. She regularly offered her talent to bring in money to charities and was always ready to entertain at any decent party or gathering. Tall, fortyish and outspoken, her tart voice brooked no nonsense.

"Abigail, dear, could you possibly spare a minute?"

"Of course. Come in."

"I need to be at the school tomorrow for my students' recital, and I hate to leave Recie alone by herself. Could you and Laura Beth spend a few hours with Recie? Just so she doesn't get lonesome?"

Recie was a teacher too, but had recently slipped on ice and broken her ankle, forcing her to a sudden house-bound leave of absence. Her love of the outdoors kept her physically in shape—and now—mentally challenged to accept her limited activity. As much as Molly's select group of elementary students and teenagers enthused over their programs, Abigail was sure the more active physical group loved Recie even more. They followed her everywhere and their invitations to join them for sandwiches and drinks at the local cafes kept her late after school and in good spirits once she arrived home.

And because she'd been invited to attend many of their functions, Abigail had seen and understood the attraction of these two sisters for the kids of the community. With many parents worried over the war and busy with keeping food on the table and bills paid, the kids had turned to the teachers, who through lack of their own families, gave special attention to them.

Abigail shook herself to attention. "We don't mind at all. We'd love to."

Molly twisted her fingers together. "We were wondering...Recie and I..."

Abigail narrowed her eyes. The only time she'd ever seen Molly flustered or hesitant was when asking for something of which she was embarrassed. What was about to be asked of her?

"Our cleaning lady quit—why on earth she'd do that when she insisted she had to work—and I don't have the time to do our place justice. Recie can't, you know, do much right now, and when she gets better, will be back to work. Would you—?"

"I will." Abigail snapped her words before Molly could change her mind. Every little bit would help pay the mounting rent due and electricity.

A breath of air puffed from between stern lips. "That's settled then. We pay good, but it's only one day a week. We'll see you tomorrow."

Abigail promised to be at their apartment by one the next day. Closing the door, she walked over and stared down at the beautiful red and green plant she'd placed on their small dining table earlier.

Why did Mrs. Owen's sons never visit? And she never went to visit either of them. Had there been a disagreement so severe, neither side was welcomed to visit? But then why did she get presents like these Poinsettias and letters with return addresses naming her sons? Odd. Very odd.

Her heart bled for the woman every time she was called down to her apartment to share in the gifts and listen to tidbits of the letters. The woman's joy was evident, and if the wording was anything to go on, the sons' love was real.

Laura Beth stirred, and Abigail strode over to gaze down at her still sleeping daughter. She pulled a corner of the small blanket, embroidered with pink elephants, over a tiny foot. Kissing her fingers, she laid them gently on the dark hair.

Abigail rocked in her oak rocker, the best piece of furniture she and Patrick owned. Right after their marriage, right before their first Christmas, he'd bought it for her—insisted on doing it even though their funds were low—smiling and explaining that someday she'd need it for their baby. He wanted her and the baby to have the best cuddling place in the world.

She adored her chair, and she'd spent many lonely hours in it since Patrick had been drafted for the service. She missed him so much. Thank God she had Laura Beth.

Her gaze was drawn to the hypnotically drifting snow outside the window. If only Patrick would come home! It had been s-u-c-h a long time. Abigail sighed and knew her bottom lip was trying to form a miniature pout. He was usually so faithful to write. She'd received a letter from him every week since he'd been shipped overseas, but now... Abigail sighed and wiggled in her chair. It had been almost a month, and nothing. Nothing at all. No letter, no phone call.

She regarded the brightly shining angel, with its synthetic blonde hair, tilting a little on the top branch. Perhaps she ought to say a prayer. If she thought it would help, she would do so.

But then, did prayer really help? Had God sent an angel to earth to look after her and her baby while Patrick was gone? Well, if he had, their angel had better get busy. He wasn't doing so well right about now.

Abigail sighed again. Her reflection in the glass showed her a young girl. In her imagination, she thought her hair drooped in the damp, and her lashes drooped from sleepiness—almost like her spirits tonight.

She jumped up, moving away from the image of her discouraging self to turn down her bed covers and lie down. "God, if you're up there, would you please send an angel to help us have a real Christmas? I suppose it would be too much to ask for Patrick to come home? And would you send a beautiful doll for Laura Beth..?"

The next morning Abigail stood at her open door, her head cocked, listening. Yes, it was the tinkle of a hand-held bell. Scooping Laura Beth from the floor, where she was making a mess with some clothespins Abigail had given her, she leaned over the banister and looked down. The third tenant of the second floor, Albert Potter, stood half-in, half-out of his doorway. His thin hand beckoned Abigail to hurry. His white hair stood out from his head as if he'd stuck his finger into an electrical socket.

"What is it, Albert?

"Come down. Come down. I need you to pick up my prescription and a few other things at Kroger's. They just called and said it was ready." The bean-thin gentleman ordered her in his scratchy voice.

Abigail glanced at the watch on her wrist. "I've got just enough time to do that before Laura Beth and I go sit with Recie. Hold on. Let me see if Dana can watch her till I'm back."

No one knew much about Dana and didn't dare ask. Her hair was thinnish and combed in a much too severe style for the shape of her face. Her clothes were well made, but hung unflatteringly on her figure. And though her conversation was brief and most times curt, once someone broke through her icy exterior, her heart was kind and her smile warm.

Three times a week, she departed early from her third-story apartment, dressed in a dark suit or a somber dress that somehow spoke of serious business. The woman had fallen in love with the only baby in the house and offered to watch her any time Abigail needed her. The offer didn't persuade Abigail to take advantage of it, but the woman's wistful eyes did. So while she was there, she might as well, this once.

"May I ask a favor, Dana?"

"Of course, Abigail. What is it?"

"Would it be possible for you to watch Laura Beth for a few hours this week while I search for work?"

"Why would you need to be searching for work when you have that precious child to care for?"

"Need a little extra money. Besides, it'll get me out of the house for a bit." Ouch. Biting her cheek wouldn't help that elaboration. But what else was she to do?

When Abigail headed out to pick up Albert's prescription, she had a promise from Dana that she'd be delighted to watch Abigail's bundle of joy.

Tomorrow, for sure, she'd spend a few hours trying to get that job.

The wind bit into her skin as she headed to the corner store. She loved this grocery. Small, yes, and a family business, but the clerks were all friendly, the food fresh, and the prices as low as the owners could go and make a profit. And they had many of the rationed foods available people like her usually did without.

Lucky for her, the first person to greet her was Bill Watson, the owner. No time like the present to ask for a job.

"Hi, Bill. Could I speak with you?"

"Sure thing." He led her to his closet-like office in the back. "What can I help you with?"

"I need a job."

Mr. Watson's face turned sober. "I don't know, Abigail. We've extended our employment about as much as we can afford, and still be able to provide the lower costs to our customers."

"I just need enough to cover my monthly rent—"

"What about Patrick? Doesn't he send money—?"

"Yes. No." Embarrassment warmed her cheeks. She could feel them reddening and looked down to avoid meeting the owner's eyes. "I mean. He usually does, but—but I haven't gotten anything from him for the last two months. That's fifty dollars I'm behind. In two weeks, we'll owe Mrs. Owen three month's rent, and I can't do that to her."

"I understand. I don't know what I can do, but let me talk with my wife, and we'll see. I can't promise anything. Maybe she'll know someone who can provide some work for you."

"Thanks, Bill. I appreciate it."

That took a little weight off her mind. But she'd keep looking while waiting on an answer from them. Working for the Watsons would be ideal. Not far from the apartment, which meant she'd not have to take a tram or taxi. And she'd be closer to Laura Beth in case she was needed.

She let her thoughts tumble back to when she and Patrick had first learned she was pregnant. They had discussed the pros and cons of her staying at home till the baby was big enough for school or getting a baby sitter while she worked and Patrick did double duty as a student and worked.

Patrick had said, "I'd really like you to stay home while our baby is little, but it's your call, Abigail. Whatever you want to do, I'll support you. Or if you want to continue working, after I finish schooling, we'll divide the chores and baby care. That will give me time to do my writing." Patrick's crooked smile flashed on and off, encouraging her to make up her own mind.

But once Laura Beth had been born, nothing or nobody could have torn her from that little bundle. She had fallen in love all over again. The question was settled of what to do with their baby. Her lips widened in a smile at the memories.

They'd been so lucky to find this apartment. Even though Florence Owen had at first been reluctant to rent to them with their newborn baby—fearful of the cries that might disturb her other tenants and wondering, Abigail was sure, what kind of tenants such a young couple would be—it'd turned out to be the right choice. Once Patrick left for the service, right after graduation, Abigail had kept busy with her baby, running errands and doing odd jobs for the other tenants. They, in turn, provided her with the extras she would've had to do without on the check Patrick sent each month.

Abigail headed for Albert Potter's front apartment as soon as she returned. His door stood open so she was sure he'd had his eyes glued to his window watching for her return.

He beckoned with his gnarled hand "Come in. Come in, Abigail. Want some tea? That dismal Dana—even if she is a good cook—brought me some gingerbread last evening. Have some. Have some. It's good even if I didn't make it. Sit down, child, for a minute." Albert toddled over to the fridge and brought out a quart of milk. "Want milk with your tea, Abigail?"

Where had he gotten *real* milk?

But she shook her head, not wanting to use up his precious supply, and sniffed. The spicy, delectable smell of the gingerbread wafted toward her, and she closed her eyes to savor it. When was the last time she'd had such a treat? Suddenly ravenous, she couldn't wait any longer and crammed her mouth full of the sweet bread. A little sound of moaning escaped from between her lips. This was so-o-o good.

"Do you know who Molly's new piano student is?" Albert went right on talking.

Abigail focused on his words.

"My, my, what is the world coming to? A grown man taking piano lessons. Why an adult would want to take piano lessons is beyond me. He should be thinking about his business instead of spending his time on such nonsense. Never heard the likes."

"Who is this strange man who wants to take piano lessons?"

"You don't know?" He gave her a suspicious glance as if thinking she was laughing, then gave his head a jerk upward. "It's Sam. From upstairs."

"Our Sam?"

The quiet, withdrawn man from the third floor was the last person Abigail would have guessed interested in such a thing.

"Yep. Saw it with my own eyes. And heard it too. They had their door open one evening after he'd gone inside. Majorly painful."

Albert smacked the table feebly with his claw-like hand, and Abigail laughed. He paid no attention, only switched topics. "Sam and Nancy stay out awfully late at nights anymore, don't they?"

Of course, he was the boarding house gossip, but he was a dear in spite of it. Abigail's heart melted like wax when she remembered Mrs. Owen's whisper one day.

"He lost his only son in the war early. You'd never guess the desolation he feels, but I hear him stumbling around at night—can't sleep, I'm sure, and every week he visits the cemetery."

"How do you know?"

Mrs. Owen simpered. "The flower shop owner goes to church with me. Says he stops every Friday to buy flowers. Who else for, but that poor son of his?"

Who else indeed?

She nodded at the old man and wiped her mouth with the thin paper napkin beside her plate. "It is Christmas, Albert, and their store must be awfully busy this time of the year."

"I should hope they would be. I wonder why they don't get a bigger apartment."

"Albert, you are a dear. Their apartment is very nice, and they love it here. Everyone is friendly—like one big family. They wouldn't move if they could." She sobered, her worry about Christmas clouding her thoughts again like annoying mosquitoes.

The old gentleman squinted at her. "What's the matter, child? Anything these old bones can help you with?"

"Well...I've been thinking...I don't want to, but...maybe I ought to get a part-time job or something to tide me over. I haven't heard from Patrick in two months."

She hated it that her voice ended in a wail and that her bottom lip trembled in spite of her teeth clenching on them. This was all she needed to get the tears flowing. Someone to listen to her boo-hooing.

Albert looked as if he were studying on her question. "Well...I don't think so, child. Not with little Laura Beth to care for. Think you can't make it till Patrick sends your next check? Is that it? You know I'll be glad to loan you..."

Temptation, and she wanted to yield.

"Albert, thanks, but no. I couldn't. I'll be okay, I think. I don't know what to do about Christmas for my daughter. Why wouldn't Patrick know I need extra for her at Christmas?" Abigail hated the accusatory tone she heard in her voice.

"Have you thought that maybe he can't write? Or send money? It's terrible times, and our men are facing drastic situations. Be patient, my dear." Albert patted her hand. "He'll come through, child. Don't you worry none about that."

But his eyes said otherwise. Two months was a long time... And he knew the danger. Death. Captivity. Injuries. A broken husband who didn't want to come home...

And the letter? What was Patrick trying to say in that? Was her husband to suffer the same fate as elderly Mr. Potter's son had? Could she bear it?

She had to. Someone had to be strong for Laura Beth.

When Abigail left, she went straight to Dana's apartment to pick up her daughter. In her hand she carried two carefully wrapped pieces of the gingerbread.

"One for tonight. One for your breakfast in the morning. You must keep up your strength. What would we do without you?" Mr. Potter's blue eyes had twinkled at her.

When she stepped into Dana's apartment, she hugged the neck of the plain little woman who always so generously shared her time for the baby. "Thank you so much for watching her. What can I do for you in return, Dana?"

Dana Smith made a deprecating gesture with her left hand, her right tweaked a strand of muddy-colored, stringy hair from her eyes. "Don't you worry about it, Abigail. I love to have Laura Beth."

"I know you do, Dana, but I'd love to do something for you in return." The plea was an old one she'd made for as often as Dana had watched her daughter.

The woman touched Laura Beth's cheek. "Caring for this little angel is all the thanks I need. It's a..."

Abigail studied the woman. There was something deeper behind the longing in Dana's voice. Was it sorrow? Wistfulness?

That was it. Perhaps she'd lost her husband in the war. Maybe a child had died or she'd failed to conceive. Whatever had happened, Abigail was sure something had happened to Dana. Only a suffering wife or mother could carry such an emotion.

"I'll tell you what. My office is having a Christmas party, and they insist I bring something even though I insisted I didn't want to attend. Would you mind baking some cookies? I'm too busy right now and afraid I'd poison someone with my endeavor—out of distraction. I have all the ingredients."

"I'd love to." She stooped to lift her drowsy child and snuggled the baby against her neck for a moment. Reaching for the grocery bag full of the ingredients she would use to bake the chocolate chip cookies tonight after Laura Beth went to sleep, she smiled at the plain woman. "Thanks, again, Dana. You're an angel."

Dana smiled and shook her head, but Abigail could see the hint of pleasure in the tired eyes of her friend.

Abigail dropped off her gingerbread and the bag of ingredients at her apartment, collected a diaper and a bag of necessities for Laura Beth and ran lightly back to the second floor, jostling a giggling baby.

When she knocked on the door, she heard Recie calling out. "Come in, Abigail and Laura Beth. It's unlocked."

Recie smiled, her happiness in their visit apparent in her bright blue eyes. Her right foot, bound with a cumbersome cast, was propped up on a round, brocade-covered footstool. Recie, the quieter of the twins, was also the more active one. Before her accident, each morning she did a three mile run before taking off for school where she counseled and taught gym classes. She loved her work as much as Molly did her musical activities. Recie suffered the leave-taking much rougher than her more out-spoken sister would have done.

Abigail leaned down to give the woman a hug before settling Laura Beth on Recie's lap. Recie jiggled the child with her good leg. "I'm sick of this hampering cast. What am I going to do for three more weeks? I'll be so out of shape it'll take me six months to get back where I should be."

"You'll be fine, Recie. You're thin as a stick now."

"Anyhow, you don't won't to hear my complaints." Recie sighed in frustration. "Want to do some typing for me? You know how I hate lengthy typing projects. I'll give you two dollars."

Abigail agreed and settled at Recie's desk and began typing the projected class work Recie had prepared for her students when she returned to her school. Abigail's fingers made a steady, low clacking hum as she half-listened to Recie and Laura Beth playing in the background. She ceased typing and turned around in her chair when Recie called to her again.

"Abigail, stop awhile. You've been typing for almost an hour. I need help in deciding on something for Molly for Christmas. What should I get her? She has everything she wants and if she doesn't, she's got plenty of money to go out and get it herself."

Abigail glanced around the familiar apartment. The ample front room was filled with warm colors and comfortable furniture—not too crowded—a Wurlitzer across the room, two comfortable corduroy chairs pulled up close to a small fireplace, and shelves of books and a couple of prints by modern artists gave it a homey feeling. She loved visiting here.

"Well... I heard on the radio yesterday that they were selling tickets to the Cincinnati Symphony. I think she would like that, don't you?"

"That's an excellent idea. And Terrance White will be in town in February for a concert. This is just the thing. I'll get her tickets to both and she'll be in seventh heaven. Why didn't I think of it?"

When Molly arrived two hours later, a sleeping Laura Beth lay on the sofa beside Recie. Abigail sat on the floor against older woman's left leg, listening to her talk of her life when she was a little girl growing up. Two empty plates with homemade toasted cinnamon bread crumbs and stained hot chocolate mugs stood on a nearby end table. Evidence of their earlier feast. Her daughter's mouth was ringed in pink, the homemade strawberry ice cream having found its way there more often than inside the small ruby-red mouth.

Molly stood with hands on her hips, a smile tugging at the corner of her mouth. She strode over to give Laura Beth a swift kiss and turned to Abigail. "Was this sister of mine good for you today?"

"Perfect. Piano students tonight, Molly?"

"Yes, and you'll never guess who my new student is." Molly chuckled when Abigail didn't answer. "Sam Nelson. He's been after me forever. Said he'd always wanted to learn."

The doorbell rang, and she glanced at her watch. "That's probably him now."

It was time to head home.

The quiet, shy man with his name brand clothes, greeted Abigail, then stopped her when she would have left.

"May I speak with you, Abigail?"

Sam wasn't tall. In fact, he was no taller than Abigail, but he was a handsome man, with his dark, slicked hair and mustached lip. And his manners were impeccable.

When Abigail nodded, he went on. "Nancy has a problem she would like to talk about with you. Perhaps tomorrow evening at seven?"

Strange. Though the woman occasionally babysat for her, she'd never specifically asked for help or called on her to talk. A passing, pleasant greeting was the most she'd ever gotten out of her. But Abigail promised to meet his wife and walked up the stairs.

Supper consisted of noodles and a bit of chicken left over from the night before, and would have been delicious if it'd had the spices she needed. Still her baby girl ate half of her mashed portion, and Abigail managed to finish the small portion she served herself. Water washed down the last bite, and then she rose, carefully placing the remainder of Laura Beth's in a small container for tomorrow's lunch.

Settling her baby on the floor close to her with her favorite toys—the clothes pins—she stirred the first batch of cookie dough. She pinched off a mini bite, tucked it into Laura Beth's mouth, and let her thoughts ramble again while she filled the cookie sheets with the moist dough.

She wondered what it was that Nancy Nelson could want. Nancy was thin to the point of attenuation, as neat as her husband, but more of a worrier, in a prim way. Childless, they devoted their time and energy to the department store, doing their best — with rations as they were — to keep it stocked with as many items as possible, even if it meant purchasing some well-made, local and one-of-a-kind pieces of clothing. Pleasant as they were with the other tenants, they nevertheless had a tendency to keep more to themselves than their more garrulous neighbors.

It was so-o-o funny to think of shy, stocky Sam taking piano lessons. But who knew? He might turn out to be really good. She hoped so. To think of wishing for something that long and finally having the chance of achieving it. Abigail sighed and glanced down at her baby playing quietly at her feet.

What a perfect little angel she was. Almost no trouble at all. What on earth would she have done while Patrick was gone if she hadn't had Laura Beth? Abigail stooped and kissed the top of the curly, dark hair. "Where's your wings, sweetie?"

She giggled when the sleepy eyes looked up.

"No, Mommy's *not* crazy. I just don't know why Daddy hasn't written, how I can pay the bills, and how I can make Christmas for you, and...and..."

Abigail abandoned the last of the cookie dough, swiped her hands on a cloth, and bent to pick up Laura Beth. She told herself it was to give her baby some snuggling time, but the truth was, *she* needed the snuggling time. Strong she might be, but her emotions lately were turning tumultuous as a tempestuous sea.

She moved to her rocker, cuddled the child in her arms, and slowly rocked, backwards and forwards, backwards and forwards, tears sliding down her cheeks as she hummed a tuneless song. One soft, baby hand reached upwards to touch a trembling teardrop on her cheek.

"Mommy's okay, Laura Beth. She's being a big baby tonight."

The tousled-headed child lay in her arms. She watched as the young eyes closed...slowly, slowly. She continued to rock, backwards and forwards, the tears drying on her cheeks, her eyes fixed now on the indigo sky outside her window and the myriad of stars hanging above the earth. "God, it's almost Christmas, and I haven't seen any evidence of my angel's help. Are you there, God? Are you listening? *Where's* my angel?"

Abigail's knock on the Nelsons' door the next evening sounded loud. What a quiet day it had been. In fact, she had wondered all day what was keeping all of her nosy, good natured neighbors so busy.

"Abigail, how are you? Are you keeping warm? Laura Beth's not catching cold?" Nancy stood in the doorway, worry lines around her eyes.

And way too chatty. What was wrong?

"We're fine, Nancy. What can I do to help you?" Abigail inquired, a little worried at the unusual request Sam had asked yesterday. The Nelsons always seemed to be so self-sufficient.

"Well, dear..."

Something was wrong. Though the woman was a worrier, she'd never been hesitant with her opinions or thoughts the few times she'd overheard her speaking with an over-zealous salesman.

"...to be quite honest, I have misplaced my personal checkbook and thought perhaps you would help me look for it."

"I'd love to, Nancy." Abigail wanted to laugh with relief. She'd been imagining all sorts of wild ideas. "Where shall I start?"

Forty-five minutes later, a red-faced Nancy pulled the checkbook out of her purse. "I had put it in the inside zipper compartment—I don't normally keep it there—and forgot about it. Can you believe it?"

What? Now she knew something was wrong. Could Nancy and Sam be having marital problems? Was their store in trouble? No, that couldn't be it. Why would she want Abigail here, with her?

Nancy and she laughed together—although hers was a bit forced—and collapsed on the matching plaid loveseats. "Worrying over nothing—as usual. Wait till Sam hears." The phone rang, and Nancy jumped up, excused herself, and went to the kitchenette.

When she returned there was an odd look on her face. "I need to fix Sam a snack. We ate a late lunch today, so we're eating light tonight, but I'm out of onion, and the man dearly loves a slice of it on his sandwiches. Would you happen to have one I could borrow?"

Nancy out of something? That worrier probably kept two of everything in this apartment.

"Mind if I walk up with you to get it?" Nancy urged and almost shooed Abigail and Laura Beth out of the apartment.

The oddest feeling swept through her, and her face warmed at the sudden sense she was being asked to leave. She followed the rambling and somewhat nervous chatter of the first floor back apartment tenant who led the way upstairs. Strange. Abigail'd never seen her act so rude.

As Abigail reached to open her own door, Nancy spoke in a kind of small gasp. "Did you think..." but the question was drowned out with the explosion of excited cries.

"Merry Christmas, Abigail and Laura Beth!"

"Surprise! Surprise!"

Later, Abigail sat rocking. She gazed peacefully at the happy faces of the tenants of 233 Darcy Road — her friends, her *family*.

Dana sitting on the worn couch, holding Laura Beth. The beautiful, antique doll, with its long dress, that Mrs. Hanson had placed in the little girl's arms, was still held tightly. Her daughter had cooed with happiness. Abigail had cried.

On the table sat stacks and stacks of food items — enough for months. Elderly Albert had quietly slipped a padded envelope to her with the words scribbled wobbly across the front, "Merry Christmas."

Abigail was sure that, in spite of her refusal for monetary help yesterday, he'd found this way to ease her worry.

Sam and Nancy had presented whole new outfits for both Laura Beth and herself, including shoes and coats. Homemade they might be, but they were well-made and doubly loved because of the generosity of her two neighbors.

Mrs. Owen had prepared a feast for all of them, and they'd all done justice to the meal. Fit for a queen and her princess, the woman had declared. And indeed it was. From where the woman had wrangled such delights as a roasted bird and real potatoes was beyond Abigail's reasoning, but no one had turned down a serving.

And Dana. While the rest of them had filled their plates with Mrs. Owen's feast, she'd slipped a small package to Abigail. "Don't open it now, but after everyone is gone."

She had gone to each one of them and whispered words of love and thanks for the gifts they had given, hugging them fiercely, loving them for thinking of her. She rocked silently, listening to their voices, smiling faintly and remembering all their assurances that the deeds she'd performed for them and sharing herself and baby with them in neighborly visits had been blessings for these older residents.

It was when her neighbors had decided it was time to leave and had moved to the hallway, turning one after another, to smile, wave, and call out their good-byes, that Abigail saw it. Her eyes widened. She blinked. Was she seeing things? A vision? Was she dreaming?

In the fading winter sunlight that streamed through the hallway window, a glow surrounded each of her friends — and, Abigail would insist afterwards — feathery, white wings waved ever so gently from behind each back.

Her friends, they looked like...could it be?

Why, they looked like angels!

Mrs. Owen in her gaudy, cheap jewelry and bright orange curls.

Dana with her quiet, unobtrusive ways.

Sam with his shy smile and budding interest in the piano.

Nancy, her worries and rather tart way of speaking.

Old Albert with his gossipy tongue but discerning eyes.

Molly and Recie, busy sisters of completely different personalities, but loving concern.

Mrs. Hanson, dear Mrs. Hanson, with her condescending ways and beautiful, but mysterious blue eyes.

Every one of them—angels.

They were the angels God had sent to look after her!

Abigail and Laura Beth, mother and daughter, watched as the Darcy House people walked slowly, still talking, to their own apartment homes and hearths. As they reached their doors, Abigail called out softly but distinctly, "God bless all of you, my friends. Merry Christmas!"

With all her heart, she hoped that her blessing on her friends would find its way to every heart.

When Abigail turned from the doorway with her daughter in her arms, she saw Dana's gift package lying on the table. Settling Laura Beth on her lap with the doll the child refused to relinquish, Abigail opened it. Inside was a note from Dana.

> *Dear Abigail,*
>
> *I knew how much you missed your husband and the confusion you felt in not hearing from him. It broke my heart knowing you were hurting so badly.*
>
> *I work for the government and put in a request for any information I could of your husband. There was bad and good news.*
>
> *Your husband was injured and in a coma for several weeks. He's just this past week recovered enough to realize how much time has passed since he's been in touch with you. He was frantic with worry, but was convinced that he couldn't leave until his health was better.*
>
> *However, he is progressing and sends this small gift and a note to you – via me.*
>
> *Merry Christmas, my dear. I do believe you'll be seeing Patrick before many more days pass.*
>
> *Dana*

With shaking fingers, Abigail ripped open the second, smaller envelope. Something stiff and flat fluttered to the floor, and ignoring the wad of money still inside the envelope, she bent to retrieve it, but stopped.

On the floor, lay a picture of Patrick, his teasing eyes staring at her, his crooked smile reassuring her of his enduring love.

On the note, he'd written: *"To my two beautiful girls, with love from your adoring husband and father. Merry Christmas, Angels!"*

Besides being a member and active participant of many writing groups, award-winning, best-selling author **Carole Brown** enjoys mentoring beginning writers. An author of ten books, she loves to weave suspense and tough topics into her books, along with a touch of romance and whimsy, and is always on the lookout for outstanding titles and catchy ideas. She and her husband reside in SE Ohio but have ministered and counseled nationally and internationally. Together, they enjoy their grandsons, traveling, gardening, good food, the simple life, and did she mention their grandsons?

Personal blog: *http://sunnebnkwrtr.blogspot.com/*

Facebook: *https://www.facebook.com/CaroleBrown.author*

Amazon Author Page: *http://www.amazon.com/Carole-Brown/e/B00EZ V4RFY/ref=sr_ntt_srch_lnk_1?qid=1427898838&sr=8-1*

Twitter: *https://twitter.com/browncarole212*

BookBub: *https://www.bookbub.com/authors/carole-brown*

Pinterest: *http://pinterest.com/sunnywrtr/boards/*

Goodreads: *http://www.goodreads.com/user/show/5237997-carole-brown*

Linkedin: *https://www.linkedin.com/in/carole-brown-79b6951a/*

Google+: *https://plus.google.com/u/0/113068871986311965415/posts*

Stitches in Time: *http://stitchesthrutime.blogspot.com/*

CPSIA information can be obtained
at www.ICGtesting.com
Printed in the USA
FFHW02n0629090918
48224532-51960FF